JEWEL OF THE NIGHT'S MANTLE

JEWEL OF THE NIGHT'S MANTLE

VALERIE STONEHOLD™
BOOK FOUR

RENÉE JAGGÉR
MICHAEL ANDERLE

THE JEWEL OF THE NIGHT'S MANTLE TEAM

Thanks to the JIT Readers

Wendy L Bonell
Diane L. Smith
Daryl McDaniel
Jeff Goode
Christopher Gilliard
Kelly O'Donnell
Dave Hicks
Jan Hunnicutt
Dorothy Lloyd

Editor
The SkyFyre Editing Team

CHAPTER ONE

Faerie dust surrounded Tetra Dupont in a golden glow that smelled like strawberries. The dust was invisible to humans, but it seemed they could smell it. Several men at the bar leaned closer as she strode past carrying a tray of beer glasses.

Val Stonehold eyed the men from her spot at the back of the bar, where she poured more beers from a hefty oaken barrel. The customers watched Tetra go wistfully, their gazes dwelling on her petite figure in black slacks and a branded golf shirt, but none rose from their seats.

Satisfied, Val returned her attention to the beer. She topped off each glass with a little flourish that delivered the perfect layer of hissing foam on top of the craft IPA, then turned to the bar.

"Tone down the dust," she muttered. "People are beginning to notice."

Tetra rolled her eyes. "You're jealous that I both look and smell good."

"*I* smell good," Val grumbled.

"You smell like smoke and iron. Did you shower after forging shit in your smithy this morning?" Tetra hissed.

Val shrugged. "Smells good to me."

Tetra scoffed. Clutching a tray of empty glasses, she stepped over the massive chestnut dog lying behind the bar.

"Tripping over your dog is enough to dim anyone's glow," she muttered. "Do you have to bring him here? He's the size of a small pony."

"I couldn't leave him home alone." Val crouched, balancing her tray on one hand, and rubbed the top of the dog's head. "That wouldn't be fair, would it, boy?"

The dog's long, fringed tail stirred gently on the hardwood floor.

"If you wanted a dog to take with you everywhere, you should've gotten a chihuahua. Would've fit in your purse." Tetra poured beer.

Val snorted. "I don't have a purse, and I don't have a dog, either."

She stepped over the dog, who lay with his forelegs extended. One bore an increasingly grubby cast. As usual, the Iron Fist was crammed. Its bouncer, a human named Jeff, stood by the doorway and kept a watchful eye on a rowdy table near the back of the tiny space. Every seat at the bar was taken as Val dispensed IPA to a group of cheering humans.

She spotted a row of familiar faces in their usual spot near the bar's end and gravitated toward them. "I didn't order a beer delivery tonight," she teased.

The pair of dwarves drooping on their stools gave her wry smiles. "You're the only bar in Brooklyn who didn't," Blair told her.

"I don't want to know how many hundreds of miles we've put on that truck today." Yuka ran a hand over her emerald-green hair, then tucked it beneath her ball cap. "The guys at the factory spent the whole day bottling, too. We've got dozens of deliveries for tomorrow."

Val grinned. "Sounds like business is booming with BrewCorp out of the way."

"Booming?" Yuka grinned. "We can hardly keep up. Brew-Corp's bad publicity was the best marketing we've ever had."

"Well, that's what happens when an asshole like Anthony Warner teams up with organized crime to sink an innocent company like yours," Val stated. "He deserves every year he'll get in prison."

"Thanks to you and Tetra." Blair chuckled. "Now, can a dwarf get a drink around here?"

"Two Iron IPAs?" Val asked.

"Merlin's beard, no," Yuka moaned. "I've seen enough Iron IPA for a lifetime today."

"Faerie wine," Blair murmured too quietly for the nearby humans to hear. "Doubles. Your best."

"That kind of day, huh?" Val raised her eyebrows. "Coming right up."

She scooped empty glasses onto her tray and hurried to the back of the bar, where Tetra was packing dirty glasses into the dishwasher.

"I want danger pay. I nearly fell over your dog," the faerie announced.

"Oh, chill." Val grabbed shot glasses from the shelf. "You actually like him. Maybe you should adopt him."

"For what?" Tetra demanded.

"He's a cute pet." Val pointed at the dog, who slept with his head on his paws. "Look at him."

"Pet?" Tetra scoffed. "In faerie culture, animals are food."

"Even dogs?" Val raised her eyebrows.

Tetra licked her lips. "Slow-roasted on a spit? Any time."

"You're horrifying," Val informed her as she poured faerie wine into the shot glasses. The noxious fumes made her sneeze.

"You're a lightweight," Tetra countered.

Val gave the faerie a friendly shove that almost knocked her head-first into the dishwasher. She then stepped over the dog and returned to the bar to find that another familiar face had joined Blair and Yuka. Jess' chestnut bob was frazzled, and her stained, wrinkled scrubs had an aroma that made the men nearby lean away.

"Let me guess." Val scooted shot glasses to Blair and Yuka. "Need a nightcap after a long shift?"

"You have no idea," Jess groaned. "I spent three hours helping Dr. West to save a pregnant bulldog and her six puppies, all doomed to a life of struggling to breathe. Then the owner lost his shit at the bill. Like, he couldn't bother to do three seconds of research when he bred his dog. He would have found out that bulldogs can only give birth via C-section!" She slammed an angry hand on the bar. "Why is this world filled with assholes?"

"I could find him for you," Val told her. "I could teach him a lesson."

Jess' gaze darted to the Damascus steel dagger on Val's hip. "Uh, it's okay. Thanks, though." She groaned. "I need a whiskey on the rocks."

"Done," Val assured her. "Hey, dog. Come over here and say hi to Jess."

The dog lumbered to his feet at the sound of Val's voice. He plodded across the hardwood floor, reared up, and planted his forepaws on the bar, towering over the patrons. Several slid their stools away, but the dog's floppy ears and waving tail attested to his good nature.

"'Hey, dog!'" Jess reached up to scratch the dog's neck. "Really? You *still* haven't given him a name?"

"He doesn't need a name. His new owners will give him one," Val asserted. "I'm not keeping him, remember?"

The dog panted like he was laughing at Val.

"Everybody knows you're keeping him, Val. It's been a month," Jess pointed out.

"He'll get a new home when his cast comes off." Val grunted. "Isn't that right, buddy?" She patted the dog's broad back. "Now, piss off. You're scaring the normies."

The dog dropped to the floor and obediently lay down two feet in front of Tetra as she marched to the bar with two trays weighed down by drinks.

"Dog!" she complained, stumbling over him. "Really!"

"You *have* to give him a name, Val," Jess chided. "Hey, where's Enzo tonight?"

"He's not here. He had family stuff to sort out," Val explained.

Blair frowned. "Is he okay? We didn't see him here two nights ago, either."

Val sighed. "He says he's okay, but he's not giving me any details. I'll keep asking if he needs help."

"Let him know we're here for him, too," Yuka told her.

Voices rose on the other side of the room, where three booths and tables stood beneath rusty old weapons hanging on the wall. Two guys argued over their half-drunk beers while their girl-friends cringed beside them, exchanging embarrassed glances.

Jeff raised his chin. Val kept a close eye on the men as she gathered empty glasses.

"I told you not to buy that stupid truck!" one barked, slam-ming an open hand on the table. "Everyone knows Ford is useless."

"Oh, you'd rather I buy a Land Rover like yours?" The other scoffed. "I can always tell where you've been from the oil slicks."

"You know my mileage is better than yours!" the first yelled.

"Humans argue over the stupidest shit," Tetra muttered.

Val chuckled. "Tell me about it."

The second guy sprang to his feet, brandishing a fist. "Say that again next time that heap of junk leaves you stranded by the roadside. I won't be the one giving you a ride this time!"

"That was *once!*" the other roared, swaying drunkenly as he tried to stand. He bunched his hands into fists.

Jeff stepped forward, but he was too slow. The dog reached the table first. Tail low and stiff, he raised his massive head, easily looking over the table. His shiny red fur, which usually lay in curly swathes on his broad back, bristled like crimson fire.

The men didn't notice him until he emitted a deep snarl that rumbled like distant thunder. He didn't expose his teeth, but the sound rolled through the Iron Fist and dragged silence in its wake.

Both men fell silent and stared at the dog. Every patron in the room froze in their seats.

Slowly, the men sank into their booths.

"Truck of yours has plenty of horsepower," one muttered.

"Nice suspension on your Land Rover," the other replied.

The dog wagged his tail and wandered back to his spot at the bar. He flopped down at Val's feet with a contented sigh.

She crouched to rub his ears. "Good job, dude."

In the booth beside the passionate car guys', three old men played cards, as they'd done every night since time immemorial. A couple of young patrons sat beside them, staring wide-eyed at the dog.

One of the old men chuckled. "Beware of the dog," he told the youngsters.

"Pray the barmaid doesn't hit you," the second added.

The third grinned. "*Never* get Val involved."

Val and Tetra exchanged a smirk as the bar settled into its usual merry ambiance, the giant dog ever-watchful at their feet.

The 1971 Mustang Mach 1 shimmered beneath the streetlights outside the Iron Fist. This late, even in the city that never sleeps, the streets surrounding Continental Army Plaza were largely empty. Genevieve was the only car outside the bar. Her beautiful lines screamed *speed* and a hunger for the open road. Black and pewter, the classic Mustang hid a V8 Cobra Jet under her hood, as well as many other secrets.

Her headlights flashed in recognition as Val and Tetra stepped out of the bar with the dog close on Val's heels. Val locked the bar's door and waved a hand. The magical ward engaged with a dull, metallic thud.

"Okay," Val acknowledged as they crossed the sidewalk. "*Now* I need a shower."

"No kidding." Tetra wrinkled her nose. "Not that it matters, considering that you let that hairy thing sleep in your bed."

The dog wagged his tail. "Where's he supposed to sleep, the floor?" Val demanded.

"Oh, I don't know. Maybe in one of the twenty expensive dog beds in each room?" Tetra teased.

Val snorted as she opened the driver's door. "He has one bed in each room, and none are as comfy as my bed."

"You smell like a dog," Tetra informed her.

"You smell like strawberries, and it's annoying," Val shot back.

The dog easily maneuvered into Genevieve, making her suspension squeak. He settled on the backseat, engulfing it, while Val and Tetra got in.

Genevieve's engine started with a fierce snarl that always gave Val goosebumps. They peeled out and sped along the plaza with the thunder of three hundred seventy-five joyous horses.

The radio crackled to life as they sped out of range of the Iron Fist's wards. The announcer was a serious, feminine para with a slight elven accent.

"Eternity Queen Julia Pendragon has spent the day in talks with her full council once more. The Eternity Council has been in session all week regarding the fate of hundreds of paranormals currently housed in the Para-Military Agency's containment units, with the most dangerous kept at the Locker in the Deadwoods," the para announced. "Prisoners of war and ordinary criminals constitute a small proportion of the prisoner population. The majority are transformed paranormals who were formerly members of the Wild Hunt."

"News," Val muttered, turning it down. "Don't they ever have anything nice to say?" She peeled away from a red light.

"You drive like a maniac," Tetra muttered.

"Hey, at least I drive," Val countered, throwing Genevieve into a screeching turn toward Bay Ridge.

Tetra rolled her eyes. "Like you'd ever let me behind the wheel of your precious Genevieve."

"The Eternity Queen's precious Genevieve, technically," Val reminded her. "Although I think she's her own person."

Genevieve gave an affirmative honk.

"You see? There's no way I'm getting behind this wheel," Tetra grouched.

Silence settled between them, holding a hint of the heaviness that had reigned a few weeks ago. Val gripped the wheel, which bore handprint-shaped scorch marks from its previous driver, and summoned her courage. "I want to talk to you about something."

The faerie tensed but kept her tone casual. "Yeah?"

Val rubbed the back of her neck. "We got off to kind of a rocky start."

"Oh, you mean a magic ritual that made me your vassal, so I have to do *everything* you tell me?" Tetra raised her eyebrow. "That was kind of rocky, yeah."

Val chuckled. "I was referring to that, yes."

"What about it?" Tetra asked.

"I don't think I ever thanked you for coming to help me in that fight at the warehouse." Val paused. "Our opponents were only human, but I couldn't have beaten them without you. I wanted you to know that I appreciate what you did."

Tetra shrugged. "I mean, if you'd died, I'd probably end up in the prison realm."

"You and I both know that's not why you did it." Val smirked. "I recall that you said something about *caring?*"

Tetra clapped her hands over her ears. "Shut up!"

Val chortled.

"You don't need to thank me," Tetra muttered, letting her hands fall to her lap. "You've been good to me. It's fine. Let's forget it ever happened."

"That's the thing, though. I want it to happen again," Val told her.

Tetra raised her eyebrows. "Which part? The nasty burns on your hand, the bit where my head nearly got blown off by a shotgun, or the epic showdown over a ledger full of evidence?"

"The part where we worked together." Val steered Genevieve onto the freeway. "Something my dad said a few weeks ago has stuck with me."

Tetra snickered. "'You really need a boyfriend, little spark.' That part?"

"No!" Val's cheeks burned. "He said I should assemble a team."

"A badass security team?" Tetra grinned. "I like that idea. You could recruit the toughest fighters from the Third Pendragon War. What about Methunoch the dragon? He can breathe ice, you know. Oh, oh, or Prince Stefrin of the Aether Elves! He slew a bunch of Hunters at the Battle of New Camelot."

"Tetra—" Val began.

"Wait, wait! I have the best idea." Tetra grinned. "I know Captain Jack Kaplan retired, but nobody's more badass than *him*."

"Tetra!" Val laughed. "I was talking about you, idiot."

Tetra froze. "You...you want me to be part of your team?"

"Well, for now, you'd *be* the team," Val told her. "I don't have anyone else in mind."

Tetra stared at her with wide, pitch-black eyes. "You want me to be your only backup? Permanently?"

Val shrugged. "We can discuss the rent, but yeah, I'd like you to be part of all my missions."

Tetra looked away, but Val saw her blinking rapidly in the reflection in Genevieve's window.

"I mean, it's not an order," Val added. "I'm extending an offer, that's all."

Tetra's shoulders heaved as she inhaled. "It's an interesting offer." A slight tremor underlined her words.

"You can have time to think about it," Val told her.

Tetra cleared her throat. "No, that won't be, uh…that's not necessary." She almost succeeded in keeping her tone casual. "I accept. It'd be fun to be part of your team."

"Cool." Val smothered a grin.

Tetra swallowed a couple of times before she could speak. "Hey, while we're on the subject of my future, there was something I wanted to ask you."

Val raised her eyebrows. "I'd say 'don't push it,' but I'm sure you're going to."

"Maybe a little." Tetra grinned. "I know the last time I left the apartment on my own was a shitstorm, but do you think you could consider giving me a little space again?"

Val bit the inside of her cheek. "It was less of a shitstorm than I turned it into with my reaction."

"You *did* completely overreact," Tetra agreed.

Val scoffed. "If this is you buttering me up, try again."

"Speaking the truth, that's all." Tetra smirked.

"Okay, I freaked out," Val confessed. "Let's see if you'll give me a reason to do the same again. What do we do when scary men piss us off?"

Tetra ticked off the items on her fingers. "Call for help. Phone Val. Self-defense only if necessary."

"And?" Val prompted.

Tetra grimaced. "Do not, under any circumstances, flip somebody's car."

"That's right." Val chuckled. "Okay, fine. You're allowed to leave the apartment on your own, provided you tell me where you're going."

"Do my old rules still apply?" Tetra ventured.

Val snorted. "The rules about not hurting people or revealing your magic to humans? Those are called Eternity Laws, Tetra. They'll always apply."

Tetra laughed. "That's fair." She paused. "Thanks, Val. I promise to be an adult about things."

Val gaped at her. "An adult? You told me one time that the faerie rite of passage is killing a moose alone with your bare hands!"

"Teeth, too. Don't forget the teeth." Tetra grinned. "Okay, point taken. I promise to be a *human-presenting* adult about things."

"Good." Val's chuckle held only a slight note of unease. "When are you willing to join the bodyguard team?"

Tetra shrugged. "Whenever."

"Good," Val repeated, "because I've got shit to do tomorrow, and I need you for backup."

CHAPTER TWO

Val was freezing. It was the height of spring in New York City, but the weather hadn't gotten the memo. Her bare toes curled on the threshold, and she regretted wearing only a pair of boxers and a baggy T-shirt.

"Dog!" she bellowed. "Where are you, asshole?"

Frigid rain pounded on the roof and splattered on the lawn in her small backyard. Yellow streetlights reflected on the pelting droplets, making it impossible to see anything more than shifting shadows, even with Val's dwarven vision.

"Dog!" Val roared. "Buddy! Dude! Boy!"

There was no response. It was three in the morning, and somewhere out there, her dog was taking the longest shit ever. A blast of wind drove a fistful of rain against Val's body. Her flesh shrank from the cold.

"I'm leaving you out here!" she roared.

The crunch of plastic heralded the return of the dog. She saw his white cast first, swinging in a merry trot. He bounded up to her, rammed his nose into her crotch, and leaped into the dining room.

Val slammed the door. "Finally, asshole."

The dog spread his paws wide and braced himself.

"No!" Val yelled, grabbing an old towel from the nearby hat stand. "Don't you—"

The dog shook his sodden coat with every sign of enjoyment. Drool, hair, and rainwater splattered all over the dining room. His jaw fell open in a happy pant, and he wagged his tail as she glared at him.

"What an idiot," she muttered.

The dog barked and pranced around her feet.

"No!" Val yelped. "Don't start with the—"

The dog took off like a shot, tucking his butt underneath him like his back legs outran his front legs. Cast flailing, he raced around the dining room, then into the kitchen. His claws clattered on linoleum, padded on the carpet as he completed his circuit, and bounded back into the dining room.

"Zoomies," Val finished with a sigh.

The dog left a damp trail of water and hair everywhere he ran. Val gave up. She flicked on the light, stomped into the living room, and fell onto the couch. The dog continued zooming, miraculously missing the coffee table by inches with every pass.

"You're an idiot," Val informed him as he leaped over her outstretched legs and almost collided with the back door.

He fell into a play bow, tail waving, clutching a rope toy in his mouth.

"Seriously?" Val observed the tatters on the toy. "You've had that thing for three days, and you're already destroying it?"

The dog took off again. Val stifled a yawn. A hundred pounds of soaking-wet dog sprang into her lap the next moment.

"Dude!" Val roared, throwing her arms around him.

The dog struggled in vain. She grabbed the towel and rubbed him vigorously, and after a moment's squirming, he submitted to being dried.

"What an oaf," she muttered when he fell onto his back, paws in the air, his broken forelimb sticking up straight because of the cast. "You're going to be impossible when this leg of yours heals, do you know that?"

The dog gave a happy grunty-growl as Val worked the towel over his thick coat.

"Hypothetically," she suggested, "how do you feel about a hair dryer?"

The dog growled for real this time.

"Okay, fine. Point taken." Val rose and crumpled the wet, hairy towel. "I think you're dry enough. Let's go back to bed."

The dog sprang to his feet, coat awry, and charged across the kitchen in front of her. She'd installed a baby gate across the stairs, and he pranced in front of it until she scooped him up and tossed him over her shoulders.

"Deadweight," she grumbled.

The dog licked her ear, his hot tongue splashing her face as well.

"Ew. Disgusting," Val chided, which made him lick her again.

She reached the top of the stairs and lowered him to his paws in the hallway. He bounded through the bedroom door and took a running leap onto her bed, landing so hard it skidded across the floor with a noisy squeak. Val switched off the light and flopped into her bed beside the dog, who enthusiastically dried himself on her pillows.

"Whatever, dude. Knock yourself out. I'm past caring," she told him, pulling the covers up to her chin. "Freakin' freezing. Assface."

The dog squirmed under the covers and wriggled to her side. Val wrapped an arm around his chest and buried her face in his thick fur.

"You reek," she mumbled.

The dog sighed happily, head on the pillow, living his best life.

"Maybe you'd come if I gave you a name," Val mused, stroking his damp fur. "I feel like an idiot standing in the doorway yelling

'Dog!' whenever I want you to come in. The neighbors must think I have no imagination."

The dog groaned with pleasure as she scratched his ear.

"Rover," she tried. "Buddy. Red. Max."

The dog snorted.

"Yeah, I know. You're not a Max." Val stifled a yawn. "My Uncle Dale had a dog called Bryce Skullcrusher, Slayer of Mountain Wyverns, Drinker of Monster Blood."

The dog yawned.

"Bryce could also breathe fire, which I doubt is in your repertoire," Val added. "It's a good name, though. Bryce? Here, Bryce!"

The dog ignored her.

"Steve," Val suggested. "Dave. Pete. Ol' Fluffy. Squishy." She tickled his tummy. "Goofball."

The dog licked her cheek.

"You're disgusting." Val rolled onto her other side and mopped drool off her face with the sheet. "So gross."

The dog scooted after her, flinging his vast, warm body against hers.

"Impossible to get rid of you," Val mumbled sleepily into her pillow. "Might as well try to shake off my shadow."

The dog sat up sharply.

Val rolled over and blinked at him. "Now that you mention it, that's got a certain ring to it."

The dog tilted his head.

Val tested it. "Shadow."

He barked.

"Come, Shadow!" Val called. "Sit, Shadow. Shadow, get your ass in here, you little shit!"

The dog barked ecstatically, planted his paws on her chest, and licked her face. Val couldn't help bursting into giggles as she tried to fend him off.

"Shadow, calm down," she ordered. "Cut it out."

The dog flopped down with his enormous head on her belly.

"Oof." Val wrapped her arms around his neck. "Good boy, Shadow."

The dog gave a colossal sigh. Val closed her eyes, smiling, and drifted off to sleep in seconds.

Val's hammer didn't clang this time. It tapped.

The sound was almost lost under the dull roar of the cast-iron forge on one side of her basement smithy, which smelled of soot and iron. Long rails held weapons: a battleax with a bent edge, a dusty katana, and a rusty broadsword among them. Wooden drawers lined one wall, each meticulously labeled in Val's strangely graceful script.

She huddled over her work at the bench against the opposite wall. Parchment on the drawing board in front of her contained a myriad of half-finished designs in charcoal pencil. The loupe before her absorbed her attention. She squinted through it as she delicately tapped the tiny hammer against a chisel with a point finer than a ballpoint pen's. The small clamp held a shiny pendant with the deep glitter of faerrous steel, an alloy of iron and faerie dust she'd invented, and diamonds encrusted most of its surface. They left only a tiny area for Val to finish the delicate carving: a swooping dragon, its back curved around the central stone, which was bigger than her thumbnail.

She tapped the hammer, finishing the dragon's left claw, and blew gently on the piece. Shadow made a comfortable footrest. He gave a deep sigh, and Val rubbed his back with her heel.

"Good boy," Val murmured.

Shadow wagged his tail, and it thumped on the floor.

Val ran a silk cloth over the weighty pendant. She'd imported the diamonds from the finest Gem Dwarven mines in the Spine, a mountain range that clove the heart of Avalon, and no earthly diamonds could rival them. Their utter clarity fractured the forge's golden light into thousands of tiny, glimmering shards.

Shadow raised his head sharply and wagged his tail again. A dull knock sounded at the open door at the top of the steps.

Val leaned back, her eyes sore from squinting through her loupe. "Oh hey, Tetra. Come in."

Tetra hovered in the doorway. "In?" she echoed. "Into your smithy?" She wore formfitting designer jeans, a lime green T-shirt, and a red cardigan that clashed hard with the shirt. Human fashion was still mostly beyond her.

"Yeah, get your ass in here," Val grunted.

Tetra almost tiptoed down the steps and gaped at her surroundings. Tools and weapons hung everywhere, and the shelves were labeled with the names of precious metals and priceless gemstones.

"What do you think?" Val asked, holding the pendant to the light.

Tetra gasped. "Whoa. How much is that thing worth?"

"A shit-ton," Val informed her, "in human currency and Avalonian dollars. That's only the diamonds. Never mind the enchantments I've woven into the metal."

"Merlin's hairy tits. It's gorgeous," Tetra whispered.

"It's also imbued with some of the most powerful wards I've ever forged," Val admitted. "This thing will protect the wearer from almost any telepathic attack. It's also useful against panic attacks and flashbacks."

"That's incredible." Tetra shook her head. "I've never seen anything like it."

"No one has," Val told her calmly. "It's unique." She gently attached the steel chain she'd forged earlier and lowered the pendant into a padded velvet box.

Tetra cleared her throat. "You, uh, you said you wanted me to help you with something today. You know. In my new capacity." Her eyes gleamed, and she grew a couple of inches taller.

"Yes." Val placed the velvet box in an iron lockbox, turned the key, and tucked it under her arm. "I need you to act as a bodyguard." She strode across the smithy, Shadow obediently jogging behind her.

"A bodyguard?" Tetra echoed. "For who?"

Val grinned as she reached the steps. "For me."

She climbed the steps into the dining room.

Tetra scrambled after her, almost tripping over Shadow. "For *you*? Excuse me?"

"Yeah. Like I said, this necklace is worth millions in any currency." Val strode through the kitchen to the living room. "It's vital that I deliver it safely to its new owner. I need you to be my eyes and ears—and backup if I run into trouble during the delivery."

Tetra swallowed. "Okay. I can do that. I think. Why don't you send it via brownie courier?"

Val raised her eyebrows. "You know brownies are six inches tall, right? They can open portals between worlds, but they're almost defenseless in a fight. This thing is so valuable that I want to deliver it myself."

"Okay." Tetra nodded, wiping her palms on her pants. "I can help."

"Great." Val grinned. "Shadow, stay."

The dog climbed onto the couch.

"No dogs on the furniture," Val chided.

Shadow placed his head on his paws and sighed blissfully.

"Whatever," Val grumbled. She stomped through the back door.

Tetra shut it behind them. "Shadow? Is that his name now?"

"Had to call him something," Val grumbled.

"Does this mean you've finally admitted he's your dog?" Tetra grinned.

Val rolled her eyes. "I'm not keeping him." She slipped the lockbox into Genevieve's trunk. "Quit mouthing off. Let's go."

"Where does your client live?" Tetra asked, sliding into the passenger seat.

Val grinned. "You'll never guess."

Tetra raised her eyebrows. "Manhattan? New Jersey? Africa? I hear that's a long-ass way away."

Val chuckled as she hit the button to open the garage door. "It's in the same dimension, unlike my client."

Tetra's body stiffened. "We're going back to Avalon?"

"Not only Avalon," Val told her. "Tintagel."

Tetra's jaw dropped. "Tintagel? The home of King Arthur and Morgan Le Fay?"

"Tintagel Village, not the castle," Val admitted, "but it's close enough. We might see it when we go past."

"Merlin's beard," Tetra breathed.

"You've got that right." Val slammed her foot on the gas, and Genevieve screeched from the garage, her engine's roar mingling with Tetra's squeals and Val's raucous laughter.

The OPMA was expecting them. Val and Tetra strode unhindered into the military wing of the squat building housing the Para-Military Agency's New York headquarters. Val only had to flash her throne-issued ID at the front desk for the elf in navy uniform to let them through.

She marched purposefully through the unadorned hallways, which had staid gray carpets and smelled of cheap disinfectant. Phones rang and footsteps echoed as dozens of paras strode past, all wearing navy uniforms with berets bearing gold insignias. Several glanced curiously at Val and Tetra, the only paras in street clothes—if Tetra's questionable ensemble could be considered fit for the street—but none tried to stop them.

Val finally reached a strong metal door labeled Portal Room.

A slender vampire awaited them, her sleeves bearing the stars of a major.

"Hey, girl!" Major Raven Ardelean chirped. "It's good to see you. I heard those asshole humans we turned over to the NYPD got what was coming to them."

"They deserved every drop." Val shook Raven's hand. "This is Tetra Dupont, my partner."

The faerie grew several inches at the word "partner." "Nice to meet you," she managed with a passable attempt at good manners.

Raven chuckled. "Oh, you're the faerie."

Tetra's eyebrows rose. "What are you gonna do about it, bitch?"

Val glared daggers.

Tetra cleared her throat. "I mean, yes, that's right, ma'am." She grimaced apologetically.

"Hey, it's cool." Raven laughed. "I can see why Julie likes you."

Tetra's eyes widened at the casual mention of the Eternity Queen.

"You're headed to Tintagel, I hear?" Raven checked her smart-watch. "I saw you on the schedule for civilian portal usage today and wondered what would persuade you to spend the *amazing* sum it takes to get access to an OPMA portal."

"Precious cargo." Val raised the small lockbox. "With an important owner."

"Ah." Raven raised her eyebrows. "I don't think there's any other kind of owner in Tintagel's area. It's crawling with Lunar Fae these days."

"I'm headed to Seraphine Wordgiver's house. Do you know her?" Val asked.

"I know *of* her. She teaches at Tintagel's school for Lunar Fae." Raven nodded soberly. "She's overcome a lot to live the life she has now. Are you sure you don't want a Special Forces unit to accompany you?"

"I brought my own army." Val smirked, flexing her biceps. "My left army and my right army."

Tetra groaned.

"Oh, and her." Val jerked a thumb at the faerie.

Raven laughed. "Okay, if you're sure." She swiped a keycard to unlock the portal door with an electronic beep and a puff of rainbow-colored magic.

They stepped into a large room far more sumptuous than the rest of the military wing. Its deep red carpet met wood-paneled walls. Classy double doors pierced two of the other walls. The tall ceiling was painted a cream color, and the room had no windows.

Magic portals pierced the walls at intervals. Amulets, buzzing thaumatechnical gadgets, and glowing runes surrounded each. About eight feet in diameter, each portal's edge hummed with either magic or electricity, and they offered crystal-clear views into worlds beyond. Val glimpsed a snowy mountainside, an underground tunnel streaked with lava, a thick jungle, a large room like a parking garage, and more as they walked into the room.

"This way," Raven announced cheerfully, leading them to a portal in the corner. "This'll take you to Tintagel's beach. It's a short ride to the village."

"*Ride?*" Tetra hissed.

"Don't worry. I arranged for transport with a livery in the village," Val reassured her.

"*Livery?*" Tetra hissed again.

"Enjoy your trip!" Raven trilled. "You know where to find us if you need backup."

Val clenched the lockbox under her arm and faced the portal, which gave her a blurred view of a pale beach and sheer white cliffs.

"Val? Hello?" Tetra nudged her. "We're riding *in* something, not *on* something, right?"

"C'mon," Val told her. "Bear down to help with the dizziness." She stepped through the portal with slight trepidation. Nausea flipped her belly, and she gritted her teeth as the interdimensional travel made her head spin. *Will I ever get used to that feeling?* she wondered. Her boots went from the soft carpet to sand, and when Val's vision cleared, she stood on a beach in Avalon.

Tetra stumbled through behind her, retching. It was an unromantic sound to complement one of the most splendid sights Val had ever seen.

"Tetra, look," she whispered. "It's Tintagel. It's really Tintagel."

The faerie looked up, and her breath hitched. Val could hardly inhale either. The castle towering above them on the steep green hills was the most glorious feat of architecture she'd ever seen. She'd driven over the Brooklyn Bridge, stood at the feet of the Statue of Liberty, and walked the halls of the Eternal Palace, but none of those could compare with the splendor of the castle.

Its two sandstone towers rose against the gray sky with understated grace. Arrow slits and stained-glass windows marked their flanks, and the banners of the Pendragon Family and the Eternity Throne flowed down their walls. A mighty bridge spanned the gap between them, its golden stone covered with scorch marks and claw scars that testified to the battles fought here during the Third Pendragon War.

"Whoa," Tetra whispered.

"It's amazing," Val murmured, awed. "Think of all the things that happened here, Tetra. Numerous battles. The reawakening of King Arthur. The incarnation of Luna. And that's only in the Third Pendragon War."

"It's pretty cool," Tetra agreed.

Hoofbeats on sand interrupted their conversation.

"Ah." Val grinned. "Our rides are here."

CHAPTER THREE

"*Horses?*" Tetra wailed.

Val grinned from ear to ear as a stout Woodland Fae strode up to them. The boy had endearing freckles, thick blond curls, and tiny nubs of antlers protruding from his head. He clutched a pair of reins in each hand, and two cobs obediently strode beside him. They were patient, sturdy beasts with long manes and hairy feet, and they regarded Val with minimal interest.

"Not *horses*," Tetra moaned.

"Eiravel Stonehold?" the fae boy asked.

"That's right." Val flipped the boy a dollar. "You'll wait here for me to bring them back, right?"

The boy nodded. "Yes, ma'am."

"Don't 'ma'am' me, boy." Val took the reins of the bigger cob, a black gelding with a white blaze and four socks. "Tetra, that one's yours."

Tetra nervously eyed the piebald mare, whose droopy lip signified that she'd gone to sleep.

"Why horses?" she demanded.

"Easiest way to get across the moor," Val told her, tucking the lockbox into her backpack.

"Don't they have roads here?" Tetra planted her hands on her hips. "What kind of place *is* this?"

"There's a main road from the castle to the village, but it's quicker and safer to go as the crow flies." Val tossed the reins over her cob's head, stuck her left foot in the stirrup, and easily swung into the saddle. "Are you getting on or what?"

The boy handed Tetra the reins, which she held like they might bite her. The piebald mare's ears flopped to the sides.

"I'm not doing this," Tetra announced.

"Suit yourself, but you'd better keep up." Val turned the cob around.

"As if horses were the only off-road option you could think of," Tetra complained, wandering to the wrong side of the mare. "Dirt bikes exist, you know. And magic carpets. I'd even take a broomstick over this thing."

The mare gave her an aggrieved look.

"You have to get over your thing about animals, Tetra," Val ordered. "Get on the horse."

"I don't—" Tetra gritted her teeth. "I don't know how."

"Good thing you booked a beginner mount for this one, miss," the boy chirped.

"Oh, shut up, you," Tetra grumbled.

"I'll help you on," the boy told her.

He cupped his hands, waiting for her knee. She planted her foot in them instead. The fae rolled with it and boosted her into the saddle, and Tetra screamed and grabbed the mare's mane.

Val golf-clapped. "Graceful."

"Shut up," Tetra growled.

The boy stuffed her feet into the stirrups and the reins into her hands. Tetra kept a white-knuckled grip on the mane.

"Ready?" Val asked.

Tetra exhaled. "Wait. *Wait.*" She straightened her spine and scanned the horizon, her black eyes intense. "Okay. I don't see any danger. Let's go."

Val hid her grin as she nudged the gelding forward. *Test passed.*

She guided the gelding to a narrow rocky trail that led up the cliff in tight switchbacks. The canny creature placed his big feet carefully, and despite Tetra's yelps and complaints, the mare plodded after him without needing guidance.

"Lean forward," Val yelled. "Makes it easier for both of you."

She tilted forward and gave the cob his head. The view of Tintagel got more splendid as the horses labored to the clifftop. The smell of equine sweat mingled with the salt of the sea and the peculiar electric fragrance of magic. This place was thick with it, and the bear-shaped amulet Val wore tingled in its presence. She felt its gentle throb on her skin like a second heartbeat.

Under the overcast sky, the moor was as harsh and wild as it was beautiful. Purple heather streaked the thick, wiry bracken. Sharp hills strewn with rocks added to the landscape's rich textures. The asphalt road that ran to Tintagel's gate seemed like an imposition on the wilderness. The castle was so old that it looked like it had grown from the rocks.

It probably had, Val thought. Lunar Fae, who'd built this place, had earth magic too.

"Glad we're not attacking the castle," Tetra grunted, swaying in the saddle as her mare scrambled to the top.

"You'd have to be an idiot to attack that place," Val agreed. Sharp wing shadows marked the sky, broader than city buses as dragons circled over Tintagel.

"Can you see the fae guards from here?" Tetra asked.

Val shook her head. "Dwarves can see well in the dark, not over long distances."

"Well, I can, and they're armed to the teeth. That's without their magic and razor wings." Tetra chuckled nervously. "They're beautiful, but they're dangerous."

"The most dangerous paras in the world," Val acknowledged. "We're not heading for the castle, though." She checked her phone. "Straight across the moor. The village is over that hill."

Val nudged the gelding into a trot. He set off at a bone-jarring jog, his feathered feet swishing in the heather and bracken, and Tetra groaned and yelped as the mare followed.

"Movement!" she squeaked. "On your left."

Val raised her head sharply, barely spotting the three milk-white deer bounding away.

"Only deer," Val yelled.

The cob didn't move fast, but his rhythm never faltered. In minutes, they reached the asphalt road. Val closed her knees, which slowed the cob to a walk, and Tetra grunted in relief as her mare did the same.

"Why horses?" she wailed.

Val chuckled as the horses crossed the road, their hooves ringing on the hard surface. "Do you want an honest answer?"

"*Yes!*" Tetra glared.

"Because I wanted to see if you could focus on your job and stay alert when you had a major uncomfortable distraction," Val confessed.

Tetra glared at her, sweating in her ugly cardigan. "This was a test?"

"It was a test, and you passed." Val laughed. "Also, Avalonians often use horses for transport."

"I grew up here too, you know," Tetra grumbled. "I know that. Do you know how many succulent young nobles I've pulled off their horses?"

Val raised a hand. "I don't want to. Thanks."

Tetra scanned the horizon again as they spoke, not letting her guard down. "Fine. I guess you have a point. I should learn to ride."

"You're not doing a bad job. Don't grab her with your legs. Just sit up straight and hang on." Val grinned wickedly. "We've gone slow so far."

"Oh, no," Tetra moaned.

Val slammed her calves against the gelding's sides. With a

snort of surprise, he took off in a canter. She kept the reins short, feeling his mouth and the rocking motion of his head and neck as he propelled them across the moor in heavy strides. Tetra squealed as the mare obediently followed.

Val's amulet hummed as they left Tintagel behind and cantered up one of the many hills. A stand of trees crowned it, and several turned to look as the horses followed a deer trail between their sturdy trunks.

"Lean back!" Val yelled as the horses bounded down the slope on the other side.

Tetra cursed fluently in numerous languages as they charged through the knee-deep heather. Moths, butterflies, and tiny birds flitted out of their wake.

"Stream!" the faerie yelped.

Val squinted and slowed her mount as a large, gleaming creature rose from the waters of the narrow brook ahead, horse-shaped and composed of water. It swung its large head toward Val, ears pricked, the water forming long, jagged fangs. Her gelding was slowing before she pulled the reins. Both cobs stumbled to a halt a few yards from the brook's edge.

"It's a backahasten," Tetra panted. "They have bigger appetites than faeries. It'll eat you and spit out your bones."

"I'm sure that's an unfair stereotype," Val grumbled, spotting a stone bridge a few yards away.

"Did you see that thing's teeth? Do you want to find out?" Tetra demanded.

"Fine. Come on." Val wheeled her horse around. "Let's take the bridge."

The backahasten watched with eerie white eyes as their horses jogged over the bridge, heads tossing, snorting with worry.

"Well done for spotting it," Val muttered. "We would've been in the stream before I saw it."

Tetra managed a thin smile. "That's what I'm here for, I guess. That and getting blisters on my ass by the feel of it."

Val laughed and squeezed her horse into a canter. He was panting when they crested the next hill and drew rein to look down at Tintagel Village. Its single street wound aimlessly between a handful of stone houses with thatched roofs. The town square featured a stone well at the center.

"Cute," she commented.

Tetra wheezed beside her, hair wild, clinging to the mare's mane. "I hate you."

Val chuckled. "Consider this payback for the heart attack at the bodega."

Tetra rolled her eyes. "Would you get over that already?"

"Not much farther," Val added. "And the horses need to cool down anyway."

She loosened the reins, and her gelding stretched his neck gratefully as they followed a sheep trail down the hill. A faun goatherd sat on a stone wall nearby, watching a flock of sheep and goats nibble grass. One of the goats burped fire, then chewed its cud contentedly. Two dogs, a lion cub, and a little elf chased a ball around the square. Merry song came from a long, low tavern, tempting Val.

Parking spaces lined the square. A pair of carthorses hitched to a large wagon dozed beside a gleaming Bentley. In the space beside them, a bright purple cow chewed her cud on the back of a huge truck with wooden rails.

Val checked her phone for the address, aware of Tetra's watchful gaze as she scanned the village. "She's down this street."

"Uh-huh," Tetra grunted. "You getting a weird vibe from that cow?"

Val eyed the cow. "It's a cow. I don't think it has vibes."

Tetra's eyes narrowed. "I don't trust it."

The ruminating cow flicked her ears at a fly and didn't bother to look as they rode past, but Tetra glared at her anyway.

Seraphine Wordgiver's cottage stood in the midst of a lovingly tended garden at the square's edge. The old sandstone walls supported a conical thatched roof. Marigolds bloomed in the window boxes, and a profusion of well-trimmed ivy climbed lattices along the picket fence. Granite stepping stones led across the neatly mowed lawn to the arched front door, which was painted a calming blue.

Val swung down from her horse and tied him to the picket fence using his reins.

Tetra slithered off the mare and almost landed flat on her ass. She bounced upright and gave the cow another suspicious glare.

Val tied Tetra's mare. "Will you wait out here and keep watch while I make the delivery?"

Tetra nodded. "Sure."

Val unzipped the backpack and retrieved the precious lockbox. She held it reverently in both hands as she followed the stepping stones to the front door and knocked. "Ms. Wordgiver? It's Val Stonehold with your delivery."

Soft footsteps shuffled to the door. A Lunar Fae opened it, her face and movements both youthful, although that meant nothing. She could be twenty, four hundred, or several thousand years old. Her eyes held the shifting rainbow colors of her species. She wore a crocheted shawl over her shoulders and a floral dress disguised most of her graceful figure.

"Hi, Val." The fae smiled with a shyness that didn't suit the aura of power that hung around her, making Val's amulet blaze. "It's nice to meet you in person." She stiffened. "Who's that outside?"

"My partner. She's here to keep a lookout and make sure the delivery goes smoothly. That's all," Val assured her.

Seraphine Wordgiver relaxed slightly. "Okay, that makes sense. Come inside."

Val stepped into the comfortably cluttered cottage. The single bed against one wall had a view of the garden through a round window. Bookshelves lined the walls, and a comfortable rocking chair faced the hearth. The kitchenette was a combination of old wooden furniture and shiny metal appliances. Bunches of herbs and onions dangled from the rafters.

"Would you like a cup of tea?" the Lunar Fae asked.

Val didn't want to be rude. "Yes, please, Ms. Wordgiver." *Fine. I'll drink your disgusting leaf water.*

"Seraphine." The fae smiled. "Call me Seraphine."

She drifted to the kitchenette and poured tea from a china teapot into mugs printed with cats. A fat ginger tom lay curled on her bed.

"Have a seat," Seraphine murmured.

Val slid into a chair by the tiny kitchen table. Seraphine placed the mugs on it and sat opposite her, then pushed the milk and sugar toward her.

"Thanks," Val murmured, adding enough sugar to make the tea bearable.

"I appreciate your willingness to deliver this in person." Seraphine eyed the lockbox on the table between them. "May I?"

"Of course." Val smiled. "It's yours." She waved a hand over the lock, and it clicked open. The lid rose, and the sparkles of the diamonds reflected in Seraphine's eyes. Her face brightened as she lifted out the glowing necklace. Tiny selenite crystals interspersed between the diamonds glowed with moonlight at the presence of Seraphine's magic.

"Oh, Val, it's beautiful," she whispered.

The joy in her voice ignited a warm glow in Val's chest. "Thank you."

"I've never seen anything like it." Seraphine laughed softly. "And that's saying something. I was in the court of King Arthur during the First Golden Age."

Val's eyes widened. That made this fae over ten thousand years old.

"I wear my age well, don't I?" Seraphine chuckled.

Val blushed. "Sorry. I didn't mean to make that face out loud."

Seraphine laughed. "You can make any face you please. I've been searching for a craftsperson to make this piece for a long time. I'm pleased Morgan referred me to you." She turned the necklace over in her hands, admiring its sparkle.

"I don't think any telepathic attack will get through this thing," Val told her. "The wards are the most powerful I could forge. Even ordinary telepathic communication will be blocked. Not even a glawackus would be able to manipulate you."

"Good, good." Seraphine nodded. "My mind has been turbulent since I lost everything in the First Pendragon War. I don't need any company inside it."

"You won't have any when you're wearing this," Val promised. "Diamond is the strongest anchor for any ward, even stronger than iron." She used layman's terms, but the glitter in Seraphine's eyes told her that she didn't have to. "It's the combination of extreme hardness and its many facets. Magic is like light, in a way. It likes to reflect."

"Fascinating." Seraphine ran her thumbs over the diamonds. "I could never make anything like this, Val, but I understand that I'm holding one of the most powerful magical objects I've ever seen." She tilted her head. "I haven't seen Iron Dwarven craftsmanship like this since the First Golden Age."

Val's breath hitched. "You have seen Iron Dwarf work from that time?"

"Of course I did. We saw every kind of work." Seraphine smiled. "King Arthur's vision of a diverse but united empire was unique. No one had ever brought all the paranormal species together the way he did. It was the first time we could share our knowledge and magic with one another. The results were astounding, and the Iron Dwarves stood out."

Val leaned forward. "I didn't learn that as a kid."

"You wouldn't have. It's not common knowledge. Mordred destroyed so much of the First Golden Age during the wars."

Seraphine sighed. "The Iron Dwarves forged Excalibur, you know."

"I do know," Val murmured. "I don't think any of us know how to create a weapon like it anymore."

"Excalibur was far from unique in those days. Iron Dwarves were King Arthur's royal blacksmiths, and they forged the most amazing things. Not only armor and weapons, either." Seraphine smiled. "Before Mordred's uprising, we had little need of those. They made monuments and mechanisms that changed our world."

"Like what?" Val leaned closer, breathless.

Seraphine lowered the necklace, shaking her head. "I'm sorry, Val. I don't..." She exhaled. "I don't remember."

Val straightened, retreating. "It's okay. I didn't mean to pry."

"Not at all." Seraphine gave a thin smile. "After I lost my family, I lost my mind, too. My memories are dim sometimes. Others..." She shivered and clutched the shawl around her shoulders. "Other times, they're far, far too vivid."

"I'm sorry," Val murmured. "I wish my necklace could help with that."

"Oh, it will." Seraphine smiled. "Wearing it, no one can prey on my mind ever again, not like Mordred tried so hard to do." She shook her head as she clasped the necklace around her neck, its gleaming diamonds incongruous against her colorful clothes. "It'll help me greatly. Thank you, Val."

Val finished her awful tea and rose. "Thank you, Seraphine. It was a pleasure to forge it for you."

"Good." Seraphine paused. "If I remember anything about the Iron Dwarves, I'll let you know."

"I would appreciate it," Val told her sincerely. She fished in the front of her shirt for her amulet and withdrew the crude cast-iron bear with ruby eyes. "You don't happen to recognize this, do you?"

Seraphine touched the amulet. "This holds tremendous

power. I've never felt anything with such deep iron magic. And it does look familiar." Her smooth brow creased. "I'm sorry. I can't remember where I've seen it before."

"It's okay." Val dropped the amulet under her shirt, letting it bump her sports bra. "Thanks for the help."

"Anything I can do, let me know." Seraphine opened the cottage door.

Val stepped outside and almost tripped over a semiconscious woman sprawled on the threshold, a nasty black bruise forming on her cheekbone. The woman had bright purple hair.

"What the—" Val jumped. "Tetra!"

"What? She was trying to steal the necklace." Tetra gripped the woman by both ankles. Judging by the state of the unlucky para's hair, the faerie had already dragged her several feet. "Oh, sorry. Let me get her out of your way." She hauled the purple-haired para onto the lawn.

"What's going on?" Seraphine quavered.

"Don't you worry, ma'am. Nothing to be afraid of. An opportunistic thief saw Val's lockbox and wanted it, that's all." Tetra strode to the garden gate, the para's head bumping on each stepping stone. "I told you that cow was totally sus."

Val glanced at the truck across the square, which now had an empty bed. Seraphine gaped as Tetra hauled the groaning werecow through the gate.

"You're safe," Val assured her. "Don't worry."

Seraphine touched her gleaming necklace. "Oh, I know I am." Her shoulders straightened as she smiled.

Val left the fae locking her front door and grabbed the werecow by the belt. She tossed the para over her gelding's shoulders like a sack of flour.

"I had to stop her," Tetra told her nervously as she struggled onto her mare.

Val chuckled. "Don't worry, Tetra. You did good."

The faerie's face lit up.

Val bit her lip in concentration as she mounted the steps in the garage that led to Tetra's apartment. She gripped two coffee mugs in one hand and tried not to trip over Shadow as he scrambled behind her, struggling with his cast.

"You can almost get rid of that thing, buddy," she promised.

The indications of dawn breaking in suburban Bay Ridge surrounded her as she reached the door: birds chirping, a cool breeze, endless honking, and drivers cursing each other in morning traffic. Val knocked on Tetra's door.

No response came from inside.

"Tetra!" Val knocked again. "I'm going to spill your coffee!"

"Go away," Tetra moaned. "It's the middle of the night."

"It's six-thirty in the morning," Val retorted.

"Go *away*," Tetra complained.

Shadow jumped up and scratched the door with the cast and the other paw.

"Dude, cut that out!" Val barked. She shoved the door with her elbows. Unlocked, it swung inward, and Shadow joyously bounded into the apartment.

Val followed him into the open-plan kitchen/living room. The bedroom door was open, and Shadow leaped through it. Tetra's angry yell became a muffled scream.

Val popped her head around the bedroom door and elected to ignore the chaos within. Tetra sprawled in the bed beneath piles of laundry. She'd pulled her covers over her head, displaying only her knuckles. Shadow straddled her, licking her knuckles, then shoving his nose under the covers.

"Geroff, you stupid mutt!" she groaned.

"That's no way to talk to him," Val chided.

"What are you both doing here?" Tetra moaned.

"We have a mission. I brought coffee." Val waved the steam in Tetra's direction.

"Get your dog off me," Tetra wailed.

"He's not my dog," Val grumbled. "Shadow, get down."

The big animal obediently dropped to the floor.

"Coffee's in the living room," Val called.

She carried the mugs to the couch in front of the TV and set them on the coffee table, then flopped on the couch. Shadow climbed into her lap like he was a chihuahua, not a hundred-pound mongrel.

"Idiot," Val muttered affectionately, rubbing his neck.

Tetra emerged from the bedroom wearing surprisingly cute silk pajamas. She perched on the couch next to Val and slurped the coffee like someone dying in a desert.

"My thighs hurt," she complained. "My calves hurt. My back hurts. Most overwhelmingly, my ass hurts. Did you know that you have bones in your ass? I do now. I think I've broken both of them."

"You're a little sore from riding, that's all." Val smirked.

"Riding? You mean clinging to a rabid moped with a mind of its own?" Tetra threw up her free hand. "Why would that make me sore?"

Val chuckled. "Not an animal person, huh?"

Shadow squirmed out of her lap and licked Tetra's face.

"Ew!" Tetra shoved him away. "Definitely not."

Shadow slid to the floor and lay on his back at Tetra's feet.

"Hateful things," Tetra muttered, rubbing Shadow's tummy with her bare foot. The dog groaned in pleasure. "You'd better have a good reason for getting me out of bed at this infernal hour."

"Grownups get up at this time," Val pointed out.

Tetra stuck out her tongue. "*I* don't. You said something about a mission."

"Yeah. Well, I think it's a mission." Val shrugged. "I have an email from Gold, Manns, and Sax requesting my presence immediately. 'In an official capacity.'" She added air quotes to the last sentence.

"Wait, who are they?" Tetra frowned. "They're the bank?"

"Yeah, that's right. I bank with them, but something tells me this has nothing to do with my finances." Val frowned. "I think this is about a security contract. Since you're officially part of the team now—"

"Your *partner*." Tetra beamed.

Val chuckled. "Don't let it go to your head."

"Too late," Tetra informed her.

Val rolled her eyes. "As I was saying, I'd like you to come along."

"Cool!" Tetra bounced to her feet. "I'm getting dressed. See you downstairs in ten."

Val grinned at the faerie's enthusiasm as she flounced to the bedroom. "I think we're making progress with her, buddy," she murmured.

Shadow barked his agreement.

Genevieve's purr sounded unique inside the Brooklyn-Battery Tunnel. Electric lights flashed past as the Mustang whined toward Manhattan, her engine's amplified hum intoxicating in the earth's embrace. Val grinned, shifted gears, and accelerated as empty asphalt extended before them. Genevieve responded with a surge of power and reached a speed that snatched her breath.

Tetra clung to the handle above the door. Val ignored her grimaces as Genevieve sped forward. She felt the earth around the tunnel, its dozens of elements throbbing with possibility. The combination of speed and being underground made her dwarven soul sing.

She slowed as daylight shimmered at the tunnel's end. They

burst into the bright morning, a bark of laughter escaping Val's lips, and ground to a halt in a tightly packed mass of traffic.

"Aw, crap," Tetra complained. "Look at this mess!"

Val chuckled. "We got lucky in the tunnel. We'll crawl the rest of the way to Wall Street, but it's cool. You haven't been in this part of town yet, have you?"

Tetra shook her head. "I've been confined to Bay Ridge and Williamsburg this whole time."

Val groaned. "Are we really going to flog that dead horse again?"

"Why would I flog a dead horse?" Tetra snorted. "It'd spoil the meat and waste the blood."

"Never mind." Val laughed. "You'll enjoy the ride. That's all I'm saying. I couldn't believe my eyes the first time I came here." She rolled down Genevieve's windows as the line of cars crawled forward. "Check these buildings out. Humans built many of them on their own!"

Tetra hung out the window, gaping at the skyscrapers towering around her. Warm sunlight flashed on sleek glass windows and caressed aging rock. Wrought iron lamp posts—human-made, judging by the amateurish work—stood beside the latest electric cars. The mishmash of old and new differed by only a few centuries, nothing compared to places Val had seen in Avalon, but it charmed her nonetheless. She guessed from the look on Tetra's face that the faerie had never seen anything like it before.

"Wow," Tetra managed.

"You ain't seen nothing yet." Val flashed a smile.

They crawled across downtown Manhattan slowly enough that Tetra could gawk to her heart's content. Val finally steered Genevieve into a parking garage on William Street and crawled into a miraculous space near the door.

"It's a short walk. A block, maybe." Val exited the car and

shrugged a denim jacket over her black turtleneck. "We're headed to one of the most iconic sights in the city."

"What's that?" Tetra asked.

"Wall Street. The financial capital of the human world," Val told her.

The faerie snorted as they strode from the parking garage. "Sounds boring."

Val laughed. "Wait 'til you see it."

Tetra's smirk vanished when they turned down Wall Street and the crowded assembly of stone pillars, glass windows, and elegant signage greeted them. The faerie's gaze traveled up 48 Wall Street's five hundred thirteen feet, her jaw dropping farther with each story.

"Yeah." Val chuckled. "Welcome to Wall Street."

CHAPTER FOUR

"That is taller than most of the Eternal Palace's towers," Tetra murmured. "It might be as tall as the round towers at Tintagel."

"Maybe," Val agreed. "C'mon. Gold, Manns, and Sax is down the block."

The bank's building fit in with the street's aging grandeur. Its endless rows of arched windows seemed uncountable, and uniformed valets bustled fastidiously around expensive cars on one side.

"There's valet parking," Tetra observed. "Why are we walking?"

Val shrugged. "I wanted you to experience Wall Street."

A smile tugged at the corners of Tetra's mouth, but she said nothing.

They crossed a polished lobby and took a vintage elevator with wood paneling and brass buttons to the thirtieth floor. A Copper Dwarf receptionist waited inside the opulent room, whose massive windows offered a view that made Val's stomach churn.

"Wow!" Tetra whispered with the confident awe of someone who could fly. "Look how high up we are!"

Val gritted her teeth. "Yeah, I noticed."

She averted her eyes from the vista of skyscraper tops and strode across the deep carpet to the receptionist. "Hi, I'm—" she began.

"Miss Stonehold, good morning." The receptionist failed to give her usual warm smile. "Please go straight to Ms. Gold's office. She's waiting for you."

Val's gut clenched. *Something's wrong.*

"Tetra," she barked, then turned on her heel and strode to the relevant office. Tetra scampered after her, and Val touched the bracelet on her left arm as she walked. The flat steel disc looked like a beautifully carved piece of art, but it unfolded into a bullet-proof shield when required.

Val thumped the door open and strode into Freya Gold's office. The banker sat behind a polished mahogany desk surrounded by elderly tomes, many with titles written in ancient runes Val couldn't read. She sprang to her feet as Val entered. Stress lines creased the corners of her eyes.

"Ms. Gold." Val's hand hovered over her dagger. "Is everything okay?"

"It won't be if we don't get this right." Freya gritted her teeth. "But there's no imminent threat. Please, Miss Stonehold, have a seat." She eyed Tetra.

"This is my partner in the bodyguarding business." Val gestured at the faerie. "Tetra Dupont."

Freya's eyes narrowed as she tried to figure out Tetra's species, but only for an instant. She sagged into her sumptuous office chair as Val skirted a glass coffee table featuring a solid gold statue of old-fashioned scales.

"What do you need?" Val asked as she sat.

Tetra followed suit and stared at the Gold Dwarf across the expanse of mahogany. The unadorned desk had files, a laptop, a notebook, and a pen lined up with fierce precision. A small crystal bowl of mints in foil wrappers stood at its center.

Freya ran a hand over her gelled helmet of golden hair. As with most female dwarves, a neatly trimmed beard adorned her jawline. "I understand that much of your work revolves around security for people and paras, Miss Stonehold. However, Her Majesty suggested I contact you to provide security for a...very important object."

Val's shoulders slumped. "That's not in my wheelhouse, Ms. Gold. I protect living things."

"Allow me to explain the mission." Freya smiled faintly. "You'll soon understand that by keeping this item safe, you would protect realms full of people and paras."

Val raised her eyebrows. "Okay. I'm listening."

"The explanation might be long, but bear with me." Freya steepled her fingers. "What do you know about the talks about the Wild Hunt at the Eternal Palace?"

Tetra shivered in her seat.

"I've heard about it on the news. Something about the Hunters they've captured and that the council can't decide what to do with them," Val replied.

Freya nodded. "We all saw the news coverage of the Wild Hunt's attacks on Queen Julia after Mordred made her a target. For centuries, no one knew who or what the Wild Hunt really was, only that the Hunters were almost impossible to kill and had sinister powers. That changed when Queen Julia's lunar power transformed the Hunters into what first appeared to be ordinary paras. However, the queen soon discovered that those 'ordinary' paras were among the worst villains in history, across time, space, and multiple cultures."

"Oh, yeah. I remember seeing several in the OPMA's containment unit," Val realized. "Baba Yaga was there, and this big snake that wanted to eat the sun or something."

"That's right. Those paranormals committed heinous crimes, including genocide. They tried to guarantee their immortality by participating in an evil rite that turned them into Hunters when they died." Freya shuddered. "It's the darkest magic of all."

"But the Wild Hunt is dead now." Tetra swallowed. "Queen Julia dragged them into the prison realm at the Battle of New Camelot. They're all gone."

"The Wild Hunt as it was no longer exists," Freya agreed. "But the Hunters the queen's lunar magic transformed are still imprisoned in containment units across both dimensions and in the Locker."

"The Wild Hunt isn't a thing, but the evil paras in their original forms still exist," Val translated. "Except for the ones who died in the prison realm."

"Precisely." Freya bit her lip. "The current difficulty the council faces is what to do with those Hunters."

"Simple." Tetra spread her hands. "Kill them."

"Tetra," Val growled.

The faerie cleared her throat. "Sorry."

"The Eternity Throne has not approved a death penalty since the discovery of the prison realm during the First Golden Age. I believe Queen Julia strives to avoid resorting to execution." Freya sat back.

"What about the prison realm? It worked on the others," Val pointed out.

Freya shook her head. "Many question the prison realm's security since Mordred escaped it. They argue that if Mordred had been beheaded after the Sylthana Elves captured him, the Third Pendragon War—and its thousands of casualties—would not have happened."

Val rubbed her chin. "I see."

"In the meantime, these dangerous paras are still captive within our dimensions. The queen is determined not to let them escape." Freya leaned forward. "That's where you and your...associate come in."

Tetra gulped and reached across the desk for a mint.

"How can we help?" Val asked.

"The queen is procuring artifacts that might assist us in containing—and, in the event of an escape, recapturing—these paras." Freya raised her chin. "The world believed them dead for centuries, and many important weapons and artifacts have gone missing. However, she has located the most important one."

Val leaned closer. "What is it?"

"Gaia's Sickle," Freya told her.

Val snorted and struggled not to laugh, but a choked snicker escaped her. Twin spots of scarlet appeared on Freya's cheeks, and the dwarf gently cleared her throat.

"'Gaia's Sickle?'" Tetra raised her eyebrows. "Why are you acting weird about it?"

Val chortled. "Do you know what Kronos did with Gaia's Sickle?"

"I don't know who any of these paras are," Tetra snapped.

Freya frowned.

"It's basic ancient history." Val cleared her throat. "I'll explain later."

"No, it's all right. We should all understand the sickle's importance." Freya rubbed her upper lip. "In the days before King Arthur, Sylthana Elves ruled a large part of this dimension, and their near-immortal king and queen subjugated elves and humans alike. That was Gaia and her husband, Uranus."

"Whose—" Tetra began but fell silent when Val leveled a glare at her.

"Kronos was their son, but Uranus was abusive and cruel. His toxicity caused Kronos to become one of the most dangerous paras ever to exist." Val folded her arms.

"Gaia and Kronos conspired against Uranus. Gaia hid her son in her bedroom. Sick of Uranus' abuse, Gaia gave Kronos her only weapon: her sickle. When Uranus came into his wife's room that night, uh..." The red spots reappeared on Freya's cheeks.

"Kronos chopped off his father's genitals with the sickle," Val finished.

Tetra snickered.

"With Uranus conquered, Kronos became king. Everyone in his reach bowed before him," Val continued. "Misguided humans even worshipped him and his successors. His Sylthana powers were off the charts. He was also an evil asshole."

"I must agree with your assessment." Freya grimaced. "A prophecy informed Kronos that one of his children would defeat him, so each time his wife and sister Rhea gave birth, he consumed the baby."

"Wait." Tetra paused. "'Consumed?'"

"He ate them," Val told her.

"All of them? Not just the runts and weaklings?" Tetra asked. "That's messed up."

"I would argue that eating any of your babies is messed up, but we'll have that conversation later," Val muttered.

"Rhea succeeded in saving one of her children, a son named Zeus," Freya went on. "She gave him to adoptive parents, who raised him to adulthood. Zeus returned to avenge his siblings. Gaia, who hated that Kronos had grown up to be worse than his father, gave Zeus the sickle that had conquered Uranus."

"So, Zeus cut off Kronos' balls, too?" Tetra inquired.

"No." Val grimaced. "He cut off Kronos' head."

"Well, that makes more sense if you think about it," Tetra acknowledged.

"No weapon had ever harmed Kronos before, but Gaia's Sickle conquered him." Freya interlaced her fingers and squeezed. "It's the only thing that can kill him, and its magic can contain him. If Kronos escaped, he could murder thousands of paras. His power and depravity are difficult to describe."

"Worse than Mordred," Val murmured.

Tetra blinked. "Shit. Really?"

"Really," Freya affirmed.

Tetra nodded and popped the mint, wrapper and all, into her mouth.

Val pretended not to notice. "You need us to transport Gaia's Sickle?"

"Yes. The OPMA tracked it to Maximilian Opulencia, a wealthy Were noble who lives in the Catskills. He has owned the sickle for hundreds of years. We are negotiating its purchase as we speak. After the sickle is secured, we wish to bring it here since our vault is among the safest places in either dimension," Freya explained. "That's where you come in."

Tetra noisily crunched the mint, wrapper crinkling.

"If the sickle is so vital, why not use an army to bring it in? Or a magic portal?" Val asked.

"Being a dangerous magical weapon, Gaia's Sickle is heavily warded. We would prefer not to risk lifting the wards to transport it by portal." Freya steepled her fingers. "We also wish to transport the sickle as inconspicuously as possible. An OPMA unit could keep it secure in the event of an attack, but we have to consider the potential for collateral damage."

She spread her arms. "We're in one of Earth's most densely populated places, Miss Stonehold. Millions of innocent human lives surround us."

"Two people, one car, one sickle." Tetra grinned, foil flashing in her smile. "Makes sense."

"You would be unlikely to attract human or paranormal attention." Freya spread her hands. "Her Majesty believes you're capable of defending the sickle against any attackers."

"Are you expecting an attack?" Val asked.

Freya paused. "It's not impossible," she conceded. "The sickle is culturally, magically, historically, and materially valuable. From opportunistic thieves to those who believe it belongs in Sylthana hands, many paras might attempt to steal it."

Val rubbed her chin. "I'm not interested in securing somebody's diamonds, Ms. Gold, but if you say that this sickle could help the Eternity Queen keep the peace, I'm all in. I have to make a delivery tomorrow, though."

"We're still negotiating with Mr. Opulencia. He is..." Freya paused again. "He is an interesting character. I will be in touch with a transport date after we finalize the negotiations. It will be several days at least."

"Perfect." Val nodded. "Tell Her Majesty I'm ready."

Freya's smile flickered. "Thank you, Miss Stonehold." The lines around her eyes eased.

Val extended a hand. "It's Val."

The dwarf smiled for real when she grasped Val's hand. "Freya."

Shadow sprawled on the table in the examination room at the vet clinic. His bulk covered the surface, leaving only glimpses of stainless steel here and there. His tail hung off the end. It faintly twitched when Val rubbed his head.

"She'll be back in a minute, boy," she promised.

Shadow shifted his weight with a groan. His front paw jutted out, trapped in its extremely grimy cast.

"Poor sad boy." Val played with his floppy ears.

Jess bustled back into the exam room, grinning.

Val straightened. "I hope your face means it's good news."

"It's *great* news." Jess's grin widened. "Here, let me show you." She turned to a computer monitor on the counter against one wall and clicked to pull up a pair of X-rays. "This is the one we took when you brought him in. See that fracture of the humerus?" She pointed at a dark line running through white bone.

Val nodded, her hand tightening on Shadow's leash. He licked her wrist.

"*This* is today's X-ray." Jess stepped aside. "Look at that!"

"Wow." Val leaned closer. "I can't see it anymore."

"Neither can I. Neither can anyone since it's healed perfectly." Jess beamed.

"Aw, good boy, Shadow." Relief washed through Val as she ran her hands over the dog's thick coat. "Does that mean we can take the cast off?"

"It sure does. He's got no reason to wear it anymore." Jess rummaged in a drawer and pulled out a tiny saw. "Hold his head for me, please."

At previous checkups, Jess had mentioned the possibility of sedating Shadow, but the big dog didn't seem to mind the sound of the saw. Val hugged his massive head against her chest, and he lay motionless, albeit trembling, as Jess cut a long slit in the pale cast. She set the saw aside, gripped the cast with both hands, and broke it open, revealing the shrunken forelimb.

"Look at that. Beautiful," Jess murmured. She moved the cast aside and gently manipulated Shadow's leg, rotating his joints. "He has full range of motion. Obviously, he's lost muscle tone, but he'll get that back quickly."

Shadow pulled his head from Val's arms and bestowed a splash of his tongue on Jess's face.

"Shadow!" Val scolded.

Jess laughed, mopping drool off her cheeks. "It's okay. You're welcome, big buddy." She scrunched her hands in the loose skin of his neck. "I'm glad you finally named him."

She turned to the monitor and closed the X-rays.

Val glimpsed the dog's chart on the screen with his name at the top: **Shadow Stonehold**. "You'll need to change that when he finds a new home," she grumbled.

"We all know he's in his forever home, Val." Jess grinned. "Want to see how he feels about having the cast off?"

Val laughed. "Absolutely."

She lifted Shadow from the table, and the big dog jogged by her side as they strolled down the tiled hall that smelled of disinfectant and cat urine. Jess opened the end door into a small courtyard in which yellowed grass clung to life.

"Okay, boy." She grinned. "Let's see what you can do."

Val unclipped the leash from Shadow's collar. "Off you go."

Shadow took off like a shot. He bounded around the tiny courtyard, his weight shaking the ground as he thundered past them, tail tucked low, ears flat, mouth wide with glee.

"Look at him go!" Jess giggled.

"He's been getting around pretty well with his cast, but he looks very happy to have it gone." Val folded her arms. "It doesn't look like his leg hurts at all."

"I doubt it will. You might want to think about starting him on a joint supplement, though. He's a big boy, and it's not a bad idea for giant breeds like him," Jess told her. "I've got several options in the store."

"Cool. You pick the best one, and I'll give him that." Val beamed as Shadow zoomed past her.

Jess chuckled. "Look at you, doting on your big pet. I spotted you picking a new toy for him when you came in."

Val shuffled her feet. "Yeah, well, he's so good during his vet visits. I reckon he deserves a treat."

"I fully agree." Jess smiled. "I'm glad he landed with you, Val. Not many abandoned pets are so lucky." She paused. "Don't take this the wrong way, but it's nice to see a large dog like this ending up with someone who has the means to care for him."

Val nodded. "It's nice to have those means. The jewelry business is growing every day. I've had to turn away a few clients because I'm so booked."

"Wow. Well done." Jess raised her eyebrows, impressed. "How about the security business?"

"I have an important new assignment coming up in the next few days. Having Tetra on my team gives me more options," Val admitted. "She's had my back more than once."

Jess nodded slowly. "I can't get a read on Tetra, but I'm glad you have backup." She paused. "Have you spoken to Liam again about the idea of him acting as your ops manager?"

Val chuckled. "He didn't seem into it, and I don't want to push him. He helped me with the BrewCorp debacle, but I get that this isn't exactly up his alley."

"Actually, I think you should talk to him again." Jess bit her lip. "I don't think he wants to tell you this because he's not expecting any handouts, but Lee's struggling for work right now."

Val tilted her head. "Not a great time in the freelance interior design business?"

"I wouldn't say that, but his depression gave his business a big knock," Jess told her.

Shadow bounced over and flopped down at Val's feet, tail wagging furiously. She rubbed his belly with the rough sole of a hobnailed boot. "It's hard to be creative when you're not in a good place emotionally," she murmured.

"His quality suffered, and he couldn't deliver on time. A few clients hung around, but many walked out on him, and it's hard to blame them. He's trying to build it up again." Jess shrugged. "I'm just saying that he's got free time and needs a paycheck."

"I'm not sure how he feels about getting involved in the security business." Val worked her boot up and down Shadow's ribs, to his delight.

"There's only one way to find out, right?" Jess smiled. "Look at his MMA obsession. Lee's not as delicate as he seems."

"You have a point." Val shrugged. "I'd love to work with Liam. I don't want to take advantage of him, though."

"Working for you would be good for him," Jess told her firmly. "I've known Lee for a long time. Trust me on this one."

Val met Jess's eyes. The woman had grown up with Liam. If anyone knew him, it was Jess. "Okay, I'll talk to him."

Jess' shoulders relaxed. "Thanks, Val. Let's go and see about that new toy, huh, Shadow?"

The word "toy" brought the big dog to his feet, and he barked, tail waving. Val and Jess laughed as Val reattached the leash, and they strode down the hallway together.

Shadow sprawled contentedly on Genevieve's backseat, engulfing it. The Mustang purred as Val steered her through Brooklyn.

"Beats me why you don't mind having dog hair and drool all over you," Val muttered.

Genevieve honked cheerfully.

"I'll have to ask Her Majesty when I see her again." Val rubbed her chin. "What do you think about what Jess said, buddy? Should we talk to Liam?"

Shadow raised his head and pricked his floppy ears but made no sound.

"Yeah, I think you're right. It *is* a good idea." Val stopped at a red light and dialed Liam's number. She put her phone aside as the light turned green, using the hands-free system magically installed in the classic Mustang.

Liam answered on the third ring. "Hey, Val. How was Shadow's check-up?"

"It was great. Jess took his cast off, and he's going to be fine." Val grinned. "Listen, Lee, are you busy right now?"

Liam missed a beat. "Um, no. Not right now. I'm, um, between clients."

Shit. Jess was right. Liam was in trouble.

"Great. I'm headed to this great sushi place Stella told me about in Brooklyn Heights. Thought I'd check it out. Do you want to come?" Val asked. "There's something I'd like to chat about if you have the time."

"Sushi? You know I'll never say no to that stuff." Liam chuckled.

"My treat. See you there in, say, twenty?" Val asked.

Liam paused again. "Make it an hour. I'm, uh, taking the subway."

Sold his car, Val concluded instantly. "That's cool. I'll take Shadow to the park in the meantime. Let him enjoy running around without a cast."

Relief filled Liam's voice. "Awesome. Thanks, Val. I'll see you there."

CHAPTER FIVE

The katanas hanging over the counter at the sushi place were fake. Val knew it the moment she stepped through the door and figured that wasn't surprising, but it still managed to piss her off.

"This place's sushi better be good," she muttered.

Plodding obediently at her heels, Shadow twitched his tail in agreement.

Val picked a booth near the door, and Shadow lay at her feet, mostly hidden in the gloom beneath the table. A curvy waitress with an impressive afro took her order for the all-you-can-eat special.

"Something to drink, ma'am?" the waitress asked.

"What's the strongest booze you've got?" Val asked.

The waitress paused. "We have excellent sake."

Val had no idea what that was. "Bring me a bottle."

The waitress gave another pause. "A whole bottle, ma'am?"

"Why not?" Val grinned.

Liam arrived at the same time as the sake. He raised his eyebrows at the bottle as the waitress placed it and two little pottery cups on the table.

"You ordered a *bottle*?" he asked.

Val hesitated. "I saw you doing shots at the Fist a few nights ago, but we can have soda instead."

Liam laughed. "No, it's cool, Val. I skirted the edge of addiction but never actually fell in. I can have a few *choko*."

"A few what?" Val raised her eyebrows.

Liam raised one of the pottery glasses. "*Choko*. Traditional sake glasses."

"Whatever, man." Val generously slopped sake into both glasses. "Let's drink!"

She knocked back the pleasant, mild fluid in a gulp. Liam sipped delicately.

"Doesn't have much of a bite, does it?" Val eyed the bottle.

"It's rice wine," Liam told her.

"Interesting." Val refilled her glass.

Shadow's tail thudded on the floor, and the big dog rested his head on Liam's knee.

"Hey, dude." Liam rumpled his ears. "Look at your leggy. Isn't that much better? Yes, it's much better. Yes, it is. Yes, it is, Shaddy-boy."

"Don't baby-talk him like that," Val grumbled. "It's an affront to his dignity."

Shadow's tail wagged faster.

"He doesn't mind." Liam kissed the top of his head. "Do you, buddy-boo?"

The waitress reappeared carrying an impressive tray of sushi. Val's mouth watered as she lowered it to the table.

"Thanks." Val grabbed her chopsticks.

The waitress glanced sidelong at Shadow and scurried away.

Liam broke his chopsticks apart and rubbed them against each other with practiced ease. "Whoa, this is a lot of sushi."

"Seems like an appropriate amount." Val grinned and grabbed a crab maki.

Liam chuckled. "I *am* hungry." He dragged a prawn nigiri through a bowl of soy sauce.

Val popped the maki into her mouth and groaned with pleasure at the fresh, varied flavors on her tongue. "So good."

"Right?" Liam mumbled around a mouthful.

"Love it." Val sipped sake. "Listen, Lee, I have an ulterior motive for bringing you here and stuffing you full of sushi."

"You said you wanted to talk." Liam lowered his chopsticks. "Is everything okay?"

"Everything's fine," Val reassured him. "I wanted to discuss making you my operations manager."

Liam scoffed. "I'm not hacking into any more major corporations for you if that's what you mean."

"Not at all." Val grinned. "Though you know we couldn't have caught BrewCorp and the gang if it wasn't for you, right?"

Liam offered a modest grin around a mouthful of uramaki. "I'm not the one who dodged bullets and shit."

"Only bullets." Val winked. "No shit."

Liam laughed and took another delicate sip of sake.

"I'm seeing potential to grow my security business." Val selected a slice of salmon sashimi. "Tetra's a big help, but we need someone to coordinate our comms and missions. I think you'd be perfect for the job."

"Oh, yeah. You looked at me, the depressed interior designer, and thought, 'Wow, that's exactly the kind of guy I need to run my operations.'" Liam raised his eyebrows.

Val met his gaze. "That's exactly what I did."

Liam froze. Neither moved until the shuffle of footsteps caught Val's attention. A fastidious little balding man approached their table, shooting glances at Shadow.

"Miss. Sir." The man bowed slightly to Val, then to Liam. "I trust you're enjoying your sushi?"

"It's great." Val gave him a don't-be-an-asshole grin. "The sake, too."

"Good, good." The man rubbed his hands; a nametag on his

shirt designated him the manager. "I'm afraid we don't allow pets in this establishment."

Val set down her chopsticks and folded her arms, aware of her muscles bulging against her coat. "You don't allow pets, huh?"

"No, miss. I'm afraid we don't." The manager failed to get the hint.

Val rubbed Shadow with her boot. He'd fallen asleep with his head on his paws. "Well, he's not a pet."

The manager hesitated. "Is...is that so?"

"Yes." Val lowered her tone to a rumbling growl. "He's my emotional support animal."

The manager's eyes popped as he scanned the knife on her hip and the width of her shoulders.

"Yes, miss," he squeaked. "That's fine, miss. Many apologies, miss." He scurried off.

"You're dreadful," Liam informed her.

Val grinned and grabbed her chopsticks. "Who says I don't need a little emotional support now and then?"

Liam rolled his eyes. "I thought this conversation was about tech support."

"It is. I need that, too." Val dunked another uramaki in soy sauce. "You'd be great at it, Lee."

"I'm not so sure." Liam dabbed his lips with a napkin. "You said you're seeing the potential for your business to grow. Are you thinking of taking on more new clients?"

"Not really." Val paused. "I've told you about my main client before."

"Yeah. The shadowy government leader who's so classified you can't tell me anything about her," Liam muttered.

"That's right. She's...anticipating trouble in her organization." Val paused. "The shit might hit the fan, and we have to try to stop it. If it *does* hit the fan, we have to be ready to clean it up."

"I assume I'll get a higher security clearance if I agree to do this," Liam suggested.

Val had no idea what Eternity Law said about human knowledge of the paranormal world. Generally, it was illegal for humans to know anything about it, but Queen Julia's adopted mom Rosa was a human who lived in the Eternal Palace. There had to be exceptions.

"I'm not sure about the technicalities," she admitted, "but if it's safe for you, I'll try."

Liam raised his hands. "No, thank you. I don't need to know anything somebody might try to kill me for."

Val scoffed. "I'd like to see them try. We'll protect your identity, Liam. The last thing I want is to put you in danger."

"That makes two of us." Liam sipped sake. "I'm not interested in getting into trouble. Or killed. Still…" His voice trailed off.

"Still?" Val prompted.

Liam ran a hand through his soft dark-blond hair. "I'm hurting for clients," he finally admitted. "And I know this gig would pay well."

"It would," Val reassured him, spearing sashimi. "But I don't want you to do it solely for the money."

"I wouldn't." Liam exhaled. "Truth is, Val, I still struggle with my life feeling pointless. I suppose it's not in the cards for me to be a kick-ass hero like you, but if I can help in a way that matters, even if it's a small way, I'd like to do that." He paused. "I'm not sure I have the skills you're looking for, that's all. BrewCorp's network security wasn't very high-tech. Don't be too impressed with what I achieved there."

"I was impressed, firstly." Val grinned. "Secondly, my client works with new tech that most people have never heard of anyway."

"Wow, that's encouraging," Liam grumbled.

Val rubbed Shadow's shoulder with her toe. "I was about to offer you help from someone in my client's organization. I know a girl who could show you the new tech and provide whatever gadgets we need. She's a fellow geek."

"Why don't you ask *her* to be your ops manager?" Liam asked.

Val met his eyes. "Because she's not you, and you're the one I trust."

Liam slumped in his seat. "You're making it hard to say no."

"I'm happy to accept that if you truly don't want to do it." Val topped up her choko. "Just be sure of your reasons for saying no. If you don't like the idea or you're not comfortable with what I do, I get that. But don't turn it down because of an inferiority complex."

"Not mincing words, are you?" Liam raised his eyebrows.

Val downed the sake. "When do I ever?"

"Good point." The corner of Liam's mouth quirked up. "Okay, sure. I'll think about it and let you know. I owe you that much."

"You don't owe me a thing, Lee." Val smiled. "I'm glad you'll think about it, though."

Liam patted his belly. "Maybe later. Right now, I'm too full to think."

Val chuckled. "Do you mind?"

Liam pushed his half-finished plate away. "Have at it."

Val tucked into her second plate of sushi with enthusiasm.

Val weighed the katana in her palm. She'd stolen it from a fae assassin—in her defense, he was trying to kill her, and he was far too dead to miss it now—and its breathtaking workmanship made it as light as air in her hand.

Her muscles tensed and she sank into a balanced stance, her feet wide apart, her weight even. Her eyes narrowed as she focused on her target.

Val moved with breathtaking speed. The katana flashed, catching the forge's yellow light, and landed hard. One, two, three swift strikes slammed into it. Val used the momentum of each ringing rebound to send another firm strike thundering home.

None touched the straw dummy she'd set up in the middle of the smithy. Each blow stopped six inches from the straw as though she'd hit cast iron. Purple magic flashed across the otherwise invisible ward with every strike.

Val stepped back and lowered the blade, grinning. The straw dummy had an amulet hanging around its neck on an iron chain. Iron, salt, and obsidian combined in the amulet to form very potent wards.

There was a knock on the smithy's door. Val glanced up, sweating, to see Tetra's form silhouetted in the doorway.

"Is everything okay down here?" she called. "It got louder than usual."

Shadow lay in a fluffy dog bed by the forge. When he heard Tetra, he raised his head and wagged his tail.

"Everything's fine, but come on down." Val tilted the katana to inspect the blade. "I could use a pair of hands." The ward had notched the katana's edge. *Impressive.*

Tetra traipsed down the steps. "What are you working on?"

"An amulet for the crown princess." Val nodded at it.

Tetra nodded sagely. "I imagine that her parents want to keep her safe."

"Obviously, but the amulet will mostly keep her from setting her babysitter on fire," Val told her. "Being half-elf doesn't seem to have reduced Lillirelda's Lunar Fae powers."

"I'd almost forgotten she's mixed-species." Tetra touched the amulet. "Ooh, that tingles. Does it have wards?"

"Heavy wards that form a bubble around her. They should protect her from everything. And everything from her." Val chuckled. "A necessity for a toddler as magical as she is."

"A necessity for most toddlers, I'll bet. I don't know since I'm not a baby person. What do you need?" Tetra asked.

Val stepped back. "I need you to hit that dummy with your

most vicious faerie dust." She grabbed a welding helmet from a nearby rack and put it on.

"Are you sure?" Tetra eyed the amulet. "It'll eat through iron like it's paper. I don't want to ruin all your hard work."

Val scoffed. "If my amulet can't protect Lillirelda from faerie dust, you might as well melt it." She unhooked a pair of goggles from the same rack and put them on Shadow, who happily submitted.

"Okay. If you say so." Tetra interlaced her fingers and stretched her arms. Her knuckles popped with a puff of rainbow-colored faerie dust. It sizzled when it hit the earthen floor and created several smoking holes. "Oops."

"Yes. That." Val flipped her welding helmet down and grabbed the fire extinguisher from its bracket on the wall. "I'd like you to do that to the amulet."

"If you're sure." Tetra gave an it's-your-funeral shrug and turned to the amulet. She clenched her fists, and a rainbow glow pulsed beneath her skin, following her veins. Her jaw clenched. She flicked both hands forward, opening her fingers, and two fistfuls of faerie dust shot toward the amulet in glowing bolts.

They hit the wards with a brilliant flash that seared Val's vision through the helmet. Tetra yelped as her clothes caught fire. Bits of faerie dust landed all over the smithy, scorching holes in the walls and floor and melting an iron bar into a goopy mess.

Val marched up with the fire extinguisher and blasted Tetra, then went around the smithy, sweeping the white foam over everything that smoked.

"Sorry," Tetra squeaked.

"Don't apologize. You did exactly what I asked." Val flipped the helmet back and grinned. "Check it out."

Tetra slapped at the smoldering holes in her baggy hot pink T-shirt and lime green leggings as she gaped at the straw dummy. It stood serene and untouched amid the carnage.

"That's some amulet," she muttered.

"I know." Val grinned. "I'm almost done testing it. One last thing."

She returned the extinguisher to its hook and bustled to a ballistic glass wall on wheels at the back of the smithy. It rumbled over the floor as she positioned it between the dummy and her workbench.

"This ought to be good," Tetra muttered.

Val handed Tetra a pair of headphones. She pulled two fat cotton balls from her pocket, stuck them in Shadow's ears, and put on her own headphones. "Ready?"

Tetra sat beside Shadow at the workbench, as far as she could get from the ballistic glass. "Ready."

Val grabbed a detonator from the workbench. "Fire in the hole!" She hit the big red button.

The straw dummy turned into a raging fireball that did not extend more than six inches in any direction. Flames boiled behind the wards, which throbbed purple but didn't falter. A muffled boom rattled the ballistic glass as the dummy vaporized into charred splinters and pale ash.

"Merlin's dangling balls," Tetra intoned.

Val chuckled. "I think it works."

"No shit." Tetra removed her headphones as the fire fizzled, leaving only the dummy's smoldering pole. "I don't think anything will get past those wards."

Val scooted the ballistic glass aside and gingerly removed the amulet from the pole with a pair of tongs. She plunged the amulet into a bucket of water, which steamed. "Mission accomplished, then. Feel like a trip to Avalon Town?"

Tetra grimaced. "You're going to deliver that thing to the queen in person?"

"Yeah." Val laughed. "No worries if you don't want to come, though. I don't need a bodyguard this time."

"I'll stay home, thanks. The palace triggers me." Tetra shuddered. "I might run into my dad, too, or my sister."

"You're only exiled from the faerie kingdom in Fernwood Deep. You can go to the palace if you want, under your vassalship to me," Val pointed out.

"Thanks, but no thanks. Enjoy your road trip. I'll be here watching *The Mandalorian*," Tetra told her.

Val gasped theatrically. "You're watching *The Mandalorian*? Have you seen the *Star Wars* movies?"

"There are movies?" Tetra asked, nonplussed.

"Liam would be disgusted." Val laughed. "I'll tell you about it later." She dried the amulet on a soft cloth and tucked it into a purple velvet bag. "Are *you* coming, Shad? I mean, Shadow?"

Shadow lay contentedly with his head on his paws.

"You put cotton in his ears, idiot," Tetra chided.

"Oh, yeah. Sorry." Val lifted the dog's ears, fished out the cotton, and pulled off his steampunk goggles. "C'mon, Shadow. Let's go to the palace."

Shadow bounded to his feet and barked.

"Is it pet-friendly?" Tetra inquired.

"I'll pass him off as a werewolf if I have to." Val shrugged on a leather trench coat and slipped the amulet into an inner pocket. "See you."

In the garage, Shadow bounded into Genevieve with a bark of excitement. The Mustang started herself before Val could insert the key.

"Excited to see the queen, huh?" Val murmured.

Genevieve's roar of affirmation rattled the garage's windows.

As Genevieve drove herself slowly through the many courtyards and passages of the Eternal Palace, Val reached back to roll down Shadow's window. "No jumping out," she warned. "Okay?"

Shadow stuck his head out, tongue lolling, his waving tail brushing the opposite window.

"Good boy." Val scrunched his ears.

The walls towered around them like Manhattan's skyscrapers. Wrought iron signs directed Genevieve across colorful cobblestones toward the guest parking near the throne room. Neatly trimmed shrubbery in the shapes of magical creatures, complete with flowers that formed their scales, feathers, eyes, or teeth, decorated the courtyards. Priceless statues carved from giant gemstones accompanied them.

A six-inch humanoid in a pinstriped suit popped out from behind one of the statues. Genevieve stopped hard before Val could jab the brakes.

"Dylan!" Val roared as Shadow barked. "Do you want to get run over?"

Dylan strutted to the driver's side, walking like he had a stick up his ass, which he did. "Miss Stonehold." He bowed stiffly. "Her Majesty awaits you in her quarters."

Val hesitated. "The queen wants me to go to, like, her house?"

"Indeed. I will show you the way," Dylan offered.

"Uh, cool. Thanks." Val swallowed.

The brownie materialized on her passenger seat, causing Val to jump so hard that she hit her head on Genevieve's roof.

"*Ow!* Shit." Val rubbed her head. "Oh, this is Shadow. I hope Her Majesty isn't allergic to dogs."

"I doubt it, miss, considering that she has spent the past three weekends dragging His Majesty across Avalon's and Earth's animal shelters," Dylan murmured.

"Oh." Val cleared her throat. "Okay. Which way?"

The brownie directed her through a maze of courtyards and finally into the palace's keep. Val tried not to look intimidated as they passed beneath a massive portcullis with a large contingent of griffins stationed before it. The powerful creatures stood taller than Genevieve, with leonine bodies and talons as thick as Val's wrists. Sharp yellow eyes followed the car through the gateway.

A round tower waited on the other side. Its many broad

windows were modern and stylish with aluminum frames, and the giant wooden doors stood slightly open. Val got out to the sound of hysterical giggling from within. The giggles turned into squeals of perfect joy.

"I'm going to get you!" someone teased in a British accent. "I'm coming to *get you*!"

A toddler burst through the doors, squealing as she sprinted on chubby little legs. Her hair streamed over her shoulders in a straight black curtain, and despite the delicate dragonfly wings amid the torrential hair, her ears were elven. She wore a grubby dress designating her *Mommy's Little Angel.*

"No catch me!" the toddler yelled.

The most powerful mage in the world plunged through the doors after her. "I'm coming for you, Lilli!" he roared.

Val gasped. She'd met Merlin Ambrosius in the flesh before, but she hadn't taken in his full splendor. His silver beard curled richly on his chest. Magnificent wings patterned in rainbow colors caught the sunlight. The blue sweatsuit covered with silver moons and stars failed to detract from his splendor.

A gust of wind snatched Lillirelda into the air and tumbled her into Merlin's arms. "Gotcha!" he cooed and smothered the tiny face with kisses as the toddler screeched in delight.

"Hat! Careful!" Queen Julia stumbled through the doors behind him. "If you make her too happy, she'll—"

"Oh, bollocks," Merlin intoned.

A whirlwind raced around Val's legs, strong enough to make her stumble. Merlin tightened his grip on Lillirelda, who giggled as the whirlwind tore at her hair and made his sweatsuit billow out. King Taylor emerged from the doorway, holding up his hands to shield his eyes.

"Lilli!" Queen Julia roared.

Lillirelda's laughter got louder.

"*Lilli!*" Queen Julia waved her arms, and the selenite in the doorway flashed so brilliantly that it scorched Val's vision. The whirlwind vanished, and Lillirelda's laughter stopped.

"Oh, double bollocks." Merlin hastily put the toddler on the ground.

"Mama's sorry, moondrop." Queen Julia crouched and held out her hands. "Mama's sorry."

Val took a step back. Lillirelda was smoking.

A car door slammed behind Val. "*Lillireeeeeeeeeelda!*" someone shrieked.

Lillirelda spun, grinning behind her wild hair. "Grandmama!" she squealed and bolted across the courtyard, arms outstretched.

"Thank Luna." King Taylor's shoulders sagged.

"As you can see, Miss Stonehold," Dylan murmured, "chaos rules here."

"Val." Queen Julia gripped Val's shoulders, her hands hot. Dark rings lay beneath her sharp eyes, which had lost none of their brilliance. Her pixie-cut dark hair stood on end. "Tell me the amulet works."

Val cleared her throat. "It works, Your Majesty."

"That's wonderful. Wait, I'm being weird. Sorry. Motherhood is hard. Motherhood while attempting to keep multiple worlds from collapsing into war is a whole 'nother story." Julie stepped back and inhaled deeply.

"It's okay, babe." Taylor wrapped an arm around his wife's shoulders. "Nobody blames you."

"I certainly don't." Val cleared her throat. "I brought my dog."

"Yay! Dog!" Queen Julia shoved past her to say hi to Shadow. Genevieve opened the driver's door for him, and Shadow bounded around the queen's legs, barking joyfully.

Taylor chuckled. "Maybe we *should* get that dog."

"Your Majesty, I beg you!" Dylan wailed. "We need order in this house, not more chaos."

The corners of Taylor's eyes creased as he smiled at his wife, who was kissing Shadow's nose. "I like our house fine, Dyl. Please come in, Val."

"Yes, Your Majesty." Val followed the king inside. She'd expected something with mansion vibes like the opulence she'd seen surrounding other monarchs. The Pendragons seemed to have left splendor to the throne and council rooms. The entrance hall was the living room: tasteful and cozy with large overstuffed couches, throw cushions, and blankets scattered everywhere. A toybox bursting with stuffed animals occupied one corner.

The TV was on, albeit muted, and Peppa Pig gamboled across the screen. A magnificent painting hung on the opposite wall, depicting the king and queen on their wedding day. The portrait was not formal. The queen sat on the rail on Tintagel's bridge, cradling her husband's head, her legs playfully wrapped around his hips. They were both laughing.

"Hey, girl!" a succubus chirped from the nearest couch.

Val dragged her eyes away from the painting and focused on the room's other occupants. The succubus, whose spiraling gazelle horns emerged from the golden curls spilling luxuriously over her shoulders, was Bianca Hartshorn, the captain of the OPMA. A slender girl in silver robes sat beside her. She looked no older than thirteen. Silver streaks and scales patterned her bald head.

"Have you met Eglantine?" Taylor asked.

"No, sir." Val bowed deeply. "It's an honor to meet you, Your Ladyship."

Lady Eglantine, the ruler of the dragons, grinned. "Oh, leave that bullshit for the court. I'm Eggy."

"Eggy!" Taylor chided. "Language."

"What? Julie says it all the time." Eglantine shrugged.

"Have a seat, Val." Taylor gestured. "I know you're here to test the amulet, but Rosa has to fawn over her only grandchild. It takes a while."

"I'm not in a hurry, Your Majesty." Val sagged onto a soft couch.

Dylan bowed. "Coffee, Miss Stonehold?"

"Black, no sugar. Thanks."

"Me too, please," Taylor chipped in.

"Her Majesty will be unamused by your caffeine intake today, Your Majesty," Dylan chided. "You've drunk over twice the recommended daily amount."

"I have a presentation in the Sylthana Islands tomorrow, Dyl. I need all the caffeine I can get. World peace depends on it," Taylor stated. His lip quirked up, but his eyes weren't joking.

The brownie bowed again and vanished.

"So, you made the thing to keep Lilli from blowing sh…stuff up?" Eglantine asked.

"Yes." Val interlaced her fingers in her lap, worrying about the platinum-blonde curls she'd chosen as today's wig. Would the dragon consider it disrespectful that she didn't go bald, too? How did hair work in draconic culture?

"I hear you'll be handling the transfer of Gaia's Sickle." Bianca grinned. "I'm more than happy to leave that one to you, girl. The last thing we need is a giant OPMA contingent trampling around New York City. We're here if you need backup, though."

"They're still negotiating," Val explained, "but yeah, I'll be moving it to Gold, Manns, and Sax."

Eglantine snickered. "Is that the ball-off-chopping sickle?"

Bianca snorted. "Gross."

Shadow bounded into the room and made the rounds, leaping onto Bianca's lap and frantically licking Eglantine's hands.

"Shadow!" Val lurched to her feet. "Dude! Cut it out!"

"Let him play, Val!" Rosa swept into the room with Lillirelda on her hip, as vibrant as ever. "He's having a good time. Come here, sweetie. Let me get a good look at you." She gave Val a crushing hug with her free arm, then stepped back and looked her up and down. "You've been working out! You need to keep your protein up. Have you tried organic grass-fed whey?"

"*Mooom*," Julie groaned, following her inside. "Leave her alone. She knows what her body needs for her workouts."

"It's much better for you than synthetic powders, dear. They're full of chemicals," Rosa warned.

Lillirelda giggled and grabbed Val's curls.

"You've got the amulet, right?" Julie asked.

Val fished the velvet bag from her pocket and tipped the amulet onto her palm. "Here it is, Your Majesty."

Julie's eyes widened. She reverently took the amulet and held it to the light. "Wow. T! Look at this, babe. Have you ever seen wrought iron like it?"

Taylor leaned closer. "Amazing. Look at that obsidian. I didn't know you could facet it like that."

"Val, it's beautiful." Julie beamed. "I love it."

"It's baby-proof, too," Val reassured her. "The wards can't hurt Lillirelda even if she drops it and activates it remotely. You gave me her hairs, so I worked her magical signature into the amulet's charms. It can't harm her no matter what, and it can't be used as a weapon. Oh, and obviously, there are no small parts for her to choke on."

"Is it fireproof?" Julie asked. "Bulletproof?" She weighed it in her palm. "It feels that way. This is powerful magic, Val."

"Almost no magic can penetrate it." Val grinned. "Nothing I could throw at it, anyway. I'm glad we're doing a last round of testing while I'm here to make adjustments if needed."

"Of course." Julie nodded. "Only the best for you, my impossible little princess." She tickled Lillirelda's cheek.

The toddler giggled. "Mama!"

"That's me, moondrop." Julie held out her arms, and Lillirelda enthusiastically climbed into them. "You okay, Hat?"

Merlin hovered in the doorway. "Fine, thank you, Julie."

"Good." Julie made a casual motion with one hand, and a

smoldering ember landed on his sweatpants. As he cursed and hopped around, slapping his smoking clothes, the queen added, "That's for psyching up my toddler right before naptime, asshole."

"She wanted to play!" Merlin protested. "Who could say no to that face?"

Lillirelda turned puppy eyes on Val.

"Don't even start. You'll have Val wrapped around your pinky in seconds." Julie hugged the toddler and kissed her head. "Are we ready to get this party started?"

"The coffee," Dylan wailed, appearing with it on a golden tray.

"Take it to go." Julie grinned. "I can't wait to see what this amulet does for my baby."

CHAPTER SIX

The training grounds at the back of the Eternal Palace were enormous. Val stood at one end, squinting at the expanse of neatly trimmed grass that stretched into the distance. She could barely make out the far wall.

"Shoo!" Julie waved her arms. "Go on, shoo!"

The herd of pegasi grazing on the training grounds paid no attention. One, a proud bay stallion whose russet wings bore the markings of a goshawk, raised his head and snorted at her.

Shadow bounded forward, barking. Lillirelda cheered him on.

"Shadow!" Val yelled. "Don't chase the royal pegasi!"

The bay stallion tossed his head and threw his wings wide. The others spooked as one, and as Shadow charged them, they sprang into the air with powerful grace. Val hung onto her wig as their wings churned the air. The pegasi were gone in moments, leaving Shadow trotting triumphantly over the grass.

"Sorry," Val offered.

"Don't apologize. Mission accomplished!" Julie beamed.

"Horsie!" Lillirelda pointed at the herd as they swooped away.

"Yes, Lilli. Horsie," Julie agreed.

Taylor carried a wooden dummy to the spot where the pegasi

had been. "Here all right, honey?" he asked, placing it on the grass.

"Maybe a little farther, babe," the queen instructed.

Taylor obediently moved the dummy. "The amulet, Val, if you please."

Val removed the amulet from its bag and stepped forward.

"Don't worry. I've got it." Taylor extended a hand. The amulet gracefully rose from Val's palm and drifted across the hundred feet separating them, then draped itself neatly over the dummy's neck.

"Oh, yeah," Val mumbled. "Telekinesis. You're an Aether Elf. Obviously."

Taylor grinned.

"Does Lillirelda have telekinesis?" Val asked.

"Not yet." Queen Julia grimaced. "Luna help us when that comes in. Aether Elves develop their magic later than Lunar Fae."

"You're going to have kick-ass powers, Lilli," Eglantine informed the toddler, who sat on the dragon's shoulders.

"She already does, honey." Rosa patted Eglantine's back.

"Ready for action?" Bianca asked.

Val grinned. "Sure." She drew her dagger. "Shall we start with this?"

"Absolutely." Taylor jogged to safety beside his wife.

Val drew back her arm. "Okay, imagine that's your daughter."

Taylor's eyes dwelled on the dagger, and the color bled from his cheeks.

"Maybe don't imagine that," Val corrected.

Julie laughed. "Show us, Val."

Val drew her arm back and flung the dagger with all her strength. She hurled her power behind the throw, propelling the iron forward on a surge of magic. It clanged hard on the amulet and ricocheted. Val reached out and barely caught it, grunting with effort.

"Remind me not to piss *her* off," Bianca muttered. "Mind if I try?"

"Go ahead," Val told her.

Bianca clenched her fists. Red magic twined between her fingers in glowing tendrils, and she punched her arms forward. Bolts of red magic thundered into the amulet and rebounded, blowing holes in the dirt around the dummy.

"Yeah, baby!" Bianca punched the air with a smoking fist. "It works!"

"But does it *contain* magic?" Merlin asked.

Val held out a hand, and the amulet's iron responded. It rose from the dummy's neck and drifted to her palm.

"I'm not the only one with tricks." Taylor chuckled.

Val handed the amulet to Merlin. "Try it out."

Julie snickered.

Merlin rolled his eyes. "Very well. Use me as a guinea pig, you insolent young dwarf." He tugged the amulet over his head, retreated a few feet, and clenched his fists. Silver fire licked over them. Merlin focused on the dummy and flung his hands forward in a flurry of attacks so fast that Val barely saw him move, only the arcs of moonfire that resulted. They hissed and churned against the wards, which flashed purple but didn't allow the flames to escape. The fire blazed harmlessly over Merlin's sweatpants.

"How does it not burn his clothes off?" she whispered to Bianca.

The succubus shrugged. "Are you complaining?"

"No!" Val hissed.

"Then don't ask," Bianca rejoined. "I don't. Lunar magic is weird shit, girlfriend."

"It contains moonfire." Queen Julia groaned with relief. "It works!"

"Fae fire is one thing." Eglantine swung Lillirelda off her

shoulders and handed her to Rosa. "Let's see what it does against real moonfire."

"I beg your pardon," Merlin spluttered.

"I'll take that, thank you." Eglantine whisked the amulet from Merlin's neck and returned it to the dummy. "All of you might want to step back."

Val beat a hasty retreat with Shadow at her heels. Rosa, Bianca, and the king followed. Only the Lunar Fae stayed nearby as Eglantine spread her arms and her outline shifted. In a heartbeat, an immense dragon stood where the slender girl had been. Her scales shimmered the color of moonlight, and steel horns swept from her head, turning to heavy spines that traced the length of her body and ended in a heavy club at the tip of her tail.

The dragon laughed, flames roaring with the movement of air in her lungs. When she inhaled, a pale glow flickered in her chest.

"Let's see what that amulet's made of," she growled.

"Eggy!" Lillirelda cheered, punching her chubby arms in the air.

The dragon opened her jaws and spewed a torrent of moonfire that made the air shimmer and forced Val back a step. The flames vaporized a swathe of grass, leaving behind bare earth.

"Shit," Val muttered. "I'm glad she's on our side."

Taylor laughed as the flames dissipated. Val grimaced, but the dummy was untouched, the amulet hanging from its neck.

"Whoa." Eglantine sat down as heavily as a clumsy puppy, making the earth shake. "I can't believe that worked!"

Julie turned to grin at Val. "I can. Bee, have you seen that thing up close? It's gorgeous!"

"Mama!" Lillirelda demanded, extending her arms.

"I'll take her." Taylor scooped his daughter from Rosa's arms and followed Bianca to Queen Julia and Merlin as they admired the amulet.

Rosa wrapped an arm around Val's waist and squeezed. "Thank you so much, Valerie."

"Any time. It's my job." Val smiled.

"You don't know what this means, honey." Rosa paused. "These talks about the Hunters have been terribly stressful for Julie and Taylor. They fought so hard for this peace and gave up so much. My sweet baby girl almost gave her life more than once."

Rosa blinked rapidly. "Now they have to maintain it, and it's harder than any of us expected. I don't think many paras out there understand how hard their rulers are working to give them this Second Golden Age."

"No," Val murmured. "I don't think we do."

"They love Lilli, but with their stress levels this high, the last thing they need is the mess of putting out fires—literally—at home every night." Rosa smiled. "Your amulet will make their lives easier. Besides, they need to travel for work now, visiting the kingdoms to talk about the Hunters. It'll give them great peace of mind to leave Lillirelda here when they enter dangerous territories."

Val was silent, realizing that the amulet would allow the king and queen more than the odd date night.

"I'll be honest." Rosa chuckled. "I love babysitting, but I'm relieved that I won't be the only one willing to put up with a fiery toddler."

Val grinned. "I like Lilli. She's cool."

"She's more than cool. She's amazing." Rosa's eyes shone. "And like plenty of amazing kids, she's a handful right now. Your amulet will make *her* life easier, too."

A familiar warm glow spread through Val's chest. She stood taller as she watched Julie hang the amulet around Lillirelda's neck. The toddler princess gripped it in both hands and giggled. "Mine!"

"All yours." Julie kissed her forehead.

Shadow pressed his cold, damp nose into Val's hand. She rubbed his ears.

Rosa touched her arm. "You mean more to this family than you know, Valerie."

"The royal family," Val murmured. "They saved the world."

"They're still saving it," Rosa told her quietly. "They're saving it daily, and you're part of that."

Val pressed a hand over her amulet as it hummed against her skin. She had no words.

The Avalonian-Earth time differences were always trippy. Bright morning light sparkled on the skyscrapers of Manhattan as Genevieve purred and wove between the traffic, dodging down side streets to avoid gridlocks when she could.

Val left the Mustang to it. She seemed to have a sixth sense that told her where traffic would be. She didn't ask questions about Genevieve's abilities. Nobody did.

She dialed Qenzi's number, hoping she'd catch the troll as she rode the subway to NYHQ. She did. When Qenzi answered, the distinctive rumble of a train underlined her words. "Hey, Val!"

"Morning, Qenz. How are things?" Val asked.

"Busier than ever. NYHQ is *swarming*. The queen has doubled down on her efforts to keep those Hunters prisoners confined. I'm not convinced it is possible to keep them all contained, but she's determined to try." Qenzi sighed. "Sorry. That turned into verbal diarrhea."

"I don't mind," Val reassured her. "I bet you guys have cool new toys to play with."

"Absolutely. They're delivering the Shirt of Nessus today. I look forward to making sure Heracles stays where he belongs." Qenzi snorted. "Asshole. The thing I can't wait to get my hands on, though, is Gaia's Sickle." She paused. "Is it true you're transporting it to Gold, Manns, and Sax?"

"Are you supposed to know that?" Val asked. "Not to be disrespectful, sorry. I'm supposed to keep it secret."

Qenzi laughed. "I appreciate your diligence, Val, but there's very little my security clearance doesn't allow me to know. Gaia's Sickle is the key to keeping Kronos contained. I mean, pretty sure he'll be triggered by the mere sight of it."

Val smirked. "Yeah, I'll bet. I'm actually calling you about something else today, though."

A mechanized voice burbled in the background. Qenzi slurped coffee. "I'm all ears."

"You remember Liam, one of my human friends?" Val asked.

"Sure. He's the one who got you the intel you needed to take down BrewCorp and its OC connection," Qenzi recalled.

"That's right. I want to make him my ops manager to coordinate missions and comms, that kind of thing. With Tetra in the mix, I could use someone like him on my team," Val explained.

Qenzi paused. "It's a good idea. I think many paras will question your choice, though."

"Because he's human?" Val asked.

Qenzi sighed. "Yes."

"It's tempting to attribute that to plain old speciesism." Val bit her lip. "But I get that the logistics could be complicated."

"Does Liam understand that there are aspects of your work he can't know about?" Qenzi asked.

"Yeah. He thinks it's classified governmental stuff. I've told him that he can't know things for his own safety, and he's cool with that," Val explained.

"You've told him as much of the truth as is safe for him. Many paras would say it's foolish to bring a human into paranormal affairs, but the world's changing, Val. Having Queen Julia grow up as a human is opening doors between the paranormal and human worlds." Excitement bubbled in Qenzi's tone. "I believe we can do far more than coexist with humans. We can cooperate with them."

"I think so too, and that's where I need your help." Val rubbed her chin. "We'll need tech that Liam can operate and understand without endangering him by revealing the secrets of the para world. Is that possible?"

"Possible?" Qenzi laughed. "It's been done, and I'm in the middle of doing it now with more. I believe humans can benefit from thaumatech, as we benefited from using human technology to develop that thaumatech. I'm working on a line of communications devices for the human market.

"I'm sticking with phones, earpieces, and tablets, but there's the potential for so much more. Imagine supplying the human world with cars that don't need to charge on electricity from nonrenewable resources. Or bringing them defibrillators and ventilators that work a hundred times better than their current tech. Is it possible? We won't know until we try. We could forge a better future for humans and paranormals."

Val waited patiently until the troll ran out of breath and fell silent. "Comms devices, you say?" she interjected.

"Yes! They're not very sophisticated yet, but your team isn't big. They could work perfectly for you since Liam could use them without knowing that the tech is part magic." Qenzi giggled. "This is a great opportunity for me, Val. I'd love to test my thaumatech on you guys."

Val smirked. "Delighted to be your guinea pig, Qenz."

"It works. I know it works," Qenzi assured her. "I'd love to see it tested in the field, but I know it works."

"Of course it does. You made it," Val told her with utter confidence. "Look, Liam's still thinking about whether he wants to join the team. If he does, can I call you and set up a meeting with him? You could show him the tech. I'm not good at that stuff."

"I'd love to do that. Liam will be using the coolest blend of magic and technology ever without knowing it," Qenzi gushed. "By the way, I think Shadow needs an Instagram account."

Val snorted in amusement at the sudden one-eighty in the conversation. "He does?"

"Yes! Look how much traffic he's brought to the Iron Fist's social media lately," Qenzi insisted. "He could be one of those Insta-famous pets that earn their people thousands of dollars."

Val grunted. "He can keep bringing traffic to the Fist's social media, thanks. He doesn't need his own."

"Suit yourself." Qenzi laughed. "Anyway, my stop is coming up. Talk to you later."

"Sure. Thanks again." Val hung up.

She leaned back and gripped the wheel, pretending to drive, as a cruiser rolled past.

"Now all we need is for Liam to say yes," she murmured.

Genevieve revved her engine in assent.

* * *

Val tipped the keg of Iron IPA to get the last drops into the jug. "We're almost out," she yelled to Tetra. "Is there another keg in the storeroom?"

Tetra bustled past with a cloth over her shoulder and a tray of empty glasses in her hands. "Shit. There is, but only one." She glanced at the crowd. "It's not going to last long."

Val checked her phone. "If Blair and Yuka were going to make a delivery, they'd have done it already. Crap. I wonder if Enzo ordered." She carefully tipped beer into glasses, raising and lowering her jug to get the perfect layer of foam on top. "Have you seen him yet tonight?"

Tetra shook her head. "No, but it's been so busy that I might have missed him. Maybe he's in the office."

"I'll check in a minute. Let me serve these people first." Val set the jug aside and lifted a tray packed with beers and whiskeys. She stepped over Shadow, who was lying in his usual spot behind the bar, and squeezed through the crowd to a booth at the center.

The three old men who'd been patrons of the Iron Fist since before Val knew it existed sat contentedly in a row, playing cards on one side of the table.

"First time at our watering hole, huh?" one of the old men asked the other group in their booth.

A gaggle of tourists dressed in the latest fashions crammed into the booth opposite them. Their eyes widened at the sight of Iron IPA, a dark fluid with flecks of scarlet at its heart.

"First time," one responded.

"You'll be regulars soon. The Fist does that to people," a second old man assured him.

"Wow, this looks like it did on your Instagram," a bearded tourist told Val as she set the beer before him. "I thought you'd edited the pic."

"Speaking of your Instagram," the girl by his side interjected, "is that big dog here? Shadow?"

"He's here," Val reassured her. "I'm sure he'll make his rounds in a minute."

"Cool." The girl grinned. "We came to see him. I have a Tibetan Mastiff at home, and I miss him."

"I get that." Val laughed as she dispensed whiskeys to the three old men. "Anything else for you guys?"

"No, thanks, Val." The tallest of the old men inclined his head.

As Val turned away, she caught the edge of their conversation.

"You're welcome here," the old man told the tourists. "Just don't anger the Guardian of the Iron Fist."

The bearded guy glanced at Val, his gaze resting on the bulges of her arms in her Iron Fist-branded sweater. "I'm not planning on it."

Val smirked as she pushed through the crowd and stepped behind the bar. "You okay here for five minutes?" she asked. "I'm going to talk to Enzo and make sure Blair and Yuka are bringing more beer."

"Got it," Tetra called over her shoulder.

Val dumped her tray on the dishwasher and hastened to the narrow door leading to the tiny office in the back of the building. She knocked loudly on the frame. "Enzo, you in here, dude?"

No response.

"Enzo?" Val knocked again.

The silence made worry curl in her belly. She pushed the door open and frowned at the tiny space. It could barely contain a rickety desk and two chairs. The single grimy window overlooked the street.

There was no sign of the orc who co-owned the Iron Fist.

Val shut the door and flopped into Enzo's chair. She dialed his number, raised the phone to her ear, and listened to it ring and ring.

"For Merlin's sake, Enzo," she muttered, scooting the beat-up desk chair back and forth, her nervous energy bubbling over.

She tried him again. When he still didn't respond, she resorted to texting.

Enzo, you okay, man?

Intense relief flowed through her when her phone buzzed almost instantly with Enzo's response.

Fine. Sorry. Can't make it tonight.

Val rolled her eyes.

Clearly. What's going on? How can I help?

Enzo typed for a long time before his text came through.

Family stuff.

Yeah, you said. I'm worried about you. Please let me help.

I'm fine, Val.

He typed for ages again.

It's someone in my family worrying me. Not ready to talk about it.

Val frowned, mentally scanning through the Lombardi family members she knew about. Enzo's sister was married to a vampire, and they both practiced law. The vampire, Bartholomew Diaz, seemed elderly. Was he sick? Could vampires get sick?

The door barged open. "Enzo, where's the beer?" Tetra yelled. "Oh, wait. Where is he?"

"Dealing with 'family stuff' again." Val made air quotes. "I'm worried about him. He says there's someone in his family causing trouble."

"Dante, maybe?" Tetra guessed.

Val raised her eyebrows. "That would make sense. He seems like a cool kid, but I hear college isn't an easy time."

"He was quiet the last few times I saw him. Seems like ages since he last picked up a shift here." Tetra snorted. "I hope Enzo drags his ass back here soon. So, where is the beer?"

Val grimaced. "I'll sort it out."

"Sort it out while helping me in the bar if you can, please." Tetra groaned. "It's madness in there. A werewolf pack came in a few minutes ago, and they all want their booze *now*."

"Coming." Val sent a quick text to Yuka Marniq, an owner of Anvil Brewery, and hurried after Tetra.

She spotted the werewolf pack instantly, although most humans would have written them off as frat boys with a dangerous air. They had no need to wear a glamour to hide their paranormal features from humans. Although their teeth were perhaps a little sharp when they smiled, and their eyes maybe a shade too pale, they seemed human despite the goosebumps that rose on Val's arms in their presence. The amulet warmed gently, acknowledging a minor threat.

Val served them quarts of Gold Pilsner and a cool smile, warning them against causing trouble.

"That crowd next to us is a little rough," the tourist girl whispered.

"Don't worry," her bearded boyfriend told her. "The Guardian's right over there." He nodded at Val.

Val hid her grin as she hustled back and started making beer shandies for the three drunken girls at the bar who didn't need any more neat beers. Her phone buzzed with a text from Yuka as she added the soda.

"Poor Blair and Yuka. They were home already, but they're headed to the brewery now to pick up a few kegs and bring them to us," she told Tetra, who loaded the dishwasher beside her. "Enzo must have forgotten to order. It's nice of them."

"Nice of them? We saved their asses," Tetra reminded her. "They owe us."

"That's not how it works, Tetra."

"That's how it works in the faerie kingdom," Tetra grumbled.

She stormed off with a tray of glasses. Val rolled her eyes as she returned to her shandy mixing.

"Get your hands off her, asshole!" The yell held the edge of a wolf's snarl, and Val whirled. Two werewolves stood, fists clenched, fine hair appearing on the backs of their hands as they bared their teeth at one another.

"She's my girlfriend!" one barked.

"Yeah, well, she doesn't want you to touch her right now!" the other snarled.

The girl lurched to her feet, her eyes like ice chips. "I don't need a whelp standing up for me," she growled.

Jeff slipped off his bar stool, but Shadow was one step ahead. The massive dog didn't run across the floor, merely strolled. Shadow sprang onto the table with an effortless shrug of his powerful muscles as the first werewolf's nails lengthened into claws.

He didn't growl. He didn't need to. His sheer presence was enough, with his hackles adding four inches to his already considerable height. The werewolves knew a *true* alpha when they saw one, so they instantly backed down.

Shadow lowered his head and directed a long, unnerving stare at each of the three werewolves, who sank demurely into their seats.

"Good boy, Shadow," Val murmured.

Shadow hopped off the table, his hackles descending over his back.

"Wait a second." The bearded tourist turned to the old men. "Is *he* the Guardian of the Iron Fist?"

The old men chuckled.

"Once you know that, you're family," one of them told the tourists warmly.

"He's even bigger in real life." The girl held out her hand to the huge dog. "Hey, big fella."

Shadow's tail twitched, and his mouth opened in its usual happy pant. He trotted over to the woman and laid his enormous head in her lap. She laughed as she played with his ears and ran her hands through his thick red coat.

Tetra hurried over to collect their empty glasses. "Anything else for you?"

"I'll have another," the girl requested.

Everyone at the table agreed. Shadow licked the girl's hands, making her smile.

"There are treats in the jar on the counter if you want to give him a few." Tetra sighed. "Val says he needs to gain weight."

"Aw, of course. Let's go get your treats, boy!" The girl rose and strode to the bar, Shadow trotting beside her with his tail high in anticipation.

Tetra shoved past Val to the bar, grumbling, "That dog gets more tips than I do." Val didn't miss that Tetra's hand trailed over Shadow's back as she moved past him.

CHAPTER SEVEN

Val chewed the inside of her cheek, squinting at the computer screen. She wished she'd paid more attention in math class at Ironforge Bastion, but she'd been busy fending off bullies half her height and twice her age as they mocked her bald head and gangly limbs. Math had taken second place to survival.

"Stupid spreadsheet," she muttered. She gingerly changed one cell and groaned when question marks and hashtags appeared everywhere.

Tetra knocked on the office door. "I've closed the bar, Val. Sweeping the floor, then I'm done."

"Cool. Be there in a minute," Val murmured.

She clicked Undo and glared at the spreadsheet. "Stupid thing," she muttered.

Lying at her feet, Shadow raised his head.

"Not you, dude. Never you." Val rubbed his head. "You're the smartest doggo I know."

Reassured, Shadow dropped his head to his paws again.

Val's phone buzzed. *Enzo?* she wondered. She picked it up, and her heart froze at the sight of a text from Liam.

Hey. I know it's late, but can you meet me at Sarah-Jane's grave?

"*Shit.*" Val lurched to her feet, sending the office chair into the wall. "*Shit, shit, shit!*" She grabbed her coat and stormed out of the office, Shadow bounding at her heels. "*Tetra!*"

Tetra emerged from the storeroom. "What?"

"Liam needs us. Let's go!" Val shouted.

Tetra's eyes widened. "It's okay, Val. You go. I'll Uber home."

Val hesitated.

"We can't leave the Fist like this. I'll tidy up and go straight home, I promise." Tetra gripped her broom with white knuckles. "You can order me to do that if it makes you feel any better."

Val's shoulders slumped. "I'm not ordering you to do anything, Tetra. We talked about more independence." She inhaled. "Maybe this is it. Okay. You can Uber home. Do you know how?"

"I'll text Isabella to help me if I need it. Go." Tetra shooed her away. "Check on Liam."

"Thanks." Val didn't worry about what Tetra might do. Her stress over Liam consumed her. She sprinted outside, and in seconds, she and Shadow were in Genevieve, speeding toward Bay Ridge.

Val and the Mustang worked together, drifting around every corner and accelerating noisily through the quietest streets. The scream of Genevieve's engine was a battle cry as she roared toward the cemetery. Streetlights flashed by faster than Val could see them.

She stomped on the brakes, which brought her screeching to a crawl at a red light, then accelerated once more. The flash of a speed camera didn't slow her down. Queen Julia would get the ticket, and she seemed to accept them as inevitable for Genevieve.

"He was doing so well, Gennie," Val whispered. "What happened?"

Genevieve threw herself into a squealing handbrake turn, missing a truck by inches, then accelerated down the street. Finally, the creeper-draped wall of the cemetery glowed in her headlights. The Mustang halted at the wrought iron gate, and Val threw herself from the driver's seat. Shadow jumped through the open window and bounded after her.

"Liam!" Val yelled, sprinting into the cemetery.

Her feet automatically found the route to Sarah-Jane's grave since she'd often come with Liam on sunny afternoons to bring flowers. In the pitch-dark, the cemetery seemed foreign and dangerous. LED spotlights cast brutal white glows here and there, illuminating tombstones' cold, lifeless granite.

Val dodged a rich asshole's mausoleum and spotted him. Liam stood at the foot of Sarah-Jane's grave, hands buried in his coat pockets, shoulders hunched.

She slowed to a walk, hobnailed boots sinking into damp turf. Her pounding heart made her amulet throb. Shadow stayed close to her heels as she approached Liam.

"Lee?" she murmured, checking to see if he had a weapon. Liam would not hurt a fly, except for himself, she feared.

Liam raised his head and lifted his empty hands from his pockets. His eyes were dry, and he was smiling.

"Oh, crap." His smile slipped. "Sorry, Val. I didn't think about how my message must have sounded." He grimaced. "It looks like I scared you."

"No, no. It's okay. I'm fine. Are you okay?" Val asked, suppressing the worry in her tone.

Liam ran a hand over his hair. "Shit. I'm sorry. I'm fine. Better than I've been in a long time, actually."

Val's shoulders sagged. "Asswipe." She grabbed him and tugged him into a crushing hug. "You scared the crap out of me."

"A *hug*?" Liam laughed as he gently returned it. "Sorry, Val."

"It's okay. I could have called and asked more questions instead of panicking." Val released him. "Now, what do you want?"

Liam smiled. "Let's sit." He gestured at a wooden bench near the grave.

Val joined him on the bench, and Shadow sat at her feet, placing his head on her lap. She stroked it as her thundering heart slowed. Liam folded his arms, gazing at the grave belonging to his younger sister.

"I texted you to meet me here so I will do what I know I should before I overthink it and back out," he began.

Val grinned. "Go on."

"I love interior decorating," Liam told her. "I always have. I like making places beautiful and seeing them make people happy. Thing is, I've felt pointless since Sarah-Jane died." His breath hitched on her name. "Taking care of her was my purpose, I guess."

Val nodded. "I can understand that."

"I know you can." Liam smiled faintly. "I felt lost for years, Val. Until you came crashing into our lives."

Val listened in respectful silence.

"I've told you that you remind me of Sarah-Jane." Liam smiled. "She was unapologetically herself, too, and she protected others any way she could. She also listened like you're doing right now." He chuckled. "Okay, so she was five foot three and a hundred pounds soaking wet, but she was much like you in other ways. I really miss her."

"Jess tells me she was an amazing person," Val murmured.

"Oh, she was. She loved me." Liam swallowed. "I was the protector's protector. I kept her safe...until I didn't. Okay, I know I'm not supposed to blame myself. I'm working through it in therapy. Still, I need something like that again. The chance to feel like I'm making a difference and helping somebody."

Val laid a hand on his shoulder.

"You're—" Liam cleared his throat, his voice still thick when he continued. "You're the sister I lost, Val. I didn't protect Sarah, and I can't kick ass in a fight like you can, but I still want to protect you."

"Hey, it's okay, dude." Val squeezed his shoulder. "I don't need protecting."

Liam laughed. "I know that, but everyone needs a friend in their corner, right?"

Val thought about the MMA cage in which she vented her frustrations. "Right."

"I want to be a part of the future you're forging," Liam told her. "I want the job."

Val punched the air. "*Yesss*! You won't regret it, Lee."

"Wait, wait." Liam held up a hand. "I have one condition."

"Name it." Val grinned.

Liam met her gaze. "You have to quit putting off your meeting with Diego Lopez at his gym. You love MMA, and I don't want to see you give it up."

Val raised her eyebrows. "*That's* your condition? Don't you want to hear about the salary I'm offering?"

"I know you'll be fair." Liam shrugged. "That's my condition. You go meet with Diego. I'll be your ops manager."

Val chuckled. "Well, in case you were wondering, the salary I had in mind is…" She named a figure that made Liam's eyes turn to saucers. "Oh, and five percent of the profits as an incentive."

"Like I need an incentive to work with the girl who saved my life." Liam nudged her with his shoulder. "Okay, now I *really* want the job. But you still have to go to the gym."

Val offered him a fist to bump. "It's a deal."

Liam laughed and knocked his knuckles against hers.

Val's phone buzzed a moment later with the best news she could have hoped for: a text from Tetra.

Home.

Despite the spring chill hanging over the East River, the air tasted of summer the next morning. Val blinked sleepiness from her eyes as she strolled down Bridge Park Drive's wide sidewalk. Sunlight poured from a perfect sky that turned the river's water a rich azure. Joggers, cyclists, and tourists crowded the drive, causing traffic to slow and honk.

After living in Brooklyn for months, Val regarded the honking as white noise. She tipped her head back and allowed the sunlight to cascade through her current favorite wig, a mass of attractive brunette waves.

Shadow panted happily at her side, strolling on a sturdy leather leash studded with spikes. Val thought the spikes were a bit fanciful, but the combination of the spiked leash and the massive dog caused many an unsavory person to cross the street, braving the morning traffic instead of Shadow's wrath.

She felt dangerous and loved it.

The Kaigo Coffee Room stood among other trendy coffee shops sporting square umbrellas and snazzy black-and-white decor. The heady scents of coffee and sugar greeted Val as she stepped inside. Liam sat at a table near the window with two glass mugs in front of him.

Val nodded at the waiter by the door, who didn't comment on Shadow's presence, and strolled to the table. "Hey, Lee."

Shadow rammed his nose into Liam's lap.

"Do you go *anywhere* without him?" Liam laughed.

"Leave him home alone? Not likely." Val sat, and Shadow lay at her feet.

"I got you a pumpkin spice latte with almond milk." Liam pushed the mug toward her.

Val glared at it with disgust.

"Relax, Val. I'm kidding." Liam chuckled. "It's a cappuccino with extra cream."

Val lived on black coffee, but the cappuccino was her special treat. She sipped and relished the balance of bitterness and creamy richness. "Wow, this is a great cappuccino."

"Right?" Liam glanced around. "Your friend here yet? Kenzie?"

Val could *hear* how he'd spelled the troll's name in his head and didn't correct him. "She texted that she'll be a couple of minutes late. Should be here any moment."

Heels clopped on the coffee shop's floor, and Liam's jaw dropped as though he were beholding a peerless beauty. Val craned her neck and saw Qenzi striding toward them, harem pants swishing around her skinny legs. The troll's chestnut bob framed a face in which her blue eyes seemed enormous behind her horn-rimmed glasses. Her tight black turtleneck hugged her bony frame.

The Veil—the powerful glamour that protected all paranormals from human eyes—didn't let Liam see her pale green skin or the yellow tusks that jutted from her lower lip.

"*Shadooow!*" Qenzi reached toward him. "Hey, dude!"

Shadow bounded to her, tail wagging joyously as he licked her hands.

Val waved. "I'm here, too."

Qenzi didn't look up from stroking the dog's rich fur. "Hey, Val."

"Hey." Val laughed.

Liam blinked, his cheeks reddening as he lifted his gaze to Qenzi's eyes. The troll straightened and flashed him a brilliant smile. "Hi. Sorry. Dogs sidetrack me."

"Same." Liam laughed as he rose and held out a hand. "Liam Miller."

"Kenzie Deacon." Qenzi gave her human cover name. "It's nice to meet you, Liam. Val's told me so much about you."

Liam shot Val a nervous look. "All good things, I hope."

"All wonderful things." Qenzi's smile widened.

Val waved at the waiter. "Here, Qenz. Order that crazy girly bullshit you like."

Qenzi ordered a whipped macchiato with soy milk, fresh strawberries, and unicorn farts for all Val knew. Val tacked a round of cinnamon buns onto the order. The waiter bustled off while Qenzi laid an old-fashioned silver attaché case on the table.

"Ready to see cool gadgets?" She grinned.

Liam returned the smile. "Who could say no to that?"

"Me," Val muttered.

"Shhh, Val, you uncultured barbarian," Qenzi told her calmly. She opened the case and pulled out a tablet, a phone, and a delicate earpiece. "I'm about to blow your mind, Liam."

"Right to business. I like it." Liam scooted closer. "Which OS do these run? Android? iOS?"

Qenzi grinned. "Neither. These run on an operating system my boss Qtana created a few years ago. I tweaked them for my needs."

"Wow." Liam blinked. "Your client's organization has serious resources, Val."

"You have no idea," Val muttered.

"What's it called?" Liam asked.

"Ether 4.1." Qenzi touched the power button on the tablet's side. "Let me show you. It's streamlined and simple. I'm still developing it, and this will be its first real field test."

"Oh?" Liam raised his eyebrows.

"Qenzi knows what she's doing. If she says it'll work, it'll work," Val assured him.

A stylized image of two humanoid figures collided on the screen and turned into the pale blue Ether logo as a cheerful start-up sound chimed from the tablet. The screen turned gray and displayed plain black buttons with white lettering. **Start Comms**, **Open Terminal**, and **Add Contact** were among them.

"Little plain, huh?" Liam commented.

Qenzi snorted. "Are you commenting on my program's aesthetics?"

"Well, yeah. User engagement would be better if you made it look cool," Liam pointed out.

Qenzi laughed. "It's a security communications program, not a video game."

Liam grinned. "You're saying people who guard stuff can't like pretty things?"

"No, I'm—" Qenzi giggled. "Okay. *After* we test this in the field, we'll talk about aesthetics. Happy?"

Liam's grin widened. "Happy."

Val and Shadow exchanged looks.

"Now that that's out of the way," Qenzi shook her head, still smiling, "let's talk about the functionality, which is kick-ass."

"I'll bet." Liam leaned closer.

"This tablet is your command center." Qenzi held it up. "It works on a network our organization developed. It extends across the globe, never loses signal, and doesn't rely on any of the networks you know about."

Liam's eyes widened. "No shit?"

"No shit," Qenzi assured him. "This thing's battery lasts up to two weeks and charges in half an hour."

"*How?*" Liam murmured.

"We discovered a pure material that offers no resistance," Qenzi explained. "It's ten times more powerful than a lithium-ion battery the same size."

"*That* is cool." Liam held out his hands.

Qenzi passed him the tablet. "I'd explain the network to you, but I don't know how it works. I'm not the one who developed it, only this comms program."

"Only a whole new operating system." Liam laughed. "Your organization has to be filled with geniuses."

A pale pink flush appeared beneath Qenzi's green skin. "Thank you."

"The tablet connects to this phone and earpiece, right?" Liam inspected them. "Looks like the earpiece will be invisible when it's in Val's ear."

"That's the idea, although it's still detectable if she's searched. I'm working on a physical implant that would be almost impossible to find. For now, this'll have to do." Qenzi sighed.

"This is sci-fi-level stuff, and I love it." Liam touched the tablet. "What's the range?"

"The range? Oh, it's global," Qenzi told him.

Liam nodded. "I'd expect nothing less. What about network security?"

Qenzi grinned. "Our firewalls are amazing, and those are my specialty. Buckle up." She rubbed her hands together eagerly. "Our intrusion prevention system has the largest attack signature databases in the world."

The conversation drifted into computer gobbledygook. Val leaned back in her chair, grinning between bites of an excellent cinnamon roll.

She couldn't begin to understand what they were talking about, but she understood the smiles on their faces just fine.

***

Val stuffed another spoonful of peanut butter into the dog toy. "The things I do for you," she grumbled.

Shadow sat at her feet on the kitchen floor, sweeping the floor with his wagging tail.

"Look at this mess." Val gestured at the peanut butter on her hands and the countertop. "All so you can stay busy while I'm not home."

Shadow smacked his lips. He eagerly followed Val to and fro as she washed her hands and carried the peanut butter-stuffed toy to the dog bed in the kitchen's corner.

"Here you go, idiot." Val dropped the toy on the floor.

Shadow pounced and pinned it between forepaws bigger than Val's hands. Delighted noisy licking commenced.

"Bye." Val rubbed his ribs with her toe. "Love you."

Shadow ignored her as she marched to the garage and locked the door, like anyone in their right mind would break into a jewelry business guarded by a hundred-pound dog. Val pulled out her phone as she strode to Genevieve and texted Jess.

Thanks. The peanut butter thing worked! No whining.

"Tetra," she yelled, opening Genevieve's door. "I'm heading to the gym."

A loud clatter rocked the ceiling. Tetra appeared in the doorway, disheveled in pajamas and a robe.

"Diego's gym?" she demanded.

Val raised her eyebrows. "Yeah. Have you not been out of bed today?"

"I want to come!" Tetra declared.

"Tetra—" Val began.

"I'm coming!" Tetra yelled, disappearing into the apartment.

Val sighed. "You're making me late!"

She had no idea what faerie dust Tetra used, but by the time she'd opened the garage door and started the engine, the faerie stood by Genevieve's passenger door with her hair and makeup done.

"Are you sure about that shirt with those jeans?" Val inquired.

"Jeans go with everything." Tetra threw herself into the passenger seat.

"I'm not sure *burgundy* jeans go with everything," Val pointed out.

"Details." Tetra waved a hand. "It's fine. C'mon. You said you were going to be late."

"Okay, but don't use faerie dust on anyone when we get to the gym, please." Val drove out of the garage and closed the door. "Remember that the fights have rules. It's sort of pretend."

"I know, I know. I'm a faerie, not an idiot," Tetra grumbled.

Val raised her eyebrows.

"Okay, sometimes I'm an idiot," Tetra conceded.

Val laughed. "I'm messing with you. Let's go!"

She flattened her foot on the gas and Genevieve took off, leaving fresh tire marks to join the others on their street. Tetra clung grimly to the handle over the door as they left Bay Ridge and took the Belt Parkway around Brooklyn to dodge the worst traffic. Lights sparkled on the water as darkness fell. The Verrazano Narrows Bridge was a string of pearlescent lights hanging over the black river.

Twenty minutes later, they eased toward the heart of Brownsville. Val had been to its darkest corners, where her amulet had pulsed in the presence of human-made danger. Here, the amulet was cool and still on her chest. Unadorned low buildings hugged narrow streets lined with battered cars. Faded signs denoted schools, churches, and community centers. People carrying grocery bags hustled down the narrow sidewalks, but they smiled at Val when she stopped at crossings to let them pass.

"I thought Bay Ridge was bad," Tetra muttered, gazing at a balcony where a young mother hung thin, faded clothes over the rail with one hand while cradling a quiet baby in her other arm. "Why do humans live like this?"

"Many don't have a choice." Val shrugged. "Not everybody has a Queen Julia looking out for them."

"Or magically binding them to random strangers," Tetra grouched.

Val raised an eyebrow. "You'd prefer the prison realm?"

Tetra held up a finger. "I didn't say that."

"In eight hundred feet, turn left," the GPS mechanically ordered.

Val obeyed and spotted Diego's gym. The long, low building

glowed warmly, in contrast to the closed and shuttered businesses surrounding it. Its windows cast a pool of golden light over the cracked asphalt street. Gawky teens hung out by the doors, sparring playfully instead of smoking. A sign over the door provided the gym's name in flowing neon-red letters: *Vanguard MMA*.

Despite the activity within, many parking spaces were open before the gym. Val guessed its customers mostly walked or took the subway. She parked Genevieve near the doors and stepped out. Upbeat music poured from the gym's open doors, calling them nearer.

Tetra stuck close to Val's side as she strode into the gym, which was a hub of light, color, and activity. Warm LEDs illuminated the interior. Posters and pictures on the walls showed the gym's fighters in action, professionally photographed, with a young Diego among them. Racks along the walls held equipment and protective gear. A couple of refrigerators flanked the counter by the door, containing snacks and drinks. A printed sign on the counter read *Take what you need!*

Three arenas occupied the center of the ample space, alive with the sounds of bodies hitting mats and the grunts of practice and combat. All were occupied. Two held teenagers who sparred and bounced with youthful bravado. A pair of muscular guys kicked and punched in the third, their movements filled with practiced grace.

The girl behind the counter played with a stylish lip piercing featuring a small blue gemstone. The workmanship was crappy, but it brought out her eyes when she smiled. "Hey, how can I help?"

"Hey." Val cleared her throat. "Name's Val Stonehold."

"I know who you are." The girl laughed. "Everybody does after you kicked Diego's ass."

Val's cheeks warmed. "I, uh, wouldn't put it that way."

"I would," a man said warmly.

Val turned and smiled at Diego Lopez, the gym's owner and her most recent MMA opponent. The bruise on his cheek was yellow. He grinned through the salt-and-pepper stubble on his cheeks and held out a hand. "It's good to see you, Val. I'd started to think you weren't coming."

"I wouldn't ignore your invitation," Val assured him, shaking his hand. "This is my friend Tetra."

Tetra raised her hands. "I'm only here to watch."

"Welcome to Vanguard, Tetra." Diego smiled. "I'm finishing a session with two of my pro fighters. You're welcome to watch while you finish the paperwork. Then I'll put you in the arena."

The girl with the piercing handed Val a clipboard, and Diego ushered them to a row of plastic chairs beside the arena where the two pros sparred. A gaggle of teenagers sprawled on the chairs, eating cheese curls and goofing around.

"Hey!" Diego barked. "These chairs aren't for messing around, guys. They're for learning. If you want to get good at this, watch the guys who are already good at it. See what they do, and listen to my instructions. Okay?"

The kids straightened and locked their eyes on the pros.

"Have a seat." Diego smiled. "They're nearly done."

He turned to the pair of guys in the arena as Val and Tetra sat. In between scribbling her details on the paper, Val watched the men. It took her a second to get past their impressive physiques to an appreciation for their fighting skills.

The taller of the two, whose muscles rippled beneath skin the color of the Iron Hills' rich earth, kept his fists close to his face as he swung toward his opponent. The shorter guy crouched, blue eyes burning, and lunged. The tall guy blocked his first blow with insulting ease…and missed the second, which landed heavily in his gut.

"Watch his left hand, Joe!" Diego ordered. "You know that. Come on."

Joe recovered quickly and delivered a swift kick to his opponent's shins. The guy's knees buckled.

"Push through the pain. Move your feet," Diego snapped.

The shorter guy danced back, dodging another kick from Joe. He seized the opportunity to deliver a jab to Joe's ribs while the taller man was off-balance.

Tetra leaned forward, watching with intent focus. "Unarmed humans can fight? I didn't know they had it in them," she whispered.

"Keep your voice down," Val warned.

"Move in, Daniel!" Diego barked. "Joe, defend!"

Daniel swung a series of haymakers at Joe, who threw his hands over his face to protect it. He sought gaps in Daniel's offense and found none.

"Sweep the legs, Joe!" Diego snapped.

Joe didn't move quickly enough. He focused on Daniel's legs, and his arms' block faltered a quarter of an inch. That was all the space Daniel needed. The shorter man moved in with an uppercut that snapped Joe's head back.

Diego was in the arena instantly. "Whoa!" He grabbed Daniel's arm.

It didn't seem necessary. Daniel stepped back as Joe thudded heavily to the mat.

"Good job." Diego slapped Daniel's back. "Joe, you good, man?"

Joe laughed and dragged a hand over his mouth, streaking his wrist with blood. "All good. You've warned me about keeping my focus on defending my face, Diego. Daniel brought that lesson home, that's all."

Daniel held out a hand and hauled Joe to his feet. "Always a good fight with you, brother." They knocked their gloves against each other. "Another round?"

"Sure." Joe grinned, revealing teeth edged with blood.

Tetra made a tiny, throaty noise.

"What?" Val hissed.

Tetra leaned close. "The blood is turning me on."

"Girl!" Val shoved her away. "TMI. *Way* TMI."

"You're done for today, Joe," Diego told the taller fighter, handing him a towel.

Joe didn't argue. "Okay." He pressed the towel to his bleeding mouth.

"Still got the energy for more, Diego." Daniel bounced on the balls of his feet.

"I know." Diego grinned. "That's why you'll spar with Val next."

Val tensed. "Me?"

"Oh, hey." Daniel leaned on the arena ropes, grinning, his gloves dangling loosely over the drop. "You're the girl who kicked Diego's ass."

"I wouldn't put it that way," Val mumbled, her cheeks blazing.

"She sure is." Diego slapped her shoulder. "She's only fought amateur so far, Daniel, but she's no stranger to real-life fighting."

"Aren't you the bodyguard who protected Nadia Stewart from that weird asshole at the school opening?" Daniel asked.

Val shrugged off her coat and kicked off her boots, leaving her in a tank top and leggings. "That's me, I guess."

"Then this is going to be fun." Daniel grinned.

"Start slow," Diego ordered. "Get to know each other. I don't need this to end in a KO. I want to see if your strength matches your spirit when you're not in front of a crowd, Val."

Val nodded. "Okay."

She fished her MMA gloves from her backpack, and Tetra helped her strap them on. Daniel pulled the ropes apart, allowing her to climb in.

"You're tall," he remarked, tilting his head back as she turned to face him.

Val inclined her head, trying to hide how much the remark stung. "You're short."

"Touché." Daniel grinned and raised his fists to his face.

"It's not your first time facing an opponent taller than you in your weight class, Danny. Take it easy at first, but I'm not saying you should hold back," Diego called.

Daniel laughed. "I'm not planning on it." He raised a gloved hand and beckoned. "C'mon. Let's see what you've got."

Val charged fast and strong, but instead of crashing into Daniel, she slammed into the ropes, which snapped her back so hard she nearly fell. Daniel's arm closed around her neck and crushed her carotids in a rear naked choke. She moved fast to dig her chin into his forearm with enough force to make him gasp, then twisted toward his chest, wrenching free of the choke.

"Good break, Val," Diego called, "but it was a mistake to let him put you there in the first place."

Val grabbed for Daniel's arm, but he was already out of reach, bouncing lightly on the balls of his feet.

"Gotta move fast if you wanna keep up!" he sang.

Val's toes curled on the mat. This little human already had her breathing hard. She raised her fists, slipped into a crouch, and then moved quickly, keeping her weight low. She strung four swift jabs together, aiming for his face.

Daniel easily blocked her blows and landed a quick kick to her knee that almost took her down. Val jumped back, and Daniel slipped around behind her and planted a quick elbow in her back. She staggered forward a few steps.

"Sloppy footwork," Diego grunted. "Move faster, Val!"

Move faster! Val urged herself. She whipped around, feeling like a lumbering minotaur compared to Daniel. He grinned wickedly and moved in fast, going for her belly. His solid sucker punch sent a bolt of pain through her guts that she refused to acknowledge. She stepped in close and stomped, trapping his right foot beneath her left. He stumbled as he tried to pull away, and Val landed a heavy punch on his shoulder that sent him reeling. She followed up with a kick he barely dodged.

"Better!" Diego barked. "Daniel, focus. Take this seriously!"

Daniel laughed as he shook his arm, dispelling the numbness from his shoulder. "Now we're talking, Val."

"I'm done talking," Val growled. "I'm fighting."

Diego laughed.

Daniel danced toward her, as quick as a cat, and Val crouched. She blocked his first punch, dodged the second, and hooked his feet out from under him with a swift swing of her leg. Daniel went down hard, and Val straddled him. She seized his arm, going for a headlock, but Daniel moved faster. He squirmed one leg free, planted his foot in her groin, and threw her over his head.

Val barely had the time to feel shock before her body slammed into the mat with enough force to knock the air from her lungs. She fought to regain her feet, but it was over. Daniel had her from behind. He wrapped his arms around her neck and pinned her head against his chest. Scarlet fog threatened the corners of her vision, and after she fought it back, Val didn't recover in time. When dark spots swarmed before her eyes, she gasped and slapped the mat.

Daniel instantly released her. Breathing hard, Val sat up and tucked her head between her knees, waiting for oxygenated blood to flow back into her brain.

"Great fight, girl." Daniel slapped her back. "I can see how you taught old Diego here a lesson."

"Who are you calling old?" Diego grumbled. "Take a water break, Daniel."

"Thanks for the fight." Daniel patted her shoulder, wandered across the mat, and sprang between the ropes with insulting agility.

Diego clambered into the arena and offered Val a hand. She gripped it, shame burning her cheeks. "Sorry," she mumbled.

Diego laughed. "What are you apologizing for? You fought one of the best MMA athletes in the UFC. You did well. Daniel's rear naked choke is legendary. Not many fighters can get out of it."

Val's tense belly relaxed. "Okay. I have a lot to learn, though."

"You do, but you're already learning. You adapted on the fly." Diego grinned and slapped her shoulder. "Okay, you've had your fun. It's time for the hard part."

Val nodded. "Fighting Daniel again?"

"Oh, no, Val." Diego chuckled. "You won't get to spar with anyone until I see *much* better footwork from you. You have the potential to be a UFC fighter, but you have a lot of training to do."

Val squared her shoulders. "Let's do it."

CHAPTER EIGHT

Val felt considerably less gung-ho forty-five minutes later after finishing the last set of sidestep, pivot, and ladder drills. Her legs trembled with fatigue as she stumbled out of the ladies' showers, which were surprisingly pleasant for an MMA gym. She pulled on her sweatsuit, groaning with the effort of lifting her feet, then grabbed her most forgiving wig—the undercut she always wore for MMA—and pulled it on before exiting the bathroom.

Tetra waited for her outside the locker rooms, watching hungrily as two other pro fighters traded kicks and punches.

"Is it normal not to feel your calves?" Val whispered.

Tetra giggled. "I mean, these guys all had to do *something* to look like *that.*"

Val wondered how many hours of exhausting drills the pro fighters had under their belts. She'd never worked so hard in her life. Even hours bent over the anvil didn't compare with the tight, focused drills she'd performed, especially not with Diego barking corrections.

"Let's go home. Genevieve's driving," Val murmured. "Better thank Diego before we leave."

They drifted toward the pro arena, where Diego watched two

guys, his arms folded and his lips pursed. Their fight had become a grapple on the mat. One grasped the other's arm and pinned it against his chest in a powerful kimura hold. Val winced on the other fighter's behalf, but he didn't panic or submit. He brought his knee up into the crook of his opponent's arm in a swift, strenuous movement that broke the lock. The two fighters rolled apart and bounced to their feet.

Diego didn't look around but knew Val was beside him. "It's not only about strength and drills, Val," he murmured. "It's about control. Can you control your opponent? That's the easy part. Can you control *yourself*? That's where the real fighters shine. Your power is impressive, but you must learn to turn that brute force into something deliberate—a dance of power and precision."

"Poetic." Val smiled. "I like it."

"You did well today. I can't wait to see you in the UFC. You'll fight female opponents there, too. Those women are tough on a different level."

"How come you don't have other girls in your gym?" Tetra asked bluntly.

Diego sighed. "I do, but they're few and far between compared to the guys. Part of it is the neighborhood we live in. Gang violence has brought a culture of fear to these streets, and it's Vanguard's mission to change that to confidence. I hold women's self-defense workshops once a month, but many ladies aren't comfortable taking advice from a man." He glanced at Val. "Maybe you and I can talk about working on those together."

"Sure." Val watched as a group of teens slouched in from the street. They made a beeline for the refrigerators and grabbed snacks and a soda each. Their ringleader, a skinny youth with saggy pants, turned to go, and a burly guy in MMA gloves intercepted him. They had a brief exchange that made the teen smile. The group followed the fighter over to one of the arenas.

"Something tells me this is more than a gym," Val murmured.

Diego shrugged. "I like to think so. We give kids something to do other than hang around on the street."

"Free snacks, too." Val raised an eyebrow.

Diego chuckled. "Use a snack to catch a teenager."

"Sounds about right." Val grinned. "You'll let me know what slots you have open for my training, then?"

"I sure will." Diego gave her a fist bump. "Thanks for coming, Val."

Tetra leaned closer as she and Val made for the door. "I love this place."

Val watched the gaggle of kids as they cheered for their favorite in a bout between novice adults. "Yeah," she murmured. "Me too."

She hauled her aching ass into Genevieve, who purred to life of her own accord like she understood Val's soreness. Val held the wheel in a pretense of driving as the Mustang backed out of the parking space.

"I didn't know how much I didn't know," she admitted quietly.

Tetra buckled up. "How do you mean?"

"I've always kicked ass in the Iron Hills. I have two or three feet on other dwarves and twice their strength." Val stretched her aching neck. "It made fighting easy. Even the amateur MMA fighters were easy to fight. But Daniel? He kicked my ass, Tetra. I might have beaten him if I'd used my superhuman strength."

"Why didn't you?" Tetra demanded.

"It wouldn't be fair, for a start," Val pointed out. "Second, I'm here to learn, not to break people's skulls."

"Fair." Tetra shrugged.

"If Daniel had had my strength? If he was an orc, say, or a vampire, with his training, there's no way I could have taken him." Val bit her lip. "I need to change the way I approach combat."

"Seems you made a good start tonight." Tetra laughed. "I've never seen you sweat like that."

"It was hard work." Val replayed the fight with Daniel in her mind. "Did you see the way he moved? I've never been so quick, but it was like he predicted my moves before I made them."

Tetra nodded, her eyes alight with excitement. "Yeah, but when you started to adapt, you anticipated his anticipation. That was when the fight really began. You were learning and growing." She paused, eyeing Val. "Except for the part where you didn't rip his head off his shoulders and drink his spilling blood, you would make a good faerie."

Val laughed. "Thanks, I think."

"It's high praise," Tetra asserted. "My people kicked ass in the Third Pendragon War, remember?"

Val did remember. A flock of faeries had helped to turn the tide at the Battle of New Camelot, the clash that had ultimately saved the world from the Wild Hunt.

"Diego's right. Fighting isn't about brute strength. Faerie dust or no, none of us can take down a moose on our own without real technique," Tetra added.

The insight struck a chord with Val. "I've always relied on my strength," she admitted, "but today, I saw the value in finesse. He was one step ahead, not only with muscle but also with his mind."

"See? You've got to use your brain," Tetra replied.

Val grinned. "Thanks for coming. It's nice to have someone to talk to on the way home."

"Not to mention my unwavering support in the gym," Tetra reminded her.

Val scoffed. "Unwavering support? I seem to recall you spending most of your time drooling over the sparring pros while I slaved away at my drills."

Tetra shrugged. "Potay-to, potah-to."

Val laughed, shaking her head. "You're an idiot."

Genevieve purred to a smooth halt at a red light. Val watched as a mother carrying grocery bags in one hand and clutching a little girl's hand in the other hastened over the crossing. Her pale, drawn face made her eyes look huge as her head swiveled left and right, alert for danger. She tensed at the sight of a young man smoking a cigarette under a nearby streetlamp. Her steps slowed and stopped, and her hand tightened on the little girl's.

Someone called to the mother. The woman turned, relaxing as a woman with a baby in a carrier on her back approached. Sticking close together, the women hurried past the smoking guy. He didn't go after them, but his head turned as they passed, taking in every detail.

"Scumbag," Tetra muttered.

The light turned green, and Genevieve pulled away.

"I think Diego's right," Val murmured. "These women want to know how to protect themselves, but they're afraid to come to him. I wouldn't want to spar with a guy if I'd been forced to live my life in fear of strange men."

"I hear you, but, like, maybe the guys should quit being assholes. Then women wouldn't have to defend themselves," Tetra pointed out.

Val shrugged. "Women are under threat now. They need to know how to keep themselves safe in the meantime."

"I guess." Tetra grinned. "Does that mean you're going to do the self-defense workshops Diego talked about?"

"Yeah, if he wants me to." Val nodded. "They sound like a great way to serve this community."

Tetra sighed. "You and your 'serving the community' thing. MMA is supposed to be your outlet, remember? Your me-time."

Val grinned. "You're my partner now, remember? Serving the community is *our* thing."

"Partners?" Tetra teased. "I thought we were liege and bitch-faerie."

"Potay-to, potah-to," Val retorted.

Tetra's laughter filled Genevieve as the Mustang rumbled through the quiet streets.

Tetra woke up after a ten-minute nap, looking annoyingly fresh. She pinged upright. "Oh, KFC!" She pointed. "Let's get some."

"On the way home," Val promised.

Tetra frowned. "Wait a second. This isn't the road by the river. Aren't we near the Iron Fist?"

"Yeah. Sorry. I decided to make a quick detour." Val stifled a yawn. "Enzo is at the Fist tonight, but he hasn't answered my texts. I want to talk to him before we go home."

"Suit yourself." Tetra settled in her seat. "As long as I get KFC, I'm happy."

In a few minutes, Genevieve backed into her familiar parking spot in front of the bar. Music and laughter spilled from the windows as Val hauled her aching body out of the Mustang. She groaned and limped into the bar, and the crowd got out of her way as she stomped across the space. Jeff bustled up and down behind the bar.

"Hey, man." Val leaned on the booze-stained wood. "Where's Enzo?"

"In the office. He had to take a call." Jeff served a round of Iron IPA.

"You okay here?" Val asked.

Jeff grinned. "I worked here when we'd think six customers was 'busy.' I'm more than happy to run around a little."

Val clapped him on the shoulder and hurried to the office. She knocked once before letting herself in.

Sitting at his desk, Enzo jumped. "Val!" A drop of faerie wine spilled from the shot glass in his hand and burned a hole in his jacket. "Aw, shit."

Val didn't apologize. "Okay, Enzo." She shut the door. "What's up?"

"I ruined my jacket. That's what's up," Enzo grumbled, setting the shot glass on the desk.

"Why are you sitting here drinking faerie wine on your own?" Val demanded, folding her arms.

Enzo stared at her.

"I know you've got something going on. Tell me how to help you." Val paused. "Please."

The orc held her gaze. Tattoos encircled his bare scalp, moving slightly under the fuzzy outline of his glamour. His once-round cheeks seemed gaunt above his tusks, and he'd allowed his sharp yellow nails to grow long.

"Stay out of this, Val," Enzo muttered, reaching for the bottle of faerie wine he kept on his desk.

Val slammed both hands on the desk. "I can't!"

Enzo's eyes narrowed. "Why in Merlin's name not?"

"Because I can't watch someone I care about suffer like this," Val whispered.

Enzo's face crumpled and he looked away, shoulders trembling.

"Tell me what's going on, Enzo. Please," Val begged.

Enzo emitted a shuddering sigh.

"Why won't you tell me?" Val asked.

"Because it's..." Enzo paused. "I don't want you to get dragged into my troubles, Val. I'm not a damsel in distress for you to save."

Val pulled up a chair. "Trust me, dude, nobody could mistake you for a beautiful damsel."

The teasing worked. The corner of Enzo's lip quirked up, a sad ghost of his usual broad grin.

"Everybody needs help now and then. I needed you when I came to New York City," Val reminded him. "I didn't know what it looked like to be a para living among humans, but you showed me. C'mon, man. Don't let that stop you from telling me what's going on."

"Okay." Enzo's shoulders sagged. "Fine. You want my family drama, I'll tell you my family drama."

Val beckoned at the bottle. "Let's hear it."

Enzo produced another shot glass from his desk and filled it, noxious vapor rising from the semi-poisonous wine. "It's Dante. He's in trouble."

Val raised her chin. "What kind of trouble?"

Enzo bit his lip. "I should back up. You know Dante's half-orc, half-vampire."

"I've met your brother-in-law, and it's no great leap of intellect to deduce that your sister is an orc," Val gently teased.

Enzo's features relaxed slightly. "Okay, smartass. I have to remind people sometimes. One can't always tell until he smiles."

Val nodded. "He takes after his mother. What kind of trouble, Enzo?"

Enzo ran a hand over his tattooed scalp. "I...don't really know."

Val frowned. "Talk to me."

"He's studying at the Eternity Throne's Royal University on Staten Island. We were very pleased when he got in. It's exclusive, and I don't say that because it's para-only. Dante studied his ass off to get accepted. His first year was so great: top of his classes, kicking ass in pegasus polo, all the good stuff." Enzo bit his lip.

"He's a great kid." Val paused. "Seems like he hasn't been here to work a shift for ages, though."

"Yeah. That's the least of my worries. When he told me he'd have to take a break from working in the bar for a few weeks, I didn't think anything of it. He's got exams coming up, and I thought he wanted to study." Enzo blew out his lips. "Seems like studying isn't high on his priority list, though. His grades tanked, and his professors called his mom to say that he's been cutting class."

Val folded her arms. "That doesn't sound like Dante."

"It's nothing like Dante, and that isn't the worst." Enzo passed a hand over his face. "Two nights ago, OPMA agents arrested him, and he spent the night in the NYHQ's containment unit."

"Merlin's anus, Enzo." Val straightened. "What for?"

"Unnecessary risk of revealing magic to humans." Enzo sighed. "I'm not clear about what happened, but that's a serious charge. He's only out because his dad's a kick-ass lawyer."

"Shit." Val bounced one leg, her heel thudding on the floor. "I'm sure you guys talked to him about it."

"He's shutting us out." Enzo threw his hands up. "He won't tell us a thing. Won't even give us the truth about what happened at the bar. He's back at school now. I mean, he's a grown para. We can't force him to do anything, but his mother is in a terrible state. She thinks he's fallen in with the wrong crowd."

"Sure seems that way," Val agreed.

"Thing is, Val, the wrong crowd could be very, *very* wrong. I'm not talking about covering his tattoos or smoking a bit of wolfsbane." Enzo bit his lip, tusks jutting. "The Golden Age is still in full swing, but you know better than anyone that Her Majesty still has opposition. She's a peace*maker*, not a peace*keeper*. A mover and shaker. She pisses people off. Rebellious kids can cause a lot of shit in a political climate like this one, stable though the throne is."

"I hear you," Val murmured.

"Many of these paras are sheltered kids, Val. Thanks to Queen Julia, the Third Pendragon War didn't affect the majority of normal paras in any meaningful way. Sure, it was hard to get hold of Bacchus mead or Fernwood flowers for a while, but many kids from the city hardly knew the war was happening."

Enzo bit his lip. "They don't know war the way we do. They don't know about its consequences."

Val thought about Uncle Dale, her dad's brother, who had given his life at the Battle of New Camelot. "They don't," she agreed.

Enzo rubbed his face. "He's a good kid, Val, but he's a *kid*. Impressionable. I don't want him to end up on the wrong side of the law. I don't want him to end up—" He stopped.

"How can I help?" Val asked. "Do you want me to talk to him? Maybe I can find out more about this bad crowd."

Enzo shook his head. "I appreciate the offer. I also appreciate you listening." A faint smile exposed the tips of his tusks. "But I'd like to resolve this between Dante, his parents, and me."

"I respect that," Val murmured, "but my offer's open."

Enzo sagged in his seat. "I know."

Shadow took up most of the couch in Val's living room. Stretched on his belly, he lay with his head and forepaws in her lap, slowly crushing the circulation from her thighs as a warm puddle of drool soaked into her leggings. His snores almost drowned out the dialogue from Val's comfort show, *Castle*, as Nathan Fillion stared earnestly into the camera.

"He's so attractive," Val muttered.

Shadow snored louder. Val tangled her fingers in his fur's thick, soft curls and raised the volume. "You're awful," she informed him. "You have nicer puppy eyes than that guy, though, and that's saying something."

Shadow sighed heavily, rolled onto his side, and then stretched, splaying his paws.

"Biiiiiiig stretch," Val crooned.

A knock at the door made Shadow fly to his feet, and he bounded through the house, baying like an angry lion.

"Shadow!" Val jumped up. "Cut it out!"

Shadow barked once more from the dining room, then fell silent. Val hurried through to his side, grabbed his collar, and opened the front door. A glowing Adonis in a white toga stood on her threshold, beaming benevolently, while a skinny bald dragon in human form cowered in his arms. The larger dragon cradled him like a damsel in distress.

"Livius! Axl!" Val grinned. "It's great to see you guys."

"Axl, put me down!" the skinny dragon hissed.

Axl obeyed, and Livius puffed out his bony chest, then produced a familiar scroll from his satchel. "Dame Valerie Stonehold, Knight of the Noble Order of—"

"Coffee?" Val asked.

Livius sighed. "Can't you let me get through it?"

"No, because you're wearing togas in broad daylight," Val pointed out. "You'll freak the humans out."

"I told you togas weren't fashionable, Livius," Axl chided.

"They were high fashion a few years ago!" Livius protested.

"Try a few *thousand* years ago," Val supplied.

"Julie did say—" Axl began.

"All right, all right." Livius stomped past Val. "Yes, good dog." He patted Shadow's head.

"Puppy!" Axl bent and kissed him on the nose.

"Axl, you disgust me," Livius moaned.

Val led them into the kitchen and started the coffee machine. The dragons sat at her kitchen table as she fetched cream and sugar.

"So, what does Queen Julia want that she can't send in a text?" Val asked.

"Texting." Livius sniffed. "There's no elegance to it. I don't own a smartphone, personally."

"Way to go," Val growled.

Her sarcasm went over Livius' head. "It *is* quite the achievement in this day and age, yes. Axl, you should follow in my footsteps."

"I like playing *My Bakery Empire*," Axl mumbled.

"Either way, it is hardly professional for a queen to send text messages to her subjects." Livius flourished the scroll. "Especially when Her Majesty has a new commission for you."

Val straightened. "A new commission? Not a new *mission*?"

"No, Dame Eiravel." Livius held out the scroll.

Val raised her eyebrows. She popped the wax seal with a

chipped thumbnail, untied the ribbon, and unrolled the parchment on the kitchen table.

Her Majesty's handwriting seemed messier than usual.

Val,

Need you meet a couple people at Waterview Bar at noon today. Find it on Google Maps.

You'll know them when you see them.

Julie.

PS Sorry to be so cryptic.

Val frowned. "Do you guys know more about this?"

Livius shook his head. "We are honored to be Her Majesty's messengers."

"It has to be top secret if she sent me a scroll instead of a message," Val murmured. She poured the coffee. "I'll be there, obviously. I'll take Tetra as bodyguard."

"We can come too if you want," Axl offered. He shrugged, making his muscles move like crunching boulders in his bare arms.

"I am extremely skilled in the fine art of fisticuffs." Livius balled his hands into bony fists and raised them in a gallant pose.

Val smothered her grin with a sip of coffee. "I'm sure you are, but it's okay. Thanks." She dropped a hand to Shadow's head where he sat beside her. "There's not much Tetra, Shadow, and I can't handle together."

CHAPTER NINE

Waterview Bar's parking lot was all but empty. Val steered Genevieve into a space beside a white minivan, narrowly missing an empty beer bottle forgotten on the asphalt.

"Classy," she muttered.

Tetra's shoulders were tense under today's frumpy cable-knit sweater, an eye-searing combination with tie-dye joggers. She scanned the parking lot, which ended at the bay's gray waters. A stray cat picked through garbage on the pebbly strip of beach. The bar's grimy windows displayed hand-painted special offers. Its sign looked homemade, and the paint had peeled, making it nearly impossible to read.

"Think it's pet-friendly?" Tetra asked, glancing at Shadow.

Val snorted. "You wanna go in there without him?"

"Not really," Tetra admitted.

"Then we try." Val exited Genevieve and held the door for Shadow. He hopped out and stiffened, eyeing the cat as Val clipped a leash to his collar. He obediently followed her into the bar.

The interior smelled of urine and stale beer, with notes of vomit. Val's nose wrinkled as Tetra stuck close beside her. Behind the counter, a heavyset human with straggly gray hair worked a grimy cloth over dull glasses. Overhead, a ceiling fan with a squeaky bearing lazily turned.

"Who are these people?" Tetra whispered.

"We'll know them when we see them, according to Her Majesty," Val murmured.

The barman lowered his dirty cloth. "What can I get you ladies?"

Val cleared her throat. "Nothing yet, thank you. We're waiting for friends."

The barman grunted. "Funny. They said the same thing."

He jerked his head at a table in a shadowed corner. When Val turned to it, her amulet responded with a low hum, the iron warming on her skin. One of the table's occupants was a pale human male. The other appeared to be a human girl, perhaps his daughter, yet Val's eyes wouldn't focus on her. Her amulet's pulses got quicker as she approached the table.

Concealment spells, Val realized. *Strong ones.*

The girl raised her head as Val approached. Red hair offset her milk-pale skin, and though her eyes seemed blue, their color shifted as the light struck them.

The man rose, keeping a protective hand on the girl's shoulder. "Are you Eiravel Stonehold?"

Val raised her eyebrows at this human's use of her paranormal name. "That's me."

"The queen sent you?" the man pressed.

Val nodded.

He scanned the bar with red-rimmed eyes. "Prove it."

"*Dad!*" the girl protested.

"Look, mister—" Tetra began.

Val held out a hand. "Tetra, chill."

The faerie backed down. Val extracted the scroll from her coat pocket and held it out to him. The man grabbed it as if she might bite him should his hand linger near hers too long, then inspected the official seal.

"Dad, come on." A scarlet flush crept over the girl's cheeks. "It's her."

"It is." The man's shoulders sagged, and he returned the scroll. "I'm sorry, Miss Stonehold. I'm...getting used to this dangerous world." He paused, his bearing awkward. "I didn't know dwarves could be tall."

"A lot of people don't." Val hid his words' sting with a smile. "Please call me Val."

"Okay." The man perched on his chair.

Val glanced at Tetra, but the faerie had already assumed her role as a lookout. She stood with her back to Val, arms folded, eyes on the door. Shadow sat beside her, his head even with her elbows.

"Tetra and Shadow won't let anyone get past us." Val slid into her seat. "We're safe."

The man swallowed hard. "Okay." He ran a hand over his receding hair. "I'm sorry if I offended you earlier. I'm still trying to come to terms with the existence of dwarves and elves and faeries."

"Fae, Dad," the girl quietly corrected.

"Fae. I'm sorry, pumpkin." The man put a hand on her knee and squeezed.

"It's okay." Val paused. "You're human, aren't you?"

The man sighed. "Yes."

"If you don't mind my asking, how do you know we're real?" Val asked.

The man rubbed the back of his neck. "Because twenty years ago, I became a father to one of you."

Val stared at the girl, her stomach dropping. Was this girl half-human, half-fae? She knew it could happen since Elspeth Feathertouch, one of the most famous heroes of the last war, was one of them, but she had never met one.

"Adoptive father," the girl corrected him again.

The man's shoulders sagged. "I suppose." He hesitated again.

"You can tell her everything, Dad," the girl gently prompted. "The queen said we could trust her."

The man bit his lip.

The girl raised her head. "I'm not human. I'm paranormal, but I grew up thinking I was human."

"Oh." Realization dawned in Val's mind, and she turned to the girl. "You're—"

"A changeling." The girl's eyes darted to the table. "Lunar Fae presenting as human."

"Wow." Val leaned back in her chair. "I knew Queen Julia's been looking for changelings and returning them to Avalon since she ascended, but I've never met one. Not knowingly, anyway."

The girl extended a pale hand across the table. "Teresa Mendoza. Nice to meet you."

Val gripped her hand. "The pleasure's all mine." When their skin touched, her amulet throbbed, scorching her skin. Teresa Mendoza's lunar power might be latent, but Val could sense it seeping through every cell in the fae's body.

"This is my dad. Adopted dad." Teresa cleared her throat. "Nicolas."

"Call me Nick." The man produced a shaky smile.

"It's nice to meet you both." Val raised her chin. "Tell me how I can help you."

Nick squeezed Teresa's knee. "Dad's worried that I'm in danger," Teresa reluctantly admitted.

"Worried? I *know* you're in danger, pumpkin." Nick shivered. "Your parents changed your identity and sent you into a different world to keep you safe. That…that's terrifying. I can't imagine how grave the danger would have to be for a dad to give up his baby girl." His voice cracked, and tears shimmered in his eyes.

"Daddy," Teresa protested.

"He's not wrong." Val smiled. "Before the Third Pendragon

War, being a Lunar Fae was extremely dangerous. Not only would Mordred's followers actively hunt down any Lunar Fae not affiliated with them, but other para species were skeptical of the Lunar Fae since Mordred was one. They found themselves with few friends, especially after Queen Esmerelda ascended, ending a Sylthana dynasty that lasted ten thousand years."

"Mordred's the one who scares me," Nick whispered.

"Mordred's dead." Val folded her arms. "Queen Julia killed him. He's never coming back."

"Yes, but he existed. If one madman could cause so much pain and chaos in a supernatural world, why couldn't there be more?" Nick shivered. "I'm still learning what we're up against, Val, and it all terrifies me. What if another Mordred crawls out of the woodwork?"

"One won't, Dad," Teresa grumbled.

Val thought about Kronos and couldn't agree. "The good news is that your daughter is the most powerful paranormal species in the world," she murmured instead. "Lunar Fae possess the strongest magic of all."

"Then why do so many of them die?" Nick rasped. "You talked about Queen Esmerelda. She was supposed to be almost immortal, but she recently died, didn't she?"

"That's right." Val sighed. "Mordred's sympathizers poisoned Queen Esmerelda with vampire blood early in her reign."

"You see?" Nick shuddered. "That could happen to my Tessie. She'd die slowly despite all your magic."

"Reassuring. Thanks, Dad," Teresa grumbled.

"I'm trying to look out for you, sweetie." Nick inhaled shakily. "Queen Julia said you might be able to help me keep Teresa safe. Something about magic things you make that protect people. Paras," he corrected himself.

Teresa admitted, "I'm hoping you can make me something that will make my dad feel better."

Val folded her arms. "Your dad's not wrong, Teresa. Queen

Julia faced opposition when she ascended the throne despite saving the world. Many paras are suspicious of Lunar Fae, and though you don't have many natural weaknesses, vampire blood is one of them."

"I want you to live your best life in this new world, Tessie." Nick's eyes filled with tears. "Not die a slow, lingering death."

"Okay, Dad," Teresa muttered.

"Can you help us?" Nick asked.

"I believe Her Majesty has a thaumatechnical poison detection system. Perhaps you should go to the trolls about it," Val suggested.

"I'm not going to spend my life waving a wand over my food every time I want to eat." Teresa scoffed.

"Perhaps—" Nick began.

"No, Dad. I'm living my life." Steel filled Teresa's gaze. "I'm not going to have a bodyguard, and I'm not doing the wand thing. I thought Val could make something I could wear. Something that wouldn't get in my way."

Val folded her arms. "I've made many commissions for Lunar Fae. Selenite boosts your powers while you're still breaking free of the changeling concealment."

"I've noticed that." Teresa raised her chin, eyes gleaming. "Can you make me something with that?"

"I certainly can. It would boost your powers and help you defend yourself." Val smiled.

"Her powers are useless against vampire blood," Nick pointed out.

Val nodded. "That's right. What you need is a piece that detects vampire blood and warns you about it at each meal."

"Yes!" Nick straightened. "That would be wonderful."

Teresa frowned. "How would that work?"

"I'd need to experiment with charms and substances," Val told them. That was code for, "I have no idea." "I'm confident that I can make it work."

"What would it look like?" Teresa asked. "Would it be a necklace or something?"

"Since vampire blood is poisonous when ingested, I had a different idea." Val grinned.

Teresa met her eyes and returned the smile.

"What?" Nick demanded.

Val chuckled. "Teresa, how would you feel about a lip piercing?"

"A what?" Nick squawked.

"I'd love that!" Teresa gushed.

"The piercing would alert her to vampire blood coming near her mouth, Mr. Mendoza," Val told him.

Nick's hesitation only lasted a heartbeat. "I guess you're getting that piercing you've always wanted, sweetie." He grinned.

Teresa squealed. "Finally!"

Val laughed as Nick wrapped his arms around his daughter. Teresa's excitement was contagious, but Nick was still shaking.

***

Val gripped the tiny gemstone with tweezers and raised it to the loupe. The gem was no bigger than a pinhead, yet her amulet sang in its presence. The forge fire emitted too feeble a glow for this work. Cold white light sparked in the gemstone's facets from a lamp on her workbench.

"Look at that," she murmured. "Isn't it magnificent, Shadow?"

Shadow's tail thudded on the floor.

The emerald's green was almost perfectly flawless. Almost. Even the best and most expensive emeralds had tiny inclusions: diminutive flecks of other minerals. Val could see none in this stone, even through her loupe.

"Incredible," she murmured. "Natural AAA emeralds are hard to find, Shadow. Emeralds like *this*? Let's just say that they aren't mined on Earth."

She'd had to call in favors from Yuka and Frode to get her hands on this emerald. The Gem Dwarves usually reserved these stones for their royalty. Queen Julia had paid a pretty penny for this, but the magnificent stone was worth it.

Val grinned. It wasn't the emerald's color or peerless clarity that made it so valuable.

"The clearer a gemstone is, the more its magic is amplified," Val told Shadow. "All gems, like all things, hold latent power for those who know how to harness it."

Shadow whined.

"Yes, even ordinary beings like you." Val rubbed his ribs with her toe. "I don't have dog magic, though. Only iron magic."

Shadow sighed.

"It's messed up, right? If I did, I'd get you to talk," Val told him. "Maybe we should get a weredog pet as a translator."

Shadow stared at her.

"I'm kidding. You and I understand each other fine." Val lowered her head. "Quit distracting me. It's time to get this party started."

She dropped the gem into her hand. It rested on her bare palm, touching skin that stung from the raw magic.

Val's amulet pulsed faster with excitement and from the emerald's magic. She closed her hand around the stone, bowed her head, and allowed the magic to course through her cells.

Is this possible? something whispered in the corner of her mind. She was an Iron Dwarf. She'd never tried to cast magic on something that contained no metal before.

The amulet throbbed harder, its heat insistent on her skin. "I'll make it possible," Val growled.

She closed her eyes. Her amulet's magic blended with hers until they were indistinguishable. It pulsed in her veins like heat, surging and ebbing at her command.

However, the gem's power seemed distant when she tried to manipulate or summon it. Her magic felt like it was pushing against an elastic, invisible wall. "Come on," Val growled. "*Come on.*"

She leaned into the magic, and her power thrummed and surged at her bidding. She sensed it pushing against the wall of the emerald's magic and felt that wall stretch but not give.

A wordless snarl leaked between Val's teeth. Scarlet fog suffused her vision behind closed eyes. Strength bounded through her, and her magic collided with the wall like a rampant bear.

The wall snapped, and her amulet blazed. Val opened her eyes to see bright green light exploding between her closed fingers. The emerald hummed on her skin as her magic flowed through its facets.

Val gasped. "It's working!"

Shadow barked gleefully, tail waving.

The raw magic made the emerald tremble in Val's hands. No, it was Val's hands that were trembling. Sweat beaded on her temples as she opened her palm and stared at the emerald's fierce green glow.

She didn't have time to celebrate. This raw, unleashed magic had to be shaped, or it would dissipate into the atmosphere.

Val mounted the stone and picked up her smallest rune cutter. The tool was familiar, yet this one seemed delicate in her hands. Like any other dwarf, she'd used many rune cutters in her lifetime—chisel-like ones with a hammer to lay basic charms on rocks, mechanized cutters with diamond blades for inscribing large jewels, and simple metal tools for engraving runes in iron.

This rune cutter was as thin as a pencil in Val's hand. The tiny on/off button rested beneath her index finger.

She leaned close to the loupe and tapped the button. A tiny red laser beam shot from the cutter and sliced into the emerald. Val held her breath to keep her hands steady. Slowly and carefully, she worked the cutter's beam across the stone's girdle, etching sharp-edged runes one by one. They'd be invisible to the naked eye.

Their effects would be conspicuous, however.

A brief flash of blue light arced through the gemstone's heart when she lasered the last rune onto the jewel. Val's amulet hummed in response.

"Gotcha," Val whispered, straightening.

She paused to stretch her aching arms and flex sore hands before lifting the emerald from its mount. It was cool and quiet now. The magic within hummed and crackled but didn't sting her skin. It had not diminished. It was focused.

"We did it, dude." Val grinned.

Shadow barked.

Val grasped the delicate labret she'd been working on for days. She placed it on the mount and peered through the loupe. The piercing was tiny, but its details were exquisite when magnified. Tiny selenite stones engraved with the finest runes surrounded an open space at the center of the gold-plated steel ring.

The work was too delicate to achieve with hand tools, so Val placed the emerald between the selenite crystals with the tweezers and closed her eyes. Her magic crept into the diminutive strip of steel, and every particle stood at attention, ready for her command. The emerald sank into its setting with the gentlest touch of her magic.

Val opened her eyes and smiled. The labret was aesthetically perfect. The only question that remained was whether it would work.

On cue, there was a knock on the door. Val raised her head.

"Val!" Tetra yelled. "Anne's here."

"Right on time." Val pushed the loupe away. "Come in, both of you."

Tetra clumped down the stairs in an oversized hoodie and sandals. Anne Dragavei-Nox, disinherited princess of the Transylvanian vampires, followed on her heels. The vampire looked like she'd stepped out of an anime movie. Jet-black hair framed a pale face in which enormous eyes belied her several thousand years. She wore an ivory suit whose classy lines traced her slender figure.

"Hey, Val," Anne called.

Val rose and strode to the door. "Hey! Thanks for coming." She tried to dissuade Anne's hug with an offered hand, but the vampire dodged it and gave her a quick embrace. Shadow snuffled Anne's hands.

"Your text said you needed help." Anne stepped back. "Is everything okay?"

"Oh, yeah. Everything's fine," Val reassured her. "I need your help for a jewelry commission."

Anne's eyes sparkled. "Anything you need. I owe you my life."

"I owe you my jewelry business, so it's cheeky of me to ask," Val pointed out.

Anne laughed. "I made a phone call to a friend, that's all. You're the one who fought vampires at odds of twenty-to-one for me. What can I do for you?"

"Can I go back to watching *The Mandalorian* now?" Tetra demanded.

"I need your help, too." Val grinned. "With my new piece."

"Tetra mentioned you were working on something for one of the changelings." Anne nodded.

"Yeah." Val turned. "Let me show you how it—"

Anne stepped into the smithy, and green light exploded from the emerald like a laser beam. It painted the ceiling, highlighting the room with its eerie glow.

"Is it supposed to do that?" Anne inquired.

"Shit." Val scrambled to the labret, from which green smoke rose. She grabbed a warded amulet from the emergency drawer in her workbench and placed it beside the labret. A blue flash announced the presence of a ward four inches across that surrounded the piece. The smoking stopped, and the green glow ebbed.

"What happened?" Tetra asked.

Val grimaced. "This labret is supposed to alert the changeling to the presence of vampire blood in her food."

"It's a lip ring?" Anne asked. "Clever."

"Yeah, only it's much too sensitive," Val muttered.

Anne laughed. "*That's* what you need help with."

"Yeah," Val teased. "I want your blood."

"As long as it stays inside my body, that's cool." Anne grinned. "I see the problem, though. Vamps are among the most populous para species."

"If it's this sensitive, she'll spend her life walking around with a smoking piercing," Tetra summarized.

Val nodded. "Exactly." She bit her lip. "I can likely use the iron inside the piercing to dull the emerald's sensitivity, and I need to alter the runes."

"What do you need me for?" Tetra asked.

"I've added wards to the selenite crystals to protect her against magical attacks. In theory, at least. I'd like you to help me test that," Val explained.

"Firing faerie dust at dummies? My favorite." Tetra grinned.

"First, could you make Anne a cup of coffee upstairs while I fix this?" Val asked.

Tetra led the vampire away, and Val removed the warding amulet. In Anne's absence, the labret lay on the mount, as plain as an ordinary emerald.

Val had to search through a couple of Frode's old magic books before she found the combination of runes that would shorten the emerald's range without reducing its sensitivity. Her laser rune cutter hummed as she carefully etched the symbols onto the emerald and its selenite companions, then added a few more runes to the gold-plated steel setting.

"Okay," she yelled after returning the emerald to its setting. "Let's try again."

Anne hovered in the smithy's door, clutching a coffee mug. "Ready?"

Val rose and placed the labret on a battered wooden dummy's head. "Ready."

Anne tiptoed down the stairs, eyeing the labret. It sparkled in the forge's light but didn't glow.

"Looks like it's working," Tetra remarked.

"Keep coming, Anne," Val coached. "I need to make sure your blood will trigger it if you get close enough."

Anne strode across the smithy floor, then stopped a couple of feet from the dummy. The emerald lay dormant.

"That's good so far," Val murmured. "She'd be able to have a conversation with a vampire without triggering the emerald."

"What if someone brushes her on the street?" Anne wondered. She moved closer to the dummy and allowed her shoulder to lightly rub it as she passed.

The emerald gleamed quickly enough that a human would mistake it for a trick of the light, then dulled.

"Perfect." Val grinned. "Now hug it."

Anne raised her eyebrows.

"You're a hugger." Val gestured at the dummy. "Hug it."

"Okay." Anne laughed as she wrapped her arms around the wooden figure.

The emerald flashed, its fierce glow painting Anne's face. She stumbled back, raising a hand to protect her eyes, and the light dimmed.

"Sorry." Val grimaced.

Anne shook her head. "Don't apologize. It works perfectly!" She paused. "If she falls in love with a vampire, she might need you to make adjustments."

"I have a feeling it's going to be a while before her dad lets her smooch anything with fangs." Val chuckled. "I'm satisfied that it works for vampire blood."

Tetra cracked her knuckles. "My turn?"

"Your turn," Val agreed.

The faerie smirked. "You guys should step back."

Val retrieved the ballistic glass panel and slid it across the smithy. "Knock yourself out," she told Tetra.

Tetra stretched out her arms. "Is that a challenge?"

"No, idiot," Val grumbled.

Tetra laughed. Val supplied Anne with a welding helmet and Shadow with his goggles. They sat by the workbench as Tetra fired bolt after bolt at the labret, and the wards Val had carved into the selenite and steel flashed blue and purple as they deflected every attack.

"Cool to watch, isn't she?" Anne murmured.

Val nodded. There was no denying Tetra's grace as she spun and flipped, her arms swift and effortless as she sent arcs of glimmering faerie dust through the air. It was a deadly dance. When she stopped, breathless, her short hair wild around her head, the smithy floor hissed, and the dummy was pocked with holes and scorch marks.

Anne applauded. Val rolled her eyes but couldn't stop grinning.

"Look at it. That's insane." Tetra shook faerie dust from her hands, then pinched the labret between finger and thumb. "It's untouched. My dust can melt diamonds."

"Diamonds, yes." Val moved the ballistic glass out of the way. "Not my wards, though."

Tetra laughed. "I reckon that will make Nick feel a lot better."

"Is that Teresa's father?" Anne asked.

Val nodded. "He's struggling to come to terms with the para world."

"Who can blame him? It can be a scary place." Anne nudged

Val with her shoulder. "I'm glad the scariest person I know is on my side."

"Always." Val mock-punched the vampire's arm. "Thanks for the help."

"Any time," Anne assured her. "Can I see?"

"Sure, but don't touch, or it'll go nuts," Val reminded her.

Tetra held out the labret, and Anne leaned closer, gazing at it as it glowed, thanks to her proximity. "Incredible. It's so simple and elegant. One would never imagine what it can do."

Val grinned. "That's exactly what I hope to achieve with Stonehold Jewelry."

"You've achieved it," Anne told her.

CHAPTER TEN

Teresa leaned close to the handheld mirror, eyes widening as she admired the labret. It rested in a piercing that looked slightly red and raw. Val guessed she hadn't mastered lunar healing yet.

"I love it," she murmured. "It's beautiful."

"The selenite will give your powers a slight boost, but we need a larger volume to get meaningful magic energy into you," Val told her. "I'll book you for a pair of selenite bracelets if you want them."

"We get issued with those at Tintagel. They're cool but not made as well as this." Teresa tilted the mirror to get a better view. "It's insane."

The emerald seemed incongruous against the grimy backdrop of Waterview Bar. Even with no vampires in sight, its natural sparkle held Val's attention as Teresa moved her head left and right.

Nick smiled. "More importantly, it protects my little girl from poisoning and magical attacks. The videos you sent me were impressive, Val. Thank you so much."

"That's what I'm here for." Val returned the smile.

Teresa turned to Nick. "This means you'll let me stay at

Tintagel for full-time training and lifting my concealment, right?" She hesitated. "We had a deal."

Nick bit his lip, pain flickering in his eyes, but he quickly hid it. "That's right, sweetie. We had a deal. I'll drop you off at Tintagel tonight."

"Yes!" Teresa squealed. She threw her arms around her father's neck. "Thanks, Dad."

Nick squeezed her. "Thank *you*, sweetie. You're a grown woman, and you didn't have to listen to me when I begged you not to go."

Teresa released him. "I couldn't leave you upset like that." She grinned at Val. "Thank you, Val. Now I can go and be everything I'm supposed to be without thinking about my dad worrying himself to death."

Val laughed. "I can understand that."

"I can't believe you approve of my lip piercing." Teresa giggled. "I never had the guts to get one before, even being, as you say, a grown woman."

Nick's features relaxed. "It's gorgeous, pumpkin. Brings out your eyes."

Val's heart tugged as she and Tetra left the bar. She pulled out her phone before getting into Genevieve and texted Frode.

You know I love you, right, Dad?

He responded instantly despite the late hour in Avalon.

Of course I know. You okay, little spark?

Standing at the driver's door, Val looked back through the bar's dirt-smeared windows. Teresa talked rapidly, her hands waving, eyes alight with excitement. The labret caught the light with every movement of her lips. Nick sat opposite her in silence, but he looked at her like she held the whole world.

More than okay.

Love you, Frode replied.

Val almost sent a huggy emoji. Almost.

Val pulled up to the drive-thru window. "What do you want? Before you answer, there's nothing raw on the menu."

Tetra sighed. "Not even sushi?"

Shadow whined.

"Or blood?" Tetra suggested. "It doesn't have to be human."

"Human blood is illegal, as you know very well," Val chided.

"Fine. I'll take the eight-piece bucket." Tetra settled in her seat.

"How do you stay so skinny?" Val wondered.

"Faerie metabolism." Tetra grinned.

Val rolled her eyes and relayed the order to the waiting server. They crawled toward the payment window, following a minivan full of crying kids.

"Teresa was so happy about that labret," Tetra murmured. "I can't believe she lets her dad order her around like that."

"I don't think he was ordering her around. He really wants to keep her safe. It took a lot of guts for him to strike this deal and let her go," Val mused.

Tetra snorted. "I would've gone anyway."

Val raised an eyebrow. "Why am I not surprised you have daddy issues?"

"I don't have daddy issues," Tetra retorted.

"You once told me that your dad made you fight a wolf alone," Val reminded her, tapping her card.

Tetra shrugged. "Yeah, well, I killed the wolf. Any issues in that relationship were my father's, not mine."

"That's what it means to—" Val began.

Her phone buzzed, and the name on Genevieve's hands-free system was **Freya Gold**.

"You'd better take that," Tetra told her.

"No shit." Val selected the handset option and raised her phone to her ear. "Hi, Ms. Gold."

"Good morning, Miss Stonehold." Freya sounded tired. "Thank you for your patience. Are you still available to transfer Gaia's Sickle?"

"Absolutely. How are the negotiations going?" Val asked.

Freya sighed. "Mr. Opulencia has finally settled on a price for the sickle, and the sale was finalized."

"Fantastic." Val grinned. "I'm glad to hear it."

"Her Majesty's coffers are less glad, but she considers imprisoning Kronos worth any price," Freya acknowledged. "I was hoping you could do the transfer very soon."

Val rubbed her chin. "I will, Ms. Gold, but I'll need to prepare. This isn't anything to be undertaken lightly."

"True," Freya agreed. "I mentioned to Mr. Opulencia that you would want to visit and reconnoiter the route before transporting the sickle."

"That's right. I'd like to drive the entire route at least once and get the lay of the land." Val checked her watch. "He lives in the Catskills, you said? A couple of hours outside the city?"

"Indeed. Mr. Opulencia has given me permission to share his location with you," Freya explained. "I will send it via an encrypted text message. Use your phone's fingerprint sensor to unlock it."

"That's great. Tell him I'll see him in the next three hours." Val drove Genevieve to the next window.

Relief drenched Freya's tone. "You're going there right now?"

"I have nothing more important to do than transfer that sickle, Ms. Gold. I'd like to get it done as soon as possible," Val told her.

Freya sighed. "Wonderful. Wonderful! Thank you, Miss

Stonehold. I'll send that location right away and let Mr. Opulencia know you're coming."

"Cool." Val grinned. "I'll keep you updated." She hung up.

"Where are we going?" Tetra inquired.

Val took the hot, greasy bucket from the server and planted it in Tetra's lap. Tetra and Shadow drooled.

"Road trip to the mountains," Val informed her. "Ready for a drive?"

Tetra tore a chunk off a drumstick with her teeth. "Let's do this!" she announced with her mouth full, spraying Genevieve's dashboard with oil.

Genevieve's gear lever clanked, transformed into a tiny, clenched fist, and punched Tetra on the elbow.

"Ow!" Tetra bellowed.

"No spilling food in the queen's car," Val ordered.

Genevieve's fist gave Val the middle finger and turned back into a gear knob.

Tetra plied her napkin. "Fine. Sorry."

Val's phone binged with a message from Freya. She opened it and plugged the location into Genevieve's Avalonian navigation system.

Numbers popped up on the screen. **2 hr 34 min**.

Val patted the dashboard. "Hear that, Gennie? That's your time to beat."

The Mustang revved her engine.

"Noooo," Tetra groaned, hugging the bucket of chicken.

Genevieve screeched out of the drive-thru with the throaty bellow of a V8 on a mission.

***

The two-lane asphalt road wound quietly between pine and aspen trees crowded close on its narrow verges. Genevieve cruised at eighty, taking every turn with effortless grace, her massive engine snarling as they climbed through the mountains. Val glimpsed a few snow-capped peaks, but for the most part, the woods were alive with late spring birdsong. Thick green foliage dappled the sunlight. Since leaving the city, Val had stopped twice to allow deer to cross the road.

Tetra shifted in her seat, sucking oil from her fingers. To Val's awe, the bucket was empty.

"Look at this view," Val murmured. They turned onto a bridge that offered a breathtaking panorama. These mountains rolled far more gently than the jagged peaks of the Spine where Val had grown up. Limpid lakes lay at their feet, reflecting the green trees. The road was a black ribbon adorning the greenery, and here and there, vast mansions and sparkling resorts jutted through the vegetation.

"Why are the trees so small?" Tetra asked.

"Small?" Val raised her eyebrows as they sped over the bridge. "They don't seem little to me."

"They're teensy. Where are the dryads?" Tetra wondered. "What kind of woods are these?"

Val snorted. "Were you expecting Fernwood Deep?"

"Someone needs to talk to the Green Man in this place," Tetra grumbled. "He's useless."

"I don't think Earth's woods have Green Men," Val suggested.

Tetra rolled her eyes. "Don't be absurd. Who ever heard of a forest without a Green Man?"

"I stand corrected." Val chuckled. "We're nearly there." They'd left the city two hours ago, but the navigation system informed her that they'd reach their destination in ten minutes.

"Do we know anything about this Opulencia guy?" Tetra asked.

Val shook her head. "All Ms. Gold told me was that he's a rich Were noble who's had the sickle for hundreds of years."

"Rich nobles." Tetra scoffed. "I'll bet he's a total shithead."

"That's a bit prejudiced," Val chided. "Her Majesty is a rich noble, too."

"Only about fifty percent shithead," Tetra acknowledged.

"What's your beef with the queen, anyway?" Val demanded.

Tetra shrugged. "Oh, apart from being made a magical slave? Nothing, really."

"We've been over this. She could have given you a far worse punishment than getting to eat fried chicken in her car while driving all over the country with me," Val pointed out.

Tetra sighed. "Fine. Twenty-five percent shithead, and that's because I don't like her sense of humor."

"Duly noted." Val laughed. "Okay, we don't know much about Maximilian Opulencia, so what do we know about Gaia's Sickle?"

"It cut off Uranus' balls." Tetra snickered.

"Do you have to be so juvenile?" Val demanded.

Tetra giggled. "His dick, too."

"Tetra!" Val scolded. "We're on a royal mission."

"Okay, okay, I won't mention anybody's genitals in front of that Opulencia guy." Tetra laughed. "What an idiot. Zeus had it more together, if you ask me. Obviously, if you want to kill somebody, you chop off their head. Sylthana-made, you said?"

"Yeah, which is interesting." Val rubbed her chin. "Gaia's Sickle was the first object ever forged from steel. I'd have thought dwarves would be the first to do that."

"Sylthana Elves have fire magic. Maybe they were the first people to realize you could melt iron and mix it with copper and shit," Tetra guessed.

Val nodded. "That makes sense. Either way, it's imbued with Sylthana magic."

"Zeus became king after he killed Kronos, right?" Tetra asked. "I mean, it's not like any of his siblings were around to challenge him for the throne."

Val shifted gears as Genevieve began a steep climb. "Actually, if I remember the story right, Zeus poisoned Kronos with copper sulfate and poppy juice before cutting off his head, and he puked up Zeus' siblings."

"First, *gross*." Tetra frowned. "Second, that seems biologically impossible."

"It's ancient magic, okay? I don't understand it either," Val admitted. "In any case, Kronos' siblings, the Titans, started a huge war with Zeus and his siblings. It lasted ten years and leveled many parts of Earth. Eventually, Zeus won and made himself king."

"Was this before or after King Arthur?" Tetra asked.

"*Long* before King Arthur. The Lunar Fae were a minority then. Zeus and company lived in Greece and ended up ruling much of Earth, although their influence didn't spread to Great Britain, where King Arthur came to power thousands of years after Zeus' reign," Val explained.

Tetra tilted her head. "How do you know all this?"

Val laughed. "I went to school."

"So did I, but they didn't teach us that shit in faerie school. We were busy learning to kill things." Tetra snorted. "Okay, so Zeus dies, the Sylthana empire gets smaller, and eventually, King Arthur rules the Lunar Fae and builds Avalon."

Val nodded. "Then he established the Eternity Throne, the first and only empire to unify all paranormals."

"But there were Sylthana Elf kings and queens of the Eternity Throne, right?" Tetra asked. "Sinatria mentioned that Queen Julia is only the third Lunar Fae monarch."

Val glanced at Tetra, surprised. She seldom mentioned her older adoptive sister.

"What?" Tetra grumbled. "I know I tried to kill her, but we lived in the same palace, okay? I heard her say shit."

Val cleared her throat. "You're right. Sylthana Elves ruled from the Eternity Throne for generations." The GPS pointed them down a narrow, unpainted asphalt path that felt like a driveway rather than a public road. She slowed Genevieve to a crawl between the thick foliage. "They helped to capture Mordred after King Arthur fell into his enchanted sleep, ending the Second Pendragon War. After that, the high council was formed, and Sylthana Elves took over the throne. Queen Esmerelda's reign started three hundred years ago."

"*That's* why they're assholes to the queen," Tetra mused. "They've ruled the Earth and paranormals longer than Lunar Fae have."

"I guess," Val conceded.

"I bet they're pissed that Queen Julia's got Gaia's Sickle now. They must want it back. Then they'd have more power, right?" Tetra guessed.

Val nodded. "Hopefully, they'll never find out, and we'll get the sickle to Gold, Manns, and Sax in peace."

Tetra chortled. "Famous last words."

"You have arrived," Genevieve's GPS announced.

Val braked the Mustang to a halt. "Uh, no, we haven't."

The asphalt road abruptly ended in a picturesque meadow on the mountainside. The woods marched around the expanse of deep grass. Wildflowers scattered color across the meadow, and butterflies dipped over their blooms. Apart from them, the space was curiously devoid of life. Val would have thought deer and birds would love a meadow like this.

"This is weird," Tetra muttered.

Val's amulet hummed, warming. "There is *something* here." She pushed the Mustang's door open and stepped out. Shadow emitted a long, low growl.

"What are you doing?" Tetra demanded.

"There's magic here." Val extended a hand. "I don't think this meadow is real."

"What are you talking about? It's right in front of you," Tetra scoffed.

"No." Val reached out and felt a springy resistance in the air. "What's right in front of me is a concealment spell."

Tetra exited Genevieve and raised her eyebrows as the air rippled blue under Val's fingers. "Not a ward?"

Val pressed harder. Her fingers sank through the spell like she'd lowered them into warm bathwater. "Not a ward. Stay close."

Her hand hovered near the dagger on her hip as she stepped forward. Shadow hopped out of Genevieve and joined them as they moved through the concealment spell. Val's vision blurred, colors melting into one another. She blinked vigorously. When she opened her eyes, the meadow was gone.

In its place, a mansion towered.

The smooth white walls and slate-gray roofs would not have been out of place in the wealthiest parts of Staten Island. Grand terraces loomed over the landscaped lawns and sternly mani-cured shrubbery. Perfect white pebbles lay in a circle at the roots of each unnaturally round tree. Palladian windows overlooked a giant swimming pool to one side.

Blue runes throbbed on every doorframe and around each window, and Val's amulet pulsed in response. Despite the absence of locked doors or iron bars, Val knew this place had intense security. No wonder nobody had pinched Gaia's Sickle from this noble in the past few hundred years.

"Swanky," Tetra commented. "I bet this place cost a fortune."

"Never mind the house. The wards and concealment spells probably cost more than the structure," Val told her. "Dad and I seldom forged wards like this in the Iron Hills. When we did, it was almost always for export to other parts of Avalon. Not many paras can afford full concealment for an estate."

"He collects fancy things." Tetra shrugged. "It follows that he's loaded."

Shadow whined at Val's heels. His tail hung low and stiff, and his hackles were up.

"What's up with him?" Tetra asked.

"I don't know." Val frowned.

"Is it the wards?" Tetra suggested.

"He doesn't usually act like this in the presence of strong magic." Val clipped his leash to his collar. "Shad, you've got to behave, dude. Otherwise, I'll leave you in Genevieve. She won't let you overheat."

Shadow growled, and his big muscles tensed. His nose twitched.

"I don't think he'll behave." Tetra stepped back.

"Me neither," Val admitted. "Shadow, come on."

She lightly tugged the leash, and Shadow turned, tail between his legs.

"What's gotten into you?" Val muttered as they squeezed back through the concealment spell. Genevieve helpfully opened her door, and Shadow scrambled inside as though he couldn't escape the mansion fast enough. He curled up on the back seat and whined.

"Sorry, boy." Val sighed. "Genevieve, take care of him, okay?"

Genevieve turned on her AC and played soothing music.

"Thanks." Val patted the Mustang's roof.

She pushed through the spell to the other side again. "Do you think we should—"

"I think we should stay here." Tetra nodded at the grandiose French doors. "Somebody's coming."

Val had never met a weremagpie in the flesh, but as Maximilian Opulencia strutted from his mansion, his species was unmistakable. He was a chubby man with thin legs clad in dark tights like humans wore a long time ago, and he moved with a high-stepping gait, his head nodding with every step. His black jacket and pure white waistcoat were laughable for the woods but fit perfectly with the mansion's splendor. Though he wore a top hat, Val glimpsed black hair streaked with white beneath it.

"Mr. Opulencia," Val called. She pulled out her Eternity Throne ID badge and raised it. "My name is—"

"Oh, I know who you are, Miss Stonehold. Please, call me

Maximilian." The weremagpie stopped a few feet away, leaning on a gold-headed cane. He tilted his chin to stare at them down his sharply beaked nose. He smiled, but his beady black eyes glittered like ice.

"Pleased to meet you," Val lied. "This is my business partner, Tetra Dupont."

Maximilian doffed his top hat. "Dear Freya told me you would be coming. The money's barely reached my bank account, and already you swoop upon my treasures like vultures."

"Gaia's Sickle isn't your treasure anymore," Tetra blurted.

Val shot her a glare.

Maximilian's eyes narrowed. "Quite right. Outspoken, aren't you?"

Tetra folded her arms, but Val's glare silenced her.

"Sir, we're not here to waste your time." Val spread her hands. "We'd simply like to see where the sickle is so we can plan the transfer accordingly."

"Yes, yes. I suppose you do," Maximilian murmured, gaze still locked with Tetra's. "It would be a terrible thing if somebody stole it, wouldn't it?"

"It would threaten the paranormal world," Val stated.

Maximilian cleared his throat and gave that cold smile again. "That too. Very well. I will show you to my vault." He beamed. "Prepare to behold the greatest collection of mythological treasures in any dimension."

The weremagpie strode away. Val and Tetra trailed behind.

The path of white pebbles leading to the front door passed between rows of stunning trees with glowing silver leaves, leaves made of jewels, or golden branches, beds of blooming four-leafed clover, and towering statues, many ancient-looking.

Val gazed at a massive wooden statue of a lady in a long robe. Its carving was more exquisite than anything she'd seen from human hands.

"Is that Shajara Elven?" she asked, curious despite herself.

"Ah, the Palladium. It's Sylthana, actually. It holds a tremendous protection charm—one that kept Troy from collapse for ten years." Maximilian paused to admire the statue. "Isn't she beautiful?"

"What about this one?" Tetra pointed at a stone statue depicting a man with ram's horns who held a decapitated head in one hand. "I like it. It's badass."

"Ah, yes, Ikenga. I brought that from Nigeria after my family first colonized it." Maximilian chuckled. "You won't believe the fuss people kicked up about it leaving the country. Isn't it magnificent? I couldn't leave it there. Come! There's much more to see."

He turned on his heel and strode away.

"Colonized?" Tetra whispered.

"I'll explain later," Val muttered. She feared Tetra might hit the weremagpie with a puff of faerie dust if she told her now.

The French doors led to a magnificent foyer with a glittering crystal chandelier suspended from a ceiling decorated with Renaissance-style paintings. Glass display cases lined the walls.

Val gasped. "Is that the Horn of Bran Galed?" She pointed at a curled ram's horn on a velvet cushion.

"Indeed it is. Good eye." Maximilian smiled. "If you raise it to your lips, it provides any drink you wish for."

"Useful," Tetra remarked.

"This is Pair Dadeni, a cauldron Luna used to combine her magic with water and create a healing potion so potent many believed it could raise the dead. If anyone could, it'd be a Lunar Fae, right?" Maximilian pointed at a cast-iron cauldron studded with selenite.

Val couldn't resist wandering between the cases, gazing at the treasures within: a crown made of glimmering blue and green strands of aurora borealis, a pair of gloves that trembled from the magic woven into their cloth, and a few links of adamantine chain stained with ancient dried blood.

She stopped short in a corner, and blood rushed in her ears. The mannequin before her wore a hauberk of the finest chain mail she'd ever seen. At first glance, it looked like silver silk. She only saw the links when she leaned closer. Her amulet had been pulsing since they reached the concealment spell. Now, it sang with fierce excitement.

"Miss Stonehold, come over here." Maximilian's tone bubbled. "I have a dried sample of the first mandioca root. Any orc would be honored to behold it."

Val wheeled around. "I'm not an orc," she barked. "Is this the silken mailcoat of Orvar-Oddr?"

Maximilian was either deaf to her tone or didn't give a shit. He joined her, gazing at the hauberk, which reflected in his beady eyes. "You know your armor, Miss Stonehold. Indeed it is. This is one of the greatest treasures of the Iron Dwarves."

"I know," Val snapped. "My people have been searching for it for centuries."

Maximilian gave a harsh, cawing laugh. "It has been safe here. Not to worry."

Scarlet fog threatened the corners of Val's vision. She clenched and unclenched her fingers, fighting to push it back.

"The sickle is this way," Maximilian added.

Val held it together as she and Tetra followed the weremagpie up one side of a double helix staircase encrusted with jewels. He pointed at paintings and statuettes lining the hall, but Val was tired of hearing about his treasures.

"Do you keep the sickle in a display room?" Val growled.

"Of course not, Miss Stonehold." Maximilian's eyes widened. "That would be foolish! Gaia's Sickle was the first steel object ever forged. It's beyond priceless. I keep it locked in a vault. We'll be there in a moment, but you must take a moment to admire my menagerie first."

He turned through another French door onto a concrete balcony covered in a fern flower creeper whose beneficial blooms dried up and fell dead to the floor. Val tried not to stare at them.

"Look!" Maximilian spread his arms. "Aren't they incredible?"

Tetra raised a hand to her mouth. The shock in the faerie's eyes dragged Val's attention from the fern flowers. Instead, she looked down into a courtyard of bare but beautifully gilded cages filled with splendid creatures. A three-headed eagle perched in one, methodically plucking small feathers out of its chest with two of its heads while the third stared into the middle distance.

A golden fox with nine tails trotted up and down one wall of its cage, tongue lolling, eyes glassy. A weasel-like ramidreju pawed at an empty bowl in the cage beside the fox. A pure white pegasus in a small cage stood with his legs wide apart and swung his weight from one side to the other, his head moving rhythmically from side to side, ears hanging listlessly.

"This is the greatest collection of creatures outside the Eternal Palace." Maximilian leaned on the railing, his gaze hungry as it rested on an empty cage beside the weaving pegasus. "Soon, it will be even greater."

Goosebumps prickled Val's skin.

"They look miserable," Tetra muttered.

"What was that?" Maximilian turned around, his half-smile mild.

Val pressed a hobnailed boot hard on Tetra's toe.

"Ow!" Tetra yelped. "I-I was saying they look magical."

"They certainly are." Maximilian laughed. "All right. Let me show you to the vault."

He turned on his heel and continued down the hallway. Val and Tetra walked silently. Val had lost her appetite for treasures and didn't bother to look as they passed tapestries, weapons on gilded racks, and mannequins bearing magical robes and cloaks. Maximilian finally halted at the door of a glaringly modern vault between deep red drapes. The gleaming steel door was featureless except for a black touchpad. Val saw no seams or hinges in the metal.

"State-of-the-art." Maximilian tapped on the tempered steel with his knuckles. "It's impossible to open without my magical signature. There's a charm on it that knows if I'm doing it under duress, too. It'll still open the vault but will also send an alert to the OPMA."

"Good to know," Val muttered. "Is the sickle inside?"

"Patience, Miss Stonehold, patience." Maximilian pressed his hand to the touchpad.

The pad flashed purple, and metal clanked inside the vault. Iron magic made Val's amulet throb, sending adrenaline through her veins. The steel compressed and folded back, forming a narrow door.

"Welcome to the home of Gaia's Sickle." Maximilian flourished. "Step inside."

Val zipped her jacket to her chin to hide the fierce red glow of her amulet's ruby eyes. She ducked to fit through the door and straightened inside a vault whose solid steel doors surrounded her like a hug. The space was too small to extend her arms and contained only one object: a sickle in a glass case against the back wall.

Excitement kicked in Val's chest. Her amulet hummed, scorching her skin and telling her she stood in the presence of the highest magic.

The sickle looked ordinary. Its long wooden handle was crude and knobby, and tool marks scarred the wood. There was still bark in places. Val imagined a desperate mother stripping a sapling with a kitchen knife. The sickle's head had a rough edge, and the hammering was unskilled at its sleek tip.

Of course it's unskilled. Val fought the urge to reach toward the sickle. The magic thrumming through its blade sang to her. *Gaia was the first to forge steel.*

Her heart galloped. She felt as though she should kneel or

perhaps fall on her face. The sickle's magic rushed through her veins, calling to every iron atom in her blood. It summoned her.

How? Val wondered. *How could a Sylthana Elf craft something like this?*

Two desires trapped her: to touch the sickle and to flee from it. If any magic item had command over a monster like Kronos, this did.

"Val!" Tetra yelled.

Val jumped, hand flying to her dagger. "What?"

"I said your name three times, and you didn't react," Tetra grumbled.

"Sorry." Val swallowed. "It's—" She didn't have words.

"It's breathtaking, isn't it?" Maximilian murmured.

"Yes, it is." Val dragged a forearm over her brow, wiping off sweat. "Are there wards or magic alarms if one removes the sickle?"

"Yes, but I disable them all when I unlock the safe." Maximilian beamed.

"Okay." Val cleared her throat. "Thank you, sir. I think we've seen what we needed to see." She found it difficult to turn her back on the sickle.

"There's so much you haven't seen, though." Maximilian's eyes gleamed as she exited the vault. "I would love to show you my collection of trophies, or the rest of the menagerie, or the gallery of—"

"We need to go." Val cleared her throat. "Thank you, sir, but we have a long drive back to the city."

"Another time, then." Maximilian gestured down the hall.

Val couldn't get out of the mansion quickly enough. She rushed down the hall, Tetra jogging in her wake. Annoyingly, Maximilian had no trouble keeping up.

"I have many wonderful treasures, as you've seen." Maximilian extended his arms. "Gaia's Sickle has always been a favorite."

"Not to worry, sir," Val ground out. "That sickle will ensure millions of paras' safety from Kronos."

"Almost as many millions as the dollars it brought me." Maximilian rubbed his hands as they passed the open door to the balcony overlooking the menagerie. "Rest assured that my collection will by no means decline in value."

His gaze slid to an empty cage beside the three-headed eagle's.

"What—" Tetra began but hesitated when Val glared. "What, uh, what a pleasure to see a place like this."

"The pleasure is all mine, Miss Dupont." Maximilian grinned. "I love showing people around my humble nest."

Stepping out of the mansion felt like freedom until Val found herself pinned between the trees and statues that didn't belong there.

"Thank you for your time, sir," she croaked, dry-mouthed.

"Yeah," Tetra muttered. "Thanks."

"Goodbye, new friends." Maximilian flourished a hand. "I will anticipate your return to take my sickle with sorrow."

Val didn't backchat him. She stretched out her arms, pushed through the concealment spell, and scrambled into Genevieve.

CHAPTER ELEVEN

"Wow." Tetra threw herself into the passenger seat. "I really hate that guy."

Shadow clambered onto the center console, whimpering, and frantically licked Val's face and neck.

"Easy, buddy. Easy," Val soothed.

Shadow returned to the backseat and lay there, panting heavily, a string of drool hanging from his tongue. A tiny compartment opened in Genevieve's back door, and a bowl extended to catch the saliva.

"Oh, so you'll give the dog a drool bowl, but you pinch my fingers each time I use a cup holder?" Tetra protested.

Genevieve revved her engine.

"You're right, Gennie." Val put her in gear. "Let's get out of here."

The Mustang wheeled around, gravel flying from her tires, and accelerated down the path. Her suspension squeaked in protest as she hurtled around the turns.

"What a shithead," Tetra announced.

"I know!" Val shook her head. "Those poor animals."

"Not to mention the artifacts and shit. Do you think Her Majesty knows that he has Luna's cauldron?" Tetra wondered.

"Her Majesty's been looking for that cauldron. I heard it on the news a few years ago. I remember because Iron Dwarves helped Luna to forge the cauldron." Val's hands tightened on the wheel. "My people have searched for the Silken Mailcoat for centuries."

"How much shit do you think he's stolen from different cultures?" Tetra asked.

"How many mythical creatures that belong in the wild?" Val murmured. "Or at least in a species-appropriate enclosure."

"Let's go back and burn down his mansion, then let the creatures free to trample him to death and bury his bones in the woods!" Tetra punched both fists in the air.

Val inhaled slowly. "No. We can't."

"Why not? You said it yourself; he's a thief. The queen would probably support us," Tetra pointed out.

Val frowned. "Yeah, maybe, but the first priority has to be Gaia's Sickle. He's agreed to let it go without a fight. We need to get it to safety."

"It's got powerful magic." Tetra paused. "I didn't feel it like you did, but I know it's there."

"It's the only thing that can contain Kronos." Val sighed. "I'll talk to the queen about Maximilian's collection. I don't know how much of it is technically illegal. But the sickle has to come first."

"Fine." Tetra sighed. "I still think my plan is cooler."

Val glanced in the rearview mirror at the illusion of the idyllic meadow that hid the collector's home. She couldn't disagree with the faerie.

Val tipped a small mountain of obscenely expensive dog food into an ant-proof dish. She clamped her phone to her ear with one shoulder as she added a scoop of joint supplement.

Shadow barked.

"Shhh," Val whispered against the dial tone.

Shadow wagged his tail, the long hairs fanning over the kitchen floor.

"Sit," Val ordered.

Shadow flopped onto his back.

"Close enough." Val lowered the bowl to the floor. "Are you a good boy? Are you the goodest boy? Are you the cutest, bestest, most squishiest—"

"Good morning, Valerie," Freya Gold greeted her on the phone.

Val straightened, her cheeks blazing. "Ms. Gold! Hi. Hello. How are you? Good morning."

A painful pause followed. Val's toes curled inside her fluffy socks.

"I'm very well, thank you," Freya returned.

Val grabbed her coffee mug from the counter and stumbled to the living room to escape Shadow's loud crunching. "Uh, good. That's great. I'm sorry to call you this late. We got back from the Catskills after office hours yesterday."

"Seeing your email when I got to work this morning was a relief." Freya paused as though she were scrolling through it. "I'm pleased that you believe you've worked out a rough route for the transport."

"I have. We'll need to iron out details with my operations manager." Val grinned at the thought. "I want to avoid places with large paranormal populations."

"If you need any data on the subject, feel free to contact the OPMA. Queen Julia has made it clear that you will have all the resources you need," Freya assured her.

"Thanks, Ms. Gold." Val sipped coffee and waited for her brain cells to warm up.

"I understand that your preparations might take several more days, but do you have a specific date in mind?" Freya asked.

Val swirled her coffee. "I need to check traffic patterns before I can confirm, but I believe the small hours on a weeknight will be our best bet. The roads need to be quiet to minimize the potential for collateral damage."

"I thoroughly agree. We must protect the humans at all costs. They have no say in our world, so it's only fair that we should shield them from the consequences of our decisions." Freya sighed. "I, for one, will sleep far better when Gaia's Sickle rests safely in our vault, Miss Stonehold."

"It's safe where it is now. I have no doubt about that." Val grimaced. "Planning the transfer will be essential."

"Then do your best, Miss Stonehold. I don't have to tell you how vital this item is." Freya paused. "Any dwarf who has stood in its presence knows the depths of its magic."

"That's for sure," Val agreed.

Her phone beeped in her ear. She raised it and frowned at the name on the screen: **Anne Dragavei-Nox**.

Val returned the phone to her ear. "I'll call you back with details, Ms. Gold."

"Of course. Thank you," Freya murmured.

Val ended the call with the dwarf and picked up the call with Anne. "Anne? Everything okay?"

"Everything's fine," Anne told her quickly.

"Phew." Val's shoulders slackened. "I know it's the middle of the night for you, so I was worried."

Anne laughed. "I'm burning the daylight oil, as vampires say, and I'm about to burn more. I have a favor to ask you on behalf of family."

"Hugo?" Val demanded. "Is the favor kicking him in the teeth? I'd gladly do that."

"No, no, not my father." Anne scoffed. "He's not getting any favors from my friends or me. It's the...other side of my family."

Val swallowed. "The Nox side?"

"I don't want to say too much over the phone," Anne hedged. "Are you busy today?"

"I finished my latest commission early, but I'm at the Fist tonight. I can try to get out of it." Val grimaced. "Trouble is, Enzo's in a difficult place, and—"

"Today is better, Val," Anne told her gently. "We don't mind staying up late."

"Okay." Val hesitated. "You sure you're okay?"

"I'm fine." Anne chuckled. "Still, please meet me in Staten Island when you can. I'll text you the address."

Val showered, changed, yelled goodbye to Tetra, and reached Staten Island in record time. Genevieve knew the way suspiciously well. The Mustang effortlessly dodged through morning traffic, outran two cops, and sped through the island's sumptuous suburbs in only ten minutes.

"Wow, dude." Val leaned forward to peer through the windshield. "I bet the doggies here all have diamond collars."

Shadow had shotgun privileges today, and although he looked cramped in the bucket seat, he wagged his tail with enthusiasm as Genevieve purred between striking mansions. Each had its own style. Many were modern marvels of metal and glass, and others had stately pillars and elegant arches. Massive gates offered glimpses of spreading lawns and splendid homes bustling with uniformed servants like it was the nineteenth century.

"I've had enough of mansions for one week, boy," Val muttered.

Shadow showed none of the trepidation he'd exhibited at

Maximilian's mansion. The dog panted happily, sticking his head out the window.

Val's GPS guided her to a solid gate in walls so tall they could have belonged to a castle. Beyond them, she glimpsed floor-to-ceiling tinted windows that reflected the morning light.

"Of course," Val murmured, rolling down the window. "The windows have to keep the sunlight out."

She hit the intercom's call button and waited.

"Nox residence," someone mumbled sleepily.

Val's foot slipped on the brake. Genevieve rolled back and jerked her emergency brake so sharply it rapped Val on the elbow.

"I'm sorry," she squeaked. "Did…did you say *Nox* residence? Which Nox?"

"Who is this?" the sleepy person demanded.

Val swallowed. "I'm sorry. I-I'm Eiravel Stonehold. Anne Dragavei-Nox sent me."

"Ah, of course. Anne told me to expect you, Dame Eiravel. Please proceed," the disembodied voice intoned.

The gates opened soundlessly, and Genevieve drove into a courtyard lined with bushes covered with fragrant white roses. All glass, the mansion towered beyond the courtyard walls, spruce trees proudly rising around it.

"Shit, Gennie," Val squeaked.

Shadow's tail wagged hard.

Genevieve parked against the wall. Val's numb fingers found the seat belt, and she stumbled out of the Mustang. Shadow bounded out behind her.

"Shadow, sit!" Val hissed. Was she insane? Why in Merlin's name had she brought her dog?

Shadow sank to his haunches beside her. "You're facing the wrong way." Val tugged his collar.

"Welcome, Dame Eiravel."

The voice came from behind her. Val nearly shat herself. She whipped around and flicked her left arm, activating the bullet-proof shield in her armband. It expanded into a glimmering disc of faerrous steel as she slipped into a fighter's crouch, right hand near her dagger.

An elegant elderly vampire in a top hat and tails gave her a smooth bow. "Master Nox is expecting you," he purred.

Val straightened and shook the shield, reducing it to an armband. She tried to ignore her burning cheeks. "Should, uh, should I leave my dog in the car?" she asked, feeling thoroughly stupid.

"He is a welcome guest in this home, Dame Eiravel," the butler murmured, "and it is not necessary to diminish Genevieve by referring to her as a mere *car*."

Genevieve honked and revved her engine. The butler tilted his head, listening. "Ah, good. I'm pleased she has respect for your greatness, Genevieve." He patted the Mustang's hood. "Anyone can have a brief lapse in word choice when startled."

"How come you speak Genevieve?" Val asked.

"She is an honored guest here," the butler told her. "This way, if you please."

He drifted through a gap in the courtyard wall. Val stomped after him, feeling loud and ungainly compared to the vampire's soundless movements. Another magnificent rose garden awaited them, blooming in dozens of colors from velvet-black to shocking magenta. A few glittered since one bush featured gems instead of flowers. Their fragrances were a symphony as Val moved through the garden, each bringing a new aroma. Many smelled like, well, roses. Others hinted at cinnamon, pine, buttered toast, fresh mint, and new leather.

"This is cool," Val commented. She brushed a fingertip against a white rose near the path. It snarled, and Val hastily shoved her hands into her pockets.

"Master Nox will receive you in the library," the butler

informed her, leading her through double doors wide enough to admit a car.

Val tried not to gape at the grandeur of the foyer, which featured marble floors and tall windows. Portraits of famous vampires hung on the walls. The Nox family banner dangled between them, as well as several flags representing the Eternity Throne.

"Uh, butler, sir?" Val began as they climbed a flight of stairs carpeted in blue.

"My name is Perkins, miss." The butler almost smiled. "Gerald Perkins, at your service."

"Okay, Gerald." Val bit her lip. "You said Master Nox. *Which* Master Nox? Anne's husband?"

Gerald's expression darkened. "Certainly not." He opened an oak door carved with wooden animals. "Sire, Dame Eiravel Stonehold is here to see you."

Val wasn't a reader, but her jaw dropped as she entered the library. The round room's walls were floor-to-ceiling book-shelves stocked with heavy tomes, their gold leaf titles sparkling in the light from a massive hearth fire. Her boots sank into a fluffy cream-colored carpet, and while an imposing desk loomed at the back of the room, the group of vampires sat on couches in the center. Cozy pillows and a collection of mugs on the coffee table cluttered the scene.

A male vampire rose from the couch and inclined his head. "Ah, Dame Eiravel. Thank you for getting here so quickly."

Val's mouth opened and shut several times before any sound came out. "Sir. Your Majesty," she croaked.

The tall vampire had deep frown lines around his eyes and mouth, but his crimson eyes held a twinkle of kindness. Gray streaks ran through his long, straight ponytail. Despite the ebony cane he leaned on, his well-cut suit and proud bearing made him exude elegance.

Val recognized him. Anyone who'd ever watched the news would. This was Julius Nox, the high king of the vampires.

He chuckled. "I go by 'Sire.'"

"Sire," Val whispered. She clumsily bowed.

Shadow didn't give a shit who King Julius was. He shoved past Val and amiably rammed his nose into the vampire's crotch.

"Shadow!" Val yelped.

"Hello, boy." King Julius rubbed the dog's ears, which propelled his wagging tail to top speed. "Don't worry, Dame Eiravel. Julie told me about your companion. I was hoping I would meet him today."

"Hey, Val." Anne rose from the couch and hurried over to give Val a quick side hug. "Thanks for coming."

"Hey," Val squeaked.

"You come highly recommended." King Julius straightened. "I'm grateful that you're able to help us."

"Sire." Gerald drifted forward. "I believe you should rest now."

"Yes, yes. I'm sure you're right." King Julius passed a hand over his eyes. "It's been another long day." He turned to the other two vampires on the couch. "Malcolm, are you sure—"

"I'm sure, Dad. I'm fine." The smiling vampire was a younger copy of his father, except that he wore his hair in a faux hawk instead of a ponytail. "Please, go rest."

"Thank you, my boy." King Julius rested a hand on Val's shoulder. "It is an honor to meet you."

Val's amulet throbbed from the vampire king's magic. "Likewise," she managed.

King Julius exited. His son watched him go with worry pinching the corners of his mouth.

"Sorry for the secrecy, Val. I'll explain everything." Anne took her arm and guided her to an armchair facing the couch. "I'd like to introduce you to Malcolm and Cassidy."

The copy of King Julius rose and shook Val's hand.

"Prince Malcolm," she murmured.

"Please. It's just Malcolm." He smiled. His father's kindness echoed in his eyes.

"You can call *me* 'Your Royal Gloriousness,'" his wife told Val. She wore bright red lipstick that matched her nails, and a fluffy white cat lay in her lap. It hissed at Shadow, who ignored it and lay at Val's feet.

"Cassidy," Malcolm chided.

"What?" Cassidy demanded.

"Yes, Your Royal Gloriousness," Val quipped, drawing a smile from Cassidy. "How can I help?"

Malcolm hooked one knee over the other and interlaced his fingers around it. His foot jiggled as he spoke. "As the councilor who represents all vampires at the Eternity Council, I'm one of few paras who know the details of the plan to transport Gaia's Sickle to Gold, Manns, and Sax. I'm grateful that you can undertake the task, Dame Eiravel, but I fear that it will be more dangerous than you anticipate."

Val raised her chin. "We're expecting trouble."

"Good. You must." Malcolm's shoulders tensed. "We're facing more resistance than we'd hoped for."

Val leaned forward. "What do you mean?"

"You know the history behind Gaia's Sickle?" Malcolm asked.

Val nodded. "I do."

Malcolm inclined his head. "I'd expect no less. You know that it's one of the most sacred artifacts of the Sylthana Elves, then."

"Permission to speak freely, sir?" Val asked.

Malcolm chuckled. "Of course."

"That dickhead Maximilian Opulencia has a lot of sacred artifacts that don't belong to him," Val growled. "It makes sense that Gaia's Sickle is one of them."

Cassidy smirked. "He *is* a dickhead. I like her."

"That's a relief, honey." Malcolm patted Cassidy's knee.

She slapped his hand. "Don't 'honey' me."

Malcolm seemed unperturbed. "Though the details of the

purchase are secret, it's public knowledge that the Eternity Throne acquired the sickle to keep Kronos imprisoned. Julie's all for laying her cards out with the public when it's safe to do so."

"Yeah, well, it wasn't safe this time," Cassidy growled.

Val tilted her head. "The Sylthana Elves aren't happy," she guessed.

"Officially, the Sylthana Elves consent to and support the throne's purchase of the sickle." Malcolm rubbed the back of his neck. "King Lotan of the Sylthana Elves is one of Julie's staunchest supporters. His court and the Sylthana councilor, Felix Kushnir, gave their permission for the purchase before negotiations began with Maximilian. They understand that the world's fate might depend on Julie having the sickle at her disposal."

"But not all the elves agree with them," Val presumed.

"No." Malcolm gritted his teeth. "Many Sylthana Elves have been bitter about losing the Eternity Throne since Queen Esmerelda ascended. They consider it no coincidence that the throne enjoyed thousands of years of peace and only collapsed into war again when a Lunar Fae ruled."

"Yeah, because the Sylthana Elves never rocked the boat, never caused shit, and never made any improvements," Cassidy muttered. "They kept the peace instead of standing up for progress the way Julie does."

Malcolm inclined his head. "Politically, I'm not allowed to agree with your position, Cass, but you're absolutely right."

"The elves want the sickle back?" Val asked.

Malcolm hesitated. "Lotan and Felix are solid in their support, but not all elves follow their example. There's a painful history regarding the sickle. Mordred stole it from the Sylthana Elves during the Second Pendragon War and used it against them. It disappeared after the elves conquered him, and they never got it back. It only resurfaced now. No one knows how Maximilian got his hands on it or where it's been for the past several thousand years."

"I bet Maximilian's not talking, either," Val growled.

Malcolm shook his head. "The OPMA hopes to get more information from him, but our priority is to secure the sickle. That hasn't gone down well with the elves. A fringe group of Sylthana Elves have been making threats online and rallying extremists on social media. We haven't pinpointed in-person gatherings yet, but Julie expects trouble."

"A Sylthana-led extremist group?" Val raised her eyebrows.

Malcolm grimaced. "I know you're thinking about the Dark Moon League."

"Hard not to." Val grunted. "They tried to burn Ironforge Bastion to the ground when I was a kid. I had to stay with Bodil while my dad went to help. It was scary shit."

"I'm sorry you went through that." Malcolm shook his head. "The Dark Moon League was a speciesist group whose focus was destroying the Lunar Fae. This group is different, though. They call themselves the Scorchborn Syndicate."

Goosebumps prickled on Val's back and arms. "That doesn't sound good."

"It isn't. We're not clear who their leader is, but we know their agenda." Malcolm shifted his weight. "They're Sylthana supremacists who believe that all species, humans and paranormals included, should be under Sylthana rule the way they were in Kronos' day."

Val exhaled. "Shit."

"We're not yet sure how much of a threat they are," Anne interjected. "So far, there have been no attacks, only angry social media posts, but these things can escalate quickly."

"I'm sure the OPMA is investigating." Val raised her eyebrows.

"Of course." Anne nodded. "But their resources are spread thin, thanks to the Wild Hunt controversy."

"We fear Gaia's Sickle will be their first target," Malcolm added.

"The Syndicate isn't our only problem. Lotan has made many enemies among his people. Sylthana Elves are nothing if not traditionalists, and many are lobbying to get the sickle back, even though Queen Julia promised to return it should Kronos be executed or banished to the prison realm," Anne explained.

Val bit the inside of her cheek, contemplating. "But the Syndicate is the only group likely to get violent."

"We believe so." Malcolm sighed. "Have you fought Sylthana Elves before, Dame Eiravel?"

"No, but I've been training." Val folded her arms. "My business partner and I will add Sylthana Elven simulations to our rota."

"Good, but that's not why I called you here." Malcolm sighed. "Julie has total faith in you, and I've learned to believe in whatever she believes in. I know you'll keep the sickle safe, but I'm afraid of compromising its safety…and yours."

Val raised her eyebrows. "Sir?"

"We're worried that the Nox family is a target for Sylthana spies," Anne explained. "We're the only royal family on the high council that currently lives in New York City, which makes us, and especially Malcolm, who knows all the particulars, a tempting target."

Val's arms relaxed in her lap. "What about the Aether Elves? I thought Queen Ilsanthia and King Victor lived in Staten Island, too."

"They do, but they're not home for the next few weeks, thank Luna," Malcolm told her. "They're touring the Forest of the Mystic Dusk. The Aether Elf councilor, Arion, lives in Avalon."

"That does make you a target. I agree that it could be a problem, sir. Would a protective detail be an option?" Val asked. "I have to do the transfer, but until then—"

"*I'm* his protective detail." Cassidy smiled, showing a lot of very sharp teeth.

Malcolm chuckled uneasily and shifted his weight. "It's not my physical safety that worries me, Dame Eiravel. Black market thaumatech and dark magic advance quickly. There are rumors of ways to steal information from my mind without me knowing it. The mansion is warded, but a para could hack into my mind from miles away."

"This kind of tech is rare and expensive, but we're worried," Anne added. "I love the faerie dust necklace you made for me." She touched the pendant hanging on her chest. "I thought you might be able to make something similar for Mal. Something to protect his mind and body from espionage."

Val rubbed her chin. "A constantly active ward that protects against magical and physical attacks. It'll be an interesting challenge, but I'm sure I can do it."

"If anyone can, it's you." Malcolm grinned. "I'm told Lilli's latest babysitter described her as 'fun' instead of running away screaming, thanks to you."

Val smiled. "Thank you, sir. I'll produce it as quickly as possible."

"That would be great." Malcolm exhaled. "Until then, I won't leave the mansion unless I must, but it's easier said than done."

Cassidy rested a hand on his knee and squeezed.

"Malcolm is not only the vampire councilor anymore," Anne murmured. "The Third Pendragon War cost Julius dearly. Malcolm also performs many of the kingly duties."

"It's okay. I owe Dad that much." Malcolm's face twisted. "Please, Val. Help me keep our world safe."

"Help us keep my husband safe, too." Cassidy's tone was gentler than Val would have thought possible. She pressed her free hand into the cat's thick white coat.

Val nodded. "I'll do my best, sir, ma'am. I promise."

Malcolm and Cassidy exchanged glances while Anne grinned proudly.

"Anne tells me your best is more than good enough," Malcolm reassured her.

CHAPTER TWELVE

Val flipped through her texts as she tossed her coat on the couch and a takeout bag in the garbage can. Shadow bounded past her to noisily slurp water from his bowl, and Val brushed by him in the kitchen as she headed for the smithy.

The first text was from Liam.

Kenzie's system works great! Familiarizing myself with the route. Will update you with traffic patterns ASAP.

Val texted her gratitude, then scrolled to a chat with another friend.

On my way. Got what you asked for.

Val grinned. She flung the smithy door open and strode inside. The ever-present forge fire's warm crackle greeted her, and her anvil's dull gleam called to her. She turned away from both and marched to a shelf of Iron Dwarven books on the wall.

Shadow clattered down the steps as Val dumped an armful of books on the workbench. He curled up in the basket at her feet.

"Anti-telepathy spells," Val murmured. "No, wait. Those won't work. It can't be the same as Seraphine's, or Malcolm will be cut off from OPMA comms. Those work on telechips."

Shadow yawned.

"It's going to test us, boy." Val opened a book, flipped through it, and traced a diagram. "Obsidian and diamond. Emerald, too. Bloodstone to enhance vampire powers. Iron to use as a shield. How do I put all those together?"

As if in response to her question, the front door banged. Shadow pricked his ears.

"It's okay," Val told him. "She's a friend." She raised her voice. "In the smithy!"

Moments later, a petite humanoid descended into the room. Sinatria, third in line to the faerie throne, wore a concealment spell that made her human-sized. Unlike Tetra's, her spell maintained her delicate wings, which bore the ragged edges of a wasp's. If one looked past the pointed gray teeth and red eyes, Sinatria was Barbie-beautiful.

"Here I am!" she trilled as she staggered under several massive books.

"Thank you!" Val rose and grabbed the books. "Wow, you got all of them."

"Avalon Town's public library is an amazing place. I don't think there are many books in the world they don't possess a copy of. Once I'd shown them your list, they found them in a matter of minutes." Sinatria beamed.

Val set the books on the workbench and was ambushed by a faerie hug. Harmless pink and purple faerie dust rose from Sinatria's skin, smelling of lavender.

Val chuckled. "It's nice to see you."

"So nice. I'm relieved that I don't have to go everywhere with a host of feral faeries anymore." Sinatria giggled. "Dad finally came to his senses when I won the melee at the last faerie tournament in Fernwood Deep."

"I saw the videos. You were kick-ass." Val offered her a fist to bump.

Sinatria gave her another hug instead. "Where, uh, where is...she?"

"Upstairs in her apartment." Val smiled. "She's doing great, Sinatria. You made the right call by letting her become my vassal. I'll admit I had my doubts, but you were right."

Sinatria's shoulders stayed tight. "Does she know I'm here?"

"No," Val admitted. "I haven't seen her all morning. She's working tonight. Usually, she sleeps in when that's the case."

Sinatria shifted her weight. "Okay." She cleared her throat. "You said you're working on an urgent commission."

"I am." Val slid into her chair and reached for the stack of books Sinatria had brought. "I need to make a bracelet that will make the wearer impervious to magical attempts to take information out of his mind, but at the same time, I don't want to block him from receiving telepathic messages from his allies."

"I don't know anything about making jewelry, but that sounds tricky." Sinatria gazed around the smithy. "I've never been down here. You've got incredible magic, Val." She rubbed her arms as though wiping away goosebumps.

"I think I have the supplies I need. I'll use the magic-blocking properties of obsidian and iron to protect him, but emerald's discernment capabilities and dwarven runes will allow the OPMA's comms to reach him. Diamonds will enhance and anchor the wards. However, I have no idea how to put it all together," Val admitted. "I need runic combinations I've never used before."

"Hence these." Sinatria nodded at the topmost book: *Advanced Runes, Volume I*. Three identical tomes rested beneath it. "You know runes, though."

"Runes are like languages. I know Iron Dwarven runes—one language—and I only know the parts of it that I need to use. I know how to strengthen wards and use runes that make armor lightweight or swords self-sharpening. This is something else," Val explained. "Runes also gain and lose power if they're combined with other languages."

"Complicated," Sinatria remarked.

Val laughed. "That's why I need the books."

Sinatria pulled up a stool and sat beside her. "Let me help. What are you looking for?"

They each took a book and skimmed the indices. Val ran her finger down the lines of text. Sinatria moved faster, flipping back and forth through the book.

Val's neck ached when Sinatria straightened. "I've found something."

Val raised her head. "What?"

"'Runic combination for selective warding.' It looks like dwarven and faerie runes, actually." Sinatria passed the book to Val and tapped the flowing figures on the bottom of the page. "I've seen those etched into the bark in Fernwood."

"We need the faerie runic alphabet," Val decided.

Sinatria combed through the remaining volumes for the alphabet while Val unrolled a piece of blank parchment and tacked it to the drawing board. Book in one hand, charcoal pencil in the other, Val copied lines of runes onto the parchment. Her amulet pulsed as steadily as a heartbeat while she worked. The dwarven runes glowed a dull blue as she finished each runic combination. Rainbow colors shimmered beneath the faerie runes.

"Wow," Sinatria murmured. She held one volume open so Val could see it for reference. "Look at that. There's strong magic in those."

"This combination isn't right." Val crossed it out. "I think I need to switch these characters around."

"Keep going. You're getting closer," Sinatria encouraged her.

Val looked from one book to the other, then added more

runes to the parchment. "You don't have to stick around, you know," she murmured. "I might not be good company."

"Bullshit. It's great spending time with you." Sinatria smiled. "Besides, this is important work. I have a feeling I know what it's for."

Val raised her eyebrows.

"I have higher clearance than you might think." Sinatria grinned. "I was supposed to get drinks with the satyr councilor today, but I can skip it to help you."

"Seriously, Sinatria, if you have somewhere to be—" Val began.

Sinatria raised a hand. "Stop right there. It's more important to help you with the bracelet than to suck up to the satyr. Come on, Val! Let me have this excuse." She chuckled. "I really hate that guy."

Val laughed.

"What?" Sinatria asked.

"Nothing." Val shook her head. "Okay, let's keep going."

They paused when the runes were almost done: Sinatria to order pizza, Val for a bathroom break and to gather supplies from the pigeonholes on the smithy's walls. She had an emergency supply of metals and gemstones, and when she tipped them onto the workbench, their sparkles filled the room. None of the diamonds or emeralds were the quality she'd used for Teresa's and Seraphine's pieces, but they'd do the trick.

She hoped.

"Starting with a standard iron armband," Val grunted, selecting one she'd forged earlier.

"If that's for the vampire I have in mind, it's too big," Sinatria pointed out.

Val grinned. "There's a simple rune to make it mold to his body. Don't worry about it." She mounted the armband in a vice and selected a hammer and a tiny chisel. "It's an easy one."

She'd carved this rune into every piece she'd made, so Val cut the angular shape into the iron with a few quick taps of her hammer.

"Right." She removed the armband. "Now to mount the gemstones. Pass me that burnisher, please."

Val extended a hand, but no tool was forthcoming. Sinatria made a tiny, strangled sound. Val's head snapped up, and she tensed, expecting danger, then froze.

Tetra stood at the top of the steps, holding a pair of pizza boxes. Her hands fell limp to her sides, and the boxes bounced down the steps, showering dough, cheese, and tomato in all directions.

Shadow ignored the bounty of fallen food. The dog was tense and motionless in his basket, ears pricked, hackles rising. Faerie dust oozed from Tetra's clenched fists and hissed where it struck the floor. Sinatria, too, froze in place. Her wide eyes locked with Tetra's.

A painful reminder rushed through Val: the fae assassin's katana plunging into her belly. Tetra had ordered him to kill Sinatria months ago, as well as anyone who stood in his way.

Val pushed the thought aside. "Easy, ladies," she growled.

Shadow emitted a warning snarl.

Sinatria blinked, and the tension snapped like an over-stretched elastic band. "Hey, Tetra." She strode forward, hands outstretched. "It's *really* good to see you."

Tetra's hands relaxed, and her voice cracked. "It...it is?"

"Of course it is. You're my sister, and I've missed you." Sinatria stopped at the foot of the stairs, hands still outstretched.

Tetra cleared her throat. Tears sparkled in her eyes before she blinked them back. "I didn't know you were coming."

"Sinatria and I are friends, too," Val murmured. "I asked her to bring these books from the library in Avalon Town."

"Okay." Tetra eyed Sinatria's outstretched hands and shoved hers into her pockets.

Sinatria took the hint. She lowered her hands and stepped

aside. "Val's working on an interesting bracelet. Do you want to see?"

"Sure." Tetra shuffled forward.

Shadow greeted her with a wagging tail, and the faeries stood on either side of Val, peering over her shoulders as she cut settings for the stones in the armband. The silence between them hung over Val's head like a wet towel. She did her best to ignore it as she set the row of stones in the armband, interspersing diamonds, emeralds, and obsidian.

"They're so pretty," Sinatria murmured.

"With kick-ass function," Tetra added, her tone sharp. "Uh, what *is* their function?"

Val shot her a look as she pressed the last gemstone into place with the help of a bit of magic. "Protecting an important para from magical espionage without blocking telepathic comms. What do you think of those runes, Tetra?" She nodded at the parchment.

Tetra rubbed her chin. "I don't know dwarven runes, but the faerie ones make sense." She tapped one. "This rune is for protection, this one for communication. How are you going to keep their spells from clashing?"

"In theory, this dwarven rune should do that." Val touched it. "It acts as a switch, applying protection and communication in different circumstances."

"I think it'll work if your iron can hold that magic," Tetra muttered.

"I was thinking that, too," Sinatria chipped in, making Tetra flinch. "I'm not sure iron alone will be powerful enough to hold this complicated magic."

"Diamond is an excellent ward anchor. It should hold the protection spells," Val muttered, "but I agree. The iron might not be strong enough to hold the more complicated bits of magic."

"What about faerrous steel?" Tetra suggested.

Sinatria raised her eyebrows. "Faerrous steel?"

"My name for the iron and fairy dust alloy." Val grimaced. "It's an excellent magic anchor, but I have to coat it with copper to keep the faerie dust from evaporating. Copper will negate the effects of diamond."

"This is more scientific than I expected," Sinatria admitted.

"It's a balancing act." Val paused with her rune cutter poised. "Maybe there's a rune that can keep the faerie dust inert."

"Maybe you can make it simpler than that." Tetra folded her arms.

"How?" Val asked.

The faerie scoffed. "Add a layer of faerie dust between the gemstones and the iron. That'll form an airtight seal. The dust will interact magically, but it won't decompose because it won't come into contact with air."

Sinatria laughed. "That's genius."

"It is." Val grinned. "And I think it'll work. Okay, let me take the gems out, and we'll give it a shot."

She delicately wriggled the gems from their settings, leaving stones and tools strewn over the workbench. "Got a bag of faerie dust somewhere," she muttered.

"Hello?" Tetra gestured up and down her body. "You also have a whole-ass *faerie* here."

"Two faeries," Sinatria added.

Val chuckled. "You're welcome to contribute a little dust."

"Which kind?" Tetra rolled up her sleeves.

"Anything that's not going to melt the metal." Val pulled on welding gloves, then held the bracelet to the loupe.

"I...I would like to contribute, too," Sinatria murmured.

Val glanced from one sister to the other. "I think you should both do it."

Tetra stiffened.

"C'mon. No arguments," Val insisted. "Get the dust in there quickly, and I'll put the gemstone over it."

"What do you say, sister?" Sinatria smiled shyly.

Tetra rubbed the back of her neck. "Listen, Sinatria..."

Val froze between them, a diamond clutched in her tweezers.

"I-I'm sorry, okay?" Tetra blurted. "I thought I was doing what I had to do to survive, but actually, I was being a total bitch. I wasn't thinking of anybody except myself. I could blame faerie culture and my upbringing or whatever, but you're nothing like me. You'd never sic a vengeful assassin on your adopted sister even if your life depended on it like I thought mine did. It was cruel and selfish, and I'm sorry." She inhaled deeply. "I really am."

Sinatria smiled. "It's okay."

"What? No, it's not. I tried to kill you." Tetra grimaced. "Val, I never apologized to you either, but I should. I mean, I've heard that you could've been killed that night, too."

"She nearly was," Sinatria murmured, "but that's over now. I can see the change in you, Tetra. Your repentance is real." She smiled. "That's not a prerequisite for forgiveness, but it sure makes it easier."

Tetra's eyes widened behind her brutally slashed bangs. "F-forgiveness?"

"Yeah. I mean, maybe you're right. Maybe it's not okay, but I still forgive you." Sinatria grinned.

Tetra sagged onto a stool beside Val like her legs had given out. "Why?"

"Because Luna forgives us all," Sinatria murmured. "Why would I not?" She held out her arms. "Can I have that hug now?"

"Tetra's not really into—" Val began.

Tetra flew to her feet and flung her arms around Sinatria, who returned the hug, laughing. For the first time, Val saw faerie dust spontaneously rise from Tetra. It was pale blue and smelled of pine trees after rain.

"Thank you," Tetra croaked.

Sinatria squeezed her. "Any time."

Shadow rolled onto his back with a happy bark.

"Okay, very cute. Reconciliation, forgiveness, all that sappy shit. Love it, but can we get back to work?" Val demanded. "We've got to finish this bracelet."

Tetra released Sinatria and cleared her throat. She brushed Sinatria's lavender dust from her clothes and discreetly wiped off a tear.

"Sure. Let's do it." Sinatria came closer.

Together, the faerie sisters extended their index fingers toward the gemstone's setting. A tiny trickle of sparkling dust ran from each finger, purple from Sinatria and blue from Tetra. Their fresh scents collided since much of the dust evaporated on the way down, but it mingled in the setting like glitter.

"Okay, that's it!" Val pressed the diamond into the hollow and felt the stone grind gently against the coarse dust. At her magic's touch, the setting closed tightly around the diamond's girdle. Her amulet hummed with pleasure.

"Did it work?" Sinatria asked eagerly. "Did it evaporate?"

Val closed her eyes, sensing every particle within the armband. The iron sang at the presence of the faerie dust's magic.

"It worked." She opened her eyes and grinned. "It worked *great*."

"Yes!" Tetra punched the air.

They spent the next hour lost in concentration. The faeries trickled dust into each setting as Val replaced the stones one by one. When each of the jewels—dark obsidian, green emerald, and sparkling diamond side by side—were in place, Val held the bracelet to the light. The faerie dust amplified the fire and brilliance of each jewel, making it shimmer brightly.

"Wow," Tetra whispered. "That's beautiful."

"Malcolm doesn't know he's making a fashion statement while keeping his mind safe, huh?" Sinatria remarked.

Val lowered the armband with studious indifference. "Who said anything about Malcolm?"

"It's okay, Val. Like I said, my security clearance is high

enough for me to know." Sinatria chuckled. "I appreciate your discretion, though."

"Malcolm, as in Malcolm Nox?" Tetra asked.

Val mounted the armband and bent over it with a diamond-tipped rune cutter and a tiny hammer. She started copying the runes on the parchment to the iron.

"Yeah, that Malcolm," Sinatria agreed.

"Oh, he's hot," Tetra told her.

Sinatria giggled. "He *is* hot."

"You guys!" Val lowered the rune cutter. "You're talking about Malcolm Nox, the future high king of the vampires and a great hero of the Third Pendragon War!"

"So?" Tetra shrugged.

"So?" Val shook her head. "You're talking about him like he's… he's—"

"A real person?" Sinatria suggested.

Val paused.

Tetra giggled. "One loses the starstruck look when you sit across from him at royal banquets and shit. Nice guy, though."

"He's undeniably a hero," Sinatria agreed, "but Tetra's right. He's an ordinary person like all of us."

Val snorted. "Yeah, you're princesses. I'm a nobody dwarf from the Iron Hills."

Tetra slapped her back. "You're not nobody to us, Val."

The faeries perched on stools beside Val as she lowered her head and lost herself in her work, cutting the runes into the armband's underside. Their light intensified as she cut the last one, and her amulet thrummed, its heat tingling her skin.

She didn't realize that the faeries had been engaged in quiet conversation until they fell silent.

"What?" Val raised her head.

"Something happened." Sinatria grinned. "Did you cut the last rune just now?"

"I did. Did you feel it?" Val asked.

Tetra nodded. "Absolutely. Strong magic."

Val raised the armband and admired its gentle glow. In her magic senses, she felt the runes take root in the armband's materials. Their magic sank deep into the iron until it was no longer a combination of metal, jewels, faerie dust, and clever workmanship. Instead, the bracelet became a whole that existed for one reason—to protect.

It looked good doing so, but protection was its identity, all its parts working together for that purpose.

"It's amazing," Tetra whispered.

"Qenzi has the tech to test it. She's coming to fetch it this afternoon and get it to Malcolm before evening." Val set it aside and cut a piece of foam to fit inside a velvet box for the armband. "I think it'll work, though."

"I know it'll work." Sinatria grinned. "You did it."

"Uh-uh." Val smiled. "*We* did it."

"Yeah." Tetra turned to her older sister, eyes wide. "I guess we did."

"Sure did, Tetra." Sinatria offered her a high-five.

Tetra accepted. "You know that most faeries will think you're a moron because you forgave me if they find out."

Sinatria shrugged. "Let them."

"Tetra's got a point." Val pressed the foam into the velvet box. "It's not the in-thing in faerie culture."

"Neither is getting your sister into a vassalship agreement instead of having her executed," Sinatria pointed out, "although our adopted dad put a different spin on that to make me seem ruthless."

"He did it for a reason, Sinatria. You're the faerie councilor. The faeries need to trust you if you continue to represent them at the high council," Tetra reminded her. "Maybe we should keep whatever this is under wraps."

"Sinatria paused. "I don't want you to think I'm ashamed of you."

"You *should* be ashamed of me. I tried to kill you," Tetra pointed out.

Val shrugged. "That's fair." She tucked the armband into the foam.

"Well, I'm not." Sinatria folded her arms.

Tetra chuckled. "It's touching. It really is. I'm not being sarcastic. I don't mind if the public never knows about this, though. Keep your image up, Sinatria."

"It's important. Otherwise, we might end up with some jackass as the faerie councilor," Val added.

"Okay," Sinatria smiled. "That seems fair. I'll stop by again, though, on the down-low."

Tetra's grin glowed. "I'd like that."

CHAPTER THIRTEEN

Val stormed through the kitchen in her gym clothes, adrenaline crackling through her veins. "You're sure?" she asked. Her phone was clamped to her ear.

"Absolutely. Sorry, Val. I know you wanted to get this done sooner," Liam told her. "But the safest time to move that weapon is Thursday morning at two. Traffic patterns don't lie. The roads will be nearly empty then."

Val sighed.

"Are you worried that the weapon isn't secure in its current location?" Liam asked. "We could make a plan to guard it better."

"No, it's secure. Nobody will steal it where it is now." Val grimaced. "My client needs it urgently, that's all."

"What on Earth does she urgently need a highly classified weapon for? Actually, don't answer that. I don't want to know."

"You don't," Val assured him. "It's legit, though."

"Of course it is. It's you," Liam murmured. "Can she wait until Thursday?"

Val gritted her teeth. "Her priority is keeping the public safe. She'll wait."

"Cool." Liam paused. "Kenzie's tech is amazing, by the way."

Val chuckled. "You told me."

"You sound tense," Liam observed.

"Pent-up energy. I thought we'd move it sooner," Val admitted. "I'm on my way to the gym anyway."

"Good. Release it. We'll meet on Wednesday to iron out the final details?" Liam asked.

"Yeah, sounds good. Your turn to bring sushi," Val told him.

Liam chuckled. "Fine by me."

Val hung up and tossed Shadow his peanut butter-stuffed toy. "Enjoy, dude."

The dog pounced on the toy, and Val strode to Genevieve. The Mustang started herself as she stepped into the garage. Her throaty snarl made energy crackle in Val's veins.

She threw herself behind the wheel as the door opened. "Punch it, baby."

Genevieve was happy to oblige.

———

"No, no, Val!" Diego barked. "Focus!"

His yell came a split second before Joe's fist, which collided with her temple hard enough that she fell to one knee. She threw her hands over her head, guarding her face from his swift jabs as they slammed into her forearms and fists.

"Come on, Val. Get him on the ground!" Diego yelled.

Val gritted her teeth. The scarlet fog encroached on her vision, threatening to take over. She could picture herself seizing Joe by the ankle and throwing him over the arena's ropes. Strength surged in her muscles, and she lunged to her feet, barely keeping herself from slamming her head into Joe's jaw in a head-butt that would have shattered his human bones.

Get a grip, Val! she urged.

"Dodge, hook!" Diego roared. "Like we practiced!"

The scarlet fog seeped through her blood. She fought it back, her amulet scorching her skin. Her dodge came clumsily and collided with Joe's swift punch to her ribs, which made her grunt. He followed up with a kick to her shin that sent her to one knee again.

"To the ground, Val!" Diego barked.

Val finally forced the fog back and hooked an arm around Joe's calf. He went down hard on his back, and Val scrambled to straddle him, but he moved too quickly. In a heartbeat, the human fighter pinned her arm in a painful triangle lock. She didn't try to squirm free, fearing she'd rip ligaments from bones, and slapped the mat.

Joe released her and rolled away. Val sprang to her feet with a roar of frustration and took it out on the ropes instead of Joe, slapping them with her palms hard enough that they creaked and bounced.

"Need a break?" Joe asked past his mouthguard, sweat trickling over his skin.

"Yeah. Sorry," Val muttered.

"Hey, it's cool." Joe slapped her shoulder with a glove. "Everybody has days like this."

I sincerely doubt it, Val thought.

Diego beckoned to her, his dark eyes sharp. "Val, come over here."

Val stomped to the ropes on the other side and flopped on the edge of the ring, letting her legs dangle over the gym's floor. She leaned her arms on the ropes and stared at Diego, breathing hard.

"What's up with you?" Her coach's tone was unexpectedly gentle. "You're not fighting like you. Why are you holding back?"

"Because I'm pissed," Val growled.

Diego raised his eyebrows.

"Work stuff." Val waved a hand. "Stress, anger. Whatever."

"Sounds like you should be wiping the floor with Joe instead of letting him kick your ass," Diego observed.

Val teased her mouthguard off her upper teeth. She wore it to keep Diego happy. She had to be careful not to bite it in half.

"In a real fight, your anger fuels you, right?" Diego smiled. "Don't deny it. Shape it. Use it."

"If I use my anger right now, I'll hurt somebody." Val met his eyes. "*Really* hurt them."

Diego met her gaze. She thought he'd question her, but he didn't. "Okay." Her coach shrugged. "Clearly, you need to let loose, though. I've wanted to correct your punching technique for a while. Let's use a bag."

He yelled at one of the teenagers forever slouching near the walls. The kid willingly jogged away and returned a moment later, dragging a heavy-duty punching bag with great effort. Val slipped under the ropes, tossed her mouthguard in her gym bag, and raised the bag with one hand to hook it up.

"Thanks, kid," she growled.

The boy's eyes were huge. He retreated to a safe distance.

A small crowd of curious teens gathered as Val steadied the punching bag.

"Okay, Val. Now you can't hurt anyone." Diego grinned. "Don't hold back. I want to see what you can do."

"Dangerous words, coach," Val grouched.

Diego shrugged. "Show me how dangerous."

I can't, Val thought. *You'll realize I'm not human.* She flashed him a smile to cover her discomfort, then raised her fists to her chin and faced the bag.

"Fix your feet," Diego growled.

Val adjusted her stance, then threw two quick jabs at the bag. They thudded against it, making it bounce and jingle on its chain.

"C'mon, Val. You've got more than that," Diego pushed.

Val hit the punching bag again. Jab-hook. Jab-hook. Jab-hook. After several drills, the pattern was familiar, and she stayed light on her feet as she drove her fists into the bag again and again. The scarlet fog grew, and she allowed it to wash over her vision.

"More!" Diego yelled. "Harder!"

A snarl of anger escaped Val's lips. The scarlet fog crackled through her bones and filled her blood with fire. She slammed her fists into the bag again and again, and it swung wildly with every blow, rebounding from her fists when she punched.

"*More!*" Diego roared.

His cry ignited something in the pit of her stomach. Her vision flashed crimson, but her punch held more than raw power this time. She rocked back on her balanced feet and generated the strike from low in her gut, putting the swing of her hips and the full power of her core behind the blow. Her fist arced through the air, trailing scarlet streaks in her blood-drenched vision, and collided with the punching bag.

Her knuckles met vinyl, which gave way to the grainy hiss of sand. A faint *clang* announced the snapping of the bag's chain. Kids yelped and scattered as the punching bag sailed through the air, trailing sand from the giant rip in its belly. It hit the wall in an explosion of falling sand and collapsed, deflated, on the floor.

Val's breaths came in heavy pants through gritted teeth. Her heaving shoulders relaxed, and the scarlet fog bled from her vision. Sound and sensation beyond the immediate returned. The sweat cooled on her skin, and shocked silence reigned in the Vanguard MMA.

Joe let out a low whistle. "Shit, Val."

She raised her head and panned her gaze across the overwhelmingly masculine crowd. Joe's eyes were huge. Others gazed at her with a mixture of shock and disgust. Daniel grinned from ear to ear, and beside him, so did Diego.

"Now, that's a punch!" he boomed, bringing his palms together in a clap so loud it made her flinch.

The handful of women present let out whoops and whistles, and the crowd erupted into applause. Most of the men grinned and cheered. Daniel clapped her on the shoulder as a handful of teenagers fetched brooms to clean up the disemboweled punching bag.

Diego patted her back. "Feel better now?"

"Much better," Val admitted.

"Good." Diego laughed. "Nice technique, by the way. Your knuckles okay?"

Val didn't feel the slight sting of pain on them until he mentioned it. Diego pulled off her gloves and nodded at the raw marks over her knuckles.

"Badge of honor?" Val guessed.

"Sign that your gloves are shit and you need new ones." Diego winked. "Good job today. Hit the shower. Come back with a fresh perspective tomorrow."

"Sure, coach. Thanks." Val stepped back.

"Val, one more thing." Diego raised an eyebrow.

"Yeah?" Val paused.

"You said you had an important security mission coming up," he murmured.

Val nodded.

Diego cracked a smile. "Heaven help the poor idiot who tries to get between you and your client. That's all I'm saying."

He strode away, leaving Val grinning as she tossed her gloves into the nearest garbage can.

Shadow's snores filled the smithy, complementing the forge fire's low crackle. Val couldn't blame him. She'd returned home at close to one in the morning after her shift at the Iron Fist, where Enzo had, once again, been conspicuously absent.

Despite the pressure release at Vanguard, Enzo's absence had her wound too tight to sleep. Instead, she sat at her workbench, turning a heavy iron pendant over in her hands.

The pendant's shape was simple, but its carvings revealed its beauty. The flowing lines depicted hills that transformed into Manhattan's skyline, and Genevieve charged across the center, her joyful speed captured by the careful taps of Val's hammer and her most delicate chisel.

Val smiled at the carving. "Got to add my other favorite nonverbal companion, right?" she murmured.

Shadow's paws twitched in his sleep.

Val mounted the pendant, swung her loupe over it, and picked up the tiny chisel and her most diminutive hammer. She leaned over the loupe and lost herself in carving the delicate lines in the dark iron. Her magic and the chisel's blade worked together, forming the image she'd imagined line by line.

When she straightened, her shoulders ached from hunching over the loupe. Beside Genevieve, a large hairy dog bounded, his paws joyously outstretched.

"Look, Shad." Val lowered the pendant. "It's you."

Shadow woke to sniff it sleepily, then curled into a ball.

"Not impressed, huh?" Val tilted the pendant to catch the light. "You're right, actually. It's missing something."

She retrieved a bag of rubies from the pigeonholes and lifted one with a tweezer. It was pinhead-sized but beautifully cut and faceted, light scintillating in its heart.

Val remounted the pendant and carefully cut a setting for the ruby in the carving of Shadow's face. She dropped the ruby into its setting and pressed it in place, her magic gently urging the iron to enfold it.

"Better?" she murmured.

Shadow snored.

"You're an ass," she told him kindly. "Now that I've made this thing valuable by putting a ruby in it," she picked up her rune cutter, "better put a simple anti-theft charm on it."

The rune she had in mind wasn't particularly strong. A powerful paranormal could push through the charm without knowing it was there. But if Val ever finished the pendant and wore it in public, the charm would guard against human opportunists. A pickpocket would find that his fingers slipped over the pendant no matter how firm his grasp was.

She'd carved the rune thousands of times, and her mind wandered as she turned the pendant over. What was going on with Enzo? Had he responded to her latest text? She feared for Dante. *The wrong crowd could be* very *wrong.*

She tapped the rune cutter one last time and lowered it, and a low rumble rose from beneath the workbench.

"Shadow?" Val pushed her stool back. "What's going on, dude?"

Shadow sat in his basket, nose raised. The low snarl vibrated through his chest. He drew back his lips, exposing long white canines.

"What's up?" Val got to her feet and touched her dagger's hilt. She scanned the smithy, but it was empty.

Had she locked the door? She heard no footsteps upstairs.

Shadow's growl continued, rising in volume, his nose raised toward her workbench.

"What is it?" Val whispered.

The dog rose stiff-legged from his basket, turned around, and pointed his nose at the mounted pendant. His hackles rose slowly as the deep growl emerged like rolling thunder.

"What?" Val lifted the pendant and moved it. Shadow's nose moved with it. "What in Merlin's name, dude? It's a pendant. It's not going to hurt either of us."

Shadow's growl intensified.

Val frowned. "What's bugging you, boy?"

Something warm brushed Val's ankles and she jumped, her fingers tightening reflexively around the pendant. The hairless cat that had rubbed her ankles hopped into her lap.

"Cleo!" Val yelled. "What in Avalon are you doing here?"

Cleo blinked huge amber eyes and purred. "Good evening, Val. You're up late tonight."

"Don't you remember the last time you were here?" Val demanded. "I had to pull you off the kitchen's ceiling fan."

"I recall," Cleo told her coolly. "Your...canine friend appears occupied with something else today."

Shadow's snarl rose in pitch. She moved the pendant away from his nose, and his hackles lowered slightly, but the growl remained.

"What's with him?" she asked.

"Ask him." Cleo hopped onto the workbench and strolled across Val's tools and precious stones.

"What's that supposed to mean?" Val demanded.

Cleo batted a ruby across the workbench. "You'll find out."

"Cut it out," Val barked.

Cleo batted the ruby in the other direction. "He's here to do more than protect you, you know."

Val stared at the tense dog. The whites of his eyes showed.

"You're here to do more than you think, too," Cleo purred. "You *are* more than you think."

"What?" Val demanded.

Cleo abandoned the ruby, sat, and curled her tail around her paws. "That's for you to find out. The answers lie in the hills."

"The Iron Hills?" Val asked.

Cleo's slow blink held no answers. "Secrets run deeper than mines in places. When you think about it, where is home?"

"Anywhere I don't have to deal with you," Val growled.

Cleo's purrs amplified. "The truth lies where you don't suspect."

"Currently, I don't suspect *you*," Val muttered.

Shadow's growl rose above Cleo's purring. The dog's tail hung between his hind legs, the tip twitching nervously.

Val turned to Cleo. "You said you're an arbiter of truth, right?"

The cat's tail flicked. "That's correct."

"Okay, so tell me the truth now." Val inclined her head at Shadow. "What's his problem?"

Cleo met Val's gaze, her amber eyes unnervingly steady. "Take a closer look at your pendant, warrior of the red bear."

"That 'red bear' bullshit again," Val grumbled.

Cleo rose and stretched, her pink-brown skin furrowing on her belly. "The bear will guide you, even in this."

She turned and sprang into midair and, unsurprisingly, disappeared.

"What an idiot," Val muttered.

Shadow pawed her leg.

"Ow!" she protested, yanking her leg away. "Dude, what gives?"

Whines combined with his growls now, and Shadow kept his nose pointed at the pendant.

"Even the cat wants me to look at the pendant." Val sighed as she flipped it over. "Not that I can imagine why you would—"

She stopped and leaned closer. Was that a dark glimmer at the base of the rune? She tilted the pendant to the light, and a cold hand clutched her belly.

The anti-theft rune was simple, but it was similar to a far more dangerous piece of magic: a vengeance rune. Technically, it was also anti-theft, but it didn't prevent things from being taken. It made thieves' hands explode five minutes after stealing.

"Shit," Val whispered, grabbing her rune cutter. Eternity Law forbade vengeance runes, and for good reason. Their power bordered on dark magic.

Val hastily pressed the rune cutter to the bottom of the shape, correcting the tiny imperfection that so nearly crossed the line into evil. Her heart pounded as a blue flash ran through the jagged figure.

Shadow's growl instantly switched off. His face dropped into its usual happy expression, and his tail wagged as he pressed his cold nose into Val's lap.

"How did I do that, Shad?" Val whispered. "That's powerful magic. I did it without thinking."

Shadow's tail wagged faster.

"Thanks, boy." Val's hand trembled as she pressed her fingers into the thick fur of his ruff. "That was close."

Shadow's warm tongue splashed on her hand.

"Qenzi wasn't kidding about those super-senses of yours, huh?" Val's racing heart slowed. "Looks like you're more than the Guardian of the Iron Fist these days. Guardian of my craft, too."

Shadow bumbled to his basket and fell into it with a sigh.

"Yeah, you're right. That's enough for tonight." Val dropped the pendant into a drawer and pushed it closed. "Time for bed."

She didn't think she'd be able to sleep, but she drifted away moments after she showered and curled around Shadow's warm, hairy form.

Food and thaumatech littered the kitchen table in equal amounts. Val sat at the head, a cup of strong coffee warming her hands while Qenzi and Liam faced each other. Shadow rummaged around on the floor, picking up crumbs. Tetra sat beside Val, contentedly shoving her third tuna sandwich into her face.

"Okay." Liam dusted fry crumbs from his black hoodie. "This is the final route as far as I'm concerned. I'd like your feedback on it."

He turned his snazzy new laptop around, narrowly avoiding the salt cellar, and showed the screen to Val and Tetra.

"This route will mainly use back roads through the mountains, utilizing service roads and farm tracks to avoid populated areas." Liam clicked and typed, zooming in and out as he spoke. "You might not see anyone else on the road until you reach the city limits."

"I doubt anyone would attack this close to the city." Val leaned forward, studying the route highlighted in blue. "There's too much risk of exposure. Too much backup nearby."

"That's what I was thinking. I know minimizing collateral damage is our priority, but whoever your client's mysterious enemies are, they'll be more likely to strike in isolation. Otherwise, they'd risk alerting people who might call the police, even assuming they don't care about hurting innocents," Liam agreed.

"Trust me." Qenzi's jaw tightened. "They don't."

"If we run into trouble, it'll be in the mountains." Val grabbed another handful of fries. "That suits me fine."

"Better to make our messes out of sight," Qenzi agreed. "I'll ensure the agency has backup in the area in case we need it."

"*Discreet* backup," Val emphasized.

Qenzi nodded. "No need to draw anyone's attention. Ideally, nobody knows that the transfer is happening, and you'll waltz into Manhattan with our enemies none the wiser."

"Where will you be, Qenzi?" Tetra asked.

"Chew, swallow, speak," Val directed.

Tetra gulped. "Sorry. Where will you be? Guarding the route?"

Val stomped on Tetra's toe under the table.

"Ow!" the faerie protested.

"I'm no warrior." Qenzi laughed. "I'll provide tech support and liaise with the agency if Liam needs it. Liam and I will be here."

"But you're—" Tetra began.

Val stomped harder.

Qenzi raised her eyebrows. "I've never guarded anything in my life."

Liam looked from Tetra to Qenzi and back, nonplussed.

"Sorry," Tetra muttered. "Sorry."

"This is the only part I'm not sure about." Liam clicked and dragged his screen. "I'm not sure if you should take the George Washington Bridge or the Lincoln Tunnel. Both will be quiet at that time of the morning. Maybe it'd be better to take the tunnel and avoid driving through the middle of Manhattan."

Val nodded. "That sounds good. We could also take the Palisades Parkway and avoid most of Newark."

"Good idea." Liam clicked around and displayed a new route. "Better?"

"Perfect." Val nodded. "If anything *does* happen on the road, we can drag it into the park instead of the suburbs."

"Yeet the assholes into the Hudson," Tetra suggested.

"Always an option." Val smothered a grin at the shock on Liam's face.

Liam asked. "All in agreement?"

Qenzi nodded. "I like it."

"Great." Liam closed his laptop. "All thanks to you, Kenzie. Your software made it easy to gather the info I needed. I had no idea your traffic pattern and population density database was so advanced."

"It's got a lot more information than that." Qenzi laughed. "I don't think you need me around anymore, either. You've got the hang of it."

"I wouldn't say that," Liam blurted.

Qenzi patted his arm, making pink spots appear on his cheeks. "Don't worry. I'll be in Mission Control with you for this one to make sure all goes smoothly with the comms."

"'Mission Control.'" Tetra snorted. "It's only the smithy."

"Mission Control sounds cooler." Liam grinned. "Speaking of which, I'll be here tomorrow morning to set everything up. I know it's early, but then I'm sure I can prepare everything."

"I'll join you," Qenzi volunteered.

Val nodded. "Sounds good to me. Qenz, is it still okay for us to come over for the training simulation tonight?"

"Yesssss." Tetra punched her fist into her opposite palm. "I'm excited."

"I'm ready whenever you are." Qenzi grinned. "I'm looking forward to it, too."

"So am I. Not the training. I know that's too top secret for me, and I'm not complaining." Liam chuckled. "I'm looking forward to the mission."

His laugh was full and genuine, and Val loved the sparkle in his eyes. She slapped his back, almost knocking his head on the table. "I'm glad to hear it."

"This is going to be great." Tetra grinned. "I hope we get into a *huge* fight."

"Uh, let's not do that," Liam squeaked. "I prefer my fights on TV."

Val snorted into her coffee and lowered the mug. "Speaking of TV, Liam, there's a serious situation you need to remedy." She jerked her head at Tetra.

"Oh?" Liam grinned. "How can I help?"

"Somebody—I'm not naming names, but Tetra—has been watching *The Mandalorian* with no context." Val clasped a dramatic hand to her chest. "She doesn't even know what *Star Wars* is!"

The color bled from Liam's face. "*What?* You're watching *Mando* without having seen the movies?"

"There are movies?" Tetra asked.

Liam clutched his chest. "Ugh. You physically pain me."

Qenzi shook her head. "Wow, Tetra. I know you're an immigrant, but wow."

"What?" Tetra demanded. "What's the big deal?"

"What's the big deal about *Star Wars*?" Liam and Qenzi chorused, then laughed together.

Tetra looked at Val. "Are they okay?"

"They're fine." Val laughed. "Well, they might not be when they find out I haven't seen *Star Wars* either. Only the memes and pop culture references."

"*What?*" Liam wailed.

"That's it." Qenzi slapped a palm on the table. "We need a movie marathon. It's official."

"Yes!" Liam beamed. "When the mission is over, I propose we spend a weekend watching every single one of the movies."

"Even the final trilogy?" Qenzi arched an eyebrow.

Liam grimaced. "I know fans are divided about it, but it's still part of the Star Wars canon."

"Is it, though?" Qenzi leaned forward. "If it deviates from what fans hoped for, is it worthy of that title?"

Tetra gaped. "What are they talking about?"

"Seems like you'll find out this weekend." Val chuckled.

Her phone hummed in her pocket, and she fished it out, expecting it to be Freya Gold asking for an update. The screen sported Enzo's name.

Fire ripped through Val's blood. "Gotta take this," she muttered, jumping to her feet. She raised the phone as she strode into the living room. "Enzo? What's up?"

"Val. I'm sorry to bother you." Enzo sighed, exhaustion and stress clashing in his voice.

"You're not bothering me. Are you okay?" Val asked.

The pause stretched.

"No." The orc's voice cracked on the syllable. "It's Dante. He's in real trouble this time. I'm sorry to ask, but—"

"Where is he?" Val grabbed her coat and whistled for Shadow. "I'm on my way."

CHAPTER FOURTEEN

The wrought iron sign over the gate said *Staten Island Private University*, but Val knew warded dwarf iron when she saw it. A gentle press of the brake brought Genevieve to an unusually civilized halt beneath the sign's elegant arch. Palisade gates barred the entrance but allowed a glimpse at the most generic college Val had ever seen: campus grounds, buildings, young humans with backpacks wandering around wearing earphones, and the odd professor in a suit.

Her eyes narrowed. This place's concealment spells were more potent than most paranormal organizations across the city, which primarily relied on the Veil to protect human eyes from their existence. Her keen eye picked out the runes in the wrought iron that made it possible. She allowed Genevieve to crawl a few inches nearer until the magical Mustang's bumper made contact with the ward's outer edge.

A bright purple ripple spread in all directions. The spell broke for Val as the motorized gates swung inward. The letters on the archway writhed and recombined, becoming *Royal University of the Eternity Throne.*

Val drove onto a campus that was anything but generic. The

U-shaped building spread its magnificent arms around a broad expanse of well-maintained lawn. No shrubbery or flowerbeds marred the lawn, but a separate domed building rose from its center, its stained-glass roof scattering the sunlight. The architecture was a mixture of medieval and baroque. Battlements clashed with bonneted roofs and dormer windows. Gilded finials decorated the apexes of each roof and window. Massive arched windows lined the large building, in which grandiose porticos sported decorative cornices and gilded knockers.

The building was far from the most eye-catching thing on campus. Paras of every species strode from door to door, talking and laughing, shoving each other. Their dress code was as varied as their species. Many wore baggy street clothes, but Val also spotted suits of armor, tunics, jerkins, tights, gold-buckled shoes, powdered wigs, loincloths, leopard skins, dresses with magnificent trains, capes trimmed in red, and elegant silk cloaks.

She steered Genevieve into a parking space between a Lamborghini Revuelto and a pumpkin-shaped carriage harnessed to six white horses. The horses chomped contentedly in their nosebags as Val disembarked and strode across the campus, Shadow jogging at her heels. No one spared the dog a second glance. Considering that the nearest group of students featured three werewolves and a werebadger in their animal forms, that was not surprising.

A shadow fell over Val as she trekked toward the main building. She squinted against the sun and spotted the spreading feathers of a soaring pegasus. Reptilian wing shadows nearby suggested dragons and wyverns, too.

Val grinned. "Maybe I should have taken Dad up on his offer to go to college, buddy."

Shadow's tail twitched in response. His nose ceaselessly worked as they marched across the lawn, taking in what must have been a cacophony of exciting scents.

He stayed close to her heels as Val pulled out her phone.

I'm here.

Meet me in the auditorium, please, the unsaved number responded. **The domed building.**

"I can read," Val grumbled. She followed the signs to the sparkling building in the lawn's center. A small door on one side stood slightly open, and Val and Shadow squeezed inside, then blinked in shock.

Like many paranormal buildings, this place was bigger on the inside. Val realized the glass roof was more than stained. Its irregular shape was designed to reflect sound. Hundreds of red suede seats in curving rows descended toward the stage at the center. It was empty now, but an industrial-sized hologram generator stood beside the wooden lectern.

Someone stirred in a seat by the door. "You're her?" its occupant asked. "I mean, you're Val Stonehold?"

Shadow wagged his tail and strained at the leash. Val let him go as they approached a skinny elf, all knees and elbows, who sat hugging a backpack on his lap. The Sylthana Elf's large blue eyes were red-rimmed with exhaustion. He clutched an energy drink in one hand and wore his silver hair in a rebellious mohawk.

"That's me," Val confirmed as Shadow tried to climb into the elf's lap.

"Cute dog." The elf fended him off, almost dropping his backpack.

"Shadow, down," Val ordered.

The dog sat at the elf's feet, tail slapping the floor. Val scooted into a seat beside him.

"I'm Aleksander Barsky." The elf made no attempt to shake her hand. "Alex."

"Good to meet you, Alex. Where's Dante?" Val asked.

"Enzo said you were coming." The elf slurped from the can for fortitude. "Dante's going to be pissed. Is Enzo mad?"

"Not yet. Not at you, either," Val added.

The elf nodded. "Okay." He bit his lip.

"Enzo tells me Dante's been hanging out with the wrong people." Val raised her eyebrows. "Does today's trouble have something to do with that?"

Alex stared at his feet and shuffled them. "Dante's going to be pissed," he repeated.

"Why?" Val asked.

Alex's shoulder slumped. "He didn't want me to tell anyone where he was going. I had trouble getting him to tell me, and we used to be besties, you know? We became roommates last fall, and we've gotten along great. Things changed a couple of weeks ago when Dante met these other guys."

"Who are they?" Val demanded.

The elf stifled a yawn and swigged from the can. "Sorry. Exams coming up. I can't remember what sleep feels like." He rubbed his eyes. "I don't know all their names, but I know that their leader is the son of a minor orc noble who thinks he's hot stuff. He's, like, this traditionalist, but he doesn't follow the traditions properly, if you know what I mean."

"I *don't* know what you mean," Val told him.

"Orcs have a thing about using their true names. Each orc has two names—the one they use in public and one their close friends know, but nobody ever says it. It's an insult to say it, basically." Alex rested his chin on his backpack. "I only know that because Dante told me his true name. That's how close we used to be. This guy, though? He goes by his true name." He winced as he spoke the syllables. "Huko."

"Okay." Val shrugged. "What's the problem?"

"He calls himself a traditionalist, but like I said, he only follows the traditions that suit him," Alex admitted. "He only eats his meat raw, practices traditional orc martial arts, and doesn't drive a car or ride the subway. He's studying history and culture,

I think. But it's more than that. That stuff's weird, but it's, like, you do you, right?"

Val smothered a smile. "Right."

"At first, I was hurt when Dante started hanging out with Huko, but I didn't get involved. He's got to figure out his identity. I thought it would be cool if Huko helped him get in touch with his orc side, but Huko underestimates what it means to be an orc...in my opinion."

Alex reddened. "I know I'm an elf, and I'm not supposed to comment, but orcs are so much more than the jungle-dweller vibe Huko gives off. Ancient orcs were the first to map the heavens. They were one of the most advanced paranormal cultures during the reigns of Kronos and Zeus. In fact, if Zeus' kingdom hadn't collapsed under the weight of his infidelity, many scholars believe orcs would have been the next ruling dynasty."

Val waved a hand. "Can we speed this along?"

"Sorry. I'm studying to be a historian. This stuff's on a loop in my head for these exams." Alex grimaced. "Anyway, Huko's messing with all the wrong shit. He's picking out all the crappy stuff from orc history, and everybody's history has crappy stuff, right?" Alex shuddered. "The raw meat thing is gross, and I feel like Dante's tattoo artist probably isn't licensed, but I didn't get worried until Huko started talking about—" He stopped.

Val leaned closer. "What is it, Alex? What's Huko getting Dante into? Wolfsbane? Silver? Garlic?"

"Nothing like that," Alex admitted reluctantly. "He's...he's been talking about an ancient orc magician with a name I can't pronounce. The guy is Huko's hero, but he—" Alex hesitated again.

"Spit it out," Val pressed.

"He practiced dark magic." Alex bit his lip, tears welling. "I thought it was all talk until today. Dante's cutting class to go somewhere with Huko and the others. He said it had something to do with a special ritual to make him one of them. To make him a real orc, he said. I'm so afraid it's dark magic, Val." Alex's breaths hitched. "Dante's not like that, but what if it is? What if—"

"Hey, it's okay, man." Val gripped Alex's shoulder as the elf hyperventilated. "You did the right thing by telling Enzo."

"Sorry. Sorry. I'm so stressed," Alex admitted. "I feel like this is my fault. I should have said something sooner."

Shadow placed his anvil-sized head in the elf's lap, and Alex's breathing slowed.

"Do you know where he went?" Val gently asked.

Alex dragged his sleeve over his eyes without spilling his energy drink. "No idea. He doesn't tell me anything anymore. But it will happen this evening, and I think it will be bad, Val." He swallowed. "Really bad."

Val reassured him. "Not if I have anything to do with it, okay?"

Alex nodded and exhaled. "Okay. You'll let me know if you find him, right?"

"Of course I will." Val squeezed his shoulder. "You're a good friend to him, Alex."

"I'm not so sure." Alex managed a shaky smile. "I don't think he'll ever talk to me again after this."

"You're doing what you believe is right for him even though it's hard. That's the definition of a good friend," Val reassured him. "You okay?"

"Yeah, I'll be fine." Alex drained his drink and pushed the empty can into his backpack. "I need to study."

He slouched off, head bowed, hands pressed beneath his backpack's straps.

"Poor guy," Val murmured, stroking Shadow's head. "C'mon, boy. Let's find Dante."

Ten minutes later, Val sat in Genevieve and grimaced into her phone as Qenzi made frustrated noises.

"Sorry, Val. I can't pick up a location on his phone. Either he's broken it, or it's got wards that even OPMA tech can't get through, which is unlikely," the troll told her.

Val grunted. "It's okay. Long shot anyway. Enzo, Alex, and his mother have been calling him all day. I reckon he ditched his old phone, and he's using a different one." She rubbed her chin. "Where would a group of orcs dabbling in the dark arts go?"

"I don't know, but Raven might. I can put you through to her office," Qenzi offered.

"That'd be great. Thanks for your help, Qenz."

"Anytime." Qenzi paused. "If you need backup—"

"I know," Val assured her. "Listen, can we do that training first thing tomorrow morning? It's important that we do it, but I can't leave Dante."

"Of course not. I'll text Tetra with an update. Putting you through to Raven now." Qenzi's words gave way to hold music.

To Val's relief, the music didn't last long.

"Major Raven Ardelean, OPMA."

Val raised her eyebrows. "I didn't know you could sound so professional," she blurted.

"Val! Hey! Great to hear your voice!" Raven trilled. "What's new in the world of badass dwarf bitches?"

"It's not a social call," Val admitted.

"When is it ever?" Raven laughed. "How can I help?"

"I'm looking for Enzo's nephew. Kid has gotten mixed up with the wrong crowd, and nobody knows where he is. He mentioned an initiation rite to his roommate, something traditionally orc, possibly with links to dark magic," Val explained.

Raven inhaled sharply. "Shit. That's the last thing we need."

"Could kids even get hold of dark magic? With Mordred and his main followers killed and imprisoned, how will they get their hands on the equipment and knowledge?" Val asked.

"It's easier than you think. Easier than any of us wants it to be. The Third Pendragon War left dark magic artifacts scattered over both dimensions. The OPMA is working hard to clean them up quietly, but we can't undo several years of war that quickly. As far as we know, there are no dark masters on the loose, but tinkering kids can be almost as dangerous. Maybe more dangerous." Raven groaned.

"I'd better find those kids quickly, then." Val buckled up. "I was hoping you'd have an idea where a bunch of orcs looking for trouble might end up. Somewhere within walking distance of the Royal University."

"Hmm." Raven paused. "The first place that comes to mind is Richmond."

"Richmond?" Val raised her eyebrows. "Where's that?"

"You'll find it on your navigation app as Historic Richmond Town. Humans have preserved it for hundreds of years as a tourist destination, but it's largely abandoned at night, and we've captured a few paras fooling around there," Raven told her. "Especially students from the RU."

Val nodded. "Sounds like a good place to start. I'll try it."

"I should warn you that it's haunted," Raven added.

Val paused. "Haunted?"

"Well, that's a little melodramatic. Humans think wraiths, ghouls, and banshees are the spirits of their dead. It's ridiculous, but they're still creepy as shit," Raven announced.

"That's a bit speciesist," Val warned her.

Raven scoffed. "Have you ever fought a ghoul? No? Seen a banshee floating around? Don't judge 'til you've done that, which you will shortly. They come out after dark." She paused. "They're attracted to dark magic. Also impervious to most ordinary weapons."

Val touched her dagger. "Good thing my weapons aren't ordinary."

"Let me know how you get on, Val. If you need backup—" Raven began.

"I'll call. Let me go in on my own first. Dante knows me, and he might cooperate better if I'm alone." Val started Genevieve's engine. "If I can't find him, I'll call you."

"We'll send in the hellhounds if we need to," Raven told her grimly. "We can't let that initiation rite take place, Val. It could be disastrous for both humans and paras."

"I hear you. I'll keep you updated," Val promised.

The sun was low and gold on the horizon as she backed Genevieve out of the parking lot. Google Maps told her the historic village was twenty minutes' drive away.

"Let's make it ten," Val whispered.

Genevieve's gas pedal sprang out from under Val's foot, and the Mustang plunged into the streets with a bellow of affirmation.

Val knew that humans' beliefs about paras they called the "undead" were speciesist and also bullshit, but goosebumps still prickled her arms as Genevieve purred down the narrow, nearly abandoned road. She didn't know places like Richmond existed in this metropolitan area. In the growing dusk, gloomy, over-grown fields surrounded her. A cow or two would not have been out of place. Tangles of dark woods loomed behind parks and hedges. The wooden buildings were old by human standards and looked like farmhouses and cottages.

Genevieve rolled past a cemetery littered with old grave-stones. Pale mist curled between the tombstones, flickering like it was only partially there. Val was beginning to regret her bravado to Raven. Hadn't ghouls and wraiths worked for Nimue?

Shadow sat on the passenger seat, tense and alert, his big head pressing against Genevieve's roof. He stared at the strip of road illuminated by her headlights.

"Raven wasn't wrong," Val whispered. "This *is* creepy as shit."

The app's blue line led Val to a road barred by metal gates. She brought Genevieve to a halt and patted the wheel. "Be ready for a quick getaway, Gennie."

The car quietly shut off her engine.

"Good girl," Val whispered.

She exited, and Shadow scrambled over the center console and jumped out behind her. Val shut the door quietly. Darkness had fallen faster than was natural. Despite her dwarven night vision, Val couldn't see into the impenetrable shadows. Shadow's hackles had half-risen.

"We're being stupid," Val whispered. "I haven't seen a single ghoul yet." She shook her wrist, activating her shield, and kept a hand near her dagger as they advanced.

Shadow stayed close enough for his shoulder to brush her hip as they edged down the main street, staying close to the houses in case Huko and his cronies had a lookout. Their symmetrical rows of small windows glared at Val like sleepy eyes as she squeezed between them. Dark woods deepened the shadows behind and between the buildings. Every hair on the back of Val's neck stood erect. An owl mournfully hooted from the woods, making Val tense. Shadow's hackles rose the rest of the way.

Val edged around a huge Gothic parsonage. It was creepy enough to satisfy a black magic-hungry orc, but no one moved within when she peered through a crack in the back window. A wind gusted uneasily through its eaves.

"Did you hear a wolf howl, or was that just me?" Val whispered.

Shadow bared his teeth, a soundless flash of white.

"Probably just me," Val squeaked.

She mounted the first step of the parsonage's front porch, and a low creak sounded beneath her boot. Val tensed, thinking the sound might wake something. Nothing else moved in the night, and she chided herself. "This is ridiculous," she announced in a normal voice.

A screech rose from the porch's rafters. Val gasped and

jumped back as dark wings swooped toward her face. She raised her shield and yanked her dagger from its sheath, ready to fight, but felt only the brush of wings on her shield.

"Bats," she muttered. "They're only bats."

She lowered the shield as the cloud of bats sped away.

Shadow whined, ears pricked, but he wasn't looking at the bats. His trembling nose pointed deeper into the village.

"Think they're that way?" Val whispered. "Okay. Let's go."

She stepped away from the parsonage, and they crept down the main street. The village was too quiet and too loud at the same time. Dozens of tiny noises underscored the silence but never fully revealed their sources. Was that a footstep or a distant car? A cricket or a spectral screech in the bushes?

Something buzzed against Val's chest, hot on her skin. She jumped and nearly shat herself before realizing it was her amulet. Its pulses came fast and hard. The red glow of its ruby eyes penetrated her sweater.

Shadow growled, the sound so low it was almost inaudible.

"I think we're going the right way," Val whispered.

The buildings were crowded closer together here. Val stayed off the road and clung to the shadows as they moved toward the end of Center Street. She peered around a tall brick building with windows as narrow and stern as a prison's and glimpsed tall white pillars at the street's end—a government building, perhaps. The fancy façade suggested a courthouse.

Shadow growled again, eyes fixed on the courthouse. Val tilted her head. Under the quiet current of the night's sounds, she thought she heard a bark of laughter from within.

"They're in there, all right," she murmured. "But we can't go in the front. Sneak in the back. Then they won't see us."

Shadow trotted at her heels as Val moved low and fast behind the brick building. She emerged on a narrow, deserted street that curved around the courthouse's flank. An American flag hung over the door, twitching in the gusty breeze. From this angle, Val saw red light flickering in the side windows.

She darted across the street and ducked behind a well-placed tree on the corner. The grass crunched beneath her boots. A few yards away, a white split-rail fence separated the grass from a paved area at the courthouse's rear.

"Jackpot," Val whispered. A railed ramp led to the back door. She doubted it was locked, or locked in a way her dwarven powers couldn't pick. None of the windows facing the back had light in them. The orcs would not see her coming.

Shadow whined softly.

"Let's do this," Val whispered. "Quick, okay? In case they have a lookout after all."

She darted from behind the tree and sprinted to the fence. Her hands closed over the top rail, and she gathered her muscles to vault over. Shadow's jaws closed over her left ankle, yanking her back.

"What in Merlin's name, dude?" Val spluttered, almost pitching head-first over the fence. Wood chafed her palm as she tightened her grip on the rail and pushed herself back.

Shadow whimpered, his tail low. His hackles stood fully upright.

Val peered over the fence. "There's nothing there," she hissed, but her amulet's accelerating pulses agreed with the dog's tension.

Shadow whimpered again.

Val bit her lip as more laughter came from within the court-house. How much time did she have? Darkness had fallen. The rite would begin soon if it hadn't already, unleashing dark magic on this peaceful, if spooky, corner of the city she had grown to love.

"Maybe I shouldn't bring you anymore," she growled.

Shadow's tail twitched between his legs, but he bared his teeth.

He's here to do more than protect you. Cleo's words drifted through Val's mind, and she hesitated. Maybe the Sphynx had a point.

She crouched and groped in the grass until her fingers closed around a rock. "Let's see if you're right," she told Shadow.

The dog remained motionless as Val tossed the rock, a gentle underarm throw. When it hit the pavement, the sound still echoed through the quiet night in a way that made her wince. The rock bounced twice, rolled a few feet, and stopped yards from the courthouse door.

Nothing else happened.

Val huffed with disappointment and grabbed Shadow by his collar. "You see? You're wasting our time by being so—"

Paving stones shattered, and earth sprayed into the air. Horrible gray hands thrust from the ground, their joints bending the wrong way, fingers moving like spider legs. Val barely bit back a girly scream as the ghoul hauled itself to the surface on all fours. Joints jutted from its naked gray skin. It was humanoid in that it had four limbs and a head, but none of its parts moved the way they should as it skittered toward the rock.

"Merlin's hemorrhoids," Val squeaked.

The thing pounced on the rock. Val didn't see its mouth, only the puffs of stone dust as the creature chomped the rock down.

"Okay. We're not going that way," Val hissed.

She backed away, Shadow following her. The ghoul snuffled the paving like it was still hungry. Hungry for a nice, juicy dwarf, perhaps. It raised its head, and Val saw its face, for lack of a better word. The dull gray eyes didn't blink. There was no nose, only a mouth that revealed a ring of sharp black teeth.

The ghoul didn't seem to see her, but it let out a low, gurgling shriek, and the courtyard trembled. More paving stones exploded as additional hands burst from the earth, and other creatures like it crawled forth from below. They swarmed over the ruined courtyard, pawing at the courthouse walls, tilting their heads this way and that like they were listening.

"Shit. Raven said they were attracted to dark magic," Val hissed.

Shadow growled.

"You're right, dude. We need to move *now!*" Val bolted around the courthouse.

As she ran, she slapped the bracelet on her right arm, her palm depressing the ruby set in the iron. With a clank of metal, a suit of armor unfolded from the bracelet, thanks to her father's magic. The reassuring dwarf-forged steel enclosed Val's body. She shook her left arm to activate the shield and unsheathed her dagger.

Val slowed as she reached the courthouse's façade. She jogged up the stone steps almost silently and pushed the door with her elbow. It swung open on well-maintained hinges. Shadow's claws clicked softly on the foyer's hardwood floor.

Voices and the crackle of flames overwhelmed the sounds of the ghouls scratching the walls outside. The door at the end of the hall was open six inches. Val stuck to the walls, staying hidden as she crept toward the door.

"There is no right," someone rumbled in an orc accent that was a little too perfect.

"There is no right," more paras echoed.

"There is no wrong," the first intoned.

"There is no wrong," the others repeated.

Val kept her back to the door. Shadow stayed by her side as she leaned forward and cautiously peered through it. The flickering light came from a black-flamed fire that hovered above the hardwood floor in the center of the large, empty courtroom. Black and red light oozed from it, as unhealthy as pus.

A chalk circle scrawled around the fire contained runes that Val didn't recognize, but they made her skin crawl, and her amulet vibrated on her chest. The artifacts placed at intervals around the circle made no sense to Val: a dead bird, somebody's fingers, a grass doll studded with pins, a scrap of sickly green fabric, and the bloody prong of a rusty pitchfork.

A group of young orcs sat cross-legged in a circle around the fire. Its light flickered on their features, illuminating tusks that bore rings of a metal that gleamed like silver. Beads of sweat shimmered on their tattooed scalps. They sat with their hands on their knees, eyes fixed on the flames. Two paras stood beside it.

"There are no rules," the first orc growled.

"There are no rules," the others chanted.

The leader was a ripped young orc whose loincloth exposed almost all of his muscle-bound body. The firelight painted red lines on his ochre skin. Tattoos and scars spread from his bald scalp to the soles of his feet, swirling in symbols Val didn't recognize, although the one on his back was painfully obvious: it was the Sign of Mordred, a yellow eagle rampant on a black field. A string of mouse skulls hung around his neck. He held a rusty dagger in one hand, and his eyes gleamed as he towered over Dante.

"We want what we want," the orc, presumably Huko, snarled.

"We want what we want," the others repeated.

Head bowed, Dante said nothing.

CHAPTER FIFTEEN

The young half-orc, half-vampire was almost unrecognizable. He'd had a thick head of dark hair. Now, his scalp gleamed in the firelight. Red inflammation surrounded the new tattoos that encircled his head.

"Why would anybody shave perfectly good hair?" Val whispered, touching her undercut wig.

"The Self is everything. The Self is all," Huko chanted.

"The Self is everything. The Self is all."

"All is excusable in service of the Self."

"All is excusable in service of the Self."

Huko grinned. The flames burned brighter, and sweat ran down Dante's face in rivulets as his body trembled.

"This is what it is to be a true orc," Huko rumbled.

Val had known a few orcs and was fairly sure that Huko's little chant wasn't part of any authentic orc tradition. Almost as sure as she was that the mouse skulls were plastic.

"To accept this truth is to become an orc." Huko raised the dagger. "You will bind yourself to your kindred by blood. Do you accept?"

Dante raised his head, and a chill crept through Val's blood.

The young para she knew and loved looked nothing like himself. His dark eyes were dull and empty, his jaw slack.

"I accept," he croaked.

"Do you bind yourself to the orc people?" Huko repeated. "Do you bind yourself to be nothing but orc all your life?"

"I bind myself," Dante croaked.

Huko gestured with the dagger, and Dante extended his hand.

"Shit," Val hissed.

The flames leaped toward the roof, reflecting in Huko's eyes. His tusks cast deep shadows over his face as he raised the dagger over Dante's unprotected palm.

The other orcs chanted, low and swift, "Orc! Orc! Orc! Orc!"

Shadow growled. Something shattered at the back of the courthouse.

"Orc! Orc! Orc! Orc!" They chanted faster now.

The objects surrounding the chalk circle glowed black and slowly rose from the floor. They levitated, and their black light changed from a dull glow to crackles like dark lightning. Shadow's growl rose in volume, and the amulet buzzed so hard on Val's skin that she got a friction burn.

"Okay, that's enough of this bullshit," she announced.

Val stepped back, raised a boot, and kicked the door open so hard it flew off its hinges and clattered to the floor. The chanting abruptly stopped, but Huko didn't look up. He raised the dagger, eyes narrowed, focusing on Dante's bare palm.

"*Nobody move!*" Val barked.

The other orcs froze. The artifacts dropped back to the floor, their light dimming. Dante's head snapped in her direction, and his dark eyes widened.

"Val?" he yelped. "What are you doing here?" Anger and relief clashed in his tone.

"You are no orc," Huko snarled. "You are not welcome here!"

"I'm here to get you out, kid." Val gripped her dagger. "Any of you idiots want to try and stop me?"

"Too late," Huko barked.

He seized Dante's hand. The younger para screamed and yanked it back, but Huko was too strong for him. Shadow lunged, barking, and the other orcs scattered.

"Dante!" Val yelled.

She plunged forward, but it was too late. The dagger missed his palm, but its rusty tip dragged down the length of his ring finger.

His scream mingled with Huko's laughter as blood gushed from Dante's hand. It didn't fall to the floor. Each droplet levitated in a circle of black light like the artifacts. The lightning crackles returned and leaped from the fingers to the dead bird to the doll and back. Huko released Dante, who fell to his knees, clutching his wounded hand. The pure-blooded orc raised a hand above his head, and dark lightning gathered between his fingers.

Val's amulet felt like a hot coal against her skin. *"No!"* she thundered.

"You're too late, fool!" Huko roared. "He is mine to command now!" Lightning and red flashes trailed from his eyes like tears. "You cannot overwhelm this magic! Your powers are useless in comparison to—"

Val swung the dagger. She had no idea if her iron magic could combat this darkness, but it was no match for Damascus steel. Her fist sailed past the creepy levitating artifacts and slammed the dagger's pommel into Huko's nose with a satisfying crunch of bone.

The orc shrieked and dropped his rusty dagger to clutch his nose. *"Ou broke by dose!"*

Darkness flashed in Val's vision. The fire roared ceiling-high for an instant, then vanished. With sad thumps of flesh, the weird artifacts thudded lifelessly to the floor.

Val kicked a hole in the chalk circle, destroying its runes. As Huko staggered around, yelling, she bent and grabbed Dante by the scruff of his neck. He wore only boxer shorts.

"V-val," Dante squeaked.

"Shut up," Val ordered. "Can you walk?"

"He's mine!" Huko bubbled through two palmfuls of blood. He whirled to face her.

"No. Uh-uh." Val waved a finger. "You don't want to do that."

Huko clenched his bloodied fists. "I will fight you!"

Wood splintered, and the slap of bare feet on hardwood echoed through the room, but it wasn't feet. It was hands, elbows, knees, and the other wrong bits of an uncomfortably not-quite-human body as a ghoul raced into the courtroom, chomping wood and stone into splinters.

Huko emitted the most high-pitched scream Val had ever heard.

She sheathed her dagger, grabbed Dante, and threw him over her shoulder. "Run, you idiot!" she roared.

Huko didn't need to be told twice. He bolted for the door, and Val thundered after him. Dante bounced on her shoulder as he clung to her breastplate with one hand. She glanced back as she reached the courtyard door to see a tide of ghouls flowing into the courtyard, baying for blood as they swarmed the dark magic artifacts.

"What are those things?" Dante screamed.

"The consequences of your actions!" Val barked.

Val, Huko, and Dante spilled down the courtyard steps. The other orcs huddled against the brick wall across the street, pinned there like sheepdogs thanks to Shadow, who crouched before them. He didn't growl. His intent stare did the trick.

"Why are you standing there?" Val roared. "*Run!*"

The ghouls exploded from the courthouse and spilled down the steps, hissing and skittering, dirt flowing from their naked bodies as they scrambled after Huko.

Shadow whirled to face the ghouls, and the other orcs scattered.

"Wait!" Huko wailed. "Wait for me!"

The other orcs didn't look back.

"What do you expect, asshole?" Val grabbed his arm. "All is excusable in service of the Self, remember?"

"Help me!" Huko wailed.

Val rolled her eyes. "Fine. Stay close. We'll go to the car!"

She would have liked to sprint down the street to Genevieve, but Huko could only manage a breathless jog that barely outpaced the scrambling, skittering ghouls. They stopped at every drop of the blood that spilled from his nose and fought each other for the right to devour it with quick snaps of their jaws. Dirt spilled between their sharp teeth as they raced after Val and Huko. Many climbed the houses' walls like lizards.

"They're really creepy," Dante moaned.

"What did you expect?" Val barked. "You're the ones who played with dark magic!"

A ghoul sprang from the nearest building and landed feet from Val. Shadow pounced on it and ripped out its throat with shocking efficiency. The creature didn't die, but the stench of its black blood stopped it in its tracks. It tried to lick its bleeding throat in the few moments before it vanished beneath a pile of others that tore it limb from limb with graphic noises.

"I think I'm gonna be sick," Huko moaned.

"Save it!" Val ordered. "Keep running!"

She yanked him forward with her shield hand. Her other hand kept Dante on her shoulder as she sprinted down the street, half-dragging Huko. Shadow bounded by her side, barking and snarling at the ghouls that kept popping out of the ground around them.

"There's more of them!" Huko wailed.

As they scrambled down the street, the sizable Gothic house loomed ahead, and ghouls sprouted from its overgrown lawn. Their hands burst through the ground, trailing dirt down their fingers, then found purchase and pulled their writhing bodies to the surface. Hungry yammering escaped their chomping jaws as they charged. Their wriggling, disjointed bodies flooded the street ahead.

Val skidded to a halt, hobnails striking sparks. "*Shit.*"

"*We're all gonna diiiieeeeeee!*" Huko screamed.

Val released his arm and slapped him. "Cut it out!"

Huko whimpered.

"Stay close to me," Val ordered. She hoisted Dante off her shoulder. "Can you walk now?"

"Yes," Dante croaked.

"Then keep up!" Val barked.

She nodded sharply, and her helmet's visor fell over her eyes, coinciding with the scarlet fog. Shadow bristled against her legs, snarling, as ghouls closed on them from all directions.

Huko shrieked, and Val whirled as a ghoul lunged toward him. She slammed the shield into the creature with bone-crunching force, and it crashed to the ground several hundred feet away after a brief flight. Power and fury surged like fire in Val's blood. Shadow's bark ended in ripping flesh as he shook another ghoul like a rat, then threw it at its charging companions. The impact knocked them back.

"Go!" Val thundered.

Shadow bounded forward, claws and teeth bared, baying. Huko and Dante bolted after him. Val slashed the head off a ghoul with her dagger, threw its wriggling body aside, and rushed after the boys.

The ghouls were faster than they looked. Shadow bit and trampled a path through the ones ahead, but more attacked from behind with every step. One lurched at Dante, its bony fingers brushing his ankle. Val stomped on its hand, and another ghoul sprang toward her face, teeth gnashing. She plunged her dagger into the soft place where its left eye should be, and black blood gushed down the hilt.

Teeth rang on her armored calf. The ghoul wailed in agony as its teeth shattered on the steel, and Val lifted her boot to kick it in the face. Its head snapped back with the crunch of shattering vertebrae, but the ghoul didn't stop moving. It clawed the earth, crawling toward her as its head flopped uselessly on its broken neck.

Val jogged after the orcs, swinging shield and dagger to keep the ghouls off their heels, but the pack of creatures thickened. The ground spat writhing bodies on both sides of the street. Shadow's deafening bark scattered the ghouls ahead, but they pressed in again, hissing as they extended their hands toward Dante and Huko. The dog sprang forward, trampling two ghouls, his claws raking black marks in their flesh. His jaws closed on a third ghoul's throat, but another lunged at him and seized two fistfuls of his thick fur.

Val threw her dagger. It darted around Dante and Huko and plunged into the ghoul's shoulder, slicing its arm off. The limb flopped to the ground, and the ghoul reared back, shrieking. Shadow kicked it aside and plunged forward, his muzzle soaked in black blood.

The dagger zipped back to Val's hand. *"Almost there!"* she roared. *"Keep going!"*

Dante screamed as a ghoul's hands closed around his bare calf. Val leaped forward and landed on the ghoul's back, shield's edge first. The steel cleaved the creature's neck, laying its tendons bare before severing them, and its head rolled between Dante's feet.

He screamed again.

"Go!" Val shoved him, whirled, and gutted a ghoul with a slash of her dagger.

Shadow yelped. Val spun as he went down with two ghouls on top of him, their hands tangled in his fur. One had its jaws locked around his front paw.

Val's vision was crimson with blood. *"Get off him!"* She leaped. The orcs cowered as her jump carried her twenty feet to Shadow's side. She had only a split second to feel shocked by her power before her boots met the asphalt with a force that cracked it. A shockwave rippled from her landing spot inches from Shadow, flinging ghouls aside.

The two ghouls on Shadow never saw her coming. She smashed her shield into them, and their bony bodies flew through the air and met the nearest brick wall so hard they splattered.

"Shadow," Val croaked.

The dog lurched to his feet. In Val's blood-drenched vision, his red coat seemed to glow. A light shone within his eyes, and the scarlet fog made it seem unnatural.

"Let's do this," Val growled.

Shadow barked once as they lunged forward, hacking and clawing, biting and slashing. Huko and Dante whimpered behind them as Val kicked ghouls aside and smashed them away with her shield. Shadow caught any that slipped past her, shattering their spines with his kill shake, yet they advanced only inches at a time. The parking lot seemed a long way away.

The snarl of a Super Cobra Jet V8 engine rose above the yowls of the ghouls like a battle cry.

"Oh, yeah." Val stomped a ghoul's skull to powder and raised her head, grinning.

Genevieve's headlights cut through the mass of ghouls, so brilliant that the creatures shrieked and raised their misshapen hands to their faces. Her tires squealed as she halted a few hundred feet away. The ghouls whirled to face her, and several peeled away and bolted or tunneled back into the ground.

A few who were courageous—or stupid—stood their ground, moaning and hissing.

Genevieve spun her wheels like a bull pawing the ground. The ghouls lunged toward her, and she charged. Bruce Springsteen's *Born to Run* spewed from her open windows as the Mustang threw herself into a long, drifting turn that spun her back end into the ghoul army.

A mass of them flew into the air. Others ended up under the wheels, tires squelching as she crushed them. When more lumbered to attack her, Genevieve shifted gears and threw herself into reverse. With her second turn, she swept a crowd of ghouls aside with her nose, leaving gooey black stains all over her pewter paint.

Genevieve skidded to a halt amid a mass of squashed ghouls. Crushed though they were, they still writhed. She flung her doors open, hitting one in the face.

"Merlin's eyeballs!" Dante yelled. "How are they not dead?"

A sea of ghouls flowed down the street from the courthouse. Many were headless; others bore bite wounds on their chests and faces. One dragged its guts behind it.

"That is disgusting," Dante moaned.

"Get in the car!" Val bellowed.

Huko bolted to Genevieve. The driver's door was nearest him, and he flung himself behind the wheel. Genevieve tilted her seat and tipped him unceremoniously onto a squishy, wiggling mass of ghoul flesh.

"Backseat, asshole," Val snapped.

Huko scrambled into the back, Dante close on his heels. Shadow sprang over the car in a mighty leap, then jumped into the passenger seat.

Genevieve's wheels were already spinning when Val crushed a last ghoul's skull and got in. She made no effort to grab the wheel.

"Go!" she barked.

The steering wheel spun. Genevieve accelerated, but not before a ghoul sprang onto the hood. It grabbed the edges and hung on, its nasty face smashed against the windshield, leaving trails of saliva as its teeth scraped the glass.

Dante and Huko screamed in unison. Shadow barked hysterically, paws on the dash. Genevieve calmly engaged her windshield wipers, which slapped the ghoul's head from side to side as the Mustang plunged down the street.

The creature hung on as Genevieve turned onto the main road at a hair-raising pace. Its teeth continued to rake the glass.

Genevieve had had enough. A metal panel slid back into the hood at the base of the windshield, and a tiny gun-shaped object rose from beneath. It emitted a plume of fire that roared like a blowtorch, reducing the ghoul to ashes in seconds as *Born to Run* reached its rousing crescendo.

Silence fell in the car as Genevieve calmly purred down the quiet street. Nothing moved on either side of the road. Shadow panted heavily, ghoul goo in his coat. Val sheathed her dagger, reduced her armor and shield to armbands, and grabbed the steering wheel.

Dante cleared his throat. Huko pulled out his phone and texted somebody. Shadow licked goo off his paws.

"Huko—" Val began.

"Yep," Huko croaked. "Yep. I get it. Not doing that again." He shifted in his seat. "You can drop me off at the next crossroads. My mom's coming to get me."

"Is she mad?" Val asked.

"Mad? You could say that," Huko admitted.

"Good. I hope she grounds your grown ass," Val barked.

Huko ducked his head. "I hear that." He glanced sideways at Dante. "Dude, I'm sorry."

"You're an asshole," Dante growled.

"That's valid. Sorry. Sorry," Huko mumbled.

Val halted at the next stop sign, where a tall orc woman leaned against a Jeep. War tattoos streaked her cheeks and hands. Her arms were folded, revealing muscles that rivaled Val's.

"Oh, shit," Huko whimpered. He got out and shuffled toward her, head hanging, resigned to his fate.

"*Andrew Willoughby Parks!*" the woman yelled.

Val would have loved to stay and watch, but she had other things to deal with.

"Gennie, take the wheel." She released it. "Let's go to the Fist. Enzo will be there."

Genevieve honked in affirmation. She purred smoothly from the stop sign as Val typed a quick text to Enzo.

Got Dante, all okay. On our way to Iron Fist.

Her phone instantly rang. She silenced it.

Can't talk now, but don't worry. Call you in a few.

Thank you, thank you!!

Two exclamation marks? Val had never seen him do that. Her lip quirked. She put the phone away as Genevieve steered calmly through Staten Island, making for the Verrazano Narrows Bridge.

"Okay, kid." Val twisted in her seat. "I know you had the fright of your life tonight, but I'll still tell you how unbelievably stupid that was."

Dante sagged. He now looked small and bony. As they passed beneath streetlights, it was increasingly apparent that his skin was far paler than Huko's.

"Don't you know anyone who lost somebody in the war?" Val demanded.

Dante mutely shook his head.

"Well, now you do. My uncle fought and died to protect the world from dark magic." Val fought the sudden lump in her throat. "He used to drink beer every weekend with my dad while they watched pegasus polo. He smelled like woodsmoke, and he gave the best hugs. His kids are growing up without him because he died at New Camelot to protect idiots like you from the effects of dark magic."

Dante shrank.

"You have no idea what that shit can do," Val continued. "Maybe your parents protected you from the news reports during the war. Maybe you never gave a shit, but I don't think that's true. I don't think the good kid I know would be cool about messing with the shit that turned ordinary paras into mindless monsters. Dark magic enslaved millions of paras during the war, and they died against their will. That's the crap you were messing with back there."

"I'm sorry," Dante whispered.

"Do you know what that thing Huko almost hit you with was?" Val demanded.

Dante shook his head.

"That was a dark geas. That was how Nimue enslaved her followers. They had to do what she wanted or die. They used to light themselves on fire to keep the dark magic from killing them if they were captured. Even with the geasa broken, those paras were mentally ill. That's what would have happened to you. Do you get that?" Val barked.

"I'm sorry," Dante repeated.

Breathless, Val stopped. She realized the young para was crying. Tears created trails in the grime on his cheeks.

She sighed. "Let me see your hand."

Dante nervously extended it, palm up. The jagged cut on his finger looked red and ugly, with the edges of the flesh turning black.

"That's a mean-ass cut," Val muttered. "That blade must've had dark magic in it, or a shit-ton of bacteria. Maybe we should stop by the para-ER."

Dante swallowed. "There's a para doctor near my house. I'd like to see my parents first." He paused. "Please."

Val relented. "Okay." She folded her arms. "That gives you

time to tell me what in Merlin's name you were thinking when you got mixed up with this bullshit."

Dante dragged his palms over his face. His voice trembled when he spoke. "Huko made me feel like I belonged."

Val tilted her head but said nothing.

"He told me I had to stop denying who I am," Dante mumbled. "That I had to embrace my nature as a true orc."

It sounded like a steaming pile of minotaur dung to Val, but she sensed it was time to stay quiet.

"I know it sounds like bullshit," Dante admitted. "It *was* bullshit, to be honest. Mom says that being an orc goes beyond tattoos and traditions, and she's right. The thing is, Huko made me feel like I could figure out who I was. If I could be an orc, that could be my identity, right?"

"There's more to identity than species," Val murmured.

"Yeah, that's what my mom says, but she didn't grow up with the shit I did." Dante wrapped his arms around himself. "Little kids on the playground in the para school I attended always asked me what I was. The orcs wouldn't play with me because I'm part vampire. The vampires wouldn't play with me because I'm part orc. It feels like I'm not one thing, you know?" Dante bit his lip. "Like I'm two half things but not complete."

Val grunted. "I know the feeling."

Dante raised his head. "Yeah," he muttered slowly. "I bet you do. I bet you heard the same thing from people where you grew up for the same reasons I did. You look different." He sighed. "Seems like that's enough for most people not to hang with paras like us."

"Doesn't explain why you'd screw around with dark magic." Val raised her eyebrows.

Dante hung his head. "That wasn't part of the deal at first. Huko and his friends seemed cool. Sure of themselves, like they knew who they were. I wanted that, so I hung with them instead of Alex."

"You owe that elf a hug, a box of chocolates, and probably your life," Val interjected.

Dante grimaced. "He's the one who called you?"

"He called your parents. They called Enzo, and Enzo called me," Val told him.

Dante ran a hand over his scalp, wincing when his fingers met the fresh tattoos. "I can't be mad. We would've died back there."

"No shit, dude." Val snorted.

Dante sighed. "I owe him an apology, too. I'll get to that. Anyway, I hung out with Huko and the others because they made me feel like I could be an orc. I don't have a problem with vampires, but it seemed simpler to be one species, you know? Even if it was only pretend. I was surprised that Huko would let me join even though I'm half-vampire."

Val nodded. "So, when he said there'd be an initiation rite, you were happy to be part of it."

Dante rubbed the back of his neck. "Yeah. I wish I could say I had no idea that there'd be dark magic, but by then, I'd seen Huko messing around with chalk circles and stuff. I told myself that it couldn't be real dark magic, or if it was, it couldn't be bad dark magic."

"All dark magic is bad, no matter how small," Val growled. "By its very nature, it can't be used for good."

"I know that. I pretended I didn't, but I do." Dante groaned. "I had no idea he could cast a geas, though."

"I believe you. It takes a special kind of stupid to allow somebody to put you under one of those." Val eyed him. "I don't think you're stupid."

"You don't?" Dante raised his head.

"I think you felt lost and wanted to be somewhere you belong —or some*one* who belongs. It was easier to throw away being half-vampire and pretend you're all orc. They didn't pick on you or call you names because of your fangs. Am I getting close?" Val asked.

Dante bit his lip. "Yeah."

"Do you know anybody else who's mixed-species?" Val asked.

Dante shrugged. "That's the thing. I don't. I mean, mixed-species marriages were illegal under most of Sylthana rule. Queen Esmerelda legalized them, but even then, it wasn't really done, you know? My parents are trailblazers." He groaned. "I know I should be happy about that, but it makes my life hard sometimes."

"I'll bet," Val empathized.

"I'm not ungrateful. I'm not against mixed-species marriage or being mixed-species," Dante added hastily. "I just...don't know how to do that. How can I be half of two things? I mean, what do I do with that? I tried pretending to be human, and all it did was leave me feeling empty."

"Look, Dante, I'm not saying it's easy." Val sighed. "I wouldn't go back to the Iron Hills if you paid me. However, things are different in the city. People are more accepting. Look at Alex. Has he ever made you feel inferior because you're mixed-species?"

"No," Dante mumbled. "He only made me feel like his friend."

"Exactly." Val paused. "Truth is, you'll never be only an orc or only a vampire. Yeah, being different can really suck, but it doesn't have to define your life."

Dante raised his head, his eyes wide and uncomprehending.

"I'm a giant-ass dwarf with no hair, but that's not the only thing I am," Val told him. "I'm a jeweler, a bodyguard, and a kick-ass MMA fighter. I own a bar, I love my friends, and I go around rescuing dumbasses like you."

Dante chuckled. "Okay, that's fair."

"You can be more than a half-orc, half-vampire, too," Val added. "You're the smart kid who always smiles at customers while working at the bar. You play Sudoku on your phone when you think nobody's looking, and you're really good at it. You like slapstick videos and stupid jokes." She smiled. "Am I right?"

Dante managed a smile. "Maybe."

"You don't have to be an orc, a vamp, neither, or both," Val told him. "You can be *you*."

Dante raised his chin. "Seems like it's worked for you, Val."

"I'm still learning," Val admitted. "You hungry?"

Dante shook his head. "I want to see my parents."

Half an hour later, Genevieve purred to the Iron Fist, where a worried family gathered before the thronging bar. Val glimpsed Jeff and Tetra inside. Enzo was on the sidewalk, his fingers interlaced over his belly. Worry had stolen much of its jovial curve.

Beside him, Val recognized his vampire brother-in-law, Bartholomew Diaz. She'd never met Enzo's sister, but family resemblance made it evident that the female orc clinging to Bartholomew's hand was Dante's mother Alessia.

Val exited the Mustang while Shadow bounded out and gamboled around Enzo's feet, smearing his pants with ghoul goo.

"He needs a few stitches, but he's okay," Val announced. "Might want to go easy on him. It's been a crazy night, and I chewed him out all the way from Staten Island."

Bartholomew gaped at the scratches on Genevieve. "What happened?"

"Dante!" Alessia cried. She released Bartholomew's hand and sprinted to her son as he got out.

"Mom," Dante croaked.

Alessia threw her arms around him despite the filth caking his bare torso.

"I'm so sorry, Mom. I'm sorry for everything," Dante whimpered.

Bartholomew shrugged off his neatly cut jacket and draped it over his son's shoulders. "We'll sort it all out, Danny," he murmured. "Don't worry about it now. All that matters is that you're here and okay."

Val leaned against Genevieve, smiling as a familiar warmth spread through her chest. Enzo sidled up to her, tears gleaming in his eyes.

"Val—" he began.

"Don't get all soppy on me." Val nudged him with her shoulder. "I'm happy everything's okay."

Enzo's tears vanished, and he chuckled. "I was going to offer you as much beer as you can drink."

Val grinned and straightened. "That sounds like a plan."

Shadow trotted at her heels as Enzo led her to the Iron Fist, leaving Dante and his family to their peaceful reunion.

CHAPTER SIXTEEN

Qenzi's eyes sparkled with excitement as the elevator hummed upward. To Val's relief, the OPMA's New York headquarters had only five stories above ground, though one elevator wall was almost covered in buttons. They displayed numbers from negative twelve to five, some letters of the Greek alphabet, pictograms, runes, and *Switzerland*.

"I can't believe Captain Hartshorn gave us permission to use the training orb," Qenzi gushed. "Usually, no one but OPMA recruits is allowed to go near it."

"Captain Hartshorn's cool," Val acknowledged.

"I bet she knows the world will explode if we don't get the sickle here in time," Tetra added.

"That too." Qenzi squealed and danced in place. "You're going to love this."

Val shifted the enormous backpack on her shoulders, and it clanked.

"Did you have to bring all that stuff?" Tetra asked.

"Obviously." Val scoffed. "I might need to make adjustments to my shield. I haven't tested it against Sylthana fire."

"Yeah, but a portable forge and anvil? Where do you suppose you'll set that up?" Tetra demanded.

"I used to work on a kitchen table. I'll figure it out," Val told her.

"If the captain lets you use the training orb, she'll let you use your forge wherever you like," Qenzi added.

The elevator halted, and they entered a staid governmental hallway with a cream-colored carpet and white walls. Qenzi led them to a pair of doors next to one another.

"This is the training room, and this is the observation room. It has screens inside that will allow me to see everything," the troll explained.

Tetra snorted. "Screens? Why not use a window?"

"You'll find out." Qenzi grinned. "Go inside. I'll talk you through what to do next."

The troll disappeared into the observation room, and Tetra turned to Val as she shrugged off her backpack. "How complicated can it be?" she grumbled. "She said she had a simulation of Sylthana Elves to help us practice. All we do is fight fancy dummies, right?"

"I guess we'll find out." Val pushed the door open.

She wasn't sure what she'd expected, but it wasn't what she encountered. Val and Tetra stepped into a featureless room, its walls, floor, and ceiling so white that they appeared seamless. A pedestal at the center of the room held a soccer-ball-sized blue orb with a sparkle in its heart, covered with indentations like handprints.

Not only handprints, Val realized. Any para species could find a place to rest their limbs on this orb. Many prints were shaped like paws, hooves, or birds' feet.

"I think we're in the wrong room," Tetra announced.

"Oh, no. You're in the right place." Qenzi's bubbly tone came from everywhere at once.

Val tilted her head. "When you said, 'training orb,' I thought it was a cool way of describing a spherical room."

"Nope, that's the orb. It's ancient and mysterious magic. Luckily for you, I know all its mysteries." Qenzi giggled. "Okay, put your hands on it."

"I'm not touching that thing." Tetra held her hands to her chest.

"It's perfectly safe. The training mortality rate is the lowest it's ever been!" Qenzi chirped.

"I'm sorry." Tetra whirled around. "The 'training mortality rate?'"

"Tetra, c'mon." Val reached toward the orb. "Do you want to learn how to fight Sylthana Elves or not?"

Tetra sighed, and their palms met the orb together. Val's fingers easily fit into the broad print she'd chosen, and the orb's warmth surprised her for an instant before the magic kicked in.

"Merlin's sake!" Val spluttered, stumbling back. The room and the pedestal had vanished. She stood in a vast hippodrome. Her boots hissed on the sand, and sunlight beat down on her as the crowd in the tiered stone seating roared their approval.

"Oh, crap," Tetra yelped beside her. "Where are we?"

Val turned, goosebumps rising on her skin as she realized that the hippodrome had an incomplete quality, like a half-finished video game. Though the crowd was distant, they moved with eerie synchrony. Val couldn't see their faces. Their cheers rose and fell like a soundtrack being played over and over.

"Welcome to the OPMA's newest innovation in combat training." Qenzi's words came from an indeterminate spot in the pixelated sky. "This is the Fully Immersive Training Experience, or FITE. My colleagues developed it last year."

"This isn't real?" Tetra guessed.

Val crouched and grasped a handful of sand. The developers had skimped on the crowd and sky, but the sand felt real.

"It's not real," Qenzi confirmed. "But it might feel that way. Ready?"

"Ready for what?" Val asked.

Her amulet prickled.

"There!" Tetra pointed.

A speck in the blue sky sped toward them—a humanoid who zoomed to the ground at an unrealistic speed. His feet hit the sand hard enough to make the ground tremble under Val's feet. With a wordless battle cry, he drew a pair of Sylthana scimitars and struck a dramatic pose. The elf wore chain mail and dark war makeup, making his blue eyes seem as bright as ice. His long silver hair streamed in a wind that hadn't existed a few moments ago.

"Ready to FITE!" Qenzi yelled in excitement.

Val shook her wrist and slapped her right armband, and shield and armor deployed. She drew her dagger and crouched.

"I'm ready," Tetra hissed. Faerie dust trickled from her fists. "Come at me, you fake asshole!"

The Sylthana Elf lunged, swinging his scimitars in movements so flowing that Val almost forgot they were deadly. His feet danced across the sand, blades sweeping around his body.

Val watched him take three steps, learned the pattern, raised her shield, and charged. She timed her attack so that her shield collided with him when he had only one foot on the ground. The elf wavered and stumbled back, and Val launched a swift dagger blow at his belly. He blocked with one scimitar and brought the armored elbow of his free arm into her temple.

Metal collided with her skin. Val's head snapped back, and pain blossomed through her scalp. She staggered aside, feeling her platinum-blonde wig slip, but recovered in time to raise her shield as the elf struck hard with both scimitars. The blow knocked her to one knee.

"Hey!" Tetra yelled. "Over here, assface!"

The elf sprang back. Val leaped to her feet as he whirled to face Tetra, who shot twin blasts of caustic faerie dust at him. He cried out as the dust melted blisters on his arms but attacked with his scimitars. Tetra dodged and wove, firing dust blasts at his feet that melted his armor.

The faerie moved in when he fell to one knee, but she wasn't quick enough. The elf slashed at her legs with both blades. Tetra jumped back and screamed as one blade caught her exposed ankle and ripped a line of blood across her skin.

Scarlet fog suffused Val's vision, and she broke into a sprint, boots slamming into the sand. Six feet from the elf, she leaped, dagger high. As he drew his scimitars back for a disemboweling blow, Val landed on his bent back. Her dagger clove his cervical vertebrae, and the elf disappeared in a shower of pixels.

"Tetra!" Val yelped.

The faerie clasped both hands around her wounded ankle, pain lining her face.

"What did you do to her, Qenzi?" Val roared.

"Nothing," Qenzi told her smoothly. "Watch."

Tetra gasped. She lifted her hands from her ankle, revealing smooth, untouched skin. Val touched her temple and found that the pain in her head had disappeared.

"The pain is simulated to make the combat more real. Sorry. I should have mentioned that," Qenzi added sheepishly. "But nothing can harm you here. Physically, you're still standing in the training room with your hands on the orb."

"Unexpectedly savage of you, Qenzi." Tetra rose.

"No shit." Val shook her head. "Effective, though."

Tetra's face split into a grin, and she slapped her fists together. "Oh, yeah. Let's do this!"

"Ready for something a little harder?" Qenzi asked.

"*Hit me!*" Tetra roared.

The distant whistle of another dramatically falling opponent reached them. Val whirled as two Sylthana Elves hit the sand.

"You take the one on the left?" Tetra suggested.

The elves charged, scimitars spinning.

"You bet!" Val charged her opponent.

Her shield met the elf's scimitars with an earth-shaking clash that ripped the scimitars out of his hands. She kicked the elf's knee, and he went down hard. Val slammed her shield against his chin, snapping his head back, and went for his chest with the dagger.

The elf raised both fists, and twin bolts of blue fire erupted from his hands, arcing toward Val's face.

She sprang back, gasping at the heat as the flames scorched her chest. The smell of burning hair rose in her nostrils.

"Hey!" she yelled. "My wig!"

"It's a simulation, remember?" Qenzi called. "Try not to get burned, though!"

The elf was on his feet, limping but determined. He spun toward Val, swinging his arms as swiftly and gracefully as leaping flames. Tongues of blue fire splashed from his fists with each movement. Val danced back, searching for a gap in his defenses. When he whirled around, she charged too slowly. He sent an arc of fire toward her, and she raised the shield to her face.

The faerrous steel conducted heat with shocking efficiency. The skin on her hand and arm blistered and peeled, and Val screamed. She staggered back, but the elf kept coming, pouring torrents of fire at her shield. The heat seared her eyeballs even after she closed her eyes. She felt her skin bubble, then go numb—

Val gasped and straightened. She stood in the training room, one hand on the orb. When she snatched it back, her flesh was undamaged, though she could swear she'd seen her muscles turn to charcoal moments before.

"Shit," she croaked.

Tetra blinked. Her hands slipped from the orb, and she looked up. "Hey, what happened?"

The door opened, and Qenzi hurried in. "I pulled you guys out. Are you okay, Val?"

"Apart from experiencing what it's like to burn to death, I'm good." Val wiped the sweat from her face. "FITE is hardcore."

"It's designed to be that way." Qenzi's face looked pinched beneath her glasses. "Sorry, Val."

"Don't apologize. This is exactly the training we need." Val shook her armband, activating the shield, and touched its edges. "It pointed out something vital. My shield isn't flameproof."

"You could have figured that out when you burned your hand at the warehouse fight," Tetra pointed out unhelpfully.

"Yeah, I know." Val detached the shield. "I need to make adjustments."

"There's an empty office across the hall. You could use that as a temporary smithy," Qenzi suggested.

Val shook her head. "Luckily for us, the shield held up to the scimitars. It doesn't need to be reforged. All I need is my rune cutter."

She took the shield to the hall and sat cross-legged on the carpet. Tetra retrieved the rune cutter from her backpack, and Val flipped the shield on her lap. She ran her fingers over the runes on the back, a shrinking charm that allowed the shield to fold into a disc on the armband, searching for the right spot for the rune combination she had in mind.

"I bet Tetra got melted before I did." Val selected her spot and poised the rune cutter.

"She did great, actually. She killed her opponent and was coming to save you when I pulled the plug," Qenzi informed her.

Val raised her eyebrows. "How?"

"Don't sound so shocked." Tetra grinned. "I can be a badass, too."

"Fire-retardant faerie dust," Qenzi supplied.

"Took the wind out of that idiot's sails. I strangled him with my bare hands." Tetra raised her chin, eyes gleaming. "It was unbelievably satisfying. You can keep your MMA, Val. I'll come let off steam here with FITE."

Qenzi delicately cleared her throat. "The throne is happy to pay for this session, but I doubt Her Majesty will fork out thousands of dollars per hour for your recreation, Tetra."

"Thousands of *Avalonian* dollars?" Tetra raised her eyebrows. "Shit. We should put our time to good use, Val."

The rune cutter's diamond point etched the last lines into the shield. Val folded it into her armband and rose. "Okay. Let's see if it works."

"That one rune will help?" Qenzi raised her eyebrows.

Val grinned. "You do the thaumatech. I'll do the rune cutting. It's a potent spell, but I've done it a hundred times before. My dad and I forged a ton of fireproof stuff in the Iron Hills."

"Let's go kill more elves!" Tetra yelled and charged into the training room.

Qenzi grimaced. "Not so loud, Tetra." She disappeared into the observation room.

Val followed Tetra inside. She hesitated half a breath before slapping her hand onto the training orb.

The hippodrome returned. Val's amulet crackled as she activated armor and shield, then drew her dagger. The unnatural light played on the wavy lines of Damascus steel as she held it high, ready to fight.

Three elves appeared from the sky.

"Yeah!" Tetra cheered. She skipped to the nearest two elves and killed one with a blast of faerie dust.

Clearly, Tetra was fine. Val turned her attention to her opponent. He charged, scimitars out to his sides like an anime hero, and sprang into the air. Val spun under his leap and rammed her shield into his shins, taking his feet out from under him. He landed on his hands and knees, and she planted a kick in his belly that sent him tumbling.

The elf yelped but rolled to his feet. Blue fire engulfed his scimitars.

"Okay, asshole," Val hissed, raising her shield to her nose. "Test my runes."

The elf charged. Val braced herself. His scimitars clanged on her shield, blue flames licking over the faerrous iron, but a flash of purple told her that her fireproofing ward was working. She charged, smashing her shield against him, and he couldn't get his scimitars out of the way in time. Val plunged her dagger into his thigh, and a spray of arterial blood splattered on her armor.

The elf's scimitars fell to the ground. He grabbed her shield in both hands, and blue flames engulfed her fingers. The fire spread across the shield, but the metal remained cool. She met his eyes and grinned. They were dull and a little pixelated but still widened in horror.

"Eat my shield, you son of a bitch," she snarled and slammed the shield into his face with skull-shattering force. He disappeared in a cloud of pixels.

"Aw, man." Tetra jogged up beside Val, flushed. "I was hoping you'd need my help. This is the most fun I've had since leaving Fernwood Deep."

Val chuckled. "I think we've got this." She held out a fist.

Tetra bumped it. "You bet."

The hippodrome fell away, and Val raised her hand from the training orb as Qenzi entered. "I think you're ready," the troll told them.

"I'm hungry," Tetra complained.

Qenzi chuckled. "Lucky for you, cafeteria meals are free."

"Cafeteria?" Tetra wrinkled her nose.

"Don't knock it 'til you try it," Qenzi chided.

Ten minutes later, Tetra was up to her eyeballs in French fries. Val had felt a moment's trepidation at the thought of cafeteria food too, but it disappeared as she bit into the best burger she'd ever tasted. Savory meat, creamy cheese, crisp lettuce, and a tart-sweet sauce melted in her mouth. The bun was the perfect balance of toasted/crunchy and soft.

"Wow," she moaned.

Tetra could only grunt as she grabbed another fistful of fries.

"This place is one of the OPMA's greatest perks." Qenzi chuckled.

The cafeteria was full of paras of every species. Val had never seen a group so diverse, all wearing the same uniforms. The spacious, wood-paneled room had banners of the seven royal families and the Eternity Throne hanging from the walls. Four long tables ran down its length. Buffet tables presenting a dizzying array of meal options stood by the walls. Val noticed several bottles of certified synthetic human blood between sodas and energy drinks. Placards on the buffet tables designated specific diets: *Low-Carb, Vegan, Keto, Raw Orc,* and *Carnivore-Specific.*

"This place is pretty cool." Val smiled. "I wish I could show Liam around."

"It feels weird training without him," Tetra murmured. "I know he didn't need to train to fight Sylthana Elves, but he's still a major part of the team."

"Keeping secrets from him isn't easy," Val agreed.

"Technically, it is." Qenzi raised her eyebrows. "I warded his tech so he can't see paranormal activity via his laptop or tablet. I developed a complicated and expensive firewall, but it'll work."

"I didn't mean physically easy," Val muttered.

Qenzi shrugged. "The thing is, Liam *knows* you're keeping secrets. He thinks they're government secrets, not the existence of the paranormal world, but he knows you're doing it for his safety."

"Still." Val chuckled. "He'd love these fries."

"Not to mention the FITE thaumatech. It'd blow his mind," Tetra added.

Qenzi's gaze softened, and she played with the cuff buttons on her blouse. "You're right. He'd enjoy this place."

Val wiped her fingers on a paper napkin. "Having a mixed human and para team isn't easy. We'll run into bigger obstacles than these, but I believe it's worth it."

"Absolutely!" Qenzi grinned.

"We can always tell him everything, then suck all the blood from his body if he threatens to tell our secrets," Tetra added brightly.

"Tetra!" Val glared.

The faerie raised her hands, laughing. "I'm kidding! I'm kidding."

Qenzi looked horrified, but Val laughed. She knew Tetra was joking.

Probably.

Val's quiet smithy was a hive of activity.

She'd pushed the racks holding tools and weapons against the walls to clear the space at the center. Workbenches and the dining room table formed a horseshoe-shaped desk in the middle, and Liam, Tetra, and Val bustled around their surfaces. Tech covered Liam's desk: laptops, tablets, earbuds, charging cables, backup power supplies, repeaters, and speakers.

He sat on the ergonomic office chair he'd insisted on bringing from his apartment and leaned over his laptop screen. His fingers flew, typing one moment, clicking the next.

Beside him, Tetra leaned over a map with highlighted routes from Maximilian's mansion to Wall Street. She traced her finger over the blue route, her lips moving silently.

Sitting at the third desk, Val smiled. "I smell burning clutch. Don't think so hard, Tetra."

The faerie didn't look up, just flipped Val off with her free hand.

Val chuckled and returned her attention to the thousands of small chain links on her desk. She raised the nearly-finished sheet of chain mail and extended a hand to the individual links on the workbench. Her power stirred the iron within, and the links rose to her hand like obedient ducklings. They locked around each other with a click of metal and formed another row on the mail.

"Okay, Tetra." Val held up the finished hauberk. "What do you think?"

"Shhh!" Tetra growled, focused. "Liam, your codenames for the escape routes are stupid. How am I supposed to remember them?"

Val left the hauberk on the desk and crossed to Tetra's. The map showed dozens of colorful escape routes labeled in Liam's meticulous hand.

"Vader? Skywalker? C3PO? What kind of codenames are those?" Tetra demanded.

Liam sniffed. "You'd know if you'd bothered to watch *Star Wars*."

Val chuckled. "I appreciate the pettiness, Lee, but maybe we should change them. They need to be easy to remember."

"One second," Liam muttered. He leaned closer to the screen. "That's it! I'm in."

"You busted through New York RTCC's security network?" Val hurried to his side.

"I did." Liam grinned, looking up. "Kenzie's tech is totally badass, not to put too fine a point on it."

"What's the RTCC?" Tetra asked.

"Real-Time Crime Center. It monitors cameras all over the state. That means I can track you everywhere you go, although there are spotty patches in the Catskills." Liam clicked through several video feeds showing busy streets and tranquil mountain roads. "I won't comment on how illegal it is to hack into the RTCC. I assume your client has it covered."

"Don't worry about it." Val waved a hand.

"Kenzie's tech makes me invisible to their servers anyway." Liam laughed in disbelief. "I'll watch you almost every moment from the mansion to Wall Street."

"Great news," Tetra sniped, "but what about these stupid-ass codenames?"

"Oh, they're not the real codenames. I only used them to prove a point." Liam smirked. "The real codenames are from *The Mandalorian*."

He came to the map and rewrote the escape route names with characters Val recognized from her avid consumption of the show starring the gun-toting, armor-wearing badass and his cute green companion.

"Much better," Tetra grumbled. "Asshole."

Val checked her phone. "Time to get serious, people. We're leaving for the mountains in an hour."

Tension crackled through the air like electricity. Liam returned to his laptop, typing fast, and Val and Tetra pored over the map. The new codenames made the escape routes effortless to memorize. Val already knew the main route by heart.

A timer beeped. Fifteen minutes to go time.

"I'm ready." Liam looked up from his laptop. "Believe it or not, I am." He exhaled shakily. "We can do this."

Val gripped his shoulder. "I believe it." She grabbed the hauberk from the workbench. "Tetra, this is for you."

Tetra's eyes widened. "Really?" She took the hauberk and held it against her body.

"Yeah." Val grinned. "Like it?"

"Um, you know Kevlar exists, right?" Liam asked.

Val and Tetra turned to stare at him.

Liam raised both hands. "I don't want to know."

"It's cool," Tetra murmured, her gleaming eyes belying her nonchalance. "Does it fit?"

"Of course it fits." Val scoffed.

Tetra slipped the hauberk over her head. Chains clinked softly as the links magically adjusted to her figure.

"Whoa!" Liam raised his eyebrows. "It sure does."

Tetra grinned. "Thanks, Val."

"Any time." Val felt the random urge to hug the faerie and hastily crushed it.

Tetra inhaled, then let the breath out slowly. "I guess we'd better go."

"Are you—" Liam cleared his throat. "Are you girls going to be okay?"

"Of course we are. We've got each other's backs," Tetra assured him.

Val grinned. "You've got both of ours, too."

Liam raised his chin. "I do."

Silence hung in the smithy until Shadow whined from his basket.

"Stay here with Lee, boy." Val crouched and rubbed his head. "It's too dangerous for you this time. Okay, Liam. We'll hear you on the road."

Liam held out a carbon fiber box containing two tiny earpieces. Val and Tetra each took one. Val's slid seamlessly into her ear, magically adjusting to comfortably fit the orifice.

"Go get the thing I'm not supposed to know anything about," Liam encouraged, smiling.

Val and Tetra exchanged fist bumps with him and each other. "Let's do this," Val growled. She shut the door on Shadow, who whimpered as she and Tetra hurried to Genevieve. "Should've made him a peanut butter toy," she muttered.

"I thought you said he ate a bunch of ghouls last night," Tetra hissed.

"I'm not exposing him to elves who shoot fire from their hands, okay?" Val growled.

"Testing," Liam announced in their ears as they strode across the garage.

Val and Tetra jumped in unison.

"Hey!" Tetra yelped.

"Dude!" Val clapped a hand to her ear. "Wow, the clarity's great. I feel like you're in my head."

"Heaven forbid," Liam muttered.

CHAPTER SEVENTEEN

Val didn't screw around this time. She kept Genevieve idling forward as they reached the pretty meadow, which looked idyllic in the fading light, and drove the Mustang through the concealment spell.

Genevieve's tires crunched on the pebble drive. Val kept her eyes on the mansion as they approached, ignoring the stolen statues on either side.

"Okay, Liam," she muttered. "Pulling up to the mansion."

"Got you." Liam paused. "Looking at these cameras. Are there weird animals in the cages around the back, or…"

"Would you believe us if we said something about mutants as a result of sinister government experiments?" Tetra asked.

Val slapped the faerie's knee. "Don't listen to her, Lee. Let's stay focused on the mission."

Maximilian Opulencia stood in the doorway as Val halted Genevieve inches from the front steps. Today, he wore a plum-purple suit with a ridiculously tall top hat, but his beakish face and black-and-white hair made his species clear.

"Good evening, Mr. Opulencia," Val greeted politely.

She braced for resistance from the collector, but he bowed

with a flourish of his hat. "Good evening to you too, Miss Stonehold!"

Tetra jutted her lower jaw and gave a belligerent nod. "What's up?"

"What is up is that I made the deal of a lifetime." Maximilian drummed his fingers against each other. "You won't believe what that sickle's money will buy me."

Val didn't want to know. "I'm sorry, sir, but we don't have time for conversation. The sooner Gaia's Sickle is safely at its destination, the better."

"Of course, of course." Maximilian stepped aside and gestured to the entrance hall. Val tried not to look at the stolen mailcoat, which was very similar to the one that rustled over Tetra's hips.

Tetra opened Genevieve's door and slid the seat forward, revealing the iron lockbox on the back seat. Blue runes glowed on its surface, its spells so strong that Val couldn't show Liam.

"Thanks, Dad," she whispered as she pressed her thumb to the sensor at the top. It read her magic signature, not her fingerprint, and a rune next to it flickered blue and went out. She'd deactivated a stickiness charm that made it impossible for the lockbox to move from its position.

She and Tetra grunted with effort as they hoisted the coffin-shaped box from Genevieve and headed into the mansion. They panted as they wrestled it up the staircase; Maximilian prattled on about "his" treasures as he led them down the hall. To Val's relief, drapes hid the balcony doors so she didn't have to look into the menagerie.

Momentary panic gripped Val as Maximilian reached the safe door and raised his hand to the touchpad, but it flashed purple, and Val's amulet pulsed in response to its magic. The door clanked open.

Goosebumps prickled on Val's arms as she gazed at Gaia's Sickle.

"Eyes on target," Tetra whispered.

"You sure it's the real one?" Liam asked. "He didn't swap it out for a fake?"

Val stepped forward and extended a hand toward the sickle. Heat washed her fingers like she'd reached for a lover's hand. The amulet blazed on her chest, its galloping pulse almost as fast as her heartbeat.

"It's the real thing," Val whispered.

"Sure is." Maximilian beamed. "I'll be sorry to see it go, but it's for a good cause, right?"

Tetra side-eyed him. "Right."

"Go ahead, Miss Stonehold. All wards are deactivated. You can touch it." Maximilian grinned. "You know you want to."

"Want" wasn't a strong enough word. Val *longed* to touch the sickle. Every iron droplet coursing through her blood and fortifying her bones screamed for her to touch it. It felt like plunging her hand into flames. She gripped the wooden shaft, startled to find it cold and ordinary, and magic crackled through her arm.

"Isn't it magnificent?" Maximilian's eyes gleamed. "Isn't it wonderful to hold something with such power, something so priceless, knowing you're the only person in the world touching—"

"Don't be gross." Tetra stepped forward. "Let's get going, Val."

Maximilian fell silent with a scowl that made his beady eyes flash. It vanished as quickly as it had come. "I suppose you're right. Better get the sickle to safety."

Val lowered Gaia's Sickle into the lockbox as gently as a mother laying her baby in a cradle. They shut the lid, which locked with the resounding metallic clank of dwarf-forged iron.

Maximilian trailed behind, prattling, as Val and Tetra hauled the lockbox down the stairs and out of the mansion. Val wasn't listening to the collector's jabber. As they stepped through the doors, she kept one hand on the lockbox's handle and the other near her dagger. Her head swiveled. Her amulet pulsed swiftly, but she couldn't tell if it was responding to the magical artifacts around them or alerting her of danger.

They hoisted the lockbox into Genevieve, and Val reactivated the sticky charm.

"Of course, they're temperamental things," Maximilian chattered on. "They mate for life, so if you have only one, it tends to starve itself. Dreadful creatures, but so beautiful, and—"

"Goodbye, Mr. Opulencia." Val half-bowed. "Thank you for your cooperation."

He blinked, but Val didn't pause to enjoy the surprise his face registered at her interruption. She flung herself behind the wheel, put Genevieve in gear, and put the Mustang into a drifting turn that sprayed gravel against Maximilian's well-pressed pants. He jumped with a yelp that made Tetra snicker as Genevieve accelerated down the drive.

Genevieve's engine made the only sound as she wove down the quiet mountain road. Random cabin lights were the only indications of civilization Val could see. Her amulet was cool on her chest, but she leaned over the wheel anyway, her gaze darting through windows and to rearview mirrors while the Mustang handled the driving.

When Tetra broke the seal on a water bottle, Val almost went through the roof.

"Merlin's teeth, Tetra!" Val squeaked.

"Sorry." Tetra shrugged. "Gotta stay hydrated, right?"

"That's true," Liam chipped in.

"Nobody asked you," Val and Tetra chorused, then smirked at each other.

Val's grin lasted for a moment before her probing gaze returned to the roadside. The shadows here were natural, unlike those in Richmond, and Val's dwarven vision penetrated the darkness but not the tangle of thick foliage crowding the verges.

"All good, Lee?" Val muttered.

"Surveillance is clear," Liam confirmed, "although you're approaching another blind spot in half a mile. Stay alert."

"Copy that," Tetra growled.

The faerie tensed at the same instant as heat scorched Val's chest where the amulet rested on her skin. Val's head swung around. She saw nothing except trees and bushes, but something crackled in the darkness.

"Liam—" Tetra began.

"Bo-Katan!" Liam yelled. "Take the Bo-Katan escape route now!"

Val jerked the wheel as signage glowed ahead. Blue fire bloomed in the night, a massive tongue splashing on Val's right. It missed Genevieve's hood by inches. The Mustang's wheels skidded, white smoke rising from her tires, and she plunged down a side road so narrow that twigs screeched on her paintwork.

"The queen's going to kill us," Tetra wailed.

"Not if that thing kills us first!" Val yelped. "What is that?"

"Someone on a motorbike," Liam barked, "with a big-ass flamethrower. Go left at the farmhouse!"

Genevieve responded before Val could. She swerved away from a whitewashed farmhouse and plunged down a rugged farm track, making her suspension squeak. The Mustang bucked, rattling Val's teeth, but the lockbox was immovable in the back seat.

Tetra gasped. "Shit. He's catching up!"

Val squinted into the rearview mirror, and her gut flipped. Unsurprisingly, their pursuer was a Sylthana Elf, his long silver hair streaming behind him. The thing he rode wasn't a motorbike.

"What *is* that?" Tetra hissed.

The animal racing down the road after Genevieve had paws in front and cloven hooves behind. It was the size of a horse, but the front half had a golden mane like a lion's, and its tail was twice the length of its body, tipped with a quivering rattle the size of a corn cob. Three heads snapped and snarled, painted scarlet by the brake lights, and all had teeth. The lion and rattlesnake heads were scary, but the goat was worse. Its amber eyes had keyhole pupils and rolled wildly in its head as it snapped at Genevieve's bumper with long yellow teeth. Blue sparks played between its jaws.

"Son of a bitch," Val yelped.

Genevieve skidded around a massive tree trunk and thundered on. The creature momentarily vanished from view, and Val rolled the window down.

"What are you doing?" Tetra barked.

"Getting it off our tail!" Val snapped, wrapping the seatbelt around her left forearm. "Gennie, don't kill me."

Genevieve honked.

As the creature skidded around the turn, Val hoisted herself out the window. She planted her ass on the windowsill and leaned against the seatbelt. The creature and its rider were gaining on them. The elf crouched over the beast's three heads, urging it on in eager whispers that drove its mismatched feet across the ground with astonishing swiftness.

"Stand down!" Val roared. "In the name of Queen Julia Artura Pendragon, stand down!"

The elf rose in his stirrups. He gripped three pairs of reins in one hand and a scimitar in the other.

"I recognize no such queen!" he yelled.

He slashed the scimitar, and a tongue of blue fire arced toward Val. She flung herself against Genevieve's roof and felt the scorching flame lick over her head. When the fire went out, Val straightened and hurled her dagger in one smooth movement. The throw was wobbly, but her powers carried the dagger forward. It ducked between the goat and lion heads and plunged into the elf's chest.

He didn't scream, but the reins dropped from his hand. He clutched at the blood welling from his chest, then tumbled silently over his mount's narrow haunches.

The bloody dagger zipped back to Val's hand. She tensed, ready to fight the creature, but it stumbled to a confused halt and watched Genevieve speed away.

"Yeah!" Liam cheered. "Great throw, Val!"

Val hauled herself back into the driver's seat. Tetra stared at her with enormous round eyes.

"Yeah," Val panted. "No sweat. That was random."

"I'm afraid it wasn't." Liam groaned. "There's more coming through the woods toward you. Brace yourselves. They're coming from your right!"

Val grabbed the seat belt.

"Not again," Tetra moaned.

Val hauled herself onto the windowsill and raised her dagger. She threw it at the first flash of movement between the trees, and a creature tumbled through the undergrowth, squealing, the dagger embedded in its front leg. Its elven rider sprang from the saddle, took two steps on the creature's rolling body, and leaped. The elf landed on Genevieve's roof before Val could regain her dagger.

"Tetra!" Val barked as she slammed her fist into the elf's jaw. His head recoiled, but his feet didn't budge from the roof, and he drew back his fist. Blue flames licked over his coiled fingers.

"On it!" Tetra slammed her hands against the roof. Caustic dust sizzled, and her fingers reached through the melting metal. Val ducked a plume of blue flame that splashed into the trees opposite and lit the night with fire. Her skin baked, and she cringed, ready for the killing blow.

The elf screamed. Tetra grabbed both his ankles and yanked him through Genevieve's melting roof. He clutched the edge for an instant, eyes wide, then vanished into the car, where his screams turned to gurgles.

"What did you do to the queen's car?" Val screamed.

"Little busy here!" Tetra yelled. The elf moaned.

Val's dagger slapped into her palm in the nick of time. Another creature sprang from the roadside, snarling, claws and fangs extended toward Genevieve. Val focused on the steel barding protecting its chest. The barding had too little iron to crush the beast to a pulp, but she slowed its leap enough that it landed clumsily several feet from the speeding car.

Its elven rider screamed at it in a language Val had never heard. The creature charged, jaws snapping at Genevieve's rear spoiler. Val aimed at the elf and threw her dagger. It plunged into the elf's shoulder with a spray of blood, and she screamed, clutching her arm, but didn't fall.

The creature seemed angrier. It sped up, snapping two of its heads toward Genevieve's tires while the third—the snake—struck at Val. She slammed a gauntleted fist into its lower jaw, and the bone shattered. Something spilled from its fangs and made Genevieve's paintwork smoke.

"The snakeheads are venomous!" Val yelled.

"No shit, but don't worry," Tetra snarled. "I got you."

She lunged through the back window and shot faerie dust at the beast's legs. Flesh melted, bone flashed, and the three-headed creature fell head over heels. Genevieve swerved to avoid its tumbling body, and Val's chest slammed into the roof. She felt the dull impact, but the scarlet fog made the pain seem distant.

"Remember the cliff ahead," Liam yelled.

Tetra scrambled to Genevieve's front. "*Gennie!*"

"One more incoming!" Liam roared. "In five, four, three, two—"

The creature launched from the undergrowth as trees gave way to a clearing behind Val. She saw a brief glimpse of a low barrier, sheer rock, and a distant river before the creature slammed into Genevieve. Tetra screamed as the Mustang skidded, her back end colliding with the barrier. It crumpled in the face of magically enhanced fifty-year-old metal, and Genevieve's wheels spun out over the gap.

The elf screamed in defiance and traded blows with Tetra through the window. The creature's three heads slammed into Genevieve's roof. Val thrust her dagger through the snake's jaws, pinning them to the roof. The lion lunged at her face, and she punched it away.

That left the goat. Its head went back, and for an instant, Val thought it was retreating. Then its jaws opened, the mouth unnaturally wide in a goat's face, and blue fire splashed over the back of its slender tongue.

"Oh, *shit*," Val growled.

She had no choice. She unwrapped her left wrist from the seatbelt.

Her shield activated as fire splashed across Genevieve's roof. Blue flames filled her vision, but no heat reached her…and she slid helplessly toward the dizzying drop below.

"Val!" Tetra screamed.

A slender hand closed around Val's knee. She quit sliding, but Genevieve didn't. Gravel spun from the wheels, fire sprayed from the goat head, and the car tilted toward the drop for a horrifying instant. Anchored by her knees, Val mustered every ounce of strength she'd developed at Vanguard MMA. She lunged and threw her body weight against Genevieve's roof. Her shield collided with the goat's head, and the fire abruptly stopped, replaced by dark blood. Genevieve swung back onto the road, and Val collapsed into the driver's seat.

The creature's front claws tore at Genevieve's body as the Mustang thundered back onto the road. Val opened her hand, and the dagger sliced through the snake's head and the Mustang's roof, landing in her hand in a shower of blood. She drew her arm back to throw, and Genevieve slammed her side against a massive tree trunk on the verge.

"Shit!" Tetra yelled, lurching back as creature blood splattered her clothes.

Val panted. "That was hardcore, Gennie."

"Okay, you guys are clear." Liam's words quavered. "Everybody okay?"

"I'm good," Tetra confirmed.

Val nodded. "Bumps and bruises." She glared at the roof. "Car damage."

Tetra grimaced and raised her hands, palm up. "Sorry."

"You can head back to the main route," Liam told them. "I'm not picking up any activity there...yet."

"Great job, Lee." Val rolled up her window and glanced over her shoulder. "Gaia's Sickle is secure. Your early warnings were great."

"Yeah, thanks," Tetra added.

Liam exhaled. "Okay. Cool. Glad to be helpful."

Val chuckled at his tone. Her racing heart slowed and the scarlet fog leached from her vision as Genevieve purred along the now-quiet roads, making for the interstate that would lead them through New Jersey. Val touched her breastplate, feeling tenderness spread through her sternum, but none of her wounds seemed severe.

Tetra elbowed her and held up her phone. Val read a series of texts between her and Qenzi.

You: Qenz, quick Q. (hehehe, see what I did there?)

Qenzi: Uh... you're aware that you're on mission, right?

You: It has to do with the mission, relax. What do you call a three-headed thing with a snake tail?

Qenzi: I really hope this is the start of a bad joke.

You: Seriously. What's it called?

Qenzi: It sounds like a chimera.

The picture following the last message depicted a beautiful creature with its long tail swept around its legs, beads braided into its mane, and gilded bridles. It was nuzzling a handsome Sylthana Elf wearing the Eternity Crown.

Qenzi: That's the last Sylthana Elven Eternity King.

Val raised her eyebrows. "Traditional Sylthana mounts?" she murmured.

Tetra nodded. "Seems like it."

"Shit," Val muttered.

Tetra's phone buzzed.

Qenzi: Tell me you haven't seen one. Not here. Not in New York.

Val grimaced. "Ask her how to fight them."

Tetra's thumbs danced across her screen, and Val gripped the wheel with white knuckles, although Genevieve steered herself down the mountain road's easy curves. *What have we gotten ourselves into?*

The interstate allowed Genevieve to open up.

Her engine's growl became a shriek, then a high-pitched whine as the magically enhanced turbo spun to its limit. The speedometer only went up to one-twenty, but Genevieve accelerated for a long time after the needle pegged. The pale ribbon of asphalt spread across the landscape, reflecting the moon's silver glow, called to the Mustang.

Val had never felt this kind of speed before.

"Shit, Val," Liam whispered, awed. "That old classic of yours packs a real punch. How souped-up is that thing?"

"She's not a "thing," Lee," Val grumbled.

Tetra hung her head out the passenger window like a happy dog, cropped hair snapping in the wind. "Woohoo!"

The ETA on Val's navigation system steadily dropped as Genevieve ate up the interstate. New York City shimmered on the horizon in minutes, a constellation of right angles and straight lines. Although the countryside spread dark and silent around them, Val felt a kick of excitement.

"Look at that," Tetra murmured. "Feels like home, doesn't it?"

Val grinned. "You bet it does."

"Ladies?" Liam cried.

"What's up, Lee?" Val straightened.

"You've got trouble five miles ahead. Lots of movement in the area. It looks like more of those motorbike guys, though they're hard to see on the cameras. Not sure why. Has to be some stealth tech I don't understand." Liam gasped. "Shit. I think they're planning to block the road."

Val and Tetra exchanged glances.

"The next escape route is ten miles away," Val growled.

"We can backtrack," Tetra suggested.

"How many buildings are in the area, Liam?" Val asked. "Any sign of traffic?"

"It's deserted as far as I can tell. It's in the middle of empty farmland, and there are no buildings within a two-mile radius." A keyboard tapped behind Liam's words. "Unless these guys are packing bombs or something, there's little risk of collateral damage."

Val met Tetra's eyes. The faerie nodded firmly.

"Then we go through them," Val growled.

"You're guaranteeing a fight." Liam's tone wavered. "You're outnumbered by more than ten to one, Val."

"Yeah, well, if we're going to fight, it might as well be somewhere far from innocent people." Val shook her wrist, deploying the shield. "Call Qenzi. Get our backup on standby."

"Yep. This could be bad," Tetra muttered.

Liam was silent.

"Liam?" Val prompted.

Liam exhaled shakily, but his tone was firm and steady when he spoke. "Copy."

Blue light danced on the horizon.

"Here we go," Tetra growled. She was grinning, her eyes alight.

Genevieve slowed. Blue light seeped from around her engine, then enveloped the car.

"Uh, what's happening?" Tetra demanded.

"I'm not sure, but hold onto your ass," Val suggested.

Tetra grabbed the leather bucket seat as Genevieve's wheels left the ground. The car levitated. Metal thudded as her panels detached themselves from her body and spun, changing form.

Tetra gasped. "She's transforming."

"No shit," Val muttered.

The panels returned to the body, and Genevieve dropped. Val and Tetra grunted as her now-massive wheels slammed into the asphalt. The racing slick Mustang tires were gone. Now, Genevieve was a monster truck. Her sixty-inch tires had treads like a tractor's that gripped the road's surface. Her exhaust ended in a fat snorkel that rose above Val's window and blared like the V8 had doubled in size.

The most significant change was to her panels. No longer was she a sleek muscle car with flawless pewter paintwork. Instead, her body was black and dented, and weapons protruded from every surface. Knives, spikes, and razor-sharp blades jutted from the roof, flanks, and hood. Val had to peer between them to see the road.

Tetra laughed. "Okay, that's badass."

"What did you do to your car?" Liam squawked.

"Our agency's got a few tricks up their sleeve." Val chuckled. "Genevieve has more than all the agents put together."

Liam chuckled. "Normally, I don't want to know, but when you guys get back safe and sound, you need to tell me more about that car." He paused. "They're blocking the road, Val."

"I can see that," Val muttered.

Dark silhouettes barricaded the freeway ahead. Sinuous tails vibrated, sending a faint rattle through the air. The figures on the chimeras' backs held drawn blades that glinted in Genevieve's headlights.

"Punch it, Gennie!" Val yelled.

Genevieve's engine roared as she accelerated, suspension bouncing, and the elves raised their swords to the sky as one. The chimeras raised their goat heads and spat gouts of fire. Blue flames caught on the road's surface and rose in a shimmering wall twelve feet high, silhouetting the creatures' graceful shapes against the bright light.

"Tetra, dust," Val barked. "I'll keep them off you."

"Deal." Tetra raised her fists, blue dust seeping between her fingers.

Val glanced at the lockbox on Genevieve's back seat before opening the window. She leaned out and raised her shield and dagger as the chimeras formed a line in front of the fire.

Genevieve's headlights painted a powerful figure in the line's center: a white chimera, its scales patterned in yellow and its mane streaked with black. A long beard hung from its goat head, and the horns curved back, almost touching its neck. The lion had fangs like a sabertooth's. Its rider wore flowing white robes that offered a glimpse of chain mail at her neck and sleeves. Instead of scimitars, she carried a slender spear, its tip shimmering with blue fire. Her helmet hid her eyes, but bright blue war paint streaked her cheeks and bare arms.

"Who's that?" Val grumbled.

"Somebody who's about to find out what we're made of!" Tetra grinned.

The white chimera reared, claws ripping the air, and its rider screamed something that made the other chimeras buck and toss their heads. Her mount hit the ground running and charged Genevieve, the other chimeras at its heels.

As Genevieve accelerated, Val flung her dagger and raised her shield to her nose. The dagger sailed true toward the white rider's face, but she batted it aside with a flick of her spear.

Shock rippled through Val as the dagger hit the ground.

Tetra splayed her hands on Genevieve's hood, sending blue dust across the vehicle. She was fireproofing the whole truck. Smart, Val thought, her powers straining to bring her dagger back to her quickly. Its hilt slapped in her hand as the white rider leveled her lance at Genevieve's engine.

Genevieve roared, and Val flung her dagger at the chimera. It swerved hard, so the dagger barely clipped its flank, but the rider's lance missed. The flaming edge screeched across Genevieve's side instead of plunging into her hood, and as the chimera scrambled past the massive truck, Val swung a punch at its rider. The elf dodged, a movement easy as water flowing. Then the white chimera was past them, and the others slammed into Genevieve.

CHAPTER EIGHTEEN

The truck bucked at the impact, and Val's hip collided with the window. She grunted, then propelled her dagger into the mass of creatures. Genevieve's spikes did their deadly work as many tumbled beneath her massive tires, and others flinched away from the hood, bleeding. Several found their way between the blades, and claws screeched on the panels. Elves leaped from their falling mounts to swarm over Genevieve, their hands filled with blue fire.

"Val!" Tetra yelped. She raised one hand from the hood and shot a bolt of fire-retardant dust at the nearest elf, blocking the blue flame he'd sent toward her.

Val grabbed the nearest spike and hoisted herself out of Genevieve. The truck struggled forward, tires spinning, but a mass of chimeras fought her progress. More elves sprang from their mounts and darted through the spikes on the hood, making for Tetra. One raised a boot to stomp on the faerie's hand.

"Nope," Val snarled.

The elf whirled, and Val punched him in the nose. He tumbled into the mass of bodies beside the vehicle.

"Come on!" Val thundered, turning to the elves as she stood

over Tetra. "Come and get me!" Her bloody dagger zipped to her hand.

The nearest elf lunged at Val, throwing bolts of blue flame. She blocked them with her shield and slashed his belly with her dagger, then kicked his body aside and roared as a scimitar rang on her steel-clad thigh. The elf's blade couldn't cleave her armor, but his other scimitar reached between her shield and her body and slashed across her breastplate, its tip meeting her cheek with a flash of dull pain.

She closed her arm around her body, pinning his wrist to her chest, and saw a flash of terror in his eyes before she kicked him in the chest so hard that his shoulder shattered. He screamed, and she flung him aside as two more elves charged her with blue fireballs flying from their fists.

Val deflected one with her shield, and it slammed into the belly of the other elf but didn't slow him down. He slapped it aside like a bug and kept coming. The fireballs rang on the shield, and Val gritted her teeth against the impact. She threw her dagger and heard the wet rip as it found its target.

Tetra screamed in fury, not pain. Val kicked a charging elf in the belly, ignoring the blade that found a chink at the back of her knee, and spun to check on her. The faerie spread fire-retardant blue dust over Genevieve with one hand. The other flung caustic dust at the chimeras, which staggered back.

Genevieve's engine thundered, and another chimera tumbled beneath her wheels.

"I can get through the wall!" Tetra yelled.

Val caught her dagger. "I can get through the elves."

She lunged at the next elf.

"Val, behind you!" Liam roared.

Val whipped around. Liam's cry gave her a split second to raise her shield as the spear flew toward her face. The white rider changed its arc at the last second, so it missed Val's face but landed in the center of her shield with the full force of the elf's leap.

Val's feet left the hood and her body sailed back helplessly, limbs trailing and weightless as she floated through the air. She had the presence of mind to tighten her grip on her dagger before she hit the road on her back. Metal screeched on asphalt as she slid across the road, and Val's grip on her dagger wavered. Darkness flickered before her eyes.

The scarlet fog surged. Her vision cleared, and Val slammed the edge of her shield into the tar, digging it several inches into the road's surface. Her skid ended, and she flipped to her feet as the white chimera reared above her.

Correction, Val thought. *The* winged *white chimera.*

Unlike the others, this one had membranous wings like a bat's. They eclipsed the night as it threw back its heads and screeched. Its rider spun the flaming spear in her hand and aimed its tip at Val, then spurred the chimera.

Val raised her shield toward the spear as the chimera charged, but she kept her eyes on its legs. Diego's words echoed in her mind. *Sweep the leg.*

She dropped at the last moment. The spear missed her by inches, and Val drove her shield's edge into the chimera's left front knee. Its limbs crossed. The chimera threw its wings open too late and went down hard, three heads hitting the dirt at the same moment, belly flashing as it went over.

The elf sprang clear of the falling beast, tumbled like a gymnast, and landed yards from Val. She spun her spear, the movement elaborate and graceful, but Val didn't let her finish the flashy motion. She charged the elf with a near-bovine bellow, then swept her dagger at the elf's chest in a devastating thrust.

The elf sprang back and blocked the blow. Val's dagger hit the spear's shaft—ironwood, she realized in the blistering clarity of the scarlet fog—and its grip clanged against the wood.

A heartbeat passed. The dwarf's and the elf's bared teeth and flashing eyes were mere inches apart. The elf's war paint made her eyes look as bright a blue as the flames on the spearhead. Her face twisted, a sneer of disgust wrinkling her upper lip. Val recognized the look in her eyes, which she hadn't seen in an opponent since she'd left the Iron Hills. She'd seen fury, terror, determination, and judgment.

But not since the barfights in her birthplace had she seen contempt.

The elf's hands caught fire. Heat scorched Val's face, and she thrust her shield up to protect herself as the elf punched both hands forward, still gripping the spear. Tongues of flame sprang from her fists and splashed over Val's shield. She dug her boots into the ground, but the fire's force sent her skidding back.

A scream tore the night. Val raised her head as Tetra's cry rang out. Genevieve was moving toward the wall of flame, crushing elves and chimeras, but her hood was on fire. Tetra held one hand over her head, a dome of blue dust protecting her from the flames. She clutched the other hand to her chest, and blood seeped between her fingers.

The elf standing over her drew back his scimitar, fire in his eyes.

"No!" Val roared.

She threw herself to the ground shield-first and rolled away from her opponent's flames. The scarlet fog surged in her blood as she found her feet, and she flung her left arm toward Tetra. Time slowed as her magic stretched the moment, giving her time to reach for the iron particles holding the shield's metal to the leather strap on her arm. They parted, and the shield detached.

Time snapped back to full speed. The shield zipped across the battlefield and collided with the elf's scimitar so hard that the blade shattered. Metal rained down around Tetra, and she recovered from the pain, slamming her bloody hand on Genevieve's hood. Fire-retardant dust spread across the spiked metal.

Val summoned her shield. It flew back to her after slamming

into the elf's knees. He fell before Tetra, and she pressed her hand to his face. His screams resounded over Genevieve's rumble as his skin and flesh melted.

Val's amulet throbbed, her senses shrieking. She whirled aside almost too late. The elven leader's spear hissed on her armor, blue flames scorching the metal. Val's shield slammed into her left arm, and she allowed its momentum to carry it toward the elf's face in a blow that would have been bone-shattering if it had landed.

The elf sprang back, fire bursting from her feet to propel her away, and followed up with a hard strike at Val's throat. Val blocked it with the shield and slashed at the elf's knees. The elf dodged, then sliced at Val's face, her spear finding its way under the shield. Val flung her head back and barely escaped the blow.

Breathing hard, Val and the elf circled one another. Both were bruised and bleeding, but neither was close to admitting defeat. Val flexed her fingers on her dagger.

"You stand between me and my birthright," the elf snarled.

Val scoffed. "Your birthright is living a free and safe life. Gaia's Sickle, in Queen Julia's hands, will help you achieve that."

"Gaia's Sickle belongs to my people," the elf hissed.

Val raised an eyebrow. "Not according to your King Lotan."

The elf's eyes narrowed. "Don't speak that spineless coward's name to me, bitch!"

She screamed and charged, and her anger did exactly what Val had hoped. Her sloppy guard exposed her chest for an instant. Val threw her dagger, and her powers propelled it toward the elf's mail-clad chest. Dwarven steel met elven mail with a hiss as her dagger penetrated.

The elf screamed as Val pushed her powers behind the dagger and felt its tip pierce her skin. Then a plume of fire came from nowhere—not nowhere, from the elf's savage kick—and scorched Val's shins.

Pain seared distantly, as though it were happening to

someone else. The elf twisted away from Val's dagger, and the movement exposed her back long enough for Val to lunge and slam her shield into her opponent. The elf went down hard on her side, and Val stabbed down. Her dagger bit into the earth as the elf rolled and swiped at Val's face with the spear. Val ducked, and the elf turned the sweep into a heavy blow that rang on the back of Val's helmet. She slammed into the ground face-down, ears ringing.

She had no time to be stunned. Val rolled, raising her shield, and the spear clanged against it with such force that the tip scratched the copper plating. Faerrous steel released a gust of faerie dust, and the elf sprang back with a grunt of surprise. Val lurched to her feet.

"Go, Gennie!" Tetra screamed.

The elf spun. The monster truck zipped backward, sending elves and chimeras flying as they lost their balance. She changed gears with a heavy crunch, and her tires spun on the battle-slick asphalt.

Only a handful of elves and their mounts remained. They gathered themselves, but their eyes were afraid.

"No!" the elven leader choked.

Val broke into a run and slammed her shield into the elf's shoulder, sending her stumbling, but she didn't have time to strike a blow.

"Pull back! Retreat!" the elf yelled.

The elves and chimeras scattered. Genevieve's back door thumped open as Val sprinted toward her.

"Come on, Val!" Tetra screamed.

A defiant elf sprang off his chimera's back, scimitars raised, and lunged at Tetra. Val threw her shield with a grunt of effort.

The shield slammed into the elf and knocked him under Genevieve's wheels as Val reached the monster truck. Her outstretched fingers closed around the door handle, and she hauled herself into the back seat. Her shield zipped through the back window, shattering the glass, and almost hit her in the belly as she scrambled on top of the lockbox.

Genevieve honked reproachfully.

"Sorry!" Val yelled. "Get us out of here!"

Tetra gasped as they thundered at the fire wall. The flames snapped above their heads. A pool of melted asphalt lay at the wall's base, and the air shimmered with heat.

"Oh, shit," Tetra yelped. She slammed both hands onto Genevieve's hood. Blue faerie dust surrounded them in a glittering bubble as they crashed into the flames. Val squeezed her eyes shut, waiting for scorching agony, but it never came. They popped through the fire wall, and a rush of cool air entered the monster truck as the dark but welcoming landscape unrolled before them.

Genevieve transformed, and as she levitated, an unseen force that felt like gravity sucked Val into the driver's seat. Familiar leather cradled her hips, and the galloping horse reappeared on the steering wheel. The spikes disappeared, and the long pewter hood extended before Val. When her wheels hit the ground, Genevieve had returned to her true form.

Val peered into the rearview mirror. Blue flames danced on the road behind them.

"Well done," Liam managed, breathless. "They're not pursuing you. Looks like they're taking their bikes into the countryside around you."

"Shiiiiiiiiiiit." Tetra drew the syllable out as she sagged in the passenger seat.

"Are you guys hurt?" Liam demanded.

Tetra inspected an ugly gash between her left finger and thumb. "Nothing major. You?"

Val shook her head. "I'm okay." As the scarlet fog ebbed, she tried not to think about the burning pain in her shins.

"Is Gaia's Sickle still secure?" Liam asked.

Val nodded. "Lockbox is on the back seat. All is well."

"Good." Liam exhaled. "That was insane."

"Shit was real," Tetra agreed.

"We're on the last stretch, everybody." Val fixed her eyes on the distinct outline of the Financial District glittering on the horizon. "Get us there, Gennie."

"Oh, crap," Liam croaked.

"Liam? What?" Tetra demanded.

"I thought they were dispersing into the woods, but they're not." Liam's tone rose. "They're trying to flank you! Take Cara Dune, now!"

The turnoff to the exit route flashed ahead before Val could grab the wheel. It spun anyway, and Genevieve screeched down the exit. She downshifted and skidded around a curve, with Val and Tetra sliding in their seats, then belted down a side road into the woods.

"How do they know we've changed route?" Liam cried. "They're still on you, and they're moving fast!"

"How can those things be that fast?" Tetra demanded.

"I don't know. I've never seen bikes like those before," Liam wailed.

"Yeah, no shit," Val growled.

Val remembered this escape route because it was intense, like the character Liam had named it after. Genevieve skidded down another side road, then crashed through the closed gates into the national park housing in the Palisades. Her tires crunched on gravel, and she belted down a narrow service road, the landscape dark but for her headlights.

"Buckle up!" Val growled.

Tetra obeyed as Genevieve swerved hard onto a covered bridge. She zipped through it, her engine's echo shivering the wooden walls, and plunged into the woods. The black hole of a tunnel appeared on her left, and Genevieve slid into a handbrake turn that sprayed gravel from her tires. She corrected, swerved, and dove into the tunnel. Tetra clung to the seatbelt with one hand and the handle over the door with the other as the Mustang popped out, sped over the service road, and bucked down a grassy embankment.

"Cliff!" Tetra shrieked. "Cliff, cliff, cliff, *cliff*!"

Genevieve's front wheels left the ground. The Mustang sailed through the air, and the dark Hudson filled Val's vision, New York sparkling on the opposite bank. Then Genevieve landed hard on another service road on the clifftops. She swerved, sending pebbles skittering down the cliffs, and skidded to a halt.

Val slammed against her seatbelt. The engine stalled. Breathless silence hung in the car except for Val's and Tetra's panting and the faint clatter of pebbles falling down the steep cliffs.

"Did we lose them?" Val whispered.

"Shit," Liam muttered. "It almost worked. They've fallen behind, but they're coming after you. It's like they're somehow tracking you." A keyboard skittered in the background. "Not now, Shadow. I have no idea how they're doing it, but I think you should ditch your phones."

"Uh, excuse me, this is an iPhone. Do you know what they cost? I'll happily fight a few elves before pitching this baby into the river," Tetra retorted.

"Tetra!" Liam barked. "Now's not the time!'

"Do you see any evidence that they're hacking our phones, Lee?" Val asked.

"No! Not even with Kenzie's sophisticated tech, but they're tracking you *somehow*!" Liam snapped.

Val and Tetra exchanged glances.

"Surely not," Tetra whispered. "The lockbox makes that impossible."

Val knew what she was thinking: the elves were tracking Gaia's Sickle using its magical signature.

"It should," she growled, "but there's only one way to find out."

She unbuckled her seatbelt and got out.

"What are you doing?" Tetra demanded.

"Get into the driver's seat," Val ordered.

"No! Where are you going?" Tetra barked.

"I'm going to cause a distraction. You and Genevieve get Gaia's Sickle to Wall Street. If I see them chasing you, I'll come after you." Val drew her dagger and activated her shield.

"What are you thinking, Val?" Tetra spluttered. "You can't fight all those elves alone!"

"Liam, tell her," Val snapped.

Liam paused, then sighed. "She's right. Splitting up is the smart move right now. It gives us the best chance of achieving our mission objective."

"It gives Val the best chance of getting killed!" Tetra yelled.

"Careful. You might make me think you care." Val smirked.

A chimera bellowed in the thick woods. The strange sound blended bleat, hiss, and roar in a single screech.

"If what you say is true, the mission objective will preserve national security." Liam's voice had stopped shaking. "This is the only way."

Tetra scowled as she scooted into the driver's seat. "I don't give a shit about the world. I don't want anything to happen to you."

"Did you miss the part where we live in the world?" Val raised her eyebrows. "Now get your shapely ass out of here, Genevieve."

The Mustang's engine started.

"Val—" Tetra began.

Whatever the faerie was going to say, her words were lost on the wind as Genevieve threw herself into reverse, skidded through a turn, and snarled down the path. Val's amulet hummed against her skin. Scarlet fog descended as she turned toward the woods, shield raised, and let out a laugh that shook the night.

"Over here, you bunch of scurvy hybrid sons-of-bitches!" she roared. She raised her dagger and slammed the flat of the blade on her shield with a deafening *clang*. "You want a piece of me? Come and get it!"

Genevieve's roar faded into the distance. Val struck her shield in a beat as rhythmic as a heart's pulses. The engine's sound was gone when the first chimera exploded from the woods.

Val didn't hesitate. She threw her dagger and rolled aside. Fire exploded on the clifftop where she'd been a moment before, but a scream came from the chimera's saddle, and the elf crashed to the ground, clutching the ragged wound in his throat. Val didn't have time for remorse. As the chimera crouched over its rider, bleating, a trio of elves on foot charged from the trees.

Footwork, Val, she reminded herself.

Her dagger returned to her hand. She threw her shield at the first elf and crossed blades with the second, blocking both scimitars with her dagger. His teeth gritted with effort, but she flung him back with a strong jerk of her shoulder, knocking him on his ass. Her shield returned as the third elf struck. His scimitars rang on the shield and Val stomped hard on his instep, then hit his jaw with the shield when he doubled over. The second elf sprang to his feet a second too slow. Val punched him in the temple, pommel first, and he crumpled to the ground like a puppet with cut strings.

"You can't keep this up, Val!" Liam cried in her ear. "There are more of them coming. A *lot* more."

"Good," Val snarled. "How many are tailing Genevieve?"

A brief pause. "None."

Trees and bushes bucked with the passage of another chimera. A blue fireball ripped through the foliage. Val deflected it with her shield, sending it flying into the second chimera as it sprang from the woods. The first chimera pounced, claws outstretched, much too fast. Val threw herself aside, and the beast's momentum carried it over her head and the cliff's edge with a drawn-out shriek.

The second chimera charged. Val sidestepped the plume of fire and jumped. Her boot found a boulder and she backflipped, then landed on the chimera's back, straddling the beast as she faced its rider. The elf yelped, and she dealt him a swift blow to the throat with her forearm. He clutched his neck and tumbled.

Val followed him in a somersault, then landed on her feet. *"Genevieve got away?"* Val yelled as two more chimeras sprang from the woods.

"She did," Liam confirmed.

"Okay. Time for me to get out of here, then," Val hissed.

She glanced over her shoulder. Her home city gleamed, an artificial constellation against the stars, calling to her, but the Hudson's dark expanse separated her from the city's comforts.

The two chimeras crouched and moved left and right, flanking Val. One chimera on either side, the cliffs behind, and elf-infested woods in front. She crouched, eyeing the beasts, but neither attacked. Venom dripped from their snake fangs and saliva from their lion teeth. Their goat jaws leaked blue sparks.

"You broke my chimera's leg, bitch!" The elven leader strode from the woods in a swirl of white robes and blue fire. Her spear glowed with flame, but it was nothing compared to the brightness of her eyes.

"Whose fault is that, idiot?" Val snorted. "You're the one who attacked us."

"Gaia's Sickle belongs to my people," the elf hissed.

Val rolled her eyes. "Yeah, yeah. I get that."

"You need a way out of there, Val," Liam yelped.

"Working on it," Val muttered.

She took a few steps toward the cliffs. The chimeras closed in, and the elven leader echoed every stride.

"You are nothing but a pawn in the Pendragon game," the elven leader snarled.

Val glanced back, ostensibly to see what lay below, but she already knew. Dark water...and a chimera splashing and screeching in the river. Its rider tried desperately to hold up all three heads as the creature whimpered and struggled.

"They can't swim," Val murmured.

"Of course motorbikes can't swim, Val. What are you thinking?" Liam demanded. "There's no way down."

"Don't you see? The Lunar Fae call themselves heroes, but they are nothing but thieves. They never stop taking what doesn't belong to them. Our lives. Our throne. Our artifacts," the elven leader snapped.

Val glanced at the water again. "There is *one* way down."

"Are you insane? You can't dive from that height! You'll never make it!" Liam yelled.

You don't know that my bones are mostly iron. Val shook her wrist, disengaging the shield, and sheathed her dagger.

"What are you doing?" the elf demanded.

Val looked up. "Not listening to your bullshit. Why are you going on and on, anyway? If you want to fight me, fight me."

The elf's eyes narrowed. "I want more than your blood. I want to know who you are." She nodded at the ruby glow of Val's amulet. "Where did you get that?"

"Where did an Iron Dwarf get an Iron Dwarven artifact?" Val raised her eyebrows. "Pretty sure it was not by killing a bunch of people the way you're doing."

"Iron Dwarf, are you?" The elf's spear burned brighter. "I should have known you were a clod."

The slur was so heinous that Val felt like a bucket of ice water had been poured over her head. It stung more than the burns on her legs, and the elf chuckled at her reaction.

"Didn't think anyone had the guts to say that anymore, did you?" she hissed. "Now, tell me where the sickle is."

"I don't think so." Val raised both hands, middle fingers outstretched. "Screw you."

The elf lunged. Val turned and bolted the few feet to the cliff's edge.

"Val!" Liam screamed. "*No!*"

Val jumped. The elves cried out. Scarlet fog drenched Val's vision as she plummeted toward the river. The elf and his struggling chimera had reached the cliff's edge, so nothing but still black water lay beneath Val.

"Kenzie? Kenzie, I need backup *now!*" Liam yelled. "Medical support to the Hudson. I'll text you the coordinates—"

Val tuned out his panicked voice and stretched her arms above her head in the most aerodynamic position. *Luna, help me,* she prayed silently.

She feared that she would hit the bottom too quickly, but hitting the water was like hitting concrete. The impact snapped her teeth shut over her tongue and rattled her bones. Blood filled her mouth, and darkness flooded her vision as she tumbled in the water. Disorientation gripped her. Her limbs flailed, but she didn't know which way was up. The scarlet fog flickered.

Heat scorched her chest, and she flailed harder. Had the elves found her? Then she realized it was the amulet, its pulses bright and hard, and the scarlet fog intensified. Pain and dizziness floated away, and Val raised her head, then struck out for the surface.

Spray shattered around her face. She sucked down a lungful of glorious cold air. Vigor surged to her limbs.

"Val!" Liam screamed.

Val coughed. "Alive," she croaked.

She'd lost her wig. Grateful for the lack of hair to get in her eyes, Val squinted at the opposite shore, and the city lights beckoned to her in the distance. She was a strong swimmer, but was she strong enough to get across the frigid Hudson?

Only one way to find out. Val reluctantly used her powers to loosen the eyelets on her boots, tugging the laces free enough for her to kick them off. They sank to the bottom of the river as she kicked away, arms gliding through the cold water.

Yells and squawks came from behind her. Val didn't have the energy to look back. She locked her gaze on the opposite bank and poured everything she had into swimming. Kick, stroke, kick, stroke. The city seemed to be getting farther away, so she closed her eyes and thought of nothing except swimming and the supernatural heat surging in her blood.

In minutes, exhaustion drained her limbs despite the scarlet fog. It kept her going but couldn't save her from cramps that racked her arms and legs. Her strokes weakened.

They didn't stop.

Finally, blessedly, her fingertips found pebbles. Val put her feet down and rose, water gushing from her armor. Her trembling knees gave way, and she fell hard. Water flooded her nostrils, and she scrambled to her feet again, coughing and wheezing. Her hands clawed the water as she waded until she was knee-deep, then fell to her hands and knees, retching.

"Val, you made it!" Liam called. "It's okay. You made it."

Val waited for her limbs to stop shaking. She fumbled to her feet and checked her wrist and hip. She still had her shield and dagger. The amulet felt like the only warm thing in the world.

A shout rose behind her. Val stumbled around, pebbles harsh on her bare feet, cold water sloshing around her ankles. Her belly flipped. The chimeras waited on the clifftop, but elves determinedly swam across the river toward her. She spotted a spear bobbing in the current as the elven leader furiously led the way.

Val groaned. "Oh, shit."

She drew her dagger, water gushing from its sheath, and activated the shield in a shower of glittering droplets. The thought of Tetra, Genevieve, and Gaia's Sickle flying toward Wall Street at that moment sustained the scarlet fog. Val moved back until she reached the dry ground and crouched, shield high, dagger raised. Her arms trembled with weakness, but she gritted her teeth. She could slow these assholes down enough for Genevieve to reach her destination.

"Hang on, Val!" Liam roared.

The elven leader was almost across the river. Her head rose as her feet found the bottom, and she held her spear above her head, blue fire reflecting on the dark water.

"Come at me, bitch," Val hissed.

A sound reached her—a roar cutting through the ripple of water. Val raised her head as two headlights filled the night, and the scream of an irate V8 ripped the air. Genevieve skidded to a halt on the road a few yards from the riverbank.

Tetra kicked the passenger door open. "Get in, idiot!"

"What in Merlin's name are you doing here?" Val roared, sprinting to the Mustang. She flung herself inside. Genevieve took off before she could close the door.

"What does it look like?" Tetra barked. "Rescuing you!"

"Liam, did you do this?" Val demanded.

"You can yell at me for saving your life later," Liam snapped.

The seat belt buckled over Val's lap and cinched tight as Genevieve threw herself down a side road and sped onto a populated street. Sleepy homes and shuttered businesses lined the road. Warm lights in windows flitted past as Genevieve accelerated.

"We're luring them into the city," Val yelped.

"Oh, I don't think they'll make it." Tetra chuckled.

Liam gasped. "What *is* that?"

A dull roar shook the world, drowning out Genevieve's rumble. Val squinted through the window. A gigantic shadow blotted out the stars. Her night vision made out massive wings and a long, spiked tail trailing behind. Fire glimmered behind scales the size of her fist.

The dragon swooped overhead, its roar like a jet engine, and vanished toward the river.

"That's the backup you asked for, Liam," Tetra informed him.

"Yeah, I know, but what is it? A new type of fighter jet? A massive drone?" Liam wondered. "Never mind. I don't want to know, but it looks capable of stopping those guys before they hurt anyone else."

Val sagged in the seat. The scarlet fog dissipated, leaving her body a shaking wad of pain. "Thanks, Liam."

"That's what I'm here for," he told her.

Tetra gripped the steering wheel. "How's my driving?"

Genevieve slapped her elbow with the gear lever.

"Ow!" Tetra protested.

"Almost there," Val murmured. She glanced at the lockbox on the back seat. "Almost."

CHAPTER NINETEEN

Everything hurt when Genevieve halted at the bottom of the towering skyscraper that housed Gold, Manns, and Sax. There was no sign of the friendly faun valet who loved the Mustang. Freya Gold stood at the door, arms wrapped tightly around herself. A uniformed PMA soldier stood on either side of her: one vampire, one werewolf.

Freya raised a hand to her mouth as Val exited Genevieve. "Merlin's beard, Miss Stonehold." Her eyes stretched wide. "Are you okay?"

Val looked down. She'd worn jeans and a tee shirt under her armor. Sylthana fire had burned holes in the jeans' legs, her shirt hung in tatters from her muscular torso, and the fabric was so wet, filthy, and bloodstained that the colors were unrecognizable. Tetra looked little better. The faerie was missing an eyebrow, and a black bruise stretched over her cheekbone.

"Oh, shit." Tetra stepped back. "The queen's not going to like this."

"Merlin's toenail fungus," Val groaned. Though Genevieve's engine rumbled with its usual fervor, the Mustang looked the worse for wear. Scratches scored her paintwork, and heavy dents were visible in her hood and roof. Claw marks bared the metal of her flanks.

"Sorry, Gennie." Val grimaced.

The Mustang cheerfully honked.

"Do you need medical attention?" Freya asked.

"Probably," Val admitted, "but let's get the sickle safe first."

Freya shook herself. "Of course. We'll drive into the vault area."

"Huh?" Tetra demanded bluntly.

"We're right on top of it." Freya turned to the building. Fancy masonry decorated the door's pillars, and she pressed her palm to a fleur-de-lys. It flashed purple and receded, stone grinding.

The sidewalk trembled under Val's feet.

"You might want to step aside," Freya told her.

Val jumped back. Slabs of sidewalk receded, then folded away, revealing a ramp that led under the building.

"This way," Freya told her.

Val and Tetra returned to the Mustang, and Val carefully piloted the car down the ramp while Freya walked alongside. The sidewalk closed behind them, sealing them in a place secure enough for Gaia's Sickle.

Val drove into a round room about fifty feet across. The nondescript walls offered little to impress her except for elevator doors.

"Where's the vault?" Tetra asked.

"Below us," Freya told her, walking toward the elevator.

"Should we unload the lockbox?" Val queried.

Freya touched the elevator button. "There's no need for that."

A metallic thump sounded far beneath them, and the floor smoothly descended. Tetra looked queasy, but Val grinned as the floor sank into the earth's heart. They passed several stories where well-dressed paras bustled along metal walkways leading in front of vault doors similar to Maximilian's, doubtlessly on their way to admire priceless treasures. One vampire exited a vault in full evening wear, caressing a diamond necklace that put Seraphine's to shame.

"I bet there's cool shit in here," Tetra loudly announced.

"Tetra," Val hissed.

Freya chuckled. "There is *very* cool shit in here, Miss Dupont."

The floor descended another story, revealing a young warlock in robes far too big for him. He stepped out of the vault, determinedly clutching a scepter with a fist-sized gem as its head. He gaped at Val and Tetra as they passed.

"I think we're alarming your clients," Val remarked.

Freya laughed. "It's all right. The bottom floor is off-limits to everyone except our security staff."

The final level was the same as the others, with walkways and vaults, but burly paranormals in black uniforms patrolled the walkways instead of clients. All carried swords and automatic rifles, and Val wouldn't have picked a fight with any of them in a bar. A werelion and a centaur strode past, giving Genevieve a quick glance. Two minotaurs approached the Mustang. One held a gun in his hands.

"All right. We can unload the sickle," Freya announced.

Val and Tetra deactivated the sticky charm, then hauled the lockbox out of the back seat. Freya led the way to a vault whose featureless door resembled Maximilian's. It scanned her palm and unlocked with a flash of wards, revealing a glass display case with warding runes etched into its wooden frame.

"You won't be able to bring the lockbox inside," Freya explained. "The wards will reject the iron's magical signature. No magical items can enter except the sickle."

"Then I should give it to you, Ms. Gold. I'm wearing a lot of magic." Val opened the lockbox and hesitated, gazing at the sickle. It gleamed dully against the black iron of the lockbox. Her amulet throbbed with its power, and when she finally lifted it, goosebumps rose on her skin. Her aches seemed distant compared to the warmth that filled her blood when she touched the sickle.

"Magnificent," Freya murmured. She took the sickle, and her eyes widened. "I've seen many a great artifact, but I've seldom felt magic like this."

"I'm glad it's where it belongs now," Val murmured.

"Indeed." Freya put the sickle in the case. The glass magically sealed itself over the sickle, and a purple flash announced the wards activating. Freya left the vault, and the door shut with a reassuringly heavy thump.

"It's safe now," Tetra murmured.

"All paras are safer now." Val turned to Genevieve. "Except me when the queen sees what I did to her car."

Freya chuckled. "I wouldn't worry about that, Miss Stonehold. Our valet service will take care of it."

"What?" Tetra demanded. "How?"

Their answer came when they returned to the top floor and found the faun valet waiting for them at the bottom of the ramp, arms folded. A small army of elves surrounded him; not tall, elegant Sylthana or Aether Elves, but two-foot-tall pointy-eared creatures with curl-toed shoes. They all wore overalls and carried toolboxes.

Val was leaning on Genevieve's roof. She hastily straightened. "Uh, hi."

"What did you *do* to her?" the faun moaned.

A gray-haired elf strode forward, brandishing a hammer. "Step aside," he ordered.

Val, Tetra, and Freya retreated to a safe distance, and the elves swarmed. They became a blur of activity around Genevieve, descending on her so thickly that the Mustang vanished from view. Clanging, hissing, barked orders, squeaking metal, and spraying paint resounded.

"Uh, do you think—" Val began.

The frantic activity lasted only a couple of minutes. Then the gray-haired elf emerged from the chaos. "She's right again now," he told Val, wiping his hands on a rag. "Try not to destroy her again. Okay?"

"Sorry. Okay," Val muttered.

The elves marched away in a neat squad. Genevieve gleamed like new again, restored from her tires to her roof.

"How did they do that?" Tetra wondered.

The faun valet rushed to Genevieve and draped his arms over her hood. "Oh, Gennie!"

"Thanks for the help, man." Val grimaced. "Will they send me an invoice?"

The faun straightened. "These weren't Genevieve's first scratches. Queen Julia has a contract with the elves to repair her whenever she needs it."

"Good to know." Val's shoulders loosened.

Freya turned to her, smiling. "Thank you again for bringing the sickle here safely. Miss Stonehold, Miss Dupont, your work is exemplary. Thank you."

They shook hands with the dwarf, drove up the ramp, and headed down Wall Street. The skyscrapers slumbered around them as dawn turned the sky pale gray.

"Liam?" Val asked.

"Here I am. The security at your destination jammed our comms," Liam explained. "I expected no less."

Val grinned at Tetra, who returned the smile.

"Gaia's Sickle is secure," Val announced. "Mission accomplished, thanks to you guys."

"Do you think any takeout places are open right now?" Tetra asked hopefully.

Val laughed. "We just helped save the world, and you're thinking about food?"

"What? I'm hungry!" Tetra shrugged.

Liam's laughter joined theirs as Genevieve sped through Manhattan.

Val winced as she rubbed bright blue cream over her burns. Dr. Olena Dovhan at the para-ER in Staten Island had mainly healed the painful wounds on her shins, but they still stung as she applied the tingling magical cream. She sat on her bed, freshly showered and wearing her most comfortable wig—the bouncy afro.

Shadow sprang onto the bed and rammed his nose into the jar of cream.

"Shadow!" Val shoved him away. "Dude! What if that's poisonous to dogs?"

Shadow licked a blob of cream off his nose.

"Shit, guy. What were you thinking?" Val yelled.

She looked up the ingredients on the paranet and learned that powdered snakestone and unspoken water had no known ill effects on dogs.

"What an ass," she grumbled. "You gave me a heart attack."

Shadow flopped onto his side, his massive head in her lap. Val bent over to kiss it and fondled his ears. The big dog sighed in pleasure.

"Idiot," she muttered.

She pulled her sweatpants' legs down to cover the wounds and tossed the cream on her nightstand, then lay back in her rumpled bed. Shadow joined her, head on the pillows like he owned the place, and she considered wrapping her arms around him and going back to sleep.

She checked the time and grimaced. "No dice, Shadow. Everyone will be here in the next half-hour or so."

Shadow whined.

"I know, dude. I know. But you can cuddle Jess on the couch. She always brings you treats." Val stifled a yawn, unlocked her phone, and selected Frode's number.

She closed her eyes and held the phone to her ear, almost

drifting off before Frode shouted, "Little spark! How good to hear from you!"

Val jumped. "Dad! Hi. Sorry."

Frode chuckled. "You called me, so why do I want to ask if I woke you?"

"It was a long night," Val admitted.

"Thanks for the text letting me know you were home safe. Are you okay?" Frode asked, his voice wobbling.

Val smiled. "A little sore, but totally fine. Our mission was successful, too."

"Of course it was. My baby girl was in charge of it." Frode laughed like that was the only possible outcome.

Val chuckled. "Thanks for forging the lockbox, Dad. It worked perfectly. Kept the sickle safe at a few hairy moments."

"I'm only too happy when I can help my girl." Frode's voice warmed. "You're saving the world, darling."

"Not so sure about that." Val grinned.

"I am. Have you watched the news today?" Frode asked.

Val sighed. "Who watches the news, Dad?"

"You should," Frode scolded.

"Okay, okay. Let me see." Val put him on speaker and pulled up a paranormal newsfeed. A headline jumped at her: **QUEEN JULIA PRESS CONFERENCE REGARDING GAIA'S SICKLE.**

"She's doing a press conference?" Val raised her eyebrows.

Frode chuckled. "You're a big deal, little spark. Listen to what she said."

Val tapped on the video, and Queen Julia appeared on her screen, looking cold and official in ceremonial Lunar Fae garments. She stood behind a lectern in the throne room as dozens of microphones bristled toward her face.

"It is my relief and pleasure to announce to all paranormals that the Eternity Throne has taken the necessary steps to ensure that we are all safe from the Wild Hunt villains currently contained around Earth and Avalon." Queen Julia held her chin high. "The throne has obtained Gaia's Sickle, the most effective weapon against Kronos, and is holding it in a secure location. The Wild Hunt villains are securely contained."

Her speech ended, and reporters crowded the lectern, a line of griffins holding them back. The queen inclined her head toward one.

"Your Majesty!" the reporter barked. "Why would you expend so much time and resources to secure the Hunters in our dimensions when they could be banished to the prison realm?"

"Many have concerns that the realm is not as safe as it used to be. The Official Para-Military Agency constantly tests and improves its security, but the council voted against transferring Hunters to the prison realm at this time," Queen Julia responded, composed.

More jabbering followed until Her Majesty indicated another reporter with a graceful gesture.

"Paranormals don't feel safe with those villains in our worlds," the reporter called. "If the prison realm can't hold them, why not execute them?"

The queen didn't waver. "The death penalty has never been part of Eternity Law. The council does not intend to change that."

"Not even to protect your people from the highest concentration of evil the world has ever seen?" the reporter countered.

Queen Julia smiled. "Little dramatic, considering we recently lived through the Third Pendragon War, don't you think? Rest assured, I don't intend to let my dominion collapse into conflict. I fought for this peace, and I will keep it. Gaia's Sickle is an integral part of that goal."

The video cut to a serious-looking satyr news anchor who glared into the camera. "The queen went on to remind the public that the Eternity Throne obtained Gaia's Sickle with the cooperation and permission of the Sylthana Elf King Lotan."

Her words became a voiceover as the studio vanished and a security camera clip of a heavily warded cell filled the screen. A tall, thin, masculine humanoid sat on the bunk, clutching his shock of gray hair and muttering. "Many paras consider the world safer thanks to the throne's purchase of Gaia's Sickle, which will assist in containing Kronos, one of the most powerful dictators of all time."

The video ended, and Val rubbed goosebumps on her arms. She was grateful that the camera angle didn't show Kronos' eyes. "Wow. This is intense, Dad."

"It is intensely *good*, my little spark. You're helping keep the peace. Did you hear that?" Frode's tone bubbled with pride. "I love you, darling."

Val thought of Frode and his cottage and smithy on a mountainside in the Iron Hills, a place safer now because of what she'd done, and her smile grew from the warmth in her chest.

"Love you too, Dad." She checked the time. "I'd better go."

"Plans this evening?" Frode asked. "Going to celebrate your victory?"

Val chuckled. "Actually, I'm staying in. We've got a case of beer and three movies to watch together."

"You're having friends over?" Excitement filled Frode's tone.

"Yeah, a few," Val murmured.

"My little spark, all of my dreams for you are coming true." Frode sighed contentedly. "Enjoy your movies, darling."

"Have a great day, Dad." Val hung up and headed downstairs to make popcorn. It wasn't long before she curled up on the couch with Qenzi, Liam, Jess, Isabella, and Tetra, Shadow at their feet, the iconic intro to *A New Hope* resounding through her living room.

***

Val raised the glass of Iron IPA to her lips. The dark, frothy fluid went down effortlessly, washing away the last of the popcorn butter. She kept drinking until the glass was empty and tapped it on the bar.

"No, no, it *was* a great twist," Tetra insisted beside her. "Who would have ever seen that coming?"

"That was why we had to watch Episode IV first," Liam enthused. "Now we can watch Episodes I through III, and you'll get the whole amazing backstory."

"I thought it was obvious," Isabella grumbled.

"Shut up, Isabella," Tetra and Liam chorused.

"*Noooo!*" Isabella dramatically threw her hands skyward. "Tetra, you're turning into one of them!"

Everyone laughed, and the sound, like the excellent beer, washed through Val pleasantly.

"I'm guessing you'd like another." Enzo approached the bar, smiling.

Val grinned. "Keep 'em coming."

"On the house." Enzo slid another beer over to her.

Val raised an eyebrow. "I own half the house, so that's my loss."

Enzo stared at her.

"I'm yanking your chain, man." Val chuckled and slapped his arm. "I'll pay for this round for all of us."

Enzo smiled, tusks protruding. "I'm trying to find a way to thank you for everything you've done for my family, Val, but there is none."

"There's no need to thank me." Val smiled and inclined her head at the booths at the back. "That's all the reward I need."

Dante stood at an empty table, industriously wiping it down. He wore baggy jeans and a black T-shirt that, to paranormal eyes, read, *Say NO to human blood!* A red line dissected the *O* of *NO*. He'd kept his scalp shaved, displaying the half-healed tattoos, and his leather jacket had a red lining. Thick leather and bone armbands encircled his wrists.

"Love the outfit," a customer told him as he gathered her empty glass.

He smiled, revealing vampire fangs and orc tusks in the same mouth, if not to human eyes. "Thanks."

"Look at him." Val smiled. "Dressed half-vampire, half-orc."

"All Dante," Enzo agreed.

"Exactly." Val chuckled. "How's he been?"

"I mean, it's only been a few days, but much better." Enzo beamed. "He's taking a short break from school since he's not ready for exams, but he'll go back next semester. He's studying at home and hanging out with Alex again in the meantime."

"I'm pleased that he made up with Alex. He's a good dude," Val told him. "A little neurotic, but good."

"Preppy college elf. Aren't they all neurotic?" Enzo shrugged.

"Stereotype much?" Val raised an eyebrow.

Enzo grimaced. "Sorry."

Dante hustled past the bar with a tray of empty glasses. He paused to look at Val, deer in the headlights, and she smiled to set him at ease. "I dig the outfit, man." She raised her fresh beer glass. "Hey, you coming to watch my next MMA fight?"

"You've got a fight coming up?" Liam asked. "Aren't you still sore?"

"Eh, nothing I can't handle." Val grinned. "It's a practice round at Vanguard. Nothing major, but spectators are allowed. Thought you might enjoy it."

Dante shyly smiled. "I'll be there."

"So will we." Liam slurped beer. "Obviously."

"Sounds good to me." Val drained her drink. "Hey, Enzo—"

"Another round." Enzo laughed. "On the house. *My* half of the house."

Val chewed her mouthguard, gloved fists close to her face as she circled Joe in the arena. The willowy fighter's muscles flexed beneath his smooth skin as he sized her up, moving fast on the balls of his feet.

A slight ache touched Val's legs as she moved, the half-healed burns making their presence known. She winced enough to get Joe's attention. His eyes dipped to the burns on her bare shins, and Val lunged.

Diego didn't call out instructions. He moved out of the way, eyes on the fight, as Val jabbed swiftly at Joe's face. He blocked with his forearms and lashed out with a kick toward her knee. She stepped out of the way, pivoted, and landed a haymaker on his temple. He stumbled back, guard slipping, and Val took him down hard on the mat. In seconds, she trapped him in a rear naked choke. He struggled against her for a heartbeat before slapping the mat.

"Release!" Diego yelled.

Val let him go and bounced to her feet. Cheers rose from the dense crowd packed around the arena. They increased in volume when Val extended a hand to Joe and helped him to his feet.

"Taking advantage of my concern? Nice," Joe teased, slapping her shoulder.

Val chuckled. "I had to get you back for nailing me in the first round."

"She's right, Joe," Diego barked. "You let your focus slip even though you knew she's been cleared to fight. It'll happen again. Fight fair and trust the rules unless you're sure the rules are wrong."

Joe nodded. "Got it, coach."

"Five minutes, and we'll start the second round," Diego ordered.

Val bounced between the padded ropes, removing her mouthguard. A crowd of friends closed around her, laughing, offering her bottled water, towels, ice packs, and a massive platter of nachos.

"Tetra!" Liam spluttered. "Get that out of her face. You're going to make her hurl."

"They smell good," Archibald acknowledged. He held an ice pack to Val's shoulder while another gigantic hockey-loving friend, Henry, bent to inspect her burns.

"I'm fine, Henry," Val chided.

"I know. They look good, but I don't want you to reopen them," Henry told her.

"He's making sure." Buck completed the trio. His slender girl-friend Sadie was on his arm. "You've got to be careful."

"I know, I know." Val grinned.

"Are you sure you don't want nachos?" Tetra asked with her mouth full. "The food is amazing tonight."

Val hadn't eaten, but she could imagine. Incredible smells permeated the Vanguard MMA. The brink of summer had brought a warm night to Brownsville, so the doors stood open. Clusters of humans had barbecues going on the sidewalk, and the gym's kitchen bustled. Long rows of plastic tables offered every-thing from gyros to fried chicken to fish tacos. Half the humans here appeared to have little interest in cage fighting. They were more into food, company, and a safe place to hang out.

"Back in the ring!" Diego called.

"Nachos after," Val promised.

She handed Buck her empty water bottle and bounded to the ring. Friends and strangers crowded together, whooping and cheering as the fight began. The spirited bout ended when Joe pinned her with an artful leg lock and she submitted. Diego solemnly awarded him a chocolate medal. Lacking champagne, Val assisted the gym kids in spraying Joe from top to bottom with a well-shaken soda bottle.

Sticky, sweaty, and laughing, the fighters retired to the showers as the spectators helped clean up. Val wanted to hurry through her shower so she could help, but getting clean without wetting her new bandages was a pain in the ass. The locker room was abandoned when she stepped out of the shower, cozy in Vanguard sweatpants, and pulled on her wig—an electric blue bob.

Val perched on a bench to lace up her new sneakers when her phone hummed. Probably her friends, wondering where she was. She picked it up, and a jolt of shock zipped through her.

Queen Julia Pendragon, the caller ID read.

Val raised the phone. "Your Majesty?"

"Hey, Val. Sorry. It's been a while. Life is crazy right now." Queen Julia chuckled. "Much less crazy now that my toddler hasn't set the curtains on fire for a few weeks, mind you. Listen, is your team nearby?"

"They're outside, Your Majesty." Val bit her lip. "Is something wrong?"

"None of you are in trouble if that's what you mean. Quite the contrary. Mind if I speak to all of you for a moment?" the queen asked.

"Sure. Give me a minute." Val put the Eternity Queen on hold, which felt wrong on several levels, and jogged into the gym. She quickly spotted Liam and Tetra helping scrub soda off the floor and pack away folding chairs, respectively. Her wave brought them over.

"A heads-up, Your Majesty," Val muttered into her phone. "I'm not sure if you know, but Liam is human. He doesn't know the para world exists."

"No worries. I speak human, as you might recall," Queen Julia reminded her drily.

Val led the other two into the locker room and cupped a hand over her phone. "It's the agency boss," she whispered. "She wants to talk to all of us."

"The *queen?*" Tetra raised her eyebrows.

"Isn't she dead?" Liam blurted.

"Not that queen, you idiot," Tetra snapped.

Val thought fast. "It's her codename. The queen."

"Oh, okay." Liam hesitated. "Wait, she's the *boss*-boss? In charge of the whole thing?"

"It doesn't get higher up than she is," Val explained.

The color bled from Liam's face. He ran a hand over his hair like Queen Julia could see him. "Okay, let's…let's see what she says."

Val put the phone on speaker. "Ma'am? You're on with my team. Liam Miller is my ops manager, and you know Tetra."

"Sure do," Tetra muttered.

"Um, hi. Hi, ma'am. Hello," Liam blurted.

There was a pause.

"That wasn't weird at all," Queen Julia commented.

"I'm sorry," Liam squeaked.

"Mr. Miller, you have nothing in the world to be sorry about. I know you don't have the clearance for many details of this mission, but allow me to praise you for your exemplary operations management," Queen Julia bubbled. "You not only ensured the success of your mission, but you also saved your team's lives. I know you might not fully understand the scope of why the mission mattered, but many lives are safer because of your work."

Liam's cheeks flushed, and he stood straighter than Val had ever seen him. She hadn't known he was so tall.

"As for you, Tetra, you blew my expectations out of the water. You were kick-ass out there. This mission could never have succeeded without you," Queen Julia went on.

Tetra's jaw dropped. Val had to elbow her before she could squeak, "Thanks, ma'am."

Queen Julia chuckled. "Val, your leadership, strategic thinking, and prowess in battle make you a tremendous asset to our organization."

"Thank you, ma'am," Val murmured.

"I would be proud to have all three of you serve in my agency.

As it is, your position outside the agency makes you neutral—and invaluable. Thank you," Queen Julia finished. "Thank you all."

"It's a privilege to serve you, ma'am." Val meant it.

Queen Julia paused. "I wish this was merely a call to congratulate you on your good work."

Liam raised an eyebrow.

"You mean we aren't done?" Tetra blurted.

"Tetra," Val hissed.

"That's right." Queen Julia sighed. "There's more."

"Tell us what we can do." Val folded her arms.

"A few hours ago, a whistleblower came forward. One who served in the rebel group that attacked you. He told us how the rebels knew when Gaia's Sickle would be moved," Queen Julia explained.

Val and Tetra exchanged glances.

"Let me guess. Maximilian was working with the rebels," Val growled.

"You knew?" Queen Julia asked.

"If I had known, I would have said something, Your Majesty. Maximilian has a certain..." Val hesitated.

"He's got bad vibes," Tetra growled.

Queen Julia groaned. "*So* bad. He's so cringe. I wasn't surprised, either. In fact, the OPMA was investigating him for those endangered creatures in his menagerie, but the whistleblower made everything easier."

Val clenched her fists, amulet throbbing with her anger. "He set us up to get killed."

"Indeed he did, Val. He sold us all out. He made an agreement with the rebels to bring Gaia's Sickle back to him for secret safekeeping on their behalf. They would obviously pay him a handsome fee," Queen Julia explained.

"So, he'd pocket your money for Gaia's Sickle, get the rebels to pay him for keeping it in his vault, *and* keep the stupid thing." Tetra huffed. "No wonder he was so smug when we arrived."

"It gets worse." Queen Julia sighed. "Did he mention what he would do with the money?"

Val and Tetra exchanged a horrified glance.

"Yeah," Val growled. "He was going to buy an endangered creature on the black market. At least, that was the impression I got."

"I'll bet, given that the creatures you reported seeing are among the most endangered in the world, and he doesn't have permits for them. That's the primary reason the agency started investigating him," Queen Julia growled.

"Will the agency handle it?" Val asked.

Queen Julia hesitated. "Their resources are stretched with everything else we have going on, but I don't want to lose sight of the importance of those cultural artifacts and the endangered creatures. So, I have someone else in mind for the job."

Val, Tetra, and Liam exchanged glances. Tetra grinned. Liam nodded.

"Say no more, ma'am." Val grabbed her duffle bag. "We're on it."

CHAPTER TWENTY

Genevieve purred up the road, peaceful in the dappled morning light. Val and Tetra had the windows down. Nicky Youre and dazy's *Sunroof* blasted through the sound system, and they ate potato chips as the Mustang effortlessly cruised around the road's many bends.

"That's the turn coming up," Tetra observed past a mouthful of chips.

"Better call Liam." Val touched her earpiece, activating it.

Shadow shoved his nose between Val and Tetra, then licked Tetra's cheek.

"Ewww!" Tetra recoiled. "Control your dog, Val!"

"He wants another chip," Val ordered.

"I don't want to give his slobbery ass a chip," Tetra protested.

Shadow licked her again.

"Give him the chip, Tetra," Val threatened.

"Okay, okay." Tetra offered him one, and Shadow crunched it with enthusiasm.

"Uh, everything okay, girls?" Liam asked in Val's ear.

"All good. We're approaching the mansion." Val took the quiet road toward the mansion, then pulled onto the grassy verge.

"Leaving Genevieve at this location. We'll go the rest of the way on foot."

"Okay. I'm still not picking up any heat signatures besides the menagerie and Maximilian. He's chilling by the pool. Who does that at this time of morning?" Liam wondered.

"Bored rich people with nothing better to do." Val exited Genevieve.

"How's your road trip companion?" Liam asked.

"He's okay." Val helped Shadow from the backseat. "He loved the drive. I hope he can take care of himself out here."

"Sorry. I really can't have him in the ops room with me while you two are on a mission." Liam groaned. "He was awful last time. He ate one of Kenzie's expensive tablets and three maps and went ballistic every time you spoke on the comm. It was like he knew you were in danger."

"It's cool, Lee. Not your fault," Val assured him. "Shadow, heel."

The big dog stayed behind her as she and Tetra headed into the woods and moved around the meadow's edge.

"Okay, good. You're approaching the back of the mansion," Liam murmured. "Keep going."

Val felt like a thundering elephant in the woods compared to Tetra. The faerie soundlessly slipped from shadow to shadow. It seemed like she barely stirred a single leaf. Val tried to move swiftly on the balls of her feet like Tetra was doing but rustled and crashed despite her best efforts.

"Can you be any louder?" Tetra hissed.

"Sorry. I'm trying," Val whispered.

"Try quieter!" Tetra grumbled.

"Okay, you're in position," Liam told them. "You're free to approach."

Val and Tetra crouched behind a fallen tree at the edge of the "meadow" with Shadow between them. Val extended a hand over the log and felt the gentle but unbreakable resistance in the air. The concealment spell and ward weren't open now.

She'd planned for this. Val fished a rune cutter from her pocket and scooped up the nearest rock. As quietly as she could, she etched a rune into the rock, a complicated shape that Frode had explained on their way over.

Her teeth gritted as she carved the last line, and her amulet pulsed in fierce, rapid waves. The rune flashed blue, and so did the dome-shaped spell. The concealment spell collapsed like burning paper, its edges blue as they fell away. Val and Tetra looked down at the menagerie at the back of the mansion.

Maximilian's abode was even more striking from this angle. The gilded cages caught the morning light. A perfectly maintained but apparently unused tennis court stood on one side of the house, the massive, clear pool on the other. The menagerie was ahead of Val, sandwiched between the pool and the court.

"Still no heat signatures, Liam?" Val whispered. The colorful blobs on his screen were magical signatures, but he didn't need to know that.

"Nothing except for Maximilian and the menagerie," Liam confirmed.

"Why doesn't he have any rebel guards?" Tetra wondered.

"No idea." Val shook her head. "Look, there he is."

She pointed at the pool, where Maximilian lay on a deckchair. A six-foot wall separated the menagerie from the pool area, and the water painted rippling reflections on the white surface. Stately palm trees lined the wall at intervals. A garden shed stood in one corner, the door open but the interior shrouded in darkness. The weremagpie wore a fluffy bathrobe, a platinum chain and pendant, and slippers, but the rope was untied and flung back to reveal a pale paunch with a hairy belly button and a shockingly pink pair of silk boxers. One arm pillowed his head. The other held his phone to his ear.

"He looks annoyed," Tetra observed.

Maximilian yelled something into the phone. Val couldn't make out the words.

"Let's get closer, but slowly," she murmured. "We might hear if he's talking to the rebels."

Shadow crawled on his belly, Val on her hands and knees, and they made their way behind the bushes to a clump of rocks a few hundred feet from Maximilian. Shadow's hackles stood upright, but he obediently lay at Val's feet as they peered over the rocks to listen in.

"You people have far too many excuses," Maximilian snapped. "We had an agreement. You said you'd bring it back."

He paused, jaw clenched, and listened for a moment.

"I don't give a shit that you didn't get it on the road! Steal it from wherever the queen has it hidden!" he yelled. "That sounds like a you problem!"

Tetra's eyes widened. "He *is* talking to the rebels."

"Keep listening," Liam encouraged. "I'm recording this."

Shadow remained motionless at Val's feet as Maximilian sat up and bellowed into the phone. "Are you threatening me, Diana? Who do you think you are? I'm warning you—"

He suddenly stopped. The color drained from his face, and he swallowed.

"Fine," he muttered. "Okay. It better come here when you've got it back. That's all I'm saying."

He lowered the phone, hung up, and stared at it briefly. Then he lunged to his feet and threw the phone with all his strength, which wasn't much. It plopped into the pool a few yards away.

Maximilian clenched his fists and threw back his head. "*I hate my life!*" he screamed at the top of his lungs.

"I guess that conversation's over," Liam quipped.

"Okay." Tetra clenched her fists. "Let's get him."

A hundred feet of smooth lawn separated the boulders from Maximilian, who was pacing up and down the pool's edge, muttering.

"We don't have cover. Wait until he turns his back again, then move in fast," Val hissed. "Remember, we're here to arrest him, not murder him."

"No murdering?" Tetra asked.

"No murdering," Val confirmed.

"Screw my life." Tetra sighed, and the faerie dust trickling from her fingers changed color from scarlet to orange.

Maximilian reached the pool's corner, turned on his heel, and paced in the other direction.

"Now!" Val hissed.

They moved out from behind the boulders and hurried across the lawn, silent and fast. Shadow jogged at Val's heels. She kept a hand near her dagger just in case. The first to reach the paving around the pool, Val sprang onto the hard surface with a tap of hobnails.

Maximilian whirled. His eyes widened as Val and Tetra came towards him.

"What are you doing here?" he screamed.

"Maximilian Opulencia, you are under arrest in the name of the OPMA!" Val barked.

Maximilian fumbled for the pendant on his shiny chain. Too late, Val realized it wasn't a pendant. It was a dog whistle.

He raised it to his lips and blew. Val heard nothing, but Shadow's ears pricked.

"Okay, and?" Tetra shrugged.

Shadow's bark tore through the air like a thunderclap. He whirled, hackles high, and a deep growl answered him.

More than one growl. Three, Val realized.

She spun. "Oh, shit!"

The dog behind them made Shadow look like a toy poodle. It emerged from what Val had thought was a garden shed and now realized was a massive kennel. The enormous paws, lean body, and short black coat could have belonged to a Great Dane if they came in horse sizes.

It bared its many teeth. Three iron chains dragged behind it, one for each head.

Cerberus flattened his six triangular ears and wrinkled his lips. His snarl got louder.

Val grabbed Shadow's collar. "Shadow, leave it!"

Cerberus lunged. Long strides diminished the distance between them as Maximilian bolted for the mansion.

Tetra aimed at the three-headed dog, orange dust bursting from her fist.

"No!" Val yelled. She tackled Tetra, and they crashed to the ground together, Shadow snarling and yelping. Cerberus gave a howl of pain. Val rolled to her feet as the three-headed hound raised his left front paw to lick an acid burn.

"I could have taken him!" Tetra bounced up, eyes flashing.

"We can't kill him," Val protested. "He's an endangered species!"

"No shit!" Tetra yelled back. "As far as I know, there's only one of him!"

"If you're not going to kill that thing, you'd better run," Liam barked. "He's coming at you!"

Cerberus' three heads swung toward Val, and he crouched.

"*Run!*" Val yelled.

They scattered. Shadow raced ahead of Val, making for the six-foot wall. Powerful muscles bunched beneath his shiny red coat, and he cleared it in a wild leap. Hot breath huffed on Val's neck, and she vaulted over the wall, landing on her feet beside Shadow on the other side.

Cerberus bayed. His paws scrabbled at the wall, saliva spraying Val as he snapped in her direction, but his choker chains drew tight around his necks. He wheezed and foamed as he tried to break free.

"If you'd quit trying to kill me, I'd take those chains off," Val growled.

Cerberus howled.

"Liam, where's Tetra?" Val demanded.

"Up here," Tetra announced.

Val looked up. Tetra bobbed serenely near the top of a palm tree, arms and legs wrapped around the trunk.

"How'd you get up there so fast?" Val asked.

"Not getting eaten was a great motivator." Tetra eyed Cerberus, who was still bent on murdering Val, and shinnied halfway down the trunk. She dropped onto the wall and hopped down beside Val. "Liam, where'd that asshole go?"

"He's inside the mansion," Liam told her. "It looks like he's going to hide instead of running. He's heading upstairs instead of down to the garage."

"Hide. From us?" Val scoffed.

"I think he was counting on our scary-ass friend to tear us to bits." Tetra jerked a thumb at Cerberus. "Wow, he's really pulling on those chains. Is he going to strangle himself?"

"Let's not find out. C'mon. There's a door into the house on the other side of the menagerie," Val reminded her.

They headed between the cages, leaving Cerberus' snarls behind. Up close, the menagerie was more horrific than before. Each cage barely allowed its occupant to turn around. Plucked feathers and excrement littered the ground, and a stench permeated the air.

Shadow's tail hung low, and he whined as they walked. Val knew how he felt. Misery hung like mist between the cages. A deer with a peacock-shaped tail made of flower petals paced up and down one wall of her cage, eyes glassy and sightless. A small cat with sapphire fur lay on a platform in its cage, staring listlessly at a bowl of old bones, flies buzzing around the reeking scraps of flesh. In a dirty tank encrusted with algae, a sea lion—lion's head, eel's body—swam in mindless circles.

"Okay, I can't do this." Tetra stamped to a halt.

"What are you doing?" Liam demanded.

"I'm not an animal person," Tetra began.

Val chuckled. "As you often remind me."

Tetra glared. "But even I can see that this isn't right. Look at these things. They should be, like, running free or something. I've been in the queen's menagerie, and it's totally different. They have more space and hiding spots and toys and shit. This isn't right."

"I agree." Val nodded. "We can't leave them here."

"The queen said the agency was investigating. Maybe they'll take care of them," Liam suggested.

"Yeah, but when?" Val demanded. "How long do these creatures have to wait in these cages? The queen's doing her best, but they're focused on saving the world now." She turned to the nearest cage, which held the splendid white pegasus. Ribs protruded through his stiff coat. His wings drooped, and he constantly wove from side to side. "We're going to save these creatures."

"We're here to arrest Maximilian!" Liam protested. "Not play animal rescue!"

Perhaps you can do both.

Val spun around. "Who said that?"

Liam hesitated. "I didn't hear anything."

"Me neither." Tetra raised her eyebrows.

The words didn't sound in Val's ears. She'd heard them in her mind. Shadow barked, tail wagging, and Val turned to the cage behind hers. It stood next to the feather-plucking eagle with three heads (what was it with three heads in this place?) and held a bird unlike anything Val had seen before.

She was sure this cage had been empty last time. She was looking at the result of Maximilian's post-sickle-sale shopping spree, and it awed her: a bird the size of a beer keg, its feathers bronze. The magnificent bird wrapped its talons around a perch that was far too small.

Those talons gleamed. They were made of solid pure copper. Val could sense it, but her pulsing amulet drew her attention to the bird's beak. Its serrated hook shape made it seem even sharper, and it held the dull gleam of pure iron, darkest where it met the bird's face but brightly polished at the tip.

The bird moved its feathers. They clinked like Tetra's mail vest, and a thrill ran through Val as she realized that the feathers were not only the color of bronze; they *were* bronze.

Hello, Eiravel Stonehold, the bird murmured, *Warrior of the Red Bear.*

Val raised her chin. "The red bear? What does that mean?"

"I think Val's gone nuts," Tetra announced.

You may speak in your mind, Eiravel, the bird told her.

The bird was speaking telepathically. Despite the warm color of her feathers, the bird had piercing gray eyes like the skies above the Iron Hills in winter, and they bored into her soul.

"Val? Val? Hello?" Tetra demanded.

Val held up a hand.

Tetra looked from Val to Shadow to the bird. "I didn't sign up to be stuck with a Disney princess."

Val ignored her, locking gazes with the bird. *Hi.*

The bird's expression didn't change, but she laughed in Val's mind. *It's good to finally meet you.*

Who are you? Val asked.

I am Gagana. Once, every Iron Dwarf knew my name. Alas, that knowledge was lost to war, but you can hear me because of a deep connection between us, the bird told her.

Val reached for the gilded cage door.

"Val? Excuse me? Have you seen that thing's talons?" Tetra demanded. "Are you trying to get us killed?"

I'm sorry you ended up here, Val told Gagana. *You should be free.*

Shadow whined and pressed his nose against the bars, his tail wagging fast. His gaze never left the bird.

Gagana tilted her head. *I thought you would have questions.*

Of course I have questions, but that doesn't matter right now. Val slid the bolt back. *I'm here to arrest the man who's held you prisoner. I'm not going to leave you in a cage.*

She swung the door open.

"Uh-uh. Nope." Tetra hid behind Val. "Take her. She's juicier." She nudged Val forward.

Gagana chuckled. *Very well, Eiravel Stonehold.* She hopped to the floor and strutted out of the cage, her tail feathers scraping the ground.

There is one thing I'd like to ask, Val added.

Gagana tilted her head, studying Val with one eye. *What?*

Can you talk to the other creatures here? Val asked.

Gagana turned to face her. Tetra cringed.

Yes, I can communicate with them, the metal bird confirmed.

Okay. Val grinned. *Would they be willing to help us capture Maximilian?*

Their captor? Gagana's crest and neck feathers rose. *We certainly would.*

Silence fell in the menagerie. Every creature turned to face their door. The glassiness left their eyes. Their bodies grew animated, and they waited as though for orders, stock-still but alert.

"What is happening?" Tetra demanded.

Val turned to Tetra. "This will sound crazy, but the animals will help us arrest Maximilian."

"Excuse me, what?" Liam squawked.

"Roll with it, Lee," Val instructed.

"I mean, backup is good." Tetra shrugged. "They can have him for dinner for all I care."

"We need him alive. I bet he's got information on the rebels." Val grimaced at Gagana. "Sorry."

The bird yawned. *We will find other, albeit less satisfying, sources of nutrition.*

"Great. We'll open the gates." Val grinned. "Oh, one more thing. The house is filled with magical artifacts that don't belong to that asshole. If they could avoid breaking those, that'd be great."

Gagana was silent for a moment. *They agree. We can all sense what is magical.* She paused. *The cadejos would like to know if they can destroy non-magical objects.*

Val chuckled. "Please do."

"Please do what?" Tetra demanded. "Can I be part of this conversation, too, please?"

"Please break Maximilian's shit, and don't break artifacts that belong to other cultures," Val translated.

Tetra grinned. "That works for me. Okay, so should I run through the menagerie and open all the doors?"

"No need for that." Val closed her eyes.

The gold plating on the cages didn't prevent her from sensing the steel beneath. Her dwarven senses detected every bar and post. She felt the bolts latching each door, and her amulet heated against her skin. Scarlet fog soaked her mind.

A clatter rose around her as the bolts trembled in response to her touch. Growls, neighs, and low whoops rang out. Gagana chirped.

The fog grew brighter. Val let out a roar, and every cage door sprang open as one.

She opened her eyes as the white pegasus in the nearest cage leaped through the door. His wing accidentally buffeted her, sending her stumbling, and his hooves clattered on the concrete as he galloped down the aisle between cages leading to the back door. The rest of the menagerie followed, scampering, skittering, bounding, and swooping, their battle cries mingling into a cacophony of rage.

Gagana spread her wings with a clink of bronze. She threw her head back and emitted a screech like ripping metal, then sprang into the air. Her wings flashed in the sun, and she soared after the others.

"C'mon, Tetra!" Val shook her wrist, activating the shield. "Let's go get that asshole."

"He thinks he can use us as pawns in his little game, huh?" Tetra reached into the empty fox cage and grabbed a sun-bleached bovine femur. She slapped the pale bone into her opposite palm like a club. "Let's show him otherwise."

Shadow bayed and bounded ahead. Val and Tetra ran after him as the tide of creatures charged the back door. An oinking, squeaking herd of winged pigs—not the potbelly pet sort Frode doted on in the Iron Hills, but hulking, wild boar-like beasts with curving tusks and wide gray wings—led the way.

They slammed into the door, and the wood shuddered. Then they drove their tusks against the bottom. The hinges squealed in protest but didn't give way until a massive bull with backward-curving horns slammed into them. They collapsed in a shower of splinters, and the creature army charged into the mansion.

Hooves skidded on marble, and the creatures fell into disarray, scrambling over the polished floor. They were in a massive ballroom with a majestic crystal chandelier and rows of glass sculptures on pedestals around its edges.

Tetra pointed at the nearest, which depicted an uncomfortably contorted female figure. "Priceless artifact?"

"Nope," Val told her.

"Awesome." Tetra swung her bone club at the figurine, and it shattered.

Gagana swooped to the crystal chandelier and perched, her talons smashing the tiny crystals. They sprayed all over the marble floor in powdery pieces. Squealing flying piglets fluttered over to join her and went to town on the chandelier with their tiny tusks and cloven trotters.

"Yeah!" Tetra cheered. She ran to the next figurine and smashed it.

The creatures rampaged around the ballroom. The blue-furred cat jumped onto the velvet drapes and shredded them with her claws. The ramidreju joined her. The peacock-tailed deer kicked out the windows. Tetra and the nine-tailed fox destroyed figurines everywhere as the white pegasus reared and smashed his iron-rimmed hooves—long overdue for shoeing, Val's practiced eye could tell—into the marble.

"What are you guys *doing*?" Liam squawked.

"The creatures are taking revenge. Is Maximilian still in his bedroom?" Val asked.

"Taking revenge? What sort of mutant science experiments are they?" Liam demanded.

"Lee. Where's Maximilian?" Val prompted.

Liam sighed. "Yes, he's still in his bedroom."

Val shoved through the carnage to the other side of the ballroom. "This way, everyone!" she roared, raising her dagger.

Gagana shrieked. The creatures rallied to her cry, and Val rushed into the entrance hall with its many stolen treasures. Even the lumbering bull didn't break a single display case. As they'd promised, the creatures left the artifacts alone.

"Spread out!" Val barked. "Catch him if he tries to escape. Gagana, Tetra, Shadow, pegasus, foxy thing, and blue kitty, follow me!"

Gagana's cry scattered the creatures. They stormed through the mansion, and as Val raced up the stairs, she heard crashes, stomps, rips, and shattering glass throughout the extravagant place.

Tetra dragged the bone club along the polished banister as she followed Val upstairs, scoring the wood. Shadow bounded by her side, and the nine-tailed fox matched his strides as the pegasus' hooves kicked holes in the stairs and ripped the carpet. The blue cat ran along the banister, sinking her claws into the wood with each step.

Val's memory of the blueprints guided her down a hallway lined with ancient art. The creatures steered clear of the paintings and tapestries on the walls but paused by a gilded sideboard covered with tiny figurines carved from diamonds.

"Priceless or not?" Tetra pointed.

Val shrugged. "They're blood diamonds from the Second Pendragon War. Mordred's followers financed their magic and military using slave labor to mine the diamonds and sell them."

"Cool." Tetra jerked a thumb at the cabinet. "Yeet it, people."

The fox and pegasus helped her shove the cabinet to a beautiful bay window overlooking the tennis court. The blue cat and Gagana pushed the window open.

Tetra stepped back. "Val, would you like to do the honors?"

"With pleasure," Val snarled. She planted her boot on the cabinet's edge and shoved. It tipped over the windowsill and plummeted to the court, then shattered in a shower of wood splinters, twisted gold, and diamonds.

"Yeah!" Tetra cheered, the creatures yelping and whinnying with her.

"*Noooo!*" Maximilian screamed. "Not my diamonds!"

Shadow bayed. His hackles rippled like flames on his back as he charged down the hallway, pawfalls heavy on the floor. The hall ended in wooden double doors with gilded lion's head knockers, but as imposing as they were, they gave way when Shadow leaped up and slammed his front paws into them.

Val, Tetra, and the other creatures spilled into a bedroom the size of Val's house's ground floor. Sumptuous leather couches crowded around a glass coffee table that looked like it was floating above its gilded supports. Lacquer doors opened to a walk-in wardrobe near a four-poster bed covered in silk blankets.

A coffee nook with a pricey coffee machine—Val knew because she was saving up for the smaller version of the same brand—stood beside the Palladian windows on the far side of the room.

Maximilian stood by one window, laden with jewelry. Strings

of pearls and heavy pendants clunked around his neck. Gold and platinum bracelets covered his arms from wrist to elbow. He clutched a wooden box so full that earrings spilled out when he jumped.

Val's gaze darted to the window. Only a small top window was open.

Shadow slipped to a crouch a few yards from Maximilian, growling. The other creatures fanned out, forming a half-moon around him, trapping him against the window.

"So, that's what you've been doing up here." Tetra slapped the bone club on her palm. "Grabbing a bunch of valuable shit. Did you think you could escape?"

Maximilian's wild, beady eyes focused on Val.

"Stand down, Mr. Opulencia." She stepped forward. "You're under arrest for high treason in the name of the queen!"

Maximilian shrieked. "You can't have this! None of it! It's mine! *Miiiiiiiiine!*"

His shriek ended in a caw, and too late, Val remembered that he was a weremagpie.

He shrank, feathers erupting over his skin. Shadow pounced. The dog's jaws snapped shut over empty air as a magpie fluttered out the top window and swooped to freedom.

"No!" Val burst out, rushing to the window.

She flung it open. The mansion's grounds were unrecognizable. Creatures rampaged over the lawns, knocking down ornamental trees and digging up the grass. The flying pigs joyfully rooted in front of the mansion, oinking in contentment.

"Look out!" Val screamed. "It's Maximilian!"

Gagana shrieked. The creatures raised their heads as the magpie transformed a few feet above the ground. Maximilian landed running, stumbling under the weight of his treasures.

"How did he do that?" Liam spluttered.

"Where's he going, Lee?" Val yelled.

"If someone hadn't taken my wings away, I could've gone after him," Tetra grumbled.

"Not the time!" Val barked.

"He's in the garage." Liam groaned. "Shit. He's starting his car!"

"I need to get down there," Val snarled.

The pegasus neighed and trotted to Val, then sank to one knee, spreading his wings.

Val sheathed her dagger, deactivated the shield, and grabbed a tangled fistful of his dirty mane.

She'd barely thrown a leg over his barrel before he surged to his feet. Val gasped and threw her arms around his neck as he charged the Palladian window. Gagana swooped a moment before his delicate outstretched nose could touch the glass and shattered the windows, and the pegasus leaped through a curtain of falling shards.

Val leaned back, fighting for balance, as the magnificent beast dove to the ground. He threw his wings open at the last moment. Her nose banged painfully on his neck as he landed, hind legs first, shaking glass from his mane.

The roar of an engine cut through Val's pain. It wasn't Genevieve's throaty rumble but a modern, high-pitched shriek. She shook her blue hair out of her eyes and looked up as a sleek scarlet Ferrari convertible sped from the garage. Maximilian clutched the wheel, wild-eyed, bracelets and necklaces streaming as he turned down the drive and accelerated in a spray of gravel.

Val flung herself from the pegasus' back and drew her dagger, but before she could throw it, the flying boar charged. His short legs carried him across the ruined lawn with surprising speed, and he leaped onto the driveway, then whirled and hunched his back.

Presented with the abundant ass of a winged pig, Maximilian stomped on the brakes. The Ferrari skidded helplessly on the gravel and smashed into the boar's butt with a resounding crunch.

Maximilian's head smacked the steering wheel. The boar barely budged as the airbags deployed.

Val sheathed her dagger. Now unhurried, she strode across the lawn and grabbed Maximilian by the scruff of the neck.

"Mine," he whimpered, dazed.

"Oh, shut up." Val hoisted him out of the convertible. Bracelets tumbled from his limp hands and scattered all over the ground.

The winged boar turned around and rooted under the Ferrari with his nose. His tusks drove into the bumper, making Val grimace. He lifted it a few inches, testing its weight, then flipped it over with an easy flick of his neck.

"*Noooo*," Maximilian moaned.

"If you'd cared more about the world than collecting flashy shit, this might not have happened to you," Val snapped.

Genevieve puttered up the drive, giving the flying pig family a wide berth since the piglets were using the Ferrari as a trampoline. Tetra and Shadow emerged from the front doors as Val grabbed a rope from Gennie's trunk and tied Maximilian's hands behind him.

"My beautiful mansion," Maximilian moaned.

The liberated creatures roamed the lawns and mansion, free at last. The three-headed eagle perched in a pine tree, amber eyes scanning the scene. The blue cat and the ramidreju chased one another among the statues. Nearby, the pegasus cropped grass, his white tail swishing over his sweaty flanks.

"Thought you could play us, huh?" Tetra swung her club onto her shoulder. "Thought we were pawns in a game we didn't know existed? Think again, asshole."

Maximilian could only groan. Val bundled him into Genevieve's trunk and slammed it shut.

"I'd tell you that you did a good job, but the wild boar

destroyed that poor Ferrari," Liam moaned in their earpieces. "Couldn't you have saved it?"

"We saved a bunch of animals and caught a criminal today, Lee. I'm happy with our performance." Val chuckled. "Please call Qenzi and ask her to send agents to collect the stolen artifacts and return them to their people. These animals might need medical help or relocation, too."

"Already on it. Qenzi has agents heading that way," Liam promised. "They're restorers and animal rescue workers, not soldiers, so they couldn't come in until you'd secured Maximilian."

Val slapped the trunk. Maximilian moaned. "He's secure. See you in the city, Lee."

"See you. Drive safely. I'll monitor your route in case his rebel friends try to save him, but judging by his conversation with whoever Diana is, I doubt it." Liam disconnected.

A rustle of metal alerted Val to Gagana's presence. The mighty bird perched on a nearby statue and studied her with those piercing gray eyes.

Is there anything I can do to help you? Val asked. *Do you need food or water? OPMA agents are on their way. We'll meet them on the road to hand Maximilian over.* She slapped the trunk. *He'll pay for what he did to you.*

Gagana studied her. *You have done what you came to do. Return home now, Warrior of the Red Bear, but rest assured, our paths will cross again.*

CHAPTER TWENTY-ONE

Tetra sighed with contentment as Val handed her the paper bag. "Ahh, Mickey D, you magical thing, you." She opened a box of chicken nuggets and beamed at them like they were the most beautiful thing she'd seen all day.

"Do you ever get tired of eating?" Val raised her eyebrows.

"Who gets tired of eating? It's so easy in this city. You don't even have to kill anything first." Tetra popped a chicken nugget into her mouth.

Val shook her head as she drove away from the drive-thru and rejoined the thick traffic on the edge of Washington Heights. She shifted in her seat, trying to ease the pressure on her shins.

"Your legs okay?" Tetra asked.

"Little sore," Val admitted. "My bed is calling me."

Shadow snored in the back seat.

"Want me to drive?" Tetra asked.

"Definitely not," Val retorted. "We're not there yet."

"You let me drive when your life depended on it," Tetra pointed out.

"My life doesn't depend on it right now." Val stretched, letting

Genevieve take the wheel. "I'm ready for a shower and a bunch of beers."

"We're not on duty at the Iron Fist tonight," Tetra pointed out.

Val laughed. "Exactly. We can drink as much as we want."

"I like the way you think." Tetra grinned. "We need to celebrate our victory, right?"

"In the best way we know how," Val agreed.

"We should movie marathon again this weekend. I want to see how Darth Vader can be Luke's dad," Tetra announced.

Val chuckled. "I'm sure that can be arranged. Liam would be delighted to…hold on."

She fished her phone out of her pocket and frowned at Freya Gold's name on the screen.

"Shit." Tetra turned pale. "Was this all a diversion? Have they pinched the sickle from Gold, Manns, and Sax?"

Val hit the answer button on Genevieve's hands-free system. "Ms. Gold, is everything okay? Is the sickle safe?"

"Gaia's Sickle is in my vault where it belongs, Miss Stonehold." Freya paused. "There's another matter we'd like to discuss with you. We've read the preliminary report your team submitted to the OPMA after this morning's events at the Opulencia manor. Could you and your associate come to our building on your way home?"

"We?" Val asked.

"Her Majesty is here. She'd like to speak with you," Freya explained.

Val and Tetra exchanged glances.

"We'll be there in twenty," Val promised.

She put her foot down, and Genevieve's mighty roar echoed around the freeway.

<hr>

The Copper Dwarf receptionist guided Val and Tetra to a spacious conference room on the same floor as Freya's office. Two walls featured gigantic windows overlooking the Financial District; Val realized she was on eye level with the tops of skyscrapers and hastily averted her gaze.

She focused instead on the room. Elegant and minimalist, the centerpiece was the long mahogany table running down the center. The leather chairs could seat a hundred people, but today, they held only two: Freya and Queen Julia.

Tetra almost hid behind Val as she stepped into the room, thanking the receptionist. Val bowed clumsily, and Tetra followed suit.

"Your Majesty," Val greeted.

Queen Julia inclined her head. "Have a seat. Sorry, the room's overkill. I wanted somewhere private for us to talk."

Val pulled out a chair opposite Queen Julia. Tetra hovered at her elbow.

"You too, Miss Dupont." Freya smiled.

Tetra sank into a chair and eyed the bowl of mints on the table but thought better of it.

"Was there a problem with my report, Your Majesty?" Val asked.

"Not with your report, Val. It was an entertaining read." Queen Julia grinned. "I especially liked the bit where the piglets destroyed the chandelier. Exactly the type of shenanigans of which I thoroughly approve."

"Mr. Opulencia's insurance company might not agree," Freya murmured.

"The insurance company can stick it. They knew that bastard had treasures that should never have belonged to him." Queen Julia paused. "Unfortunately, this is about far more than one idiot hoarder."

"It is?" Val raised her eyebrows.

"I listened to the recording your excellent pal Liam made of

Maximilian's conversation on his phone, but I wanted to be sure." Queen Julia leaned forward, hands interlaced on the table. "Are you certain he said 'Diana?'"

"Yeah, absolutely." Val glanced at Tetra.

The faerie nodded. "Yes, Your Majesty."

Freya and Queen Julia exchanged glances.

"Shit," Queen Julia muttered.

"Who is she?" Val asked. "Is it the elf woman who led the rebel group that attacked us?"

"Probably, but she's far more than an ordinary rebel leader." Queen Julia sat back. "Many Sylthana Elves would argue that Diana is the rightful heir to the throne."

Val's eyebrows shot up. "What?"

"It was all over the news…what, ninety or a hundred years ago," Freya murmured. "Long enough for many paras to forget."

"The current Sylthana king, Lotan, wasn't born the crown prince." Queen Julia sighed. "He was the second child of King Bohdan and Queen Daryna. Their eldest was a girl, Diana. They groomed her to become queen for decades. That's probably why Lotan was such an ass, come to think of it."

"King Lotan has become an admirable ruler, Your Majesty, in no small part thanks to you," Freya told her.

"He put in plenty of work. I wasn't sorry when King Bohdan stepped down after losing Daryna to illness. Lotan easily outperforms both his parents." Queen Julia grimaced. "But Diana could still be very problematic."

"Why didn't she become queen, Your Majesty?" Val asked.

"Diana was too radical even for Bohdan and Daryna, Val. Even when tensions between the Sylthana Elves and the throne were at their height before the Pendragon Peace Treaty, they never withdrew from the high council, unlike the dragons.

"They didn't want real war with the Eternity Throne under my mother. They came close at New Camelot, but it was more of a dick-measuring contest than anything. Diana, though, was the real deal when it came to Sylthana radicalism. She started a Sylthana supremacist movement that eventually resurrected the Dark Moon League. Of course, by the time the Dark Moons became a problem, Queen Esmerelda had ordered Daryna and Bohdan to control their daughter. They didn't want her arrested, so they exiled her."

"They threw their kid out of the house?" Tetra asked.

"She was hardly a kid. She was a grown-ass woman who caused a lot of shit," Queen Julia grumbled.

"They did more than remove her from the royal family," Freya added. "Diana was ordered never to enter Sylthana lands again. Officially, she was exiled to one of the Sylthana Islands on the edge of their territory, but there have long been rumors that they couldn't contain her there."

"I'd hoped she'd quietly died or retired to be a hermit on a hillside somewhere," Queen Julia muttered. "But it seems she's back, Val, and rallying the most radical Sylthana group we've seen since the Dark Moons."

"Did Liam get video of her?" Val asked. "Maybe you can make a positive ID from that."

"Hard to tell with the war paint, but it sounded like her." Queen Julia grimaced. "I heard what she called you. I'm sorry. I'd hoped never to hear slurs like that in my dominion again."

Val shivered, remembering how the elf's face twisted around the word "clod." Tetra laid a supportive hand on Val's arm.

"Diana has shown up at the worst possible moment," Queen Julia continued. "The para world is already divided over the Wild Hunt issue, and now this."

"I'll do whatever I can to help, Your Majesty." Val leaned her elbows on the table. "Tell me what I can do."

Queen Julia grinned. "Keep doing what you're doing. I will need your services more and more in the coming months, Val, and not only for security threats like this one." She tilted her head. "Malcolm won't stop talking about the bracelet you made him. Tess Mendoza loves her classes at Tintagel, thanks to her labret, and Seraphine is so confident since you made her that necklace. We will need more work like that to keep paras safe."

Val raised her chin. "I can make that happen, Your Majesty."

"Her Majesty is not the only one with a task for you, Miss Stonehold." Freya smiled. "We understand that you have little interest in protecting the pricey trinkets of the rich, but Gold, Manns, and Sax has many dealings with clients and artifacts that are vital to keeping the peace. Would you be open to helping us with more missions like this one?"

Val hesitated. "I would, but there's a lot to do, and not many of us available to do it," she admitted.

Queen Julia chuckled. "Looks like you'll need to look at expanding your operations, Val."

The queen rose, and everyone in the room followed suit. Tetra stayed silent, but her eyes widened when the queen held out a hand.

"It's good seeing you like this, Tetra," Queen Julia told her.

Tetra warily shook her hand, saying nothing.

Freya gripped Val's hand, tilting her head back to look Val in the eye. "Miss Stonehold, suffice it to say that Gold, Manns, and Sax are extremely impressed with your service. Not only did you bring Gaia's Sickle safely to the vault, but you did it without any collateral damage or human exposure to the paranormal world. We acknowledge your skill and discretion, and we thank you for your courage."

Val released Freya's hand and turned to the queen, who shook her hand, too. The amulet hummed in the presence of her powerful magic.

"It's good to have an ally like you in times like these." Queen Julia smiled. "Thank you, Val."

Val and Tetra left Wall Street in silence except for the steady hum of Genevieve's engine. Several minutes passed before Tetra rediscovered her cold chicken nuggets and popped one into her mouth.

"I guess the work we're doing is important," she muttered with her mouth full.

"Maybe more important than we realize," Val agreed.

Tetra slurped from the soda cup. "Hey, what did you think about what the queen said about expanding operations? Are you going to hire more security people?"

"Not yet. I was thinking of hiring more jewelers," Val told her. "There's plenty of room to expand the smithy. I'm sure my contractors can use a simple bigger-on-the-inside charm to make that happen."

"Are you sure other dwarves can do the magic you do?" Tetra asked.

Val smiled. "I'm far from the most powerful Iron Dwarf I know, Tetra." She shifted gears as they approached the tunnel. "Besides, I was thinking of hiring lower-level smiths skilled in the basics. They can forge the iron parts, and I'll assemble the jewelry and add the wards. It'll save me enough time to increase my output."

Tetra chuckled. "Sounds like you're keen on that idea."

Val inclined her head. "The more paras we can help, the better."

"Do you have any particular smiths in mind?" Tetra asked.

Val bit her lip. "I know a few dwarves who would be perfect for the job. There's only one hitch."

"What's that?" Tetra raised her eyebrows.

Val grimaced. "The last time I saw them, they beat the crap out of me in the Iron Hills."

A pregnant pause hung in the air.

"I can see how that might be a problem," Tetra acknowledged.

Val laughed. "We've tackled bigger ones."

"You got that right." The faerie held out a fist.

Val bumped it and put her foot on the gas. Genevieve surged

through the tunnel, her horses bellowing in the bowels of the earth.

***

The Iron Fist was a riot of laughter and camaraderie. Sunday nights were often on the slow side, though Val and Enzo were brainstorming ways to change that, but tonight, she appreciated the relative quiet. A few patrons sat in the booths, with a handful of tourists alongside the usual three old men. The real party was at the bar.

Liam came in, his nose red with cold, holding his phone. Val lowered her beer glass as he grinned and raised the device.

"That was Kenzie," he announced. "The agency rounded up the animals that needed medical attention or to be released in a more suitable habitat. They left the others to roam free in the mountains. They've also boxed up all the stolen artifacts, and they're on their way back to where they belong as we speak."

"Yeah!" Val raised her glass.

Her friends at the bar joined in her roar of approval.

"To justice!" Tetra announced.

"Justice!" Val echoed, tapping her glass on the faerie's. She raised it to her lips and drained it.

Dante slid another quart across the bar, smiling shyly, then bustled away with a tray of empty glasses. Shadow lay at Val's feet.

Seated at Val's left, Jess rubbed the big dog's haunches with her foot as she nursed a rum and coke. "What kind of endangered animals were in there?"

Liam slid into his seat next to Jess. "Creepy mutant shit."

"Liam!" Val scolded.

"Sorry. I think that was classified," Liam admitted.

"I wish I could show you pictures, Jess. You'd have loved them." Val grinned.

"I still want to know how you got them to corner Maximilian like that. Does the agency have tech that allows you to talk to animals?" Liam demanded.

Jess raised her head. "Does it?"

Val laughed. "No. Sorry."

"Bummer. It'd be much easier if they could tell us where it hurt." Jess smiled. "Maybe I should join your operation. I could run the animal rescue branch."

"Enough animals," Tetra complained. "I'm not an animal person."

"Sure," Val muttered into her drink.

"Are you being sarcastic, Valerie Stonehold?" Tetra demanded.

"You're playing a dangerous game, Val." Isabella laughed. "Tetra will kick your ass when it comes to sarcasm."

"I sure will." Tetra balled her hands into fists. "Bring it, bitch."

"Whoa, whoa, whoa." Henry, sitting on Tetra's left, burst out laughing. "Were you there last night? Did you see how this slugger knocked Daniel Davies on his ass? That's a UFC fighter. Take her on in sarcasm, not fisticuffs."

"Fisticuffs?" Archibald chuckled. "What is this, the eighteenth century?"

"You're the one whose name is Archibald, dude," Val retorted.

Laughter resounded around the bar. Enzo joined in, belly rocking with mirth. He leaned on the counter, holding a beer bottle featuring the Anvil Brewery logo.

As he took another swig, Blair leaned closer. "Hey, Enzo, how is that?"

"Goes down well." Enzo held the bottle to the light. "Never liked the non-alcoholic stuff, but this is the best I've had."

"I like it, too." Liam raised his bottle.

"I'll have an Iron IPA as soon as I'm off duty." Enzo winked. "But this'll do in the meantime."

"Much appreciated over here, too." Jeff gestured with his bottle.

"See?" Yuka smiled. "I told you they'd like it, honey."

"Of course." Blair wrapped an arm around her shoulders.

"Hey, Val." Isabella leaned back to look past Jess and Liam. "When will you have a cool client again? All this spy stuff is bull-shit. I want to watch you kick ass on TV."

"She has an excellent point." Liam folded his arms. "Since I've joined, all you do is run around after artifacts. When do I get to work with the likes of Nadia Stewart?"

"You'd rather we protect an actress than save the world?" Val teased.

Liam clasped a hand to his chest in mock indignation. "Are you saying that caring for individuals doesn't matter?"

"You know I'm not." Val rolled her eyes.

"Do you still have the video, Enzo?" Buck asked.

Enzo grinned. "Sure do." He bustled to the TV in the corner.

Val groaned. "Do we have to watch me beat that guy again?"

"Of course we do." Jess elbowed her. "It was epic."

"Tell us the story again, Val." Archibald scooted nearer. "I love this story."

"You're about to see the video." Val gestured.

A clamor rose from her friends as they waved their drinks and demanded the story. Val stared at them silently as Enzo got the video on the screen and Dante served another round of drinks. Her smile grew. Her dog snored at her feet. Her heart swelled, warm and buoyant, filling her throat.

These people were more than friends. They were her family, and their mission bound them together.

There were forces in the world that sought to destroy and harm the peace that allowed these humans and paras to thrive. The thought made her amulet pulse and scarlet fog gather in her vision. Nothing could be allowed to harm them. Diana, Kronos, or whoever else threatened the peace that had given rise to this Golden Age would not enact their evil plans unopposed.

Come what evil may, Val Stonehold would stand in their path with her friends by her side.

"Tell us! Tell us! Tell us!" the group chanted, laughing and spilling their drinks in excitement.

Val blinked, and the scarlet fog faded. "Okay, okay. I'll tell the story."

Everyone cheered, and the patrons leaned closer as Val wet her lips with another sip of beer.

"We were at the opening of an acting school Nadia supported," she began, "and little did we know that an assassin was out to get her..."

Her words rolled through the Iron Fist, as warm as the lighting. Val enjoyed the peace she was fighting for.

AUTHOR NOTES RENÉE JAGGÉR

JULY 3, 2024

Thank you for reading book four and here to the back! This series is so much fun to write!

A Southwestern Hobbit

The other day, I was ~~wasting time on~~ scrolling through posts on Facebook, and I ran across one that resonated with me.

A Hobbit's Life

- A lovely garden
- Daily teatime
- Potatoes on the menu
- Bread and cheese in the pantry
- Second breakfast
- Walk around barefoot

As I've said before, I love my garden. In summer, it's full of roses, and I got my first Saturn peach off my new tree today. They look like donuts, but the flesh is white and sweet. The grapevines are crazy this year, so I have an enormous shady retreat under the trellis, which is twenty feet by twenty-eight feet. On a Zoom the other day, Michael Anderle thought I was in some hip California restaurant. When I told him I was in my yard, he was shocked.

Thanks to our Nat Roberts and Izzie Campbell, teatime is a must. In summer, it's iced tea, but needs must when the devil Arizona heat drives. Today's teatime was iced chocolate chai. Nat would faint, but Izzie might try it. I made a Meyer lemon cake yesterday, and it paired well with the tea. Who am I kidding? I would have eaten it anyway.

Potatoes are always on the menu. The other day, I tried a variation on a favorite version of coleslaw, but for potato salad. You use a ramen packet, and you mix the soup with the dressing, then crumble the noodles on the salad. It was much better than you would expect. I like the coleslaw version better, but one must experiment, mustn't one?

I haven't been baking much, and…sob…I used the last of my sourdough starter. I'm just not cut out for keeping something alive that you have to remember to feed when it's at the back of the fridge, Alexa reminders be damned. Since it was always on the edge of expiring, I think I'll just buy Rustic Sourdough slices and make fake sourdough crackers (involves buttermilk and yogurt) and live a happy life anyway. As for cheese, the larder is always full. My current favorite is manchego with apples or bourbon jam (or both), but I came across some Stilton with apricots the other day, and that sounded good too.

Which brings us to second breakfast. Sourdough and cheese sounds good to me. It's clearly time for second breakfast. As a child, when someone made me order food at "normal" breakfast time, I ordered cheeseburgers. Never liked bacon and eggs, except on sandwiches. Therefore, any meal can be second breakfast. Even better if it involves pizza. Yum, sourdough pizza with garlic white sauce and lots of cheese. Nah, too hot to turn on the oven.

Finally, walk around barefoot. I have never understood people who wear shoes in the house. You're bringing all the outside dirt in! Why would you do that? I have a shoes-off-at-the-front-door house, and my floors stay much cleaner for it. I am sure some of my readers are on the other side of this argument, but that's my position, and I'm sticking to it.

I am often sorry I didn't buy a sign I saw in Hawaii:

Aloha

Please Remove Your Slippahs

But No Take Mo'

Bettah Ones When You Leave

Mahalo

As always...

Mahalo to everyone at LMBPN as well. I sincerely appreciate my editor, the JIT team, and you, the readers! We authors couldn't do it without you. Kelly, as always, you rock!

Until we speak again, I hope your skies are sunny and your days are filled with happiness and good books.

Renée

BOOKS FROM RENÉE

Para-Military Recruiter
(with Michael Anderle)
Drafted (Book 1)
Recruiter (Book 2)
Accepted (Book 3)
Lead (Book 4)
Recruited (Book 5)
Soldier (Book 6)
Tactical (Book 7)
Officer (Book 8)
Leader (Book 9)
Victor (Book 10)
Appointed (Book 11)
Councilor (Book 12)
Royal (Book 13)
Princess (Book 14)
Peacemaker (Book 15)
Queen (Book 16)

Valerie Stonehold
Security For Hire (Book 1)
Shieldmaiden of the Modern Realm (Book 2)
Arbiter of Shadows (Book 3)
Jewel of the Night's Mantle (Book 4)
Echoes of the Anvil (Book 5)

Piercing the Veil
Dangerous Opportunities (Book 1)
Dangerous Responsibilities (Book 2)
Decisions To Make (Book 3)

Reincarnation of the Morrigan
Birth of a Goddess (Book One)
The Way of Wisdom (Book Two)
Angelic Death (Book Three)
A Cold War (Book Four)
A Battle Tune (Book Five)
Broken Ice (Book Six)
A Torn Veil (Book Seven)
Sins of the Past (Book Eight)
The Wild Hunt Comes (*Book Nine*)

The WereWitch Series
Bad Attitude (Book One)
A Bit Aggressive (Book Two)
Too Much Magic (Book Three)
Were War (Book Four)
Were Rages (Book Five)
God Ender (Book Six)
God Trials (Book Seven)
The Troll Solution (Book Eight)
Winner Takes All (Book Nine)

Callie Hart Series
Thin Ice (Book One)
Cold Blood (Book Two)
Feelings Run Deep (Book Three)